The Good Father

Marion Husband

Published by Accent Press Ltd – 2007
ISBN 1906125031/9781906125035
Copyright © Marion Husband 2007

Printed and bound in the UK

Cover Design by Red Dot Design

For my father Ted Donkin 1913 – 2003

Chapter 1

Thorp,
Spring, 1959

Hope came to the funeral. I noticed her as I followed the coffin through the church porch, where I had to pause whilst the bearers shifted their load discreetly on their shoulders. Standing at the back of the church, she turned to me and smiled that delicate schoolgirl's smile of hers, lowering her eyes almost at once, not expecting me to respond perhaps, possibly believing that smiling was some breach of funeral etiquette. And maybe it was, but I smiled all the same, although she didn't see me. No one saw me because my father's coffin blocked the congregation's view of my face. For those few seconds, as the undertaker's men synchronised themselves and Hope lowered her eyes from her brief, shy smile, I thought how lovely she was; if I were poetical I would say that my heart seemed to expand a little, that I felt suddenly generous and good and hopeful. As the bearers began their slow progress up the aisle, I made my face solemn again.

We sang 'I Vow to Thee My Country' and 'Jerusalem' and 'The Lord's My Shepherd', hymns my father had chosen years ago, planning for his death well in advance, as he planned everything. There were not many mourners. Dr Walker was there of course, Mrs Hall, Mr Hall, a few of the neighbours my father so despised. I had informed cousins whom he had not seen for years and I have never met, but they declined to attend, citing ill-health and old age. So I stood in the front pew alone. The wreath of white chrysanthemums that graced the dark coffin filled the air with its peppery scent, and the bright cubes of light from the stained-glass window were cast at my feet as I sang the hymns and said the prayers, all the time thinking that if I turned around I would see Hope, her head bowed to her hymn book. I thought I could hear her voice above all the others, sweet and clear, singing the too-familiar words of lambs and green pastures; I thought too that I could feel her eyes on me, her soft, concerned gaze. How wrong it would be to turn around, what a bad impression I would give of myself, a man who couldn't concentrate on his grief, on the solemnity of the occasion, but glanced about the church like a tourist. But it would have only been a glance. And although I longed to, I didn't. I was as well-behaved as ever in my father's presence. I was right and proper and straight-backed, and I sang not too quietly, not too loudly but clearly and with my head raised so that I looked straight at the window that shed its coloured light at my feet, the window that depicted the Good Shepherd, a benign and sadly smiling Christ, pale and blond and tender as Hope herself.

The vicar, the congregation and I followed the coffin out into the graveyard. The sun shone and the sky was a rare, beautiful blue, the blue one only ever sees in England in springtime. Earlier, the verger had cut the grass around the old graves and there was a neatness and tidiness about the place, enhanced by the daffodils that grew beneath the sticky-budded chestnut trees and along the gravel path. The gravel whitened my shoes and felt sharp beneath their thin soles, making me think of penances and returning my mind to the funeral lunch. Mrs Hall had prepared a tongue and salads, bread and butter and a fruit cake. Too much food, as though she was expecting hungry hordes of mourners and not just this sad little gathering. I thought she knew my father better.

Beside the grave with its mound of lumpy clay earth, I

2

watched Hope walk away along the path that led through the graveyard. Of course she would not stay, would not come back to the house as I had hoped. She would not wish to 'intrude' as she would think of it. I had to hold myself back from running after her. I had to bow my head and clasp my hands together and close my eyes in prayer, as sons do at their father's funeral as the coffin is lowered and the words said.

Hope was wearing her school uniform, the navy blazer and skirt and long, brown socks that show her pale, still childish knees. Although she is very slim and tall, the blazer makes her look rather square and bulky. There was a long, golden hair on her shoulder, shining against the dark cloth. Lately there has been a kind of shyness between us. We are all awkward smiles and side-steps; she bristles away from me when once she would throw herself with such force into my arms I'd be momentarily winded. I tell myself I always knew that one day she'd grow away from me.

Later, when I had the house to myself again, when even Mrs Hall had gone home, having cleared away the sorry remains of the funeral lunch, I walked through the empty house, going from room to room and thinking how silent it was, how full of silent things. Oil paintings, china ornaments of flower baskets and pug dogs, tapestry fire-screens in dull faded threads that made me wonder why their makers worked in such dismal colours. All I now own seems to be in a shade of brown that was chosen for its ugliness. The heavy drapes and swags at the windows are an odd shade of mink, faded because they've hung at these windows all my life at least.

Everything in this house is as it was in my childhood. Even when I returned home from the war I realised after a few days, not really caring, that in the six years of my absence not so much as an umbrella had been moved from its place. It seemed too that my father had hardly moved,

3

sitting at his desk when I returned just as he had been when I left. I remember how, on my return, he looked up at me from a letter he was writing, saw what a poor, wretched shadow I had become and shook his head. 'So,' he said, 'you're back.' No bunting for me, then, no girls to throw flowers or children waving flags, no mother to cry and laugh with relief. The war – even my war, the Japanese war – had been over for almost a year. No one cared at all that I should have returned. Not even I cared very much. In those days I felt nothing but the cold.

As I stood in the window, framed by the faded swags and tails, I remembered how my father had got up from his desk and crossed the room to stand before me. He looked me up and down quite deliberately, theatrically almost, frowning sardonically. He was shorter and stockier than me, and I felt like a great, lanky weed beside him, just waiting to be cut down. Nothing had changed between us; six years of experience might just as well have been six hours, the time I had spent away from his study nothing more than an evening at the pictures for all it helped me to stand up to him. I left as a boy and returned as a boy, only with worse dreams, nightmares that could compare with his. Soon both of us would be screaming the house down at night, neither admitting to the other that he had been disturbed.

A week ago, Dr Walker had come down from my father's sickbed and found me in the kitchen preparing my lunch. I felt embarrassed, caught in the greedy act of seeing to my stomach as my father lay dying upstairs. Ham, bread, butter and mustard pot were arranged on the kitchen table, the kettle whistling cheerily on the stove; the wireless was on, BBC voices discussing the news, and I was spooning tea from the caddy into the teapot when, from the kitchen doorway, Walker cleared his throat.

'Sorry,' he said, 'I didn't mean to startle you.'

I quite often look startled, I think. Scared, even. I flinch often, on buses, in the street when someone brushes past me

4

too closely or shouts out too loudly. I am a bag of nerves that was once merely a bag of bones. Now I am fleshed out a little, my nerves have jangled and jolted back to life, and Dr Walker was right – he did startle me. I had been lost in thoughts of the illustration of the Frog Prince I'd been working on, the minute changes I might make to improve the gravity of the Prince's expression, and I hadn't expected the doctor to be finished upstairs so quickly.

Stepping towards me, he placed a steadying hand on my arm, and said, 'Should I make the tea?'

Dr Walker had fought in the trenches, as had my father. It should have been possible to imagine that my father would have liked him more because of this – although I know as well as anyone that it isn't necessarily so that we should bond over the horrors. As it was, my father disliked Walker as he disliked everyone – more, perhaps, because the doctor is kind and patient, qualities my father thought of as weaknesses. Now this kind, patient man sat opposite me at the kitchen table, regarding me with some concern. He made me feel squirmy, inadequate. I remember that I hadn't shaved and that I wore a soft, collarless shirt, its sleeves rolled up; no doubt my fingers were inky. I itched to get back to the Prince and knew that I would lose the thought I had, about his expression and how it should convey his longing, if I didn't finish him soon. But it was obvious that Dr Walker wanted to talk, so I made myself look as though I wanted to listen.

He said, 'How are you coping, my boy?'

'Fine!' I smiled, bright as a button, hoping he would take my word for it and allow me to get on but he only searched my face as though he longed to examine me. I hold quite a fascination for doctors – they'd like to know how I survived. I said, 'I'm coping very well, and Mrs Hall is a great help. She sits with him if I have to go out.'

'You look tired.'

'No, not really.'

As if I hadn't spoken he went on, 'And your father is worried about you.'

I laughed, astonished that this sensible man should be so taken in by the old devil.

Gently, Walker said, 'Peter, you know you can talk to me if anything is worrying you, if you feel uneasy in yourself, anxious . . .'

It dawned on me just what he was getting at: my father, even as close to death as he was, still had the energy for malice. I imagined him clutching the doctor's hand, attempting to sit up as he desperately tried to impress on him how sick I was, on the verge of a nervous-breakdown so that it would only take his dying to push me over the edge. He would like the good doctor to certify me, of course that was it, and so he sowed his seeds of doubt about my ability to cope, gloating no doubt as he imagined this conversation we were having.

Firmly I said, 'Doctor Walker, I'm quite well, you don't have to concern yourself with me.' I almost said that I was fitter, happier even, than I had ever been, that I felt like a prisoner who had been told that his release was only a matter of days away. He would think that my eagerness for my father's death was heartless, perhaps even one of the manifestations of madness. So I only repeated that I was well, saying for good measure that perhaps I *was* tired, just to keep him happy.

The doctor is a handsome man, tall and blond as a Viking, although his fine hair is thinning. He has the resigned look of a man who has seen a great deal of suffering and over the years has realised he can't do much to put a stop to it, that he has failed in his youthful ambition to do good. I would like to sketch him; his could be the face of the benevolent King in *Sleeping Beauty*. As I sat opposite him at the kitchen table I realised I was studying his face rather too closely – his eyes are a particularly pale shade of blue – and sensed that I was making him self-conscious. I looked away at once, apologising. He stood up, patting my arm as he made to leave. 'If ever you need to talk, Peter. . .'

What would I talk about, I wonder.

I was a prisoner of the Japanese for four years.

I have no idea now how I survived, although I believe a great deal in luck.

I illustrate collections of fairy tales.

I think about Hope often. She is sixteen and the most beautiful, precious thing in my life.

What would Walker say to this last confession? How would those near-colourless eyes look at me then?

At the graveside today was a man I didn't recognise – a tall, distinguished-looking figure. He stood a little way back from us few official mourners, his head bowed respectfully; I noticed that he crossed himself when the vicar said the final amen – a Catholic. Interested, I watched him, and he caught me watching and held my gaze, frank, unsmiling, sad. He looked as though he truly mourned my father, the only one amongst us that did. I began to make up a story for him, that he is an old soldier, an officer by that expression of his, and wealthy. I imagined ways he might have made his fortune – gun-running, perhaps, because he had a look of new money, of having come from nowhere. But old soldiers don't make money from wars, they would risk too many ghosts coming back to haunt them.

As I considered, the vicar interrupted my thoughts, briskly solicitous, wanting me out of his churchyard and safely home. As I was escorted away, I glanced back to see if the stranger still stood there. He did, close to the grave's edge now, ignoring the grave-digger who moved in from his hiding-place with his shovel. I saw this stranger toss a handful of dry earth down onto the coffin. Perhaps it's a ritual Catholics feel they have to attend to. Hope is a Catholic. I remember her in white at her first Holy Communion; she looked so breathtakingly beautiful and innocent as a lamb.

Weary from the business of the funeral, I went upstairs for a rest. Downstairs, the house is stuffed with furniture – old, ugly, heavy furniture that collects dust in its intricate carvings, scrolls and beading; my room, however, is quite bare, like a servant's room, empty but for my wardrobe, bed and bedside table. I suddenly realised that I could get rid of everything that belonged to my father and clear the house once and for all of his brooding presence. Never again would I enter a room and get dragged into some unhappy moment in the past by merely glancing at a sideboard or a chair. I could make the house bright and modern. I could make it so I would be less ashamed when Hope came for her lessons.

Yes, I resolved, that is what I would do. More than anything, I wanted for Hope to be happy when she came here, to treat this house as her home. Charged with purpose, I went downstairs again and made a start.

Chapter 2

Hope watched her father comb his hair in front of the hall mirror, watched him smile experimentally at his reflection, the self-conscious smile that hid his slightly crooked teeth so that it seemed like no smile at all – not one he used on them, at least.

'So,' he said, 'you'll make sure the boys are in bed by eight o'clock?' He glanced into the mirror again, then turned away to lift his coat from the hallstand. Shrugging it on he said, 'I told you that we're going to the Grand for dinner, didn't I? It's a dinner dance.' He smiled his ordinary smile. 'I thought I might bring her back here, afterwards . . . How would you feel about that?'

The girl shrugged.

'Hope . . .' He sighed. 'You like Val?'

'Yes.'

'Yes? So it's all right if we come back here for a night-cap? If you want to stay up, that's fine. If not, well – that's fine too.'

'I'll see.'

Frowning at her he said again, 'You do like Val, don't you? She's nice, isn't she? And the boys like her . . .' He trailed off. Distractedly he said, 'Anyway. I should dash.'

His coat buttoned, his gloves pulled on, he said, 'I've left you a bar of chocolate in the cupboard beside the tea caddy. Save it until the boys are in bed. It's your treat, for being my best girl.'

She went to the door with him, watching as he walked to the end of their road and turned the corner on to Oxhill

Avenue, before closing the front door and locking it, just as he had told her she must.

Martin and Stephen were already in their pyjamas, their father insisting that they be bathed and bed-ready, as he called it, before he left. He had warned them that they must be good for Hope; he always said this, every time he left them in her care. Always she thought that he might just as well save his breath. Climbing the stairs to their room, Hope heard the boys shouting and she opened their bedroom door to see them bouncing on Martin's bed, competing to see who could jump the highest.

Between bounces, Martin said, 'Has Daddy gone?'

'Yes.'

'You can't make us go to bed, you know.'

'Stay up, then,' she said. 'See if I care.'

The two of them fell on to the bed together. Breathlessly, Stephen said, 'We think he's going to kiss her.'

'Do you now?'

'Do *you*?' The boys looked at her, an odd mix of hope and anxiety on their faces. Martin said, 'If he kisses her he'll have to marry her.'

'Only if she likes it,' Stephen said. Still looking at her, he added, 'And she probably won't.'

Martin rolled his pyjama leg up and began picking at a scab on his knee. 'She'll like it if she's after his money.'

Stephen was outraged. 'He hasn't got any money!' He shoved his brother. 'Bloody idiot.'

'Stephen!'

'He *is* an idiot! Daddy won't marry anyone!'

They began to fight, two identical little boys grasping and pulling at one another as they rolled about the bed and bumped onto the floor. Hope watched them, thinking that she could leave them to it, that eventually they would tire themselves out and fall asleep, probably on the rug, curled up together like puppies. She thought about the chocolate her father had told her about and the novel she was reading, *The Masked Ball* by a woman called Avril D'Vere. The book was rubbish, terrible, slushy rubbish, but the hero was handsome; she had built him up in her head and made him more interesting, hoping to fall in love with him. So far, that magic hadn't happened. She couldn't concentrate on stories; her mind wandered.

This afternoon, her mind had wandered constantly to Peter. She thought of him in the church porch, in his dark coat, white collar and black tie; she thought of the way he had smiled at her, as though he was terribly pleased that she was there. She'd had to look away, and the horrible creeping feeling she had so often lately, that she had somehow encouraged him to look at her so longingly, had sent a hot rush of blood to her face.

The last time they were alone in his house, as he took out the paper and pencils she was to sketch with, she had asked how he was. For a moment he had stood quite still, frowning as though trying to make sense of what she'd said. What had been only a polite question all at once began to seem inappropriate, insensitive even. Then she realised that no one ever asked him how he was, and that her asking had touched him too deeply. Appalled, she'd seen that he looked as if he might cry, gazing at her with this desperate expression until the atmosphere between them became so charged she had to turn away. At once he began to fuss with the sharpened pencils, lining them up just so; she noticed that his hands shook a little.

She'd wanted to go home. Ashamed of this lack of pity, she had touched his arm, smiling at him as sympathetically as she could. He had laughed painfully, his embarrassment compounding hers. 'I'm sorry,' he said, and she had said no, no, it was fine, wanting only to reassure him so he wouldn't look at her like that again.

Peter was her father's oldest friend, and she had loved him for as long as she could remember. But lately she was embarrassed by this love, its childishness and its over-demonstrative enthusiasm; she squirmed whenever she remembered her silly exclamations of just how much she loved her Uncle Peter. But she had been a little girl then, had known nothing. She knew more now, she had been made to understand what some men hid away in their hearts.

As well as being her father's friend, Peter had been her mother's, too. She remembered her mother and Peter together in the kitchen a few years ago, her mother hugely pregnant with the twins. They had been talking – serious, intent on each other – until Peter had seen her watching them from the kitchen doorway and had immediately held out his hand to her. 'Hope,' he'd said softly, and her name had sounded like a gentle warning.

This morning, her father had said, 'Damn and blast and damn!' Standing by the phone in the hallway, he turned to her. 'That was Mr Davies. He's insisting I come to the office – some problem with the accounts that must be sorted today.' He exhaled sharply. 'Blast the man!'

He had been wearing his best suit, a black armband around its left sleeve, his black tie draped around his up-turned collar, the phone call from his boss catching him out in the process of tying it. He looked down at the tie and suddenly gave it a sharp, hard tug so that it rasped against his shirt.

'Aren't you going to the funeral?' she asked.

He tossed the black tie down so that it fell against the phone, only to slither to the floor. 'No, I can't, not unless I want to lose my job. I'll have to call Peter.' He turned back to the telephone as though he couldn't think of a worse call to make. 'Damn,' he said again, but quietly now. She'd had an idea that he was deciding whether to make the call or not, whether he could simply not go and explain later. Reluctantly he picked up the phone.

Their conversation had been very short. When it was

12

over and her father had hung up, he turned to her. 'I suppose I'm relieved, in a way.'

She had nodded; of course he was relieved. Her father was bad at sympathy; he liked it best when those around him were happy enough to be ignored. All the same, he had looked bleak for a moment, only to quickly pull himself together. 'Listen – why don't you go instead? I think one of us should, after all.'

'No!' Appalled, she'd shaken her head.

'I know it's horrible.' Smiling suddenly he went on, 'Look, it's an Anglican funeral. They have you in and out of the church as if they were renting the place out by the half-hour – nothing too over-wrought. And it will be good for Pete to see a friendly face. Go on, Hope, do it for him, if not for me.'

Desperately she said, 'I can't – the school won't allow it.'

'Oh, for goodness sake!' Her father sighed, exasperated. 'I'll write you a note – give it to the teacher. Does it matter anyway? You'll be leaving there in a few weeks.' He touched her arm as he stepped towards the stairs on his way to change out of his funeral suit. 'Are the boys ready for school?'

'Dad, please don't make me go.'

He turned, frowning at her. 'Hope, don't be silly. I know funerals are a bit daunting, but just think of it as a more sombre church service.'

Then he went upstairs and she heard him shouting at the boys to stop fighting and get ready for school or he'd box their ears – another empty threat: her father had a hundred of them. It had occurred to her that if she didn't go to the funeral he would only bluster for a few minutes and then forget he had cared. She had thought about Peter and guessed that if her father didn't attend the funeral – if *she* didn't – he would be alone in that church with his father's coffin. She'd shuddered, resolving not to go, only to

13

remember how much she had loved Peter until so recently, only to think how much she pitied the sudden image she had of him alone at his father's graveside.

After assembly this morning, she had gone to Miss Vine's office and handed in her father's hurriedly scrawled note. A few weeks earlier, in the same room with its photographs of hockey and netball teams and its display cabinet full of trophies, Miss Vine had told her that she didn't think she should stay on for her second year at sixth form. 'I know your heart's not in your work, Hope.' Her voice had been stern but then her face had softened and she had taken off her glasses so that Hope had known she was about to fake concern. 'I think you should learn some shorthand and typing, some office skills. Not everyone is cut out for higher academic achievement – becoming a good wife and mother are vitally important roles.'

This morning, sitting at her desk, Miss Vine had peered at her over the rim of her tortoiseshell spectacles, the spectacles chain around her neck catching the morning sun streaming through the high windows. 'I heard that Mr Wright had died. And if your father insists you attend his funeral . . .' The woman had sighed, as though she knew how unthinking her father could be. 'All right. Go, of course you should go.'

And that is how she had found herself at the funeral in her father's place.

Martin said, 'Are you going to make us go to bed?'

Hope looked at her little brother. 'No. I'll tell you a story, if you like.'

'One of Uncle Peter's stories?'

'Yes, all right.'

The boys whooped and began bouncing again as Hope lay down on the other bed. 'Hush now,' she said. 'Lie down and listen quietly.'

Halfway through the story, she remembered it was one Peter used to tell her years ago in the months after her mother's death, when she would sit beside him on the sofa downstairs, his arm light around her shoulders. She would place her head very deliberately so that she could hear the beat of his heart and feel the resonance of his soft voice vibrating through his chest. He would smell of carbolic soap, a clean, harsh scent that comforted her in its adult right and properness; at that time her father had begun to smell of unchanged beds and unwashed hair; his face had become blue-black and rough with bristles and his eyes looked as though someone had just said something horrid to him. Sometimes her father would grab her and hold her too tightly, and sometimes he would lock himself in his bedroom for hours. Peter would come then, as if he sensed she was alone with just her baby brothers. Peter would feed them and put the boys to bed; he would tap gently on her father's door.

Hope came to believe that this gentle tap-tap-tap was a sign to her father that all was well; Peter never opened the door, never went inside the room, just tapped out this signal before taking her hand and leading her downstairs. There they would settle on the sofa and he would tell her the story of *Cinderella* or *The Tin Soldier*. Or this story that now, on her brother's bed, had brought such memories back to her – *Tom Thumb*.

Her voice trailed off and Stephen said, 'Hope! Don't go to sleep. We want to know what happens next.'

She closed her eyes, remembering how once, in the middle of *Tom Thumb*, she had asked Peter if he had ever wished for a little boy of his own. He had only laughed a little, kissed the top of her head as she'd gazed up at him, and told her, 'One day, perhaps.'

'After I'm grown up?'

He'd gazed back at her. 'Yes, after that.'

She had been satisfied, realising that she didn't want to share him with other children he might love more than her and her brothers. Boldly, because her mother's bewildering absence had made her demanding, she'd said, 'You're not to get married until I'm old.'

Recalling this, Hope opened her eyes, anxious suddenly that he might have taken her demand seriously. Of course he hadn't – he had probably forgotten all about his promise that he wouldn't marry, but all the same she felt a guilty kind of fear dart through her. Had he had stayed unmarried and unhappy because of *her*?

Stephen had come to stand beside the bed. Hands on hips, he stamped his foot. 'Hope! Finish the story now!'

She sat up, not wanting to go on with Peter's story, not wanting to be reminded. Quickly she said, 'They all lived happily ever after. Now, let's go downstairs – Dad's left us some chocolate.'

The band began to play 'Rock Around the Clock' and Val Campbell tapped her foot beneath the table, thinking that she and Jack Jackson were too old to dance to music like this and that she shouldn't look as if she wanted to dance so badly because that might make her seem too flighty. She looked at Jack surreptitiously, thinking that he didn't really look his age. He was slim and slight and his dark hair was still thick, with no grey that she could see. When he smiled unguardedly – which wasn't often – he looked even younger. She had been told that she looked younger than her years, so that was one thing they had in common, at least. She was as blonde as he was dark and not particularly slim, certainly not slight – *buxom*, Harry used to call her. Harry would slap her bottom and laugh and call her 'wench'. Vulgar and vivid, Harry would be on his feet now, throwing himself around the dance floor, the first to laugh if he fell on his face. Too big, too loud, she sensed Harry's presence most strongly in places like this where there was food and music and drink and the air was blue with tobacco smoke. Harry had smoked cigars as fat as his chubby fingers. His clothes, those beautifully cut suits and hand-made shirts, had smelled of cigars, his breath of sweet, ruby port. Naked, he had smelled of sandalwood, clean, expensive, subtle; the naked Harry was a different, calmer, gentler man.

But she had told herself not to think of Harry, and especially not to compare him with this man who sat beside her. Impossible to compare the two of them, anyway – like putting a terrier in competition with a wolfhound. And Jack Jackson was handsome – at least, the girls in the typing pool thought he was. More than one or two of them had their eye on him; she had seen the looks they exchanged behind his back. And Jack had been a pilot during the war, had flown bombers over Berlin. Val guessed how many of the girls liked to imagine him in his RAF uniform flying through exploding, fiery skies. Harry had been in the Army, a translator, disarming Nazi prisoners with his perfect German. 'I wasn't their idea of an English Army Major,' Harry laughed as though remembering SS Officers' astonished faces when he opened his mouth. 'I looked like Oliver Hardy and sounded liked Hindenburg!'

He was wrong. He didn't look like Oliver Hardy. And in bed, his face soft with desire, he was the most beautiful man alive.

Hadn't she told herself *not* to think about him? She turned to the dance floor. A few couples had begun to jive but mostly this was a place older couples frequented, couples who expected waltzes. The band seemed to take the hint, and began to play 'Moonlight Serenade'.

'Would you like to dance?' Jack stood up, holding out his hand to her. He smiled and she thought that he was handsome in a way that she might grow to appreciate. Smiling back at him, she stood up and took his hand.

Jack Jackson had first asked her to have dinner with him one bleak Monday lunchtime as they both queued in the canteen. Clutching her tin tray and bent cutlery, wondering whether to have the meat pie or the boiled fish, Val had turned to Jack and asked him what he thought looked less horrendous. He had laughed and said that yes, it was the usual Hobson's choice but he'd probably risk the meat pie. She and Jack had been exchanging friendly remarks like this for years, in the canteen, in corridors and on stairs as they passed each other on the way to meetings and minute-takings. She had worked for Davies & Sons for only a week when Joan, one of the other secretaries, had told her that Jack Jackson was a widower and wasn't it tragic to have your wife killed like that, leaving you to look after three small children! Joan had sighed, a mixture of sympathy and wistfulness that Val would come to associate closely with Jack over the coming years.

Joan was only one of many who would have liked to comfort this widowed man, although it seemed to Val that he didn't much notice any of these women. He was cool and professional; she appreciated his good manners, the fact that he wasn't a groper or a bottom-pincher; she liked that he talked to her more or less as an equal and not in the absurdly patronising tones used by most of his male colleagues. She thought that he was aloof and attributed this to his status as office curiosity. Obviously, he knew he was talked about. Obviously, he had decided that the best way to deal with the gossip was to keep a dignified silence.

But that Monday lunchtime, amidst the canteen's din and clatter, the stink of boiled cod all around them, Jack had said suddenly, 'I know a little restaurant where the food is pretty good – Italian. It's only a backstreet place, off the High Street . . .'

He smiled awkwardly and she'd realised he was asking her on a date. Handsome Jack Jackson, the man all the women of a certain age mooned after, had asked *her* on a date. She had almost laughed because it seemed so unlikely; instead she had looked down at the plate of pie and mashed potato she had just been served before joking to him. 'Well, if the food is better than this . . .'

He had smiled back – in relief, it seemed to her. They had sat down together at one of the long tables as they often had before, and their date wasn't mentioned again until Jack began on his treacle pudding. 'How about this Saturday?' he said. His eyes were dark, serious, and at once she had regretted her earlier glibness. She shouldn't have encouraged him; she imagined the gossip there would be when it came out that she and Jack had been out together. But then she thought how pleasant and ordinary it would be to have dinner with this man, perhaps even an antidote to Harry. That any man could be an antidote to Harry was such a foolish idea that now she could hardly believe it had crossed her mind. But then she had smiled and said, 'Yes, dinner on Saturday would be nice.' Nice! Niceness had never figured in anything to do with Harry.

On that first date with Jack she had dressed carefully, believing that she should look demure but also as though she hadn't made too much effort; she didn't want this quiet, family man to think she was out to seduce him. So she left the clothes she would have worn for Harry in her wardrobe, clothes he had bought her – jewel-coloured cashmere sweaters and slim-fitting pencil skirts, her favourite black dress that nipped in her waist and emphasised her breasts. Instead she had worn a dress in a busy, floral print, its circular skirt boosted with a net petticoat. In the full-length mirror in her bedroom she realised that the dress was too young for her. She was thirty and the mirror reflected a woman who seemed to want to look ten years younger, sweeter, and less experienced. 'Mutton dressed as lamb,' she had said aloud. But it was too late to change; Jack was already waiting downstairs, she could hear him making stilted conversation with her father in the front room – a room her father Matthew kept only for those he considered class. As she came downstairs, Matthew had come out into the hall. He had winked at her then said loudly, for Jack's ears, 'By, you look a proper Bobby Dazzler!' Her father wanted her to like Jack, and Jack to like her. He wanted there to be happy endings, for Harry to be forgotten.

On the Grand Hotel's dance floor, Jack held her closely, leading her expertly, a good, competent dancer. She imagined this slim, deft man was good and competent at most tasks he set his mind to. He liked machines; he liked numbers, things that could be fixed and controlled and predicted. On their first date in the Italian restaurant, he had told her about his twin boys in a way that had made her believe he wished he could occasionally tidy them away in a cupboard. Then he had mentioned his daughter Hope, and his expression softened. 'She's a little mother to the boys, of course.' He had laughed self-consciously as though he felt he'd been boasting, only to add, 'She's just so terribly sensible.'

He hadn't told her just how beautiful Hope was, or how self-contained, although she might have guessed. Cool, confident, beautiful Hope had smiled at her when Jack had introduced them, had said in her clipped, careful voice, 'I'm very pleased to meet you, Miss Campbell.' And Val had thought she saw a glint in the girl's eye that belied her good manners – something like suspicion mixed with a determination not to appear too friendly, too eager to be liked.

'Moonlight Serenade' ended. Jack stepped back from her. To her surprise, he took both her hands, lifting one to his lips. 'Val,' he said, glancing over his shoulder then back to her. 'Val, I thought we could go back to my house – for a nightcap. The children will be in bed . . .'

'All right.'

'Yes? I mean, if you don't want to, if you're tired . . .'

'Jack, it's all right. Let's go.'

He nodded gravely, as if the whole idea had been hers. 'Very well. Let's get our coats.'

He murmured, 'Oh God, Val, oh sweet Christ . . .'

He lay on top of her on the sofa, his hand on her bare thigh between her stocking-top and cami-knickers. He had unbuttoned her blouse and unhooked her bra and had lifted his mouth from her nipple to gaze at her with such desperation that she had pressed her hand to his cheek. 'Jack,' she whispered, 'it's all right, it doesn't matter. Hush now, hush . . .'

It seemed he was unable to look at her. Scrambling away from her, he got to his feet and hastily cleaned himself up with a handkerchief before buttoning his flies and thrusting the soiled, crumpled hanky into his pocket. 'I'm sorry.'

Val sat up and held out her hand to him. 'Sit down.'

'No.' He glanced up, towards the rooms where his children slept. 'I'll walk you home.'

Her breasts were uncovered still, heavy, too white in the yellow light from the standard lamp behind her. Her nipple stood out, glistening with his saliva, expectant-looking. For all his clumsiness, for all his weight on top of her, his frantic roughness, she was wet, ready for him; she had thrust her groin against his, opened her mouth wide as he kissed her, searching out his tongue and grasping his head, her fingers pressing hard against his scalp, making him groan, just as she had groaned when he'd pushed his hand up her skirt. She had been much too wanton altogether, and she had robbed him of control. As she fastened her bra she had a feeling that this might be the end of their pretending they were suited.

Her head bowed, her hands busy with the buttons of her blouse, she heard him light a cigarette. After a moment he said, 'It's been a long time for me.' He laughed painfully. 'You wouldn't believe how long. Sometimes I don't believe it.'

He was standing over her. Gently nudging her foot with his he said, 'I've never felt so much like a fifteen-year-old boy – not even when I was fifteen. Your fault – you shouldn't be so sexy.'

Standing up, she took the cigarette from him and inhaled deeply before handing it back. 'Perhaps it would be better if I got a taxi home, Jack.'

He stepped back from her. 'If you like.'

'We're both tired.'

'Yes. Of course.' Then, tapping the cigarette ash into the dead fire, he said, 'Did you enjoy this evening?'

'Yes, thank you.'

'I mean apart from just now. Apart from my disappointing performance.'

She sighed. 'Jack . . .'

'You're very cool, aren't you? It's almost as if you want to give the impression . . .' He snorted, shaking his head, his voice becoming bitter as he said, 'Oh well, never mind, eh? Put it down to yet another experience.'

She brushed past him. 'Good night, Jack.'

'Wait.' He caught her arm. 'Val, wait . . . I'm sorry.'

Shaking free of his grasp she gazed at him, keeping her anger in check only because he looked so miserable. He attempted to smile but his eyes gave him away. Perhaps they should just call it a day – but that was too cruel a thing to say to a man who looked like he was about to cry, who already felt himself to be humiliated. She pressed her hand against his cheek; softly she said, 'I think you're a lovely man.'

He grasped her wrist, lifting her hand away from his face. 'You think I'm a lovely man?' He laughed nastily. 'Jesus! Do you want to make that sound a little less patronising? What's the next line? And I really like you but? Don't you dare brush me off like this.' He let go of her wrist abruptly. 'Don't you dare!'

'Because if there's any brushing off to be done, you're the one to do it?' she retorted. Then, 'Look, I think I should just go home.'

22

'Not yet. You can't go yet.'

'You're upset.' Wearily she added, 'Like I already said, we're both tired.'

'I'm not tired. I'm not upset.' He burst out: 'I wanted tonight to be special.'

'I know.'

'Well, you don't have to sound so bloody resigned. You wanted it too – I know you did.'

His hair was sticking up. Earlier she had undone some of his shirt buttons and now she could see his grey-white vest and a few wisps of chest hair dark against his pale skin. She remembered how lean and angular his body had felt against hers, how his urgent need for her had been a savage, mindless thrill. She had thought she'd experienced too much to ever feel so desperate for sex again.

Reaching out, Jack touched her arm lightly. 'Val? Don't look like that.'

'Like what?'

'Like you've made a dreadful mistake.' Suddenly he said, 'I'm not boring really.'

She laughed, astonished. 'I never said you were!'

'But you think it. Actually, I am boring. Not when I was younger, but now . . .' He pulled himself together. 'You want to go home. I'll walk you there.'

They walked along the quiet streets in silence and Jack kept a small distance from her so that she felt stiffly self-conscious, as though she took up too much room on the pavement. The semi-detached houses of Jack's suburb began to give way to the rows of terraces that in turn gave way to the High Street.

As they turned into the last of these terraced streets, Inkerman Terrace where she lived with her father, Jack stopped. Taking her hand, he pulled her into an alleyway, backing her against the wall as he guided her hand to his erection. His lips close against her ear, he groaned, such a longing, needy sound, infecting her with his lust. Her free

23

hand pressed against the damp wall, the filthy old brick crumbling in her curling fingers as Jack ground himself against her; he grunted, bending his knees, pushing up her skirt and tugging at her knickers until they fell around her ankles. Covering her mouth with his, he thrust his fingers inside her.

She turned her face away from his. 'Jack, wait . . .'

'Let me, please.' His fingers still inside her, he rested his forehead against hers, his breath warm on her face as he whispered, 'Please . . . I love you, you know I love you.'

She closed her eyes. He had withdrawn his fingers, had begun to work on that place that would bring her to climax. She groaned, opening her legs a little more as she felt herself slump against the wall. He kissed her and she heard the smile in his voice as he said, 'There, you like that. You're so wet. Little hussy, little bitch on heat . . . there!'

She came, arching her body against his, her head back so that her throat was exposed. He bit into her neck delicately even as he put his leg between hers so that she could ride out her orgasm. Then, quickly, he was unbuttoning his flies and closing her hand around his cock as he took a Johnny from his pocket.

'Ready?'

She nodded, wrapping her legs around his waist as he entered her. Deep inside he stopped, drawing his head back a little to look at her. 'Good?'

'Yes.'

He grinned, but then his face became anonymous again, that of every man who had ever fucked. She closed her eyes, catching the dog-piss-and-rain stink of the wall as he reached his own climax.

Chapter 3

It's very odd how empty and silent the house feels now. Even though in the last few months of his life he never left his bedroom, my father's presence made itself felt. I was always listening for the thump of his walking stick on the bedroom floor whenever he wanted me to attend to him, a noise that seemed to travel along the crack in the dining-room ceiling and threaten to bring down lumps of plaster. Much as I was used to this noise, it would almost always startle me, concentrating as I was on my work, lost in it, often, so that I'd managed almost to forget about him completely. Sometimes, not often, I would make him wait, but the thump-thump-thump would come again – and besides, I had been put on edge, unable to continue. Best if I went to him immediately; he would be calmer then and less inclined to be a swine.

I was meant to excuse his foul temper, his insults, because he was dying and in pain. But he had been foul and insulting to me all my life, and although I cared for him as best I could, I never felt the pity that most people would have felt. I suppose I never really believed in his pain either, because he seemed so unchanged by it, remaining the nasty, spiteful man he had always been. Only sometimes, when I washed him, or later when I had to move him often to prevent sores, would I see the pain manifest itself in his expression. He would never betray his agony to me in any other way, never tell me that I hurt him, not directly. He would just shout out how clumsy I was, a bloody clumsy half-wit. I tried to be as gentle as I could; I tried to keep him quiet.

Sometimes, when he was in a more reflective mood, he would tell me how much like my mother I was: useless and ungrateful. 'That slut,' he would say, 'that flighty piece – she cared for nothing and no one, interested only in her fancy men, her own pleasure.' His lip would curl then and his nostrils flare as if he could still smell her scent on his sheets. He always used the same stock words about her, the same stock phrases. From these words and phrases I've gathered that she was blonde and very young, and that she left shortly after I was born with a man I know only as That Bastard. There are no photographs of her that I have ever seen; I'm pretty certain there are none in existence. I imagine that she was a bottle-blonde, that she laughed a lot and wasn't afraid of my father. So not like me at all, then.

There was a time in my childhood when I thought about her a lot, even imagined that she would soon come back for me. But even then I knew I was only making up stories for myself, like the story I invented where a wealthy-looking, handsome man helped her into a fast, fancy car. The man was That Bastard, of course, and he was about to whisk her away.

I wanted my mother to be film-star bright and daring when I was a young child. Later, I didn't want her to be anything at all. She had left me and wasn't worth thinking about. I remember feeling sullen when I decided it would be best to forget about her, as though I was stubbornly refusing to apologise for something bad that I'd done, knowing that it would weigh on my conscience. But that feeling didn't last. I'd started at Thorp Grammar School by then and it took all my concentration, all my energy, just to pretend to be normal enough to fit in.

This morning, I worked in the garden. After all the quiet respectfulness of the last week, I felt that I needed to do some hard work in the fresh air, work that would make me ache with weariness so that I looked forward to going to bed rather than dreading the sleepless night ahead. I dug out the old roses that had grown so leggy and spotted with mildew; I made a bonfire of last year's leaves and thought I could toss into the flames some of the rubbish that had accumulated in the house – the old bills and bank statements and such that my father refused to throw away. As I watched the smoke drift into the sky, I heard my name being called, and turned to see Jack, Martin and Stephen. The boys ran to me, almost knocking me off my feet. Jack said, 'Oh, steady you two,' as though he was terribly exasperated with them both. I looked past him, wanting to see Hope following him into the garden, but they were alone and I made myself smile through my disappointment.

Martin said, 'Can we go and play in the tree-house, Uncle Peter?'

They didn't wait for my answer, but ran off towards the oak tree with its trailing rope ladder. Jack gazed after them. After a little while he said, 'Monkeys. It's just like living with a pair of tireless monkeys.' He turned to me. 'Listen – I'm so sorry about yesterday, terribly sorry –'

'It's all right. You explained on the phone, there's no need to apologise.'

He thrust his hands into his trouser pockets, hunching his shoulders a little as he does when he feels awkward. Watching the bonfire spark and smoke, he said, 'I suppose letting one's friends down is just another consequence of being a damn wage-slave.'

The boys came down from the tree-house having found the pop guns, holsters and cowboy hats I'd left there for them, and began to chase each other around the lawn making shooting noises. Jack turned his attention on them, frowning. 'I don't remember being so noisy when I was their age. But then I suppose there was only one of me.'

I laughed, patting his shoulder because he looked so weary. 'Come on in. I'll make you a cup of tea.'

* * *

In the kitchen, as I busied myself making tea, Jack stood at the window and watched the boys run around the bonfire. I have known Jack Jackson since we sat next to each other on our first day at Thorp Grammar, listening to our new form master telling us how we were to behave. The form master – Mr Jeavons – had a wooden leg with which he would threaten to bash our stupid heads in; he was a veteran of the First War and scary as a devil. He knew my father – they had the war in common; he made me believe that all the men who returned from the trenches were vicious, that the fearfulness of it all had knocked out any kindly feelings they might once have had. Jack sat beside me as Jeavons ranted, as rigid with terror as I was, only smaller and weedier-looking. Jeavons singled Jack out because of this weediness; I was singled out just for being me. Thus a bond was created between us.

Jack turned to me. He said, 'So, he's dead. Odd, really – somehow he gave the impression that he'd see us all off.'

My father liked Jack – as much as he liked anyone. He used to ask him why he was friends with a fool like me. Now, Jack glanced up at the ceiling, as though my father really was still alive, aiming at immortality, about to start his banging. Looking at me, he said, 'You look a bit knackered, if you don't mind me saying so.'

'I'm fine.'

I wanted to mention that Hope came to the funeral, to ask him if he had sent her, his envoy, but I'm almost certain he didn't. I thought of her again in the church, how she looked so concerned and yet timid all at once. As casually as I could I asked, 'Where's Hope today?'

He didn't hear me, as he was back at the window, scowling at some antic of the boys. He rapped on the glass. Turning to me again he said, 'How would you like to adopt two six-year-old boys? I'm sure they'd much rather live here with you – you're the one who builds tree-houses, after all.'

He sat down at the table and I poured him a cup of tea. Taking out his cigarettes he lit one, impatiently thrusting the case and lighter back into his pocket and exhaling smoke down his nose. Just as impatiently he said, 'I'm not sure what to say to you, Peter.'

'You don't have to say anything.'

'I know. It's just that I remember how it was when my old man died.' He rolled his cigarette around the rim of the ashtray. 'To say it was bloody awful – well, that's understating it.'

I wanted to laugh, to say, But you loved your father, Jack! Your father loved you! I'd expected him, of all people, not to behave like everyone else. Yet it seemed that this man, who knew more about grief than anyone, still wanted me to make a show of my grieving, still susceptible to these lies the bereaved have to tell. Bitterly, because sometimes I am jealous of him, I said, 'I don't feel awful, Jack, only relieved.'

'I felt numb at first, too.'

'I'm not numb.'

He looked at me, baffled as though he hadn't understood. Perhaps he hadn't; people who loved their parents speak a different language from those of us who didn't. At last he said, 'Anyway, I know what it's like and if there's anything I can do . . .' He smiled awkwardly. 'There. Enough said.'

Clearly he thought he had embarrassed me and went back to the window to watch his sons. I watched them too, thinking of the imps and sprites I'd drawn early that morning, sharp-faced creatures climbing through tangled ivy leaves and thorns, shaking down blossom to fall at the feet of the princess lost in the dark woods. I realised that I had put too much malicious glee in their expressions, but of course, they wanted the princess to be terrified: her fear was entertainment, a spectacle. I had been right to draw them as I did; it's only when I'm away from my work that the doubts begin.

Jack said, 'Do you know that it's been almost five years since Carol died? It doesn't seem that long and yet sometimes . . . Well, sometimes it seems a lifetime ago. At least no one can accuse me of rushing into the arms of another woman.' Looking down at his cigarette, suddenly he ground it out as though it sickened him. Sharply he said, 'I went out with Val again last night.' He glanced up at me, only to look away again. 'I'm never sure what to make of her.'

'Does she know what to make of you?'

He frowned at me with that same, puzzled expression that I realised he has been using rather a lot on me lately. All at once I had the feeling that our friendship was slipping, that I could lose him if I didn't try harder to be more like the other men he knew and less like an eccentric relic from his childhood. Quickly I said, 'Did that sound glib? I'm sorry.'

It was as if I hadn't spoken. He said, 'Carol would have wanted me to be happy, wouldn't she? Not mourning her for ever. But I still feel disloyal! And Val, well – she's been around the block, I know. Sometimes I get the feeling she thinks I'm incredibly dull.'

'I'm sure she doesn't.'

'Sure?' He shook his head dismissively. 'Well, you weren't there.'

No, I wasn't there, and so my opinion was worthless. And I'm sure he believed that it would have been worthless even if I *had* been there, knowing as I do so little about women, about anything very much of the real, manly world in which he strides about. There, I'm bitter and I'm jealous. These low feelings must have shown on my face because he said, 'Oh listen, I'm sorry – going on like this when you've just buried your father.'

I laughed, imagining my father not dead but only buried – thumping on the lid of his coffin for me to come and dig him up again. My laughter must have sounded deranged because Jack gazed at me with such a look of pity that for the first time in my life I was angry with him. I couldn't sit there enduring his wrong-headed concern any longer. I got up and went out into the garden. The twins ran to me, grasping my hands.

'Come and see what we've found, Uncle Peter. Come on!'

I was tugged along, a boy holding each hand, their fingers warm and damp with sweat, soft, dirty little hands I had held so often before without ever feeling as I did then, suddenly and forcefully, a sense of furtiveness. Since their birth I have always been intimate with these children; I know the bony feel of them, their scent, and their salty, sharp taste when I kissed them. I have held them both on my knee and thought nothing of our easiness together. But now I wanted to pull my hands away from theirs and I would have, only I knew Jack was watching me. More than that, I had the idea that he was assessing my behaviour. I would have to act as I always had, the loving uncle, not the oddity I felt myself to be.

The boys led me behind the garden shed where three headless mice were lying in a neat row, their tails artfully arranged so that they appeared tied together. Next to these pathetic little corpses was a dead blackbird, intact, glossy still, its bright yellow beak the last vivid colour left in this gruesome little world. Still holding my hands, the boys looked up at me, grinning.

'We've been finding as many dead things as we can.'

Behind us Jack said, 'For goodness sake, you two!'

Martin and Stephen turned to him. Proudly Martin said, 'It's our cemetery, Daddy.'

'Go and wait for me in the front garden.' Making an effort to control the anger in his voice, he looked at me. 'I'm sorry –'

'It's all right.'

'No, it's not.' He turned to the boys again. 'Didn't I just tell you to leave us? Go on, quick about it.'

'We want to stay with Uncle Peter!'

'Well, you can't. You've done a horrible, disgusting thing and you're to go home.'

'Jack, it's all right, it's nothing.'

He stared down at the dead creatures, his lip curling in disgust. Martin made to speak and his father shouted, 'Get out of my sight, both of you!' His voice was so loud that the boys' faces paled. They stepped back from him, stumbling a little before turning to run across the garden and along the path leading to the front of the house. Jack watched them, anger setting his mouth into a thin hard line. When the boys were out of sight he said stiffly, 'I'm sorry, Peter, I shouldn't have brought them here.'

'Of course you should have.' I attempted to laugh. 'You're always welcome, all of you.'

He glanced down at the dead mice. 'I'll have to scrub their hands when we get home – God knows what diseases these vermin carry. Christ, they're disgusting. Were we ever as vile?'

'It's just a few dead mice, Jack, and they're just boys being boys. Don't be hard on them, not for my sake.'

Prodding the blackbird's corpse with the toe of his shoe he said, 'A cat must have killed them – some well-fed cat killing for the sake of it. I'll get rid of them for you. Do you have a shovel?'

I stooped down, picked the mice up by their tails and tossed them into the weedy, overgrown flowerbeds. The bird I picked up more gently and placed it under the laurel bush that grew beside the shed. It would decay into the earth soon enough. Turning to Jack I said, 'There, there's no harm done.'

'Peter.' He placed a hand gently on my arm. 'Why don't you come to us for lunch tomorrow?' Glancing in the direction the boys had gone he said, 'I had better go, before they take it into their heads to do something even more horrible.' He looked at me, that same furrowed-brow concern. 'Come for lunch, eh?'

I nodded. Wanting him to go, I began to walk across the lawn, leading him to the boys. I could hear them calling to one another, another game already started.

Later, as I threw the stewed tea down the sink and washed the teacups, I thought how during my time in the POW camps I would have eaten those mice, and the bird, and that they would have been a very welcome addition to my diet. I thought too how Jack was disgusted by the poor dead things, how he would have needed a shovel to get rid of them. Jack, of course, had a very different war to mine. From his Lancaster bomber, he saw death from a completely different perspective. I would be surprised if he had ever seen the dead close up.

I was taken prisoner in 1942, at the fall of Singapore. I was twenty and had seen nothing, done nothing – was, in fact, as green as green could be. And four years later I had still done nothing, still seen nothing except the worst, most perverted cruelties, which I think count as nothing because I learned nothing from them, only what it feels like to be terribly afraid, perpetually cowed and ashamed. In 1942 I stepped innocently into chaos and all normality, all ordinary experience that would have contributed to my growing up ended; now my twenty-year-old self is petrified inside the body of a thirty-seven-year-old – a middle-aged man. No wonder Jack looks at me the way he does. What is he to make of me, after all?

Before he left with the boys, Jack told me – incidentally, having almost forgotten – that Hope would not be coming for her drawing lesson as usual this afternoon. He didn't say why and of course I couldn't question him, couldn't allow my disappointment to show. I've been thinking that perhaps she's only shy of me now because of my newly bereaved status. I shall see how she behaves towards me tomorrow at lunch, and not mention the missed lesson. I have begun a drawing for her, and next Saturday, if she still doesn't come, I shall take it to her and hope that it will dispel any new awkwardness between us.

Chapter 4

Harry sat by his wife's bed. The injection Dr Walker had given her was doing its work because Ava was sleeping peacefully, or so it seemed. He wondered if such unnaturally induced sleep could be peaceful, but at least her expression was relaxed, her lips slightly parted as if about to speak, to smile even. Beneath her closed lids, her eyes had stopped their restless flickering, she was breathing steadily and a little colour had returned to her cheeks. Lying on her back, her long blonde hair fanned out on the white pillow, she looked like one of the porcelain dolls she had once loved so much. Harry hunched forward in his chair, kissing her hand that he had been holding since the doctor stuck the needle in her arm. 'Ava,' he said softly. '*Liebchen*. I must go.'

He placed her hand down on the counterpane, watching her for a moment to be certain she slept on before getting to his feet. Standing over her, he watched again for signs that she might be about to wake, to reach out and grab at his hand, to weep and rave and throw herself about the room. It had taken both him and Esther to contain her, and only when she was a little subdued by exhaustion could he send Esther to fetch Walker. By the time the doctor came Ava was curled on her bed, weeping; she had made the pillow wet with her snot and tears. Walker had sat beside her, stroking her hair and saying, '*There now, there now*,' over and over. Every time Harry saw this man he could have cried with relief for his kindness. Few doctors were so good; his goodness meant that Harry was in danger of

35

telling him everything. Already, Walker was his saint, his saviour; it wouldn't take much before he became his father-confessor.

Harry went to the window and closed the curtains. It would be dusk soon and besides, the thickly-lined curtains would muffle the noise from the road. He went to Ava's dressing-table and turned on the lamp; she was afraid of the dark and always slept with the light on. Tonight more than ever she needed the reassurance of the lamp's soft glow.

Next to the lamp stood the silver-framed photograph taken on their wedding day, bride and groom on the register office steps – her favourite photograph of him, she said, because he looked so handsome. 'My knight in shining armour.' She'd laughed, thrusting the photo at him. 'Look – look how grave and serious you are!' And she'd made a frowning face that was supposed to be an impersonation of him in the picture. It was true he hadn't smiled, but only because the photographer had caught him unawares. He had been happy enough. *Enough!* He exhaled sharply, knowing he was lying to himself. He hadn't been happy then, not by any measure. Besides, happy seemed too frivolous a word to apply to anything at that time.

In the photograph Ava wore a flower-sprigged cotton dress, belted at the waist, the skirt sagging to just below her knees. Several sizes too big for her, the dress hung on her like a sack on a scarecrow, the girlish puff-sleeves loose where they should have fitted closely and showing off her poor, emaciated arms. The dress had had a detachable lace collar; he remembered how it would flutter up around her face in the breeze. The lace should have been stiffened, an Elizabethan ruff to frame her beautiful, delicate face. But such delicacy had been fashioned by starvation and she hated the way she looked; she wouldn't have wanted to emphasise any part of herself. So she had worn a matronly, flower-sprigged dress and sensible, lace-up shoes. Man's shoes, from the Red Cross – she had stuffed newspaper in

36

their toes to help them fit. And she had grinned at him when he met her outside the register office, 'Am I not the most pretty girl?' her eyebrows raised, ironic. Except, of course, she *was* the most pretty girl – more than pretty, incandescently lovely. She had made him worry that, big fat man as he was, he would crush her.

Harry put the photograph down as quietly as he could. He turned to his sleeping wife; she hadn't moved. He tiptoed across the room, wincing at every squeak of floorboard beneath his heavy tread.

From the doorway Guy said, 'Are we going to get some peace now?' He walked into the room and went to stand at Ava's bedside. 'I wonder what drug he gave her?' Frowning thoughtfully, he turned to Harry. 'Perhaps he could leave a few injections for us to administer – what do you think? I would stick the needle in if you're too squeamish.'

Harry sighed. 'Guy, let's leave your stepmother in peace, eh? Let her rest.'

Guy ignored him. Gazing down at Ava he said, 'I'll sit with her, if you like.' He smoothed a strand of her hair back from her face; he picked up her wrist and seemed to time her pulse before allowing her hand to fall limply back onto the bed. Itching to drag him away, Harry only watched his son impotently, knowing that if he acted on his natural impulse he would only be playing into Guy's hands. Lately Harry had decided that he would try to ignore Guy's efforts to provoke him; he had decided that he would treat him as a rather tiresome child with whom he had to be patient.

As evenly as he could he said, 'Guy, I was going to have some supper. Have you eaten?'

Guy glanced at him, only to return his attention to Ava. 'I'm not hungry. And anyway, shouldn't you be dieting?'

'Guy, please. Come downstairs with me now. I'll make us some cheese on toast – you like that.'

Turning from the bed, Guy gazed at him. In the dim

37

lamplight, he looked younger than his eighteen years, a slight, slim boy who so resembled his mother. A week ago he had been expelled from his boarding school, the last school in a long line that had failed to tolerate his oddness and disruptiveness, his absolute refusal to conform to any set of rules. 'He believes he's rather too clever for us,' his last headmaster had told Harry when he had gone to collect Guy. 'And perhaps he is. I believe he is quite brilliant – but I'm afraid brilliance may be quite wasted on him.'

Harry believed that brilliance wasted his son, charging him up so that he was unable to concentrate on anything except his own frustrations at the slow stupidity of the rest of the world.

Placing himself on the chair beside Ava's bed, Guy said, 'I'll sit with her for a while.'

'There's really no point.'

'All the same. Go on – you go and eat. We'll be fine.'

Harry decided he wasn't hungry and went to his study to work. He reread Tom Wright's will, and, just as he had when the old man had first sat in his office, he thought how nasty he was. Then, and even more so now, he wished that Wright had found some other solicitor in Thorp to do his dirty work; but, a year ago, Wright had walked into his office on the High Street, leaning heavily on his walking stick, his knuckles white around its brass handle. Wright's face was a deathly, putty grey, and Harry would have pitied him for the pain he was obviously suffering, and because death so closely shadowed him, had it not been for the malicious glint in his eye. Those glittering eyes of his never seemed to tire of being amused by the rotten joke he was about to play on his son, Peter. Sitting on the edge of his seat, his big, knobbly hands clasped on top of his walking stick, Tom Wright had smiled his death's-head smile.

'My son needs to be shaken up, Mr Dunn,' he said. 'He needs to make his own way in this world. My money, my house will only hold him back, make him even more feeble than he is now. So,' he sat back, making an effort to appear inconvenienced rather than overwhelmed by pain, and drew breath. 'So, I have decided to leave everything to a family friend – a man in great need, I might add, a man who has children, who has made more of his life than my son ever will. I am here to make my will to that effect.'

He was to leave his son, Peter Wright, nothing. He was matter-of-fact about this, too matter-of-fact, rather over-playing his hand so that ironically there seemed to Harry to be an absurd theatricality about Wright's manner as he told him everything was to be left to John Jackson. In the unlikely event that John should die before him it would all go to Jackson's three children, divided equally among them. Harry had wanted to ask him why; rarely curious any more about his clients' motivations, he found that he did want to know what had caused this old man to hate his son enough to disinherit him. Wright must have expected to be questioned because he smiled that dreadful smile, his unnaturally bright eyes searching Harry's face. 'Fathers are not legally bound to love their children, Mr Dunn.'

This was to be his answer then to a question that in his professional capacity he hadn't and couldn't have asked, but which the old man had anticipated with relish. The son simply wasn't loved. Nor, he had no doubt, was the father. Perhaps, he'd thought at the time, they deserved such a miserable relationship, each as meanly vindictive as the other. At the time he hadn't seen Peter Wright. Because he had only to see him to know what type of man he was.

Standing in the cemetery as Wright's coffin was lowered into the grave, having observed the son's conduct throughout the funeral, he knew that Peter Wright was not a man at all, but a ghost, a shadow, one who smiled and smiled to try to fool real, substantial men and women that he was just as vital as they were.

Harry leaned back in his chair; he covered his face with

39

his hands and groaned softly. He hadn't wanted Peter Wright to be like this; he had wanted him to be as resilient as his father so he wouldn't have to think about him. On Monday he was to tell him that he was about to become homeless – penniless too, for all he knew, because he couldn't imagine that Wright had much money to his name. The old man had told him that his son was a draughtsman. Harry could still hear the sneer in his voice, the way his face had become even more pinched. He remembered that there had been a silence between them then as he'd watched Tom Wright contemplate just how worthless his son was. The silence went on and Harry had shifted in his chair, beginning to feel the kind of discomfort he had not felt since the war when other, younger men had sat opposite him, men who were just as steeped in the justifications of their own hatreds. Not wanting to, he had thought of Hans and had begun to tidy papers on his desk to distract himself from such thoughts. Tom Wright had laughed shortly, as though he guessed at the effect he was having. 'Shall we get down to business, Mr Dunn?'

Putting the will back in his desk drawer, Harry got up and poured himself a gin. He drank it down in one and poured another, taking it back to his desk. He wouldn't drink any more than this tonight; he would be strict with himself. Lately, with each drink he was reminded of his father, saw his reddened, coarsened face smiling with all the unfocused, good-natured befuddlement of his permanently half-cut state. When he was growing up, everyone told him that he was the image of his father; that had been fine by him. His father was a grand man, the most generous man in the whole world – all fathers should be like his, their pockets full of sweets and pennies to be given away with smiles and winks. Those smiles and winks! Sometimes as a young child he half-expected his father to ask him his name, just like some affable uncle at a friend's house. His father's spiritual absence was disguised by his jolly generosity –

how could such a magical, larger-than-life presence not actually be there? – but it was an absence, all the same.

He had told Val that he had been brought up by Father Christmas. She hadn't laughed as he had expected her to. Instead she had gazed at him, her expression soft with concern. 'Tell me about him,' she'd said. They had been in bed, in that hotel where the huge bay window looked out over the sea, where he and Val had stood on the balcony and he had, for a few seconds, been able to imagine them both far, far away, free of anxiety and guilt. And for a few seconds in that hotel bed he had imagined telling her about his father as she'd asked him to, but his father mattered less and less to him; he had almost forgotten his name; it was only when he took comfort in a drink that he was reminded. Besides, in that bed, time was exquisitely precious. Val lay in his arms, such a wonderful luxury that could not be squandered on remembering. He had kissed her breasts, felt her fingers curl into his hair. Soon he would be groaning her name, all thoughts, all memories annihilated – the greatest luxury of all.

Val. Thinking about her, he imagined bowing his head and banging it repeatedly against his desk, to clear her from his thoughts, to punish himself for remembering, for being an ordinary, faithless man. Hadn't he so prided himself on his restraint? Hadn't he always despised men who were governed by their cocks? After Ava's accident he had told himself he could live an orderly, celibate life. Laughable now, he supposed, but still admirable, still something he might have achieved, perhaps, if he had been blinded, or deafened, if he hadn't ever been close enough to Val to smell her, to wonder what it would be like to fuck her, that filthy, dehumanising speculation when his heart and soul suddenly became those of a rapist's. The moment he saw Val Campbell all his noble ideas were unmasked, too feeble to survive his lust.

The moment he saw her he heard himself saying, 'I'd

41

be delighted if you would care to dance with me later, Miss Campbell.'

They had been standing at the bar of the Grand Hotel's ballroom, where he had been introduced to her by Stanley Davies, who had organised this Christmas party for his staff at Davies & Sons, the engineering firm where Val worked and to which, by way of being Stanley Davies's solicitor, Harry had been invited. He hadn't intended to go, suspecting that Stanley would only corner him until he'd paid for his supper with advice. Then he would be on his own, watching Stanley's employees drink themselves into indiscretions. But he had been feeling melancholic that day, the same melancholy that came every year with Christmas trees and the sight of Esther helping Ava to thread paper chains. Esther, sensing this mood of his, had said, 'Why don't you go, sir' her voice that odd mix of shyness and encouragement as always. 'Mrs Dunn and I will have a lovely time here, cheering the place up for when you get back.'

Guy, sitting beside his step-mother, had looked up from the book he was reading. In that sardonic tone Harry had come to loathe, he had said, 'Yes, Papa, do go. Do have a lovely time and don't think of us at all!'

So he had dressed in his dinner suit, complete with black dickie bow and black satin stripe down the trouser legs, a black cummerbund holding in his belly. Esther had smiled at Ava when she saw him. 'Doesn't Mr Dunn look the part, Miss?' Ava had only looked at him as though he was a stranger, Esther's expression adding to her confusion. What *part* was he fit for, anyway? He was a middle-aged man in an old-fashioned evening suit, weary, dreading the boredom that awaited him, dreading the return to a house that had been cheered by paper chains. In that time before Val he had begun to feel that he'd had his life – even though it was not one he would have wholly chosen – and that there was nothing left but waiting.

Val had danced with him. Val had worn a green satin dress, close-fitting, even straining a little at the seam that ran down the middle of her backside. He'd imagined the stitches giving way, hot, fervent imaginings that had him wanting to grind his erection hard against her as they danced. The green satin dress was low cut, back and front, that straining seam giving way to a daring split that showed how erotic the backs of a woman's knees could be. She wore no jewellery, nothing to distract from the sheer magnificence of her body, those curves encased so tightly, so perversely restrained. It had been all he could do not to pant, not to take her hand and press it against his cock. He worried that his own hand would leave a big, sweaty print on the small of her back.

As they danced he had asked if he could drive her home and she had declined, of course, afraid of gossip probably, afraid of him too no doubt – that he would be all over her the moment they were alone. But then she had smiled at him. 'You're a very good dancer – I just wanted to tell you that.'

'For a fat man, you mean?'

She'd laughed. 'You're not fat! You're imposing . . . Statuesque.'

She went on smiling, smiling and smiling, and he saw that she was teasing him so that he relaxed a little, his filthy thoughts becoming a little less rampant. He'd even managed to smile at her almost normally, only spoiling the effect by saying, 'You're the sexiest woman I've ever seen in my life – I just wanted to tell *you* that.'

'For a spinster, you mean?'

He'd looked away, wanting to close his eyes and groan to release some of the pent-up frustration, at the same time wanting to laugh at the ridiculousness of being forty-five-year-old Harry Dunn who had told himself sex was a joy he could live without. He forced himself to look at her. She gazed back at him, no longer teasing but serious, appraising. No woman had looked at him with such direct honesty; he searched her face, wondering if he could dare to be so honest in return. When she smiled, eyebrows raised, he laughed despairingly.

'All right. I admit it.'

Her smile became archer. 'Admit what?'

'That I want to fuck you.'

She gasped, astonished.

'I'm sorry.' He stopped dancing. 'I can't believe I said that.'

'No, neither can I.'

They stood at the edge of the dance floor and she was still in his arms, still notionally at least his partner. He thought that she should have slapped his face and walked away; he imagined her proud, indignant exit from his life. Instead she seemed to be waiting for something.

Just as he was about to apologise again she said, 'I heard you're married.'

'Yes. I am,' he told her.

'Where is she tonight?'

He was unable to look at her, feeling that she had manoeuvred him into a trap, resenting her even as he felt he deserved his humiliation. At the hotel's bar, he saw Stanley Davies lift his drink in a silent, smirking salute. He thought he had never felt so ashamed, so nakedly foolish in all his life. Quickly he said, 'I'm sorry, forgive me.'

She followed him off the dance floor and out into the hotel's deserted lobby. Facing her he said, 'I've never spoken to a woman like that before.'

She stepped back, startled, as though he had swung round too suddenly when she had expected him not to turn around at all. Awkwardly she said, 'It was flattering really, in a way.'

'Was it?'

'No, not really. You made me feel cheap and it was a shock, a nasty little fizzing shock darting through me.'

44

Looking at him she said, 'Humiliating, how your body reacts, isn't it?'

'I'm sorry.'

She sat down on the hotel's stairs. 'Is your wife at home looking after the babies?'

He thought of Guy, his son, who wasn't a child, who sometimes, it seemed to him, had never been a child at all, and told himself he wasn't really lying when he said, 'We don't have children.'

'So she doesn't like parties, then?' Val took a packet of cigarettes from her handbag and he stepped forward, offering her a light. As she accepted, she met his eyes, that same honest look sizing him up. At last she said, 'Why don't you sit down?'

He sat beside her on the stair, relieved that it was good and wide and could accommodate them both without any part of their bodies touching. He sat stiffly, straight-backed, feeling huge beside her; in an effort to feel easier, he took out his own cigarettes and they smoked together in silence, music from the ballroom a steady beat he concentrated on. The music and the cigarette combined to calm him; he began to think that perhaps he could get away with behaving so badly. She was a stranger, after all; he would never have to pass her desk in his office or nod to her in his street. He would never see her again after tonight; she would never *want* to see him after tonight. The thought of never seeing her again was bleakly comforting; he knew he would wallow in the sweet agonies of unrequited lust.

He got up to fetch an ashtray. When he came back she had stood up too. She stepped towards him, grinding her cigarette out hard, the force pressing the ashtray against his palm; he imagined he could feel the stub burning through the thin tin. She stood close to him; he could smell her perfume that earlier he had tried not to inhale, not wanting to be more overwhelmed by her than he already was. Now though, he had an urge to press his face against her neck, not only to smell but to taste her. Feeling his unruly cock begin to stiffen again, he stepped back.

'Your wife . . .'

He shook his head; he had the terrible, absurd feeling that he might cry. She stepped towards him, close again, and touched his hand.

'My wife.' He laughed painfully, remembering how Ava had looked at him so blankly over the coiled links of bright paper. All at once he felt angry, a surge of animating feeling that made him desperate, selfish. 'I want to take you home. I want to be with you, alone in my car.'

'You want what you wanted on the dance floor.'

He gazed at her just as she had looked at him, honestly, coolly, despite his raging hard-on. When she looked away, he caught her hand and held it tightly. 'Shall we go?'

In his study, Harry picked up his glass of gin only to put it down again. He thought of Val in his car, arching her back in response to his kisses, to his hand cupping her breast. They were still in the front seats and the gear stick had got in the way; he was too big a man to climb all over a woman on the back seat of a car, even a car like his, built to impress, for comfort rather than speed. He had pulled away from her groaning in frustration and despair, his head back, eyes closed, so that it was a surprise when he felt her hand unbuttoning his flies and closing around him. Her hand was cool, soft, and she was tentative at first, as though she had never touched a man before. But she was expert, really, an expertise he had guessed at, of course. Her experience was one of the things he loved about her. When he was with her he didn't have to be careful; she was his equal, he could relinquish control.

He got up and went to the window, staring out at his neat and tidy garden, kept neat and tidy by a gardener, just as his home was kept thus by a cleaner, just as Ava was kept by Esther, just as a series of boarding schools had

46

temporarily at least managed to keep control of his son. His life ran rather smoothly, considering, considering there was a hole in his chest where his heart had been.

He thought of Hans – unexpectedly, because thoughts of that man always crept up on him, ambushing him in his weakest moments – Hans leaning across the table in the interrogation room, his handsome face frowning as though the question Harry had asked of him was deeply puzzling. 'You ask me *why,* Major Dunn?' He'd smiled that film-star smile of his. 'Now, that's not an *official* question, is it? Come – you are being prurient!' Sitting back in his seat, he'd laughed. 'Why: I don't have to tell you why. Just as you don't have to tell me how many women have refused to fuck you.'

Turning away from the window, from his white-faced, flabby reflection, Harry went to his desk again, took out Tom Wright's will and put it in his briefcase ready for Monday morning. He thought of Peter Wright, a man whom Lieutenant Hans Gruber would have shot through the head if Hans had cared to look at him more than twice. Gentle people like Peter Wright incensed Hans; they wasted the air they breathed. So, without Hans to carry out an execution, he would have to deal with him. Harry sighed. Picking up his glass, he drank its contents down in one and went to pour himself another.

Chapter 5

Hope stood on the street outside the church, waiting for her father to finish with the polite, necessary business of shaking Father O'Brien's hand and exchanging pleasantries. A little way along the street, the twins hung off the railings surrounding the church, their feet on the low wall, their bottoms swinging out so that those leaving the church had to step in the gutter to walk round them. The boys were wearing their best Sunday clothes, and she thought that she should call at them to climb down, to stand and wait nicely, to be good rather than risk tearing their trousers and dirtying their white shirts. But she knew they wouldn't take any notice. Besides, lately she had begun to think rebellious thoughts about her father, because weren't these two naughty little boys *his* responsibility? She heard her father laugh, saw Father O'Brien clap him on the shoulder as he shook his hand. Then Jack Jackson put on his hat, straightened it and pulled on his gloves. He took a handkerchief from his pocket and blew his nose. At last he was ready to leave and Hope felt her relief mix with exasperation at her father's inability to do anything quickly and decisively, or to ever consider her – her time, her impatience at being kept waiting. Today of all days he should have been quick. Today she had somewhere to go.

Last week, Irene Redman had invited her to her birthday party. Irene was in the second year of the sixth form, a girl she knew only slightly, but all the same, this pretty, popular girl had stopped her outside the school gates and said, 'Here, this is for you.' She'd thrust an envelope at

48

her, smiling. 'It would be jolly nice if you could come.'

Then, Irene had gone, leaving Hope looking down in surprise at the invitation to her eighteenth birthday party.

Ever since she had received the invitation she had wondered why she'd been asked, and whether or not she should go; worrying that she wouldn't know anyone well enough, that she would stand on the edge of the party, ignored. The Redmans lived in a huge house overlooking the park. Mr Redman was a lawyer, Mrs Redman was known for her charity work; her photograph was often in the *Gazette* where she'd be posed surrounded by nurses or nuns or little sick children. When Hope told her father that she had been invited to this party he had merely raised his eyebrows. 'Moving in high society, eh? Excellent!' He'd grinned ironically; she'd thought how useless he was as an only parent because he understood so little. She began to worry again why Irene Redman had condescended to invite her.

Her father walked down the church path and went immediately to the boys, scooping them down from the wall and snapping, 'Behave yourselves!' Turning to her he said, 'Right, are we ready?'

They began to walk home, the boys holding their father's hands, Hope trailing a little way behind. As they crossed the road leading to their house, he said, 'I did mention that Peter was coming to lunch, didn't I?'

'No!'

'Well, no need to look so alarmed – the chicken's quite big enough, isn't it? We'll just have to peel a few more potatoes.' He grinned at each of the boys in turn. 'It'll be fun having Uncle Peter over, won't it?'

The boys agreed excitedly as Hope felt a creeping anxiety that had nothing to do with chickens or potatoes. She had been trying not to think about Peter. She had lied to her father about having too much school-work to go to Peter's lessons, but now it dawned on her that of course she couldn't get out of seeing him altogether; he was still her father's oldest, closest friend, still liable to call at their house at any time. Realising this, she felt a kind of panic as she remembered how he had looked at her at his father's funeral. She remembered too that last lesson, and how he had smiled at her as he'd taken the pencil from her hand, finishing the bird she had attempted to draw with such quick, fluid skill he'd barely needed to take his eyes off her. His smile was too warm, his gaze lingering on her too long after he'd placed the pencil down. She tried to tell herself that he smiled like that only because he was amused by the clumsy way she'd drawn the bird's wing; but in her heart she knew it was more than that. He had turned the same smile on her as she stood at the back of that church feeling lumpy and childish in her school blazer. It was a smile that wanted too much. The panicky feeling grew stronger. She knew that he would never stop coming to their house, never stop looking at her in a way that made her feel naked, and that there was absolutely nothing she could do about it.

As she followed her father and brothers up the path to their house she said sullenly, 'Why did you ask him today, of all days, when you knew I was going to Irene's party?'

'I'd forgotten about that,' Jack admitted, 'but it won't make any difference, will it? I know – Peter could give you a lift to the party on his way home. Save me and the boys having to walk you there, eh?' He beamed, pleased with this idea.

Horrified, Hope said quickly, 'Don't ask him to drive me there. Honestly – don't.'

'Don't be silly! He'd be only too pleased. There,' Jack unlocked the front door and ushered the boys inside, 'that's decided. Come on, I'll help you with the lunch.'

Peter said, 'This is delicious, Hope.'

Hope looked up from her plate of roast chicken, mashed potato and peas to smile at him briefly, the first

50

time she had looked at him directly since he'd arrived. All afternoon she had avoided his gaze, becoming more and more self-conscious, convinced that he was watching everything she did, listening too attentively to everything she said. His attention made her clumsy, her skin prickling whenever she couldn't avoid dodging past him. She had even dropped the gravy boat on the kitchen floor as she became more flustered and felt her face burn as Peter at once took out the dustpan and brush from beneath the sink and swept up the broken shards of pottery, despite her protests that he really shouldn't bother. As he'd replaced the dustpan it occurred to her that he knew the house too well, knew where every last thing was kept just as if he lived with them. Her father, lounging against the kitchen dresser with a glass of beer in one hand and a cigarette in the other, had smiled at her behind Peter's back, an eyebrow raised, mocking look as if he thought Peter fussed too much. His contempt only made her feel more anxious; if her father believed this man was odd, then he truly must be.

Now, finishing his meal and placing his knife and fork neatly together on his plate, her father said, 'Hope's been invited to a party this afternoon, Peter. At the Redmans', no less, and at such an odd time. I can't decide if this Redman girl is rather too old for a tea-party or much too young for a cocktail party – seems a bit rum to me.'

'It's just a party.' Hope glared at him, wanting him to see from her expression that he shouldn't say anything more.

He only grinned and went on, 'Anyway, Hope is rather nervous – you know, over whom to curtsey to, all that . . .'

Peter smiled at her – an ordinary, kindly smile. Ever since she could remember he had sympathised with her over her father's relentless teasing. Instinctively, out of long habit, she found herself smiling back. Angry with herself for this lapse, she looked down at her half-finished meal and pushed her plate away.

Peter said, 'I daresay the Redmans will be very kind, Hope. I'm sure you'll have a lovely time.'

'Of course she will!' Her father sounded exasperated. 'My God – *I* would like to go! You'd like to go too, wouldn't you, boys? Have a good old snoop around? They have a tennis court in their garden, isn't that the bees' knees?'

The twins said together, 'Can we come, Hope? Can we – please? We'll be good.'

Peter laughed. 'You haven't been invited, only Hope. How would it have looked if Cinderella had taken two little rascals like you to the ball, eh? It wouldn't have done at all.'

'She isn't going to a ball and she's not Cinderella!'

Peter glanced at her then turned to the boys again. 'It's not a children's party, boys. We'll have a party of our own here.'

'I rather hoped you'd give Hope a lift to the Redmans', Peter.'

Peter looked at her, questioningly. 'Is that all right, Hope?'

Her father shook his head. 'What'd you mean? Of course it's all right. Hope doesn't care who takes her, do you, Hope?'

Feebly, knowing she would be over-ruled, she said, 'I could walk.'

'Nonsense. You'll want your posh new friends to see you getting out of a car, not arriving all flushed and sweaty. Peter will take you, he doesn't mind. You'll pick her up too, won't you, Pete?'

Peter nodded, glancing at her as if to gauge her reaction.

Satisfied that he wouldn't have to be saddled with the tedious business of walking her home from the party, Jack said cheerfully, 'Right, let's get this table cleared. There's apple pie and custard waiting!'

They lived in a semi-detached house, brand new when her father had bought it the year the boys were born. Her mother had liked its clean modern fireplaces, its kitchen with its many fitted cupboards, its bright, white, tiled bathroom. There was a lounge and a dining room, and of the three bedrooms, one – the smallest – would be hers to do just as she liked with. This is what her mother had told her, crouching in front of her awkwardly, big with the twins: 'You'll have the cosiest, most lovely little room all to yourself.' But unlike the room she had shared with her parents in her grandmother's house, this new room had space only for her bed and a wardrobe. There was nowhere for her dolls' house or rocking horse, nowhere for her baby dolls and their pram. All of these toys had once belonged to her mother and were now hers, her grandparents having lovingly kept their only child's possessions. Hope remembered sitting on her bed in her new little box of a room and thinking how rotten it was that she should have the baby room. But the doctor had already discovered the second heartbeat in her mother's tummy – she was to have two new brothers or sisters, and wasn't that twice as much fun, twice as exciting? So, of course, she was to have this little room so the babies could have the space they needed. It was rotten, but she conceded that it wasn't unfair. She had always been, as her father kept reminding everyone, including her, sensible.

Her bedroom remained unchanged since that day, still papered with the same, pink rosebud-covered paper her mother had helped her to choose, the matching curtains still hanging at the window that looked out over the street. Standing at the window, Hope could hear her father and Peter talking in the lounge below; she heard her father laugh, heard Peter's soft, smiling voice say something in return, unable to make out words, only tone. She had to admit that Peter had a nice voice, quiet – too quiet sometimes because he could never control the classes he taught. She remembered her discomfort when the girls in her class took advantage of him, his weakness – his *oddness* as she had come to see it. Sitting in that art class, as her friends talked and laughed and ignored his efforts to teach them, she had found her embarrassment turning to anger. He should simply behave like all their other teachers and be firm, as strict as the art mistress who eventually took over from him and wrote such critical reports about her inability to sketch.

Her father had told her once, 'Uncle Peter has had a lot to put up with in his life.'

She had thought he meant Peter's father, a terrifying old man who would sometimes grab her hand and pull her to him, forcing her to sit on his knee and holding her too tightly, his heavy hand hot on her thigh. The old man had difficulty breathing. She remembered how wet his laboured breath seemed, how it smelled of the peppermints he sucked constantly – sweets he would offer to her, smiling his sly smile. His wheezing was terrible, like that of one of the monstrous creatures Peter drew for his handsome princes to slay. This man would be a lot to put up with, she thought. She had thought then, when she was younger and Peter was still *uncle*, that he didn't deserve such a father.

Lately though, her father had begun to tell her a little about his war and, from his incidental comments about Peter's war, she had learned that the *lot* Peter had had to put up with also included being held prisoner by the Japanese. 'I can't imagine what he must have suffered,' her father had said in a rare reflective moment of serious sympathy. She remembered feeling hardly any sympathy for Peter at all, only pleasure that her father had finally begun to talk to her as an adult. After all, he had always treated her as an adult, ever since her mother's death.

Hope went to her wardrobe and, opening its mirrored door, stared at her small selection of clothes. The dress she had thought she might wear to the party was pale yellow, with a sweetheart neckline, short puff sleeves and a cinched waist above a full skirt. She was afraid that it would make her look too young, not fit to be invited to an eighteenth birthday party. Fleetingly, it crossed her mind that if this dress did make her look like a child, then Peter would stop looking at her as though she was a grown-up. She let this thought go, not wanting to look like a little girl for whatever reason. She had decided as she'd washed the dishes after lunch that she would begin to treat Peter with a disdainful aloofness. If he wanted to behave badly, then so would she. The decision had steadied her; she felt less afraid of him now she had a planned response to those smiles of his.

Chapter 6

Hope hardly spoke in the car. As I drove her to the Redmans' house I tried to think of something to say to her so she'd feel easier about this party. Try as I might, I couldn't; every opening I thought of seemed too stilted or worse, too childish. I imagined telling her about the drawing I intended to give her of the woodcutter's encounter with the goblin. But isn't *goblin* such a silly word? It certainly struck me as such as I drove Hope to the party. And the drawing itself is silly – why would a sixteen-year-old girl want such a thing? As I desperately hunted for something to say, I couldn't help taking my eyes off the road to glance at her from time to time. I thought how lovely she looked in her pretty party dress. She wore a necklace around her slender neck that had belonged to her mother Carol. More and more these days, she looks like her mother. She has the same quiet determination, too; I remember that Carol was always very single-minded in getting her own way.

At last, laughing inanely, I said, 'Do you think there'll be jelly and ice cream, or canapés?'

She gazed out of the window. 'I don't know.'

Blundering on, I said, 'Perhaps there'll be champagne.'

I was ignored. She was resolutely turned away from me, her hands clasping the neatly-wrapped present on her lap. Her hands are very small and white, her fingernails short and round and pink as the inside of shells.

I said, 'What did you buy her?'

'Chocolates.' She looked down at the gift, smoothing

the wrapping paper before turning back to the car window. After a moment she said, 'Milk Tray.'

Her necklace was a silver crucifix, the tiny figure of Christ suffering at her throat. Her fingers went to it as if to check that the crucified figure faced outwards, a nervous gesture that made my heart ache with sympathy for her. I know how shy she is, like me, know how difficult it would be for her to walk into a room full of people like the Redmans. I'm afraid I allowed my sympathy for her to run away with me because I said clumsily, 'You look lovely, Hope, there's no need to feel awkward . . .'

She glanced at me, a sharp, frowning look, only to look away again.

Of course, I couldn't take the hint and be quiet. I was too full of the idea that I could somehow make her feel less nervous, a near evangelical zeal to make her understand that I empathised with her. Too fervently, I said, 'You imagine that you'll say or do something foolish, but you won't. You are young and lovely and charming –'

'Could you stop, please. I can walk from here.'

I looked at her in surprise, already slowing the car for a red light. As we came to a stop she opened the car door. 'Thank you for the lift.'

'Hope –'

She turned to me. 'It's not far from here, I can walk.'

'No.' Dismayed, I caught her arm to prevent her from getting out of the car. 'I promised Jack I'd see you safely there.'

She pulled back from me as though desperate to get away. The lights had changed to green; the driver behind me honked his horn. Hope jumped from the car and began to walk quickly. Crossing the junction, I pulled the car into the side of the road and got out to stand in front of her.

Hope stopped, then made to walk round me. Following her, I said, 'Hope, please get back in the car and let me take you to the party as I promised Jack.'

'I'd rather walk.' She looked at me with the kind of insolent dislike I'd seen so often before on the faces of her schoolmates. She might just as well have slapped me for the pain it caused. I stepped back from her, that familiar sense of humiliation having its usual, shaming effect. I smiled, and it was the kind of creeping, ingratiating smile one gives to bullies, even though this was Hope. Through the pain I felt an even greater sense of shame that she could make me feel so abject.

She moved past me and all I could do was watch her walk away.

Late afternoons have always been the worst time of day for me, the time when I can no longer concentrate enough to work and the evening stretches out ahead of me, time I have to somehow fill with reading, or listening to the wireless, passive pastimes that make me feel as though I've been caged, although when I actually was imprisoned I would long – pray, in fact – for such routine, such small comforts. At times in the camps, I would organise lectures to help pass the dark evenings. The lecturers were only fellow prisoners, of course, men who'd had interesting professions in their former lives and felt up to entertaining us. More often than not we were all too exhausted, too ill and listless either to talk or to listen, but sometimes the effort was made. I look back on those few times with a kind of wonder that we could behave so normally.

This afternoon I drove home and went straight to bed, thinking I could block out the anger I felt with myself – and with Hope if I am scrupulously honest – if I slept. I wanted to sleep the whole of the wretched evening away, sleep right through until morning when I'd have the will to work. But of course, I had to go and collect Hope, risking her scorn again. I found myself staring at the ceiling, going over and over that journey with her in the car and the way she had looked at me on the street with such contempt. I am a grown man and yet I was made to feel like a schoolboy with that look of hers. Of course, my feelings are my own responsibility and she was anxious about that party – this is the excuse I give her to comfort myself with – only to remember that she looked at me as though I was despicable.

But shouldn't I be used to being despised? I have been despised and humiliated by masters of the craft, by true sadists. Humiliation is standing naked before a fellow officer while he slaps you across the face, knowing you have to slap his face in return – a bizarre ritual punishment we all too often had to perform. Humiliation is being kicked up the backside by a tiny Korean guard, and being kicked again when you stumble. It is not merely being dismissed by a young girl in a tantrum. Her eyes were so angry, bright and blazing, her pale cheeks flushed. Even feeling as pathetic as I did, I couldn't help thinking that she was beautiful.

But I *am* despicable, in reality, and possibly she senses just how despicable I am.

Perhaps I should write my story down so that she might read it and imagine I'm ordinary. *Once upon a time . . .*

Once upon a time, a young man of twenty knelt at the feet of a Japanese soldier, the point of a bayonet scratching at his throat. This Japanese soldier – an officer –spoke remarkably good English with the slightest trace of an American accent. Odd what one notices even when one thinks death is imminent. I believed truly that I would be killed right there and then. I trembled. I had been ordered to place my hands on my head so that my elbows stuck out at sharp angles and I trembled so badly I could feel my fearful vibrations through my skull. I wasn't a very edifying sight for my men. They knelt too, behind me and to one side; I could hear Johnson praying softly until one of the Japanese soldiers used his rifle butt to silence him. I spoke then, and I tried to sound reasonable, although my voice quavered and faltered and the bayonet seemed about to slice through my vocal cords. I said, 'We have surrendered. We are prisoners of war and should be treated accordingly.' I waffled, woolly-headed with fear, although some sharp, defiant part of me wanted to say that if they killed us, they would be murderers. Some men would have said that, I think. Some men would have been beheaded right there and then.

The officer withdrew his bayonet. He gazed over my head, a distant look on his face as though wrestling with his conscience. He looked weary, almost as dishevelled and sweat-stained as we were, and for a moment of absurd naivety I thought he might empathise with us and thus take pity because he had been through the same bloody experience. But then he looked at me, and it seemed he saw for the first time what a pathetic creature I was – an excuse for a soldier. He shouldn't have been demeaned by having to converse with me, nor have his conscience troubled by our continued existence; we should have been lying butchered at his feet – the honourable dead. Because I wasn't a respectable corpse, he drew back his arm and hit me hard across the face. I toppled to the ground and felt his boots smash against my ribs.

What if I were to tell all this to Hope? What if I were to tell anyone, in fact, as I have not spoken about my experiences to a soul. Jack suspects a little, I think. On reflection *suspects* is the right word. It wasn't quite the *done thing* to have been taken captive by the little yellow men in Jack's opinion, I'm sure. Not that he would say as much. We all keep very quiet on this shameful subject.

That Japanese officer broke two of my ribs. I never saw him again, he was just the first in what I began to believe was a never-ending line of sadists and bullies. At first it was hard for me to take in the fact that there were so many such men and none that would take the slightest pity on us. We were contemptible, and the more they starved and beat us, the more ragged and naked and wasted we became, the less it seemed we deserved. Then, as I write this, I remember that of course in their eyes we didn't ever deserve anything, we were merely tools to be thrown away when broken. There was nothing personal, apart from the irredeemable disgrace of being captured in the first place.

I try not to dwell on the past.

Paradoxically, the past has held me captive, just as surely as if this house was surrounded by impenetrable jungle.

Still, I tell myself everything is grand, now. My father is finally dead and freedom is within my grasp. The jungle beckons, full of dangers and rewards.

Then I think of Hope and am as scared as I ever was that the past and all its truths will come out. I think of Carol, her mother, and am doubly ashamed.

I knew Carol before Jack did. We met one fine Sunday afternoon when I was sketching the ducks on Thorp Park lake. She stopped and stood a little behind me, watching, and so of course I became self-conscious – I would never sketch in public nowadays. I eventually put my pencil and pad down, wanting to pretend I had not been doing anything as ridiculously pretentious as sketching. But she went on standing there and I was so aware of her eyes on me that I hardly dared move, afraid that if I did she would laugh or make some jeering comment. My ears began to burn. On the lake, the ducks began to gather, swans too, because if people stop near them they expect bread as much as I expect ridicule. At last, she came to stand in front of me.

'Have you finished it?'

'Pardon?'

She nodded her head towards my sketchpad. 'Your drawing – it's very good. I wish I could draw. I can't draw a thing! Stick men, maybe, stick men standing outside square houses with triangular roofs.'

The pad had begun to flap in the breeze and I held it down on my knee, my hands covering it so she couldn't see my drawings of mallards. To my surprise she sat down beside me, gazing at the ducks. 'Will you draw the swans, too? They're so elegant.'

'They're vicious,' I said, and blushed.

She smiled at me. 'My name's Carol, by the way. They called me Carol because I was born on Christmas Eve – isn't that horribly embarrassing?'

'No, not really.'

'Well, I think it is. Silly, anyway. If I had been a boy they would have called me Noel. Dreadful. Still, they're all right, really.'

'They?'

'Mummy and Daddy.' She twisted round and pointed to the big houses behind us, their gardens running down to the park's boundary. 'I live there, in that house with the flagpole. Daddy's *very* patriotic. I have no brothers or sisters, do you?'

'No.'

'Rotten, isn't it? They both have *masses* of brothers and sisters, but they all went to live in India or Canada or Australia – I have an uncle in South Africa, even. He sent me a real-life Zulu's shrunken head – would you like to see it?'

'I don't think Zulus shrunk heads.'

'It wasn't shrunk by a Zulu – it *belonged* to a Zulu, as it were . . .' She trailed off, puzzled for a moment before her face brightened again. 'Anyway, it is rather interesting. Horrible, but interesting. You're probably right though, being a boy.'

I laughed, astonished by her because I had never heard anyone talk so freely, so happily about nothing very much. She wore a bright pink and green tartan tam-o'-shanter and a matching scarf and mittens, muffled up like a little girl, her cheeks pink with the cold. Her eyes were the clearest, most brilliant blue, as lively as the sunlight on the lake. A strand of her thick, golden hair fell out from beneath her hat and she pushed it back, smiling at me.

62

Later – years later – the day I was sent overseas, she told me that in the park that afternoon she had wanted me to say something, ask something, just so she would have to stop talking. 'You know how much I talk . . .'

'No.' I kissed her. Held her face between my hands and kissed her again and again, her mouth, her eyes. She didn't return my kisses. She was crying, and I tried to comfort her, to say that I would be home in no time, no time at all. She only drew back from me, placing her hands on my chest as if to ward me off, her palms flat against my chest, pushing gently, her head bowed because she couldn't meet my eyes.

Quietly she said, 'Keep safe.'

I laughed. 'I will, of course. You know me.'

'Yes, I know you. I know that you don't realise how precious you are.'

Precious. As if I was a stone dug from the earth, a hard, inanimate thing without feeling. I should have told her that I loved her. That, in fact, I had loved her since the moment in the park when she first smiled at me. I thought she didn't want to hear me say that; perhaps she did.

In the camps sometimes we would receive letters, rarely, but sometimes the Japanese would allow us a little contact from home. For many men it was a great comfort; they would go off on their own to find a private place to read their letters from wives and sweethearts, from mothers and fathers. Needless to say, I received no letter at all. She thought I was dead. That's what she told me, that was her excuse. She thought that I wasn't the type of man who could survive. I was a will-o'-the-wisp, a fey boy who drew ducks in the park. She looked so shocked when she saw me on the street a few weeks after my return. Her face paled so dramatically I thought she was about to faint.

I wrote earlier that when I came home, I didn't feel anything – and that's true, in essence. That day though, when Carol stared at me with such horror – I was quite a sight, let's not forget – I did feel that it would be better if she no longer existed. It wasn't a very robust thought. I didn't want her dead – didn't want to kill her or even Jack. I just had an idea that it would be easier for me if she didn't exist. As it was, we had to go through the rigmarole of greetings, of explanations, the awful, embarrassing smiling and hand-shaking it all entailed. Jack cried when he saw me. He actually cried – hard to believe; a tight-lipped, manly crying, but crying all the same. Guilt, I thought then, not caring very much, not *feeling* very much, except of course that runt of an idea that it would be easier for me to live if Carol had never been born.

I got up from bed and went downstairs. I began to draw, fitfully, finishing the picture for Hope. In the end, I picked it up and tore it in two.

Chapter 7

Hope sat on the edge of the Redmans' pale silk couch, a plate of birthday cake balanced on her knee. She watched as Irene and her friends danced to 'Move It'. Irene was a great fan of Cliff Richard. His records were piled up beside the gramophone on the sideboard, his poster had gazed down from her bedroom wall, seen when Hope had gone to put her coat on Irene's bed. She'd noticed how big Irene's bedroom was, and how pink and frilled and smelling of a sweet, violet perfume. Perfume bottles, jewellery boxes and a silver-backed brush, mirror and comb set were laid out neatly on the dressing-table that was complete with pink velvet cushioned stool and triple mirror. Hope, lingering in Irene's bedroom a little too long, shy of returning to the thronged rooms downstairs, had imagined Irene sitting at this dressing-table each morning, brushing her hair, dabbing her nose with face powder from the silver compact beside the perfume bottles. Standing in front of the mirror, reflected in triplicate, Hope had smoothed down her skirt and thought how young she looked. Young and nervous and uncertain of whether to be ashamed or proud of the way she had jumped out of Peter's car and walked away from him.

She'd gone downstairs and had hung about the edges of the dining room where guests helped themselves to the buffet that was spread over two large tables. She thought that perhaps she should take one of the stacked white china plates and a napkin and gather a few bits of food. But her nervousness had robbed her of her appetite, and besides, she believed she would look greedy, tucking into vol-au-vents alone in a corner. She smiled at a man who brushed past her, only to feel her face colour as he ignored her. Turning away to hide her embarrassment, she caught the eye of a boy across the room. He gazed at her. After a moment he raised his hand to his mouth and blew her a kiss. She'd felt her blush darken and had looked away quickly, bumping into Irene's mother who had taken pity on her. 'Come, my dear,' she'd said. 'Allow me to introduce you to some people.'

Some people had told her they knew her father and asked after him, asking too about those *darling little brothers of yours*. These people who knew her father knew also about her mother's death. Hope couldn't help noticing the expression in their eyes that over the years had become so familiar: pity, concern, curiosity all mixed together with a sympathetic smile so that she wouldn't think them prurient. After all, the fact that she had lost her mother had been headline news for a few days that horrible winter. *Young Mother Killed by Hit & Run Driver – Latest!* Hope remembered how the newspaper-stands were full of it, at the time.

She had escaped from these adults and their questions to sit alone on the couch with her layered pink and white wedge of cake. Now she tapped her feet to 'Move It' and smiled to try and appear as though she was having a nice time. She wondered how she might dispose of the cake she couldn't bring herself to eat because it looked so dry and sickly and because she knew the crumbs would spill down her dress. Thinking that she could perhaps slip the plate under the couch, she realised that the boy who had blown her the kiss was watching her. He turned to the boy beside him, said something and then began to weave through the dancing girls towards her. Irene caught his hand, laughing as she tried to make him dance, but he pulled away from her crossly, determined not to be stopped. As the song ended, the boy sat down beside Hope.

Watching Irene select another Cliff Richard record, he said, 'I suppose you like him, too, don't you?'

Hope glanced at him, only to return her gaze to the girls who had begun to dance again, not wanting to be polite to someone who had deliberately made her blush. Stiffly she said, 'Like who?'

'*Whom*.' He snorted. '*Cliff*, as my cousin calls him.' Suddenly he held out his hand to her. 'I'm Guy Dunn, Irene's distant, distant cousin. Hello.'

She took his hand and immediately he grasped it tightly and pulled her towards him. With his lips close to her ear he whispered, 'Listen, and smile as you do. You see Irene's brother over there? We have a bet that you won't dance with me because you think I'm rotten for blowing you that kiss just now. He thinks you'll freeze me out all evening.' Letting go of her hand he sat back, his eyes searching her face. 'You blush really easily, don't you?'

'No!'

He laughed. To her surprise he reached out and hooked a strand of her hair behind her ear. 'I'll lose half a crown if he wins the bet. So – will you dance with me?'

He was gazing at her still; she noticed how bright his eyes were, as though he was laughing at her. Then she saw that there was something not quite right about his left eye; the green of its pupil seemed to have run in a jagged line into the surrounding white. She found herself frowning at him, fascinated by the eye's strangeness. Instead of turning away, he touched his cheek beneath the damaged eye.

'When I was six, a boy at my boarding school threw a dart at me. *Bull's eye*! They thought I'd lose it, but as you can see . . .'

'Can you see through it?'

He laughed. 'Yes. I see you looking appalled and fascinated all at once.' Softly he said, 'What most people ask next is *did it hurt?*'

'Did it?'

'Can't remember.' He got to his feet in a quick, graceful moment and held out his hand to her. 'Come on. There's half a crown at stake.'

He was eighteen; he was only a little taller than her and slim. His dark brown hair was cut very short, showing off small, neat ears. She supposed he was handsome although she couldn't bring herself to really look at him properly; she found herself glancing to one side of him, afraid that if she looked at him too directly she would seem too forward. And she had stared at his eye, and said 'who' instead of 'whom', so perhaps he already thought she was lacking in social etiquette. He held her lightly as they danced; his hand in hers was hard and dry and he smelled clean, like a beach that has had the hot sun on its sands all day. She wanted to lean in closer to him to inhale his warm, salty scent. Wanting this, she felt a softening inside her and was appalled to feel a blush spreading across her face and throat and skin exposed by her sweetheart neckline. When the music stopped, he stepped back from her and she thought he might tease her over this blush, but he only smiled. 'Would you like to see the garden?'

Holding her hand, he led her through the crowded house and out onto a terrace, its steps leading down onto a huge lawn. Groups of guests stood about, laughing and talking a little too loudly; all evening, waiters had patrolled the rooms with napkin-wrapped bottles of champagne, filling the guests' glasses so that no one was ever without a drink. Each time a waiter had approached her Hope had covered her half-empty glass with her hand; she thought the champagne tasted bitter.

Guy said, 'So – this is the Redman mansion and grounds. Are you suitably impressed?'

She thought that he was the kind of boy who talked too much, confident that he wouldn't be ignored or hushed. She was, she knew, intended to consider his showing-off as ironic whilst at the same time recognising his superiority, and so she made an attempt to smile at him as knowingly as she could. He only laughed.

'All right,' he said, 'I'm being an idiot.' He gazed at her, his face becoming serious. At last he said, 'I asked Irene to invite you to the party. I wasn't going to tell you but I think you should know. I wanted you to come.'

She felt that same soft feeling inside her, as though he had touched her intimately. Imagining that he had, she found she couldn't look at him, afraid of what her face might betray. He stepped closer to her and her skin tingled.

'Hope?' His fingers brushed against hers and she stepped back, stumbling as her heels sank into the soft grass. He caught her elbow.

Managing to look at him, she thought what a poor impression she must be making on this confident boy. Attempting boldness, she said, 'Why don't you show me the rest of the garden?'

There was a vegetable garden behind a high copper hedge where a square of bare soil had been dug over ready to be planted. There was a greenhouse full of plant pots, each stuck with a white marker to remind the gardener which seed had been poked into its compost, and against an ancient-looking wall an espalier tree traced its dark trunk and branches, clinging tight to its own shadow. Guy led her to a rough wooden bench beside the greenhouse. Taking off his jacket, he laid it over the wood so that it showed its blue silk lining. 'I don't want you to snag your dress,' he said.

'Really, there's no need –'

'Sit,' he commanded. Then frowning he said, 'You're not really shy of me, are you?'

As she sat down carefully on his jacket, he sat beside her and took her hand again. Looking out over the broken ground he said, 'This is my part of the garden. Uncle David allowed me to take over this little square. I grow things.' He glanced at her from the corner of his eye and for the first time he himself seemed shy. 'I grow vegetables, mainly,' he went on. 'Last year I entered the Biggest Onion competition at the allotment society.'

She laughed and felt him squeeze her hand briefly.

'I know,' he said. 'Idiotic, really.'

'Did you win?'

He gazed at her. 'No. You have to have been at it for years . . . I came third.'

'Well done!'

'Hope, are you laughing at me?'

'No, honestly.'

'Honestly?' Then he asked, 'Do you mind that it was me who wanted you at this party and not Irene?' Quickly he added, 'Of course, Irene was quite happy to invite you. She didn't *not* want you here. Sorry, this is coming out all wrong.'

'I don't mind.'

'Good. That's good. Listen . . .' His hand tightened its grip on hers as though he was afraid she was about to run away. 'Why don't you and I go to the cinema sometime?'

She thought of sitting in the Odeon with him, in the darkness, in the back row perhaps – or would that be too fast for a first date? Her friends at school talked about first-date rules, the length of time a kiss should last, the number of blouse buttons that could be safely undone, how there should be no touching below the waist – either his or your own. She remembered how Janet Gibson had shrieked at this last rule, saying how she wouldn't ever, *ever* want to touch a boy's *thing* anyway! Something had stirred inside Hope then at the idea of a boy's anatomy changing just because he wanted you. She had known that she *would* want to touch it; she had wondered if this made her odd.

Guy glanced at her. 'Hope?'

'Yes,' she said. 'I'd like to go to the pictures.'

He grinned. 'Friday?'

70

She nodded, holding his gaze, until it seemed that they were moving closer as if some gentle, outside force was pushing them together. Her nose brushed his; she felt his lips on hers, dry and soft, and she moved still closer as she heard him groan, a part of her embarrassed at this noise he made, a bigger part wanting to groan too. As it was, eyes closed tight, she pressed her mouth harder against his until she felt his hand on the back of her head, his fingers curling into her hair and massaging her scalp. And then she did groan, wriggling still closer to him so that his mouth opened wider, his tongue searching out hers as he moved closer too, so close he was almost on top of her, his hand below her breast to steady himself. He drew away, breathing heavily.

'Hope . . .' He closed his eyes and kissed her again, his hand moving upwards until it was light on her breast.

She pulled away.

'Sorry,' he said.

'It's all right.'

He laughed self-consciously, looking away. She wondered if he felt as she did, so sensitive and engorged that if he were to touch her again, she would guide his hand to that place between her legs that she sometimes found for herself, wanting him to press hard – roughly, even – until she felt that blissful, shaming sense of release. He only moved away from her a little, clasping his hands together as if to stop himself from reaching out again.

He cleared his throat, a noise so self-conscious that again she found herself embarrassed by his betrayal of emotion. She noticed that he had an angry red spot just above his collar and another high on his forehead. When he had blown her that kiss earlier, it hadn't occurred to her that such a boy might have spots or ever feel as awkward and self-conscious as her. He had seemed arrogant. She found herself wishing that some of that arrogance would return.

Catching her eye he smiled a little, almost back to the boy she imagined he was, partly granting her wish. 'I daren't kiss you again – you know that, don't you?'

She pretended to be a tease. 'Why not?'

He looked away towards the house beyond the copper hedge. 'We should go back inside. *Not* that I want to . . .'

'We don't have to.'

He turned to her, giving her a long hard look. At last he said, 'You'll get into trouble saying things like that.' He stood up abruptly. 'Inside, now. You didn't eat your cake.'

Peter was standing in the dining room, a little way from the French windows Guy led her through. He looked shy and out of place, even though Irene's mother was chatting to him, smiling and laughing her light, tinkling laugh, doing her best to put him at ease. Except Hope thought she saw a look of desperation in Mrs Redman's eyes, as though this strange man was really too, too difficult.

Hope guessed that he'd been worried about her, her seeming absence from the party. His face changed when he saw her, his expression one of relief that she had appeared. It was this look that she hated most of all the things she suddenly hated about Peter, the look that implied she was his concern, his responsibility, signalling to these people that they were somehow related. More strongly than ever at that moment, with Guy at her side, she didn't want to be associated with this man who looked so pathetically eccentric beside the Redmans and their friends. To her shame she saw that he was wearing his most ancient-looking jacket, the leather patches at its elbows cracked, a button dangling by a thread; worse, its sleeves were just that bit too short, so that his big, bony hands stuck out and appeared even bigger.

Peter smiled with all the force of his relief. 'Hope! There you are.'

'Mr Wright,' Irene's mother said, 'this is my cousin, Guy – he must have been showing Hope the garden.'

Guy thrust his hand out at Peter, confident and smiling,

superior again. 'Hello, sir.'

'Hello.' At once Peter turned to her. 'Hope, if you like I can come back later . . .'

'Oh no, Mr Wright,' Mrs Redman said, 'please, you must stay and have a drink with us. I won't hear of you driving away only to have to come back. Guy, darling, go and fetch Mr Wright a glass of champagne. I don't know where all those waiters have got to.'

Laconically, Guy said, 'I think they're packing up, Diana. I think all the champagne has been drunk.'

'*Really*? Oh dear.' She turned to Peter. 'Oh well, you could have a proper drink . . .'

'No, thank you, Mrs Redman.'

'Oh, do call me Diana!' She touched his arm, a flirtatious gesture that made Hope imagine that she was drunk. Grinning at Peter, Diana Redman said, 'Why don't I know you?'

Peter laughed so easily that Hope was surprised. 'I don't know,' he said. 'Some oversight on my part?'

Mrs Redman giggled and touched his arm again. 'Oversights can be remedied.'

Hope heard Guy groan softly. He glanced at her, a mock-despairing look. To Peter he said, 'May I fetch you a drink, sir?'

'No, thank you.' He looked around the almost empty room as if to make the point that most of the other guests had already left.

Diana Redman sighed. 'Well, I suppose the party *is* over,' she said. 'Guy, why don't you go and fetch Hope's coat?'

When Guy had gone, Irene's mother returned her attention back to Peter, and said lightly, 'I really feel I should know you.'

To Hope's astonishment, she realised that Diana Redman wasn't drunk, but was actually attracted to Peter, was actually flirting with him, and that Peter was behaving quite as if this happened to him often, with a kind of grace of which she would never have suspected him to be capable. Mrs Redman seemed not to see his shabbiness, his oddness; Hope made herself look at Peter, trying to see him as this woman did. Peter caught her eye and smiled his ordinary, familiar smile and it seemed that Irene's mother moved closer to him as if she wanted him to smile like that at her, too.

Guy came back and helped her on with her coat. He saw her to the door and on the Redmans' sweeping drive he again held out his hand to Peter.

'A pleasure to meet you, sir.'

Suddenly it occurred to Hope that Guy thought Peter was actually her father. Without thinking, wanting only for there to be no suspicion that they were in any way blood related, she blurted out, 'You know he's not my father, don't you?'

Guy laughed awkwardly, and she realised at once how rude she must have sounded to him. She blushed darkly and he made an immediate effort to ease the embarrassment that radiated out from her.

'Yes, I know,' he said. 'You have a different surname.' He glanced at Peter. 'Well, goodbye, sir.' To her he smiled. 'See you on Friday?'

She nodded, knowing her face was still blazing, hating Peter even more bitterly for causing her such embarrassment.

Chapter 8

On his way to visit Peter Wright, Harry drove along Inkerman Terrace and stopped the car outside Val's house. For a moment he just sat, clutching the steering wheel, thinking that if he drove away now he would only feel angry with himself for a few minutes, and he could bear such frustration, that it would be nothing compared to the kind of humiliating show he was about to make of himself. He couldn't resist it though, knew that if he didn't do it now he would only come back later, and if his nerve failed again, he would try again, again and again, because he had reached a decision and he would not give in.

Taking the keys from the ignition, he pulled on the handbrake and got out of the car. The street was empty, its children already taken to school, mothers returned behind the closed doors. Monday was wash day; these women had their routines, according to Val at least, time-tables they followed, just like her own mother had. The men were at work, many of them at Davies & Sons. He wondered how many of Val's male neighbours watched out for her as she shimmied back and forth from the typing pool. Some of them, she had told him, wolf-whistled after her.

Knocking on the door of number ten, Harry stood back and looked up at the house. Her bedroom was at the front, the double room her father Matthew had conceded to her. He slept in the back bedroom, looking out over the yard and his pigeon loft. It was Matthew Harry had come to see. He wondered if he should knock again, or go around to the back where the man was more likely to be.

Glancing down the street to the alley that ran along the back of the terrace, he saw Matthew walking towards him. The man was frowning, ready for an argument, belligerent as ever. Harry stepped towards him, unconsciously raising his hands in a placating gesture.

'Matt –'

Val's father brushed past him, taking his house key from his pocket and stabbing it into the lock. As he opened the door he said, 'Bugger off. Bugger off and leave us alone.'

'Please.' Harry caught his arm, afraid that he would slam the door in his face. 'Please, I just want to talk.'

'There's nowt you've got to say to me.' He turned to him. 'Christ, you've got a nerve, coming here.' Nodding towards Harry's car, he said, 'Why didn't you tie a few balloons to it – make an even bigger show of yourself? Aye – and us! Don't you think she's talked about enough already, you silly bastard?'

'I'm sorry.'

'Sorry? Listen – go now, before I thump you. You're not too big a bastard for a bloody nose.' Matthew shrugged him off, about to go inside, and Harry moved quickly to put his foot in the door.

'Let me in, Matthew. Let me in or the neighbours really will have something to talk about.'

Matthew gazed at him; he seemed to be considering. At last he said, 'You're a lousy bastard, you know that, don't you?'

Harry nodded.

'*Christ*!' Shaking his head, the older man stepped aside. 'Come in. Be quick – I can see the bloody curtains twitching already.'

Matthew led him through to the kitchen, a room big enough for a dining table and two armchairs, a sideboard beneath the window that looked out onto the yard. Rag rugs Val's

76

mother had made were laid over the worn lino; there was a print of Van Gogh's *Sunflowers* on the wall, the orange and yellows startlingly bright in this room washed out by the grey light of a cold northern spring. On the draining board was a folded tea towel, a dishcloth was draped over the taps; there was a stink of bleach vying with the mince-and-onion smells coming from the pan simmering on the stove. Matthew had been a Corporal in the Durham Light Infantry, had fought in the Great War and had been in the Home Guard in the last. When his wife had died a few years ago, he had taken over the running of his home, scorning the work, Val had said, but all the same managing to be better at it than her mother had ever had the heart to be. Matthew kept the house with military precision, everywhere so neat and tidy it seemed only the most disciplined of men lived there, and not Val, not the Val Harry knew at least, who strewed her stockings and knickers about, who spilled face powder on polished surfaces and left the tops off her perfumes and lotions.

Standing in this pristine kitchen where Val had been so recently, Harry felt the familiar, panicky desperation at the idea that he might not ever see her again; his despair sounded in his voice as he said, 'Matthew, I have to talk to her. Would you give her a message?'

'No.'

'You must. At least tell her I've been here.'

Matthew shook his head, as implacable as a child. 'No. No, no, no.'

'Yes! Please, Matt – please.'

'Don't *Matt* me. I'm not your pal. Never was.' He laughed shortly. 'Most men would kick your backside out onto the street. I should. I bloody should.'

'Except you know how much I love her.'

'Love! Do you think I'm a fool? What do you think I'm going to say? That if you *love* her it's all right? Bugger off back to your wife. *Love* her.'

Harry sank down onto one of the chairs. He held his head in his hands, knowing that he must appear ridiculously theatrical to this man. Matthew Campbell had been married to the same woman for forty years, a till-death-do-us-part marriage so that his heart had been broken predictably, cleanly, and had mended in the same straightforward way. He couldn't imagine that Campbell had ever felt as he did now, Val's father had too much right on his side. Looking up at this straight-backed, merciless old soldier, Harry said, 'I told Val I'd divorce my wife.'

'Aye, I know. I know it's not all you told her, neither.' He shook his head, frowning. 'Divorce her but go on living with her after you'd married Val – that was to be the set-up, wasn't it? Jesus!'

'It's the best I can offer.'

'Best for who? You. No one else. Now get out, go on. She's told you what she thinks of your best – now you know what I think of it too. Bloody crack-pot!'

Harry got to his feet. 'Matthew, please tell her I've been here. Tell her that there will never be anyone else, and that if she should ever change her mind –'

'I'll tell her nowt. I won't have you messing up her life any more. She's courting someone anyways, a decent man.'

'She's seeing another man?'

'Don't you look so horrified – she's nothing to do with you.'

'Who? What's his name?'

Matthew smirked as though he was enjoying Harry's panic. 'I'm not telling you his name. I'll tell you that he's honest and decent though, a widower. His wife really *is* dead – he doesn't just wish her dead.'

'I don't wish my wife dead.'

'No? Then you'll be the only adulterous bastard who doesn't.' Gazing at him Matthew said, 'Listen, I know you've got your troubles –'

'*Troubles*?' Harry laughed; even to his own ears he

sounded unhinged.

Matthew held up his hand to silence him. 'Listen, son. You just accept that there's nothing you can do. I can see that it's hard for you, I can understand that, but in the end, well – you're married. It doesn't matter how sick your wife is, how much you think you love someone else, in the end you're married and there's nothing you can do.'

'You think so? Well, we'll see about that, eh? We'll see!'

And Harry walked out, slamming the door behind him so that it seemed the whole terrace shook. He was in his car, driving too fast down the cobbled street when he realised that the anger he felt was the purest, most unadulterated feeling he'd ever experienced; he could punch Val's *widower's* head in and it would be the most fantastic, liberating act he could imagine.

A red light showed and he slammed on his brakes, drumming his fingers on the wheel and honking his horn when the car in front failed to move off quickly enough as the lights turned green. He was breathing heavily, his heart beating too quickly; he knew how red in the face he would be, apoplectic, an ambulance case if he wasn't careful. As he calmed a little, he tried to imagine what he might do next, but all he could think of was finding the man Val was seeing and giving him a good kicking.

Unbidden, as ever, Hans came into his head, beaten so that his eyes were no more than slits in his swollen face. Hans still had the energy to smile at him, having wiped the blood from his mouth with the back of his hand, having spat one of his perfect white teeth into his other hand, his beautiful voice slurring only a little as he said, 'A fellow officer accused me of being a traitor. I ask you, Major Dunn – what is a man to do?'

He remembered handing him his handkerchief so that he might clean himself up more effectively and how Hans had stopped smiling and had looked almost ashamed that

Harry should see him in such a state. Catching his eye as he thrust the hanky into his pocket, Hans had said, 'Will this be over soon?'

'Soon enough.'

Hans had nodded, drawing himself up as if he felt he had betrayed too much weakness. Placing his tooth down gently on the table between them he said, 'For the Tooth Fairy, eh? Maybe you'll get sixpence in return for your handkerchief, Major.'

Sometimes Hans spoke the most impeccable English.

Harry found that he had reached the tree-lined avenue where Peter Wright lived. He stopped the car but went on sitting, the engine running, unable for a moment to contemplate getting out and carrying on with his normal business. There was nothing much normal about what he was here for, anyway. Looking at the house where, for the time being, Peter Wright lived, he thought about shoving the car into gear and driving home. This morning he had left Esther trying to coax Ava into eating a little scrambled egg, holding the spoon up to her lips and making soft, encouraging noises. He guessed that Esther could be doing this still, a task that often took all morning. Guy would be idling around; no doubt if he arrived home so unexpectedly his son would make some sarcastic comment. He realised that he wanted to face Guy even less than he wanted to speak to Wright.

Finally, he turned off the engine and got out of the car, taking his briefcase with its life-changing documents from the back seat. Squaring his shoulders, he walked up the path to Wright's house.

Chapter 9

I spent the morning working; believe it or not, I have deadlines and my publisher telephoned me just after breakfast to ask after my progress. He is a kind man, his hints are gentle. He is another who thinks I should be deep in mourning; he said he hardly liked to bother me at *a time like this*. Well, bother away, I thought. The illustrations he's after are almost finished, and I told him so. I have to be reliable, after all, if the work isn't to dry up – my income with it.

I worked, but my thoughts kept returning to Hope, how as I drove her home from that wretched party I so much wanted to ask her about that boy – this Guy – who was so confident, so cocky, so suddenly possessive of her. I'd seen how he looked at her, how he held on to her hand; I hadn't missed the smirk in his eyes each time he called me *sir*. All those *sirs*! Arrogant little puppy! And Hope could hardly bear to look at me. Her face was flushed, her throat and chest too, all the pale skin exposed by her party dress mottled pink and red. When the boy helped her on with her coat, his hands lingered on her shoulder. Unobserved, no doubt, he would have kissed that place below her ear where wisps of her hair escaped from her ponytail. But he looked up and caught my eye, holding my gaze for a long moment. He's an odd-looking boy, not handsome in a conventional sense. His left eye is damaged. I know a girl like Hope would find this fault touching.

Of course, she is angry with me after the foolish way I'd behaved as I drove her to the party. I only wish I had kept my feelings to myself. Lately though, it seems that my feelings are not as manageable as they once were when my father was around to keep them in check.

A man came to visit me today. His name is Harry Dunn and he is the same man who came anonymously to the funeral, the stranger I made up stories about.

I could not have invented Harry Dunn; he is extraordinary in every way one could care to imagine. I felt rather as if I had been visited by a king of some ancient, recently exterminated civilisation. There was such sadness about him, a depth of grief I have rarely come across. He is a huge man, the expensive cut of his clothes showing off his broad shoulders; I couldn't help noticing the girth of his thighs. He is the most beautiful, most imposing human being I have ever seen and he pities me. He believes I am the most pitiable wretch alive.

Harry Dunn called at midday. Even the way he rang the doorbell was authoritative, a sharp, short burst of noise. I got up at once, grateful for the distraction. Callers at this house have always been rare. On my way to the front door I paused momentarily at the hall mirror and saw that my hair was sticking up where I'd pushed my hand through it – a habit I have when I'm concentrating. I smoothed it down hastily; I also took off my glasses and put them in my pocket because I only need them when I'm working. I suppose I wanted to make the best impression on whoever it was. I only wish I had been wearing shoes and that my big toe had not been sticking through the hole in my sock, even that I'd been wearing a collar and tie rather than the soft plaid shirt and corduroys I had on. If I'd made a real effort, however, I could not have looked any more ineffectual than I did.

When I finally opened the door to Harry Dunn he smiled at me as if I was a child.

'Mr Peter Wright? Harry Dunn – my secretary spoke to you on the phone.'

I hadn't had any such phone call. Mrs Hall often forgets to pass messages on to me – I'm sure she has the subconscious idea that nothing in my life is important enough to warrant her attention. I must have looked bemused because he said, 'You seem not to remember?'

'Your secretary may have spoken to my housekeeper, Mr Dunn. I'm afraid she didn't pass the message on.'

'Oh. Then I'm sorry, this may be an inconvenient time.' He glanced over his shoulder to his car and I had the idea that he wanted to go, but then he looked at me again as if he had resigned himself to staying, his voice worryingly gentle as he said, 'I'm your late father's solicitor, Mr Wright. May I come in?'

I made him coffee and cut him a slice of the cake left over from the funeral, carrying it through on a tray to the dining room where I'd left him taking papers from his briefcase. He had filled the room with his scent, a rich mix of expensive cologne and cigar smoke. An envelope was in front of him on the table where he now sat, another of the dining chairs pulled out ready for me to be seated, as though this was no longer my house but his office. At the very least he was in command. He said, 'Ah, coffee, thank you,' and I laughed a little, imagining that perhaps he'd forgotten I didn't actually work for him. He looked at me, puzzled, as though laughter was the very last sound he expected me to make.

Thinking it would be best not to attempt to explain my amusement to him, I said only, 'My housekeeper made the cake. She's a good cook but a poor secretary, I'm afraid.'

'I'm sorry about the confusion, Mr Wright. I should have made certain that you knew I was coming.'

'Well, no harm done.'

'No.' He cleared his throat. 'No, but all the same . . .' He pulled the envelope towards him and opened it. I saw the heavy velum paper, the deeply black, ornately scrolling letters. I had guessed what it was, of course. My father had told me he had made a will; he used to try to make me guess who he had left everything to. I wouldn't rise to his goading but kept silent whenever he raised the subject; nothing could have frustrated him more than my silence.

Dunn looked grave. He gazed down at my father's last will and testament as if he knew it off by heart but wanted to make doubly certain he had it straight before reading it to me. I presumed he would read it, formally, leadenly, like those actors playing his role in films as a motley crew of would-be murderers wait on the edge of their seats. But he looked up at me and, gently he said, 'Mr Wright, I should let you know now that your father has left everything to a man named John Philip Jackson. Everything. He has made no provision for you, none at all. I'm sorry.'

John Philip Jackson. For a moment I had absolutely no idea who he was talking about; it crossed my mind that my father had picked out someone randomly from the telephone directory. Then I realised that he meant Jack. I laughed shortly. I should have guessed – of course, how obvious it was!

'Mr Wright?'

Dunn looked even more worried; perhaps he thought he had an imbecile on his hands because his voice became soft and rather slow, his pronunciation even clearer. 'Mr Wright, your late father has left everything to this man, John Jackson. I think you should know that you can contest the will, if you wish.'

'Would there be any point? He was of sound mind, wasn't he?'

'Arguably.'

I laughed again. 'He was, Mr Dunn. More than *sound,* I would say. Pain made his wits even sharper. You haven't drunk your coffee. Please, don't let it grow cold.' Suddenly puzzled, I said, 'Shouldn't Jack have been present, to hear this?'

'Jack?'

'John Jackson.'

Dunn looked down at the will again. 'It was a stipulation of the will that you should know first.'

I nodded. 'Is it also a stipulation that I should be the one to tell Jack?'

The man frowned at me as though rather shocked at such an idea; he obviously didn't know my father very well. 'No, Mr Wright. I shall write to Mr Jackson.'

Because he looked so concerned, so anxious for me, I said again, 'Drink your coffee, Mr Dunn, please. And do try the cake – it's really very good.'

He ignored me. 'Do you know Mr Jackson?'

'Yes.' I edged the plate of cake towards him. 'If you enjoy the cake I'll give you some to take home. I'll never get through it, although I haven't the heart to tell Mrs Hall. I know I'll end up surreptitiously throwing it to the birds. Actually I should give it to Jack, for him and the children, although I suppose it's his anyway, now. How does this work, Mr Dunn? Am I to just pack a suitcase and go? But then really the suitcases belong to Jack now, too. My clothes are my own, I suppose? Not that he'd want them.'

'I'm sure Mr Jackson will give you time to organise your affairs, Mr Wright.' In that preposterously gentle voice of his he said, 'How well do you know him?'

'I don't want to be rude, but I don't think that's any of your business.' Tired of his demeaning concern I said, 'This isn't a shock to me, Mr Dunn, as I believe you imagine it to be. I neither want nor expect your sympathy.'

'I understand.' He sighed. To my surprise he began to eat the cake, taking sips of coffee between bites. He ate with great concentration and delicacy, his eyes fixed blankly on the middle distance; I don't believe I have ever seen anyone look so sad whilst eating cake, so absent from the pleasure of it. He had obviously never known starvation. At once I realised how unfair this bitter thought was; after all, often enough I took no joy from food. Besides, I wouldn't wish starvation on anyone.

He caught me looking at him and smiled rather bleakly. 'You're right, it's good cake.' As if he felt the need to make conversation he said, 'Your father told me that you're a draughtsman, Mr Wright. Where do you work?'

'A draughtsman?' This was a new one on me. Usually he would say only that I was an invalid; sometimes he would say that I was feeble-minded to boot. I daresay he thought he would appear too cruel in disinheriting a feeble-minded invalid, so he had to think up some other description of me. I don't know why he should have had such contempt for draughtsmen as to describe me as one of their number.

Dunn said, 'I presume that's not what you do?'

'No. I illustrate children's books.'

'Really?' His face became more animated as though this was terribly fascinating. 'That must be very rewarding.' He went on smiling at me. 'What kind of books do you illustrate?'

'Collections of fairy tales, mainly.'

He nodded enthusiastically. 'Wonderful! I know the Grimm Brothers' stories very well. My wife . . .' His smile slipped a little. Quickly he said, 'My wife came from the place where they were born. Jakob Grimm was a great German linguist.' He breathed out sharply. 'Anyway, Mr Wright, if there's anything I can do to help in any way . . .'

I laughed. 'Do you have a spare room, at all?'

He gazed at me and for a brief moment I truly believed he was about to cry. 'I'm very sorry, Mr Wright.'

I wanted to comfort him. I said, 'It's all right, Jack is a friend. Perhaps he'll keep me as his lodger, eh?' He didn't look much comforted so I went on, 'Don't worry, Mr Dunn. Things have a habit of working out, in my experience.'

'Do they?'

I nodded and he frowned at me. All at once he said, 'Your father also told me you were a prisoner of war. Was

86

that a lie, too?'

'No.' I glanced away from him, imagining the contempt in my father's voice as he told him this. Knowing that this kind man would have been embarrassed by such contempt made me feel ashamed. After all, what type of man has a father who despises him so much? I made myself look at him. I said, 'I'd like to tell Jack about this business myself. Is that all right? I know you'll need to write to him officially, but all the same, I don't want him to think that I don't know about it. I don't want this to be any more awkward than it need be.'

'Of course you must do what you think best, Mr Wright.' He hesitated then. 'Were you a prisoner in Germany?'

'No. In Burma.'

His eyes widened, a mixture of shock and pity on his face – the same expression I've seen before when I've told people how I'd spent the war. 'I'm sorry.'

So, I'd earned myself yet more sympathy. Standing up, wanting more than anything to get him out of the house, I said blithely, 'Yes, well – I did hear the Germans were a little kinder to their POWs. Now, there wasn't anything else, was there?'

He got up, this big, commanding man who pitied me to the point of being insufferable. If my father had not tried to poison his mind against me he might have treated me normally, without his bloody kid gloves. He might have noticed that I was a man just as he was and not some terribly wronged child. I saw him to the door; I held out my hand to him and thanked him for coming. I have my dignity. At least I have always had that.

After Dunn left, I went upstairs to my father's bedroom and sat down on his stripped-bare bed. I stared at his wardrobe where his shirts and suits still hung, where his shoes were neatly lined up together in their pairs, where his ties were coiled into a drawer like snakes. Above the hanging rail are box files, made of heavy, marbled cardboard in dark reds and greys, pristine because I bought them from the stationer's only last week. The files are stacked one on top of the other; they contain my father's diaries.

My father kept a diary every day of his life from when he was a boy. Not all his diaries are in the files, of course, there were many that I burned. Amongst those I kept were the ones he wrote during the 1914-18 war, and during the time when he met and married my mother, because on the pages of those diaries he seems like a different person; he is brave and optimistic, a good soldier and a thoughtful lover. He writes of my mother tenderly, with words that remind me of the old music-hall songs popular when he was a young man: she is his love, his turtle dove, his sweetheart. He cannot quite believe she could care enough even to look twice at him. She is the sweetest, loveliest thing and he is crazy for her, half-mad with love. Time and again he wishes that she would be nice to him and not tease him so cruelly.

He promises himself he will ask her to marry him and his nerve fails. Then, when he finally asks her and she says yes – well, that is a day in May that is full of exclamation marks, of flowers and cupids and hearts pierced with arrows so that his joy and excitement leap from the page. I found myself smiling, as pleased for him as if I hadn't already known her answer or knew what was to come. I found myself liking him, and it was an unsettling feeling that too quickly became grief for this father that I never knew. I cried for him, the tears that have been expected of me these last few days.

My father under-estimated his illness; he didn't expect it to rob him of his mobility quite as quickly or as suddenly as it did. I know he intended to burn all the diaries himself before he gave himself up to the cancer. Instead, much to his horror, he had left it too late.

One afternoon, I heard him fall and ran upstairs to find

him on his hands and knees by the fireplace in his bedroom, his face as white as the paper he was trying to destroy. I hadn't seen his diaries before, I had no idea he kept them. As I carried him back to bed he raged at me, gasping through his agony that I was not to read a word – not a word! I laid him on the bed, reassuring him, saying anything at all that I thought might quieten him. He grasped my arm and pulled himself up so that his face was near mine.

'You will burn them, every page.'

'Yes, of course. Of course.'

'And you must promise me – promise me most faithfully that you won't read a word.'

'Hush. Hush now.' As I tried to ease him down onto his pillows, I had an idea he was delirious. He was certainly not himself, not the man who would ever dream of extracting a promise from me, being certain that I would never keep it.

He gazed up at me and for a moment his face cleared of pain. Then he said, 'What does it matter now?' He snorted. 'Nothing matters now. Read them all – burn them all, do what you like.'

I sat with him until he slept, until it was almost dark, so that when I got up I stumbled over the diary he had been about to burn when he fell. I picked it up and saw that it was for the year 1954. I put it down on the mantelpiece; I had no interest in what he wanted to write about that terrible year. I went into my own room and got ready for bed. Then I went downstairs and made cocoa and listened to the news on the wireless before locking the doors and climbing the stairs. I did all these habitual things automatically and thought only of 1954, that November when Carol was killed.

1954 had been, until its end, a rather good year for me. My recovery had been a slow process, so slow, so many tiny, shuffling steps towards believing I could have something of an ordinary life – the first time I went to the

89

cinema on my own, for instance, and managed to convince myself that I wasn't being stared at or whispered about because I looked so strange, a skeleton whose clothes had miraculously failed to rot along with his flesh. Dressing one morning, I'd caught a glimpse of my naked body in my wardrobe mirror and was startled. I made myself confront my reflection full on, something I hadn't done for years, since my discharge from hospital where there always seemed to be mirrors and weighing scales and tape measures to alienate me from myself. That morning in the spring of 1954 I saw in the mirror an almost ordinary man. Because it was Sunday, as usual I walked to Carol's house to sit with the twins while she, Jack and Hope went to Mass. Carol smiled at me, puzzled.

'What's happened?' She took a step back as if to see me better. Looking me up and down she said, 'Something's changed.'

I grinned, scooping up the boys, one in each arm. 'Nothing's changed – nothing of any consequence.'

She put her hand to her mouth, her eyes wide. 'You've met someone – I can see it in your eyes. Jack!' She turned to him as he came out from the kitchen, rushed as usual, frowning. 'Jack – Pete's met someone!'

He turned his frown on me. 'Really?'

'No. Carol's jumping to conclusions.' I smiled at her, hoping to see something in her eyes that betrayed even a little jealousy of this suddenly invented woman. 'There's no one else. I just feel happy this morning, that's all.' I kissed the boys and put them down; immediately they clamoured at my legs to be lifted up again. Carol went on gazing at me, unconvinced. Perhaps there *was* some jealousy in her eyes, in the way her smile faltered. She became brusque, scolding the boys for being too noisy for poor Uncle Peter; she wouldn't look at me as she kissed my cheek before she left. Behind her back, Jack rolled his eyes. He patted my arm. 'My wife wants everyone married off,' he said. He laughed shortly. 'God alone knows why!' There were times like that when I thought that he hardly knew his wife – that he barely even looked at her; at those times I could have punched him.

So, in 1954 I had stepped a little from the shade into the light, and I had my work – lots of it. I had found a publisher of children's books who liked my drawings and there seemed so many children about in those days, so many new parents to buy storybooks to read at bedtime. I saw pregnant women everywhere, many already pushing a pram and tugging a toddler along by his hand. I drew these mothers and children for a series of schoolbooks designed to help infants learn to read – my bread-and-butter work – and so I was able to save a little money, beginning to hope that the woman Carol had invented for me might come along. If she did, I would have enough for us to set up our own home, away from my father. I began to imagine I was ready to leave him in the autumn of 1954.

My father was still working at the bank at that time, the manager of the Leeds & Pennine on the High Street, leaving the house at eight-thirty prompt every morning, returning just as promptly at five. Mrs Hall cooked our meals, cleaned the house and did our laundry. I discovered how little my father paid her and increased her wages with my own money. I discovered too, quite soon after I returned home in 1946, just how much my father was drinking.

He drank each morning, a swift, stiff short to see him to the bank. He filled a silver hip flask with Scotch and slipped it discreetly into the inside pocket of his jacket to be reached for just as discreetly whenever he felt the need; it was reverently added to his morning coffee, served at eleven in his office by one of the bank girls, and just as reverently to his afternoon tea. He called these sneaked drinks his *tipples*, his *little snifters*, and it was a kind of boasting because he knew I hadn't the stomach for alcohol – another of my many failings at manliness in his eyes. He drank steadily all day, seemingly immune. At night he drank himself into oblivion and this suited me. I'm ashamed of how much his drinking suited me.

After Carol was killed I had reason to be ashamed, more reason than enough to be sick with shame and guilt – so sick that I lost the little weight I'd managed to gain. Not that I cared, not that I ever looked in a mirror again after Carol was killed.

He killed her. There. I shall be honest now and not look at her death obliquely as I always have in an effort to excuse him – to excuse myself – and to somehow make her death less cruel. After all, it's kinder to believe that a loved one was killed by accident than to know that she was murdered. But even at the time I knew my father murdered Carol as surely as if he had squeezed his hands around her throat.

He had been drinking all day, as usual, only that November evening he had a dinner to go to, a rare enough occurrence – he disliked socialising with colleagues, with anyone. I remember that he threw himself about his room, looking for cufflinks, turning out drawers in a search for clean handkerchiefs that were properly folded and pressed for his breast pocket. He asked me to help him fasten his bow tie, scolding me for not being quick enough, but never the less subjecting himself to my ministrations – a foretaste of what lay in store for us both in the years to come. He cursed the bloody fool who had organised this dinner for branch managers, wiping his mouth with the back of his hand as he swallowed a mouthful of Scotch from the tumbler on his dressing-table. I suggested that he shouldn't go – only wishing that he would. He gazed at me scornfully. Of course he had to go! Of course he had to, if one believes in unchangeable fates.

The house was so peaceful when he'd gone; I haven't known such peace since. I worked on an illustration of Snow White finding the dwarves' cottage in the woods; it was never finished. Weeks later, I crumpled it into the hearth and burned it, unable even to look at it because it seemed so invested with hope, my foolish, optimistic hopes for a future that ended that night.

I was in bed by the time he came home. I heard the front door slam, heard him blunder about in the hall, and thought that I would turn out my lamp in case it should encourage him to come into my room and berate me for something I had neglected to do. Instead, I placed my book down, listening. He was weeping, crying and moaning an anguished stream of words. I heard him stumble on the stairs, his crying becoming louder. Such a sense of dread filled me, and a panic that had me tossing my bedcovers aside and running to him. He was in the lavatory, on his knees, vomiting and vomiting; at last he fell against the wall, dishevelled, there was mud on his shoes and trousers, a dark stain on his white evening shirt. I crouched beside him.

He grasped my hands. He looked at me with the kind of desperate relief I had seen only on the faces of men who believed I could save them from dying. 'Help me,' he said. He jerked me towards him and I could smell the vomit and alcohol on his breath. His tears splashed onto the backs of my hands. 'Help me, Peter.'

I don't think he had ever used my name before that night; I know he never used it since. At that moment, for the first and only time in my life, I felt that I was his son and he was my father and that there was a bond of love between us. I remember that I brushed away the strand of his hair that had fallen across his eyes and that I tried not to betray my panic. I spoke to him then as I was soon to speak to Hope and the twins, saying that everything would be all right, soothing them with a conviction that shamed me and that later I was to marvel at: I had no idea I could lie so well.

He told me what had happened falteringly – at times I

could barely make out what he was saying through his sobs. At times I wanted not to hear, to get up and leave him there, crumpled on the lavatory floor. I thought I might be sick as he had been, throwing up until my guts ached and there was nothing left but bile. But I went on crouching beside him, his hands clasping mine as he staggered over his confession. He had killed Jack and Carol, he had killed them and he hadn't meant to, Christ forgive him he hadn't meant to, he hadn't meant to. But they were dead – they were dead on the side of the road. They were dead. He tugged his hands away from mine and covered his face. He cried and his whole being shook so that I pulled him into my arms and rocked him. And I hushed him, and I saw in my mind's eye his car plough into Carol and Jack. I saw her face white in the headlights, her eyes big with awe that this should be happening to her. In my mind's eye she isn't afraid, only astonished. And a moment earlier she had been laughing with Jack and a trace of that laughter was still in her eyes, and she looked as beautiful and young and full of life as she always looked. Not frightened, not frightened at all; I comfort myself with the thought that it was all too quick for fear.

He stopped crying eventually. I helped him up and supported him along the passage to his room. There, I partly undressed him and put him to bed. I gathered up his clothes and saw that the stain on his shirt was blood. I took the shirt and his muddied evening suit and shoes downstairs and out into the garden, soaked them in petrol from a jerry can in the garage and watched the flames devour them until there was nothing left but ashes. It was dawn by then; in the grey light I pushed the car into the garage. I told myself I didn't want to wake the neighbours, but that was only a tiny part of it. In truth I couldn't bear to sit in the seat where he had been, or turn the key in the ignition and hear the engine come to life, knowing she was dead. I had an idea that the engine's noise would bring me to my senses, that I would find myself in the house telephoning the police. In silence then I pushed the car out of sight of the road and covered it with its tarpaulin. I didn't look closely at the damage to its front bumper and wing. I went inside to the kitchen and vomited into the sink.

And what was next? What else was there to do but wait stiffly, without warmth from the fire I couldn't bring myself to light, without allowing myself even to switch on a lamp. I waited, certain that at any moment the police would come.

After hours and hours of waiting, I slept, fitfully, waking to find him standing over me, his face swollen from crying. At first I believed I had woken from a nightmare, but then the truth of it came quick and relentless as a bamboo-cane beating. I staggered as I stood up, stiff with cold, and he grasped my arm. 'You must go,' he said. He sounded quite mad, his voice hardly recognisable in its intensity. 'Go and see them. Find out what's happened.'

I stank of the smoke from the bonfire I'd made of his clothes, I needed to bathe, to shave, but such was his agitation he only allowed me time to dress. He followed me upstairs and waited outside my room, then followed me down again close on my heels, watching as I put on my coat, telling me over and over that I should be quick. And then, as I was about to go, he said, 'Stay! They might come for me! If you're not here . . .' He began to cry, but I couldn't bear to touch him now. As calmly as I could I said, 'Go back to bed. Don't answer the door if anyone calls.'

In the room where he died, I went to his wardrobe, taking down the box files one by one. I found the diary for 1954 and for every year until 1958, when he no longer had the strength or the will to write. Really I should have burned these diaries, but what held me back was the idea that one day I would be strong enough to read them. Now though, all I could think of was the idea that they must be destroyed; I imagined Jack walking from room to room, going through every cupboard, every drawer, every bookcase and shelf, making his inventory. Jack is very thorough.

Bundling the five diaries together, I carried them into the garden and made a bonfire of them.

Chapter 10

Val's father had made supper, a cottage pie with cabbage and tinned pineapple and custard to follow. He finished his own meal quickly as always, and then got up to make a pot of tea. Filling the kettle, he said over his shoulder, 'You look tired – that place not getting you down, is it?'

'Don't start, Dad.'

'What? I'm only asking. You've been at Davies's years now, you must be sick to death of it.'

Val finished off her last spoonful of pineapple and took her plate to the sink to begin the washing-up.

Matthew said, 'Leave that, I'll see to it.'

'It's all right –'

'No, I'll do it. Sit down, have a rest with this cup of tea. That lad will be here soon – are you going out like that, or are you going to get changed?'

'I'm going to get changed.' She sighed. 'Dad, I'll tell you this so as you know. I like working at Davies. Jack is not a *lad*, he's a grown man with kids. And . . .' She stopped herself from saying what she had been about to say, that she didn't much care if he turned up for their date tonight at all, whether he saw her in her work clothes or dressed to the nines. She thought about the sex they'd had, how wrong and horrible it seemed now, that the first time he'd made to love to her it should have been up against a back alley wall. And he had behaved coldly afterwards, as though he believed she was as cheap as he'd made her feel.

She sat down and a cup of tea was placed in front of her. Standing at her side, Matthew said, 'I think he's a decent fella, anyway. And if he's got kids . . . Well, at your age you can't expect a man not to have them.' He snorted. Under his breath he said, 'At least he's not got a wife.'

'Dad, don't. Just don't go on.'

'I'll go on until you see sense.'

'See sense about what, for goodness sake?'

'About going after that lad with everything you've got! A man like that – with a good job and his own home, a nice, smart-looking lad – you should be counting your lucky stars. They're not queuing round the block, you know, men like him.'

'*And I'm not getting any younger.*'

'Well, you said it. You said it, not me. But now you have said it, I'll say this – you've wasted enough time. And one day you'll look in the mirror and know the truth of it. There. I won't say any more.'

'Yes, you will.' She shook her head, exasperated. 'You like Jack, then?'

'Aye!'

'You think Mam would have liked him?'

'Your mam would be telling you the same as me.'

Val stirred sugar into her tea. Looking down at her cup she said, '*I* don't think she would have liked him.'

'Why not?'

He asked so sharply that she looked at him, thinking that perhaps he had the same suspicions she had about Jack Jackson. Carefully she said, 'Maybe I'm wrong. He's smart, like you said.'

'What are his kiddies like? Well-behaved, are they?'

'Yes.' She didn't want to think about his children, especially not the cool, haughty Hope. Unable to help herself she said, 'They're posh little brats, really. Snooty. Their grandparents pay for them to go to private schools. The boys will be going to boarding school eventually.'

'That's good – gets them out the way.' He smiled at her. 'No one's ideal, pet.'

'No.'

'And I think your mam would have thought he was dapper.'

'*Dapper*!' Val laughed. 'Did she think you were dapper?'

'She might have.' After a moment he said, 'You like him well enough, don't you? He seems pretty keen on you.'

She thought of the way Jack had pushed her against that stinking wall, how he had entered her so roughly, how his face was taken up so much with his own satisfaction, his expression closed to her, contemptuous, even. He didn't seem very *keen* on her after he'd withdrawn, after he'd tossed the slimy Johnny down and buttoned his flies. Without wanting to, she thought of Harry, his gentleness, how he had always looked at her with such love. Even in the early days of their relationship, when there had only been lust between them, when his desire for her had been so exciting, so flattering, he had always treated her with respect.

Gently, her father said, 'Don't look so sad, pet.'

'I'm not, not really.'

'If you don't like this Jack enough, well . . . '

'Plenty more fish in the sea?'

'It's no good crying over that bastard, anyway.'

Belligerently she said, 'Which bastard?'

'You know who I'm talking about – the Big I Am.'

'Don't call him that! You liked him! You liked him more than you've liked anyone. *Anyone*! So don't pretend you didn't.'

'I liked him well enough until I found out he had a wife at home.'

She got up. 'I'm going upstairs.'

Matthew caught her hand. 'Listen.' His voice changed. 'Don't think about going back to him, you hear? I don't want to see you hurt again.'

'I wasn't thinking of it.'

99

'Good.' He let go of her hand. 'That's good.' More gently he said, 'Now, off you go. When Jack comes I'll give you a shout.'

In the bathroom, stripped to her waist, Val washed. She brushed her teeth; she combed her hair and sprayed perfume on her wrists and at her throat. She peered at herself in the mirror and thought that perhaps she was beginning to look her age. She had put on weight recently because she ate too much when she was unhappy. She should have been losing weight again, too love-sick to eat, just as she was when she first met Harry. Closing her eyes, she gripped the edge of the hand-basin. 'I don't love you any more, Harry.' She said this every day, like a spell to ward off spirits.

Dressed in slacks and one of the cashmere sweaters Harry had bought her, she went downstairs again. She put her coat on to be ready to leave at once when Jack arrived, and her father came out from the kitchen. 'You have a good time.'

There was a knock on the door. As she was about to go, Matthew said, 'Don't be late, Val.' He looked at her pointedly, concerned. 'I mean it. Don't be late.'

They went to the cinema and saw a film about the Battle of Britain. During the scenes where the pilots ran across the air-field to their waiting Spitfires, Val glanced at Jack who was smoking steadily, his eyes fixed on the screen, his expression unreadable. Once, he caught her looking at him and he smiled, eyebrows raised as if he thought the film was absurd.

As the lights came up, as the rest of the audience began putting on their coats, Jack sat on, yet another cigarette only half-finished between his fingers. She sat still too, thinking that it was probably best to wait until the scrum in the cinema's lobby cleared – more dignified. It suited Jack to be dignified, just like those frightfully, frightfully proper men they'd just witnessed shooting up the skies. It seemed that all the men she had ever known had been involved in war, even her father, whose old wounds still ached in the cold, who still missed his brothers lost at the Somme.

Gazing at the yards and yards of plush red velvet curtains that had been drawn across the screen, she remembered her father's words to her as she'd left the house. He knew she'd had sex with Jack – he presumed so at least, because he knew for certain she had slept with Harry. Feeling ashamed all over again, she stood up too quickly so that the cinema seat flew up, trapping her coat that she'd been sitting on.

Jack smiled at her. 'Are you in a hurry?'

'No, but they'll come and shoo us out any minute now.'

He sighed cigarette smoke. 'What did you think of the picture?'

'What did you think?'

He laughed bleakly. Standing up, he released her coat from the seat and helped her on with it before squeezing her arms. 'Let's go and have a drink, eh?'

In the snug of the Castle and Anchor, Jack was quiet, smoking more than he usually did. She wondered what memories the film had stirred up in him, and she wished that there had been something else on instead. A comedy would have been best, even if it hadn't been funny. She managed to glance at him without him noticing and she saw how tired he looked, even sad, so that she felt herself soften towards him. He was a good man, after all; a good man who had wanted her too desperately and so had behaved as desperate men do. He would never have treated his wife like that. This thought had come to her unbidden, meant in his defence, but at once it had become an accusation. Her heart hardened a little, although she still noted how vulnerable he looked; she thought of those pilots she had just watched, and despite her bitterness, thought how much she would have liked to have known Lieutenant Jack Jackson splendid in his blue uniform.

Jack picked up his pint of beer and took a long drink. Stubbing out his cigarette, he turned to her. 'We're two sad sacks tonight, aren't we?' Gazing at her, he said, 'I'm so sorry about the other night. Truly. It was unforgivable.'

'I forgive you.'

'It's all I've thought about. I was amazed when you agreed to see me tonight.'

He had come into the typing pool, pretending he needed a document copied urgently. As head typist, it had been her job to take the bundle of papers from him, to make a note of how many copies he needed, and he had stood a little too close to her, his voice too clipped so that she knew how embarrassed he was, how aware of the many pairs of eyes watching him over the clattering typewriters. Very quickly and quietly, as he was about to go, he said, 'Will you come out with me tonight?' She'd nodded, also aware of the girls' eyes on them. As he left, June and Barbara had wolf-whistled after him.

He took another long drink. He said, 'Am I really forgiven?'

'Yes. And anyway, it takes two, doesn't it?'

He laughed, turning his glass round and around on its beer mat. Eventually he said, 'Are we the talk of the typing pool?'

'Probably.'

'Do you care?'

'No.'

He put his glass down and reached for her hand. 'Well, they've always talked about me, so I don't care either.'

She thought of his wife and the shocking way she was killed. Carol Jackson had been beautiful, by all accounts, a fittingly lovely bride for the dashing bomber pilot. There were rumours that she had been pregnant when she was killed; but then the gossips liked to make even the most horrible tragedy worse. One of the women in Accounts had told her that Jack had gone mad with grief and had to be restrained from throwing himself into his wife's grave.

Val sipped the gin and tonic he had bought her. There was a jukebox in the corner of the pub by the cigarette machine and she watched a young boy, his hair combed into an elaborate quiff, his jacket fashionably long, feed coins into its slot and deliberate over his choice. After punching a few buttons, the boy walked back to his girlfriend and 'Peggy Sue' began to play from the speakers. Jack too had been watching the boy and he turned to her.

'Would you prefer to go somewhere quieter?'

'No.' She smiled at him. 'Actually, I like this song.'

Jack sang softly and tunefully, *'Pretty, pretty, pretty, pretty Peggy Sue . . .'* Then he breathed out heavily and said, 'Something's happened.'

'Oh?'

'It's odd, really. It's rather thrown me.' Quickly he said, 'And the person I would normally talk to about something like this . . . Well, I can't talk to him about it, since he's involved.'

'Would you like to talk about it with me?'

He began turning his glass again so that she longed to take it from him. At last he said, 'I have a friend, Peter. Friends since school, you know? He's a bit of an odd bod – always was. Anyway, his father died last week.' He laughed, as though he couldn't quite believe what he was about to say. Turning to her, he said, 'Well, he died and he's left me all his money, house – everything. Peter came to see me last night and he told me, calm as you like. I'm rich now, apparently. Or I would be, if I wanted anything to do with it.'

'And you don't?'

'No!' He frowned at her. 'I don't want to make Peter homeless – penniless. I couldn't live with myself. Pete has nothing – no wife, no family, not even a proper job. God

103

knows where he'd end up. Living rough, probably. I told him, as far as I'm concerned, he can tear up the bloody will – burn it, for all I care.'

'He must have been relieved.'

'That was the funny thing. He said no, that he wanted me and the children to have it.' Jack sighed. 'He's a very. . . oh, I don't know. He's my friend, a good, true friend – probably the best I've ever had.'

She waited for him to go on, but he remained silent. Finally he said, 'When we were at school, he was the boy who'd get his head flushed down the lavatory, you know? I used to be embarrassed to know him. But I knew he was having a lousy time at home – his father was a real old bastard – and I felt sorry for him. And he's had a rotten life, a really rotten bloody life . . . *Jesus*. That old bastard is stirring things up even from his pit in hell! I don't want his stinking money!'

'Peggy Sue' ended and Jack looked towards the jukebox, as if he couldn't say anything until he knew what song was to be played next. When Elvis Presley's 'Hound Dog' began, he snorted. Finishing his drink, he said, 'Should we have another? I'm going to have one, anyway.'

He came back from the bar with a pint and a gin, sat down and lit another cigarette. Suddenly he said, 'All I ever wanted was a nice, quiet life.' He looked at her from the corner of his eye. 'I'm a boring accountant. Peter's an *artist*.' Less mockingly he said, 'He's a very good artist really, except he earns a pittance, except he doesn't know his arse from his elbow . . . except he looks like a scarecrow that's been pulled through a hedge. Poor sod.' Taking her hand he squeezed it. 'So, I don't know what to do. He wants me to have the money, the house, says he can manage – although he can't. I say no, I don't want it, and he says yes, I must take it. I've been thinking that it would probably be best if I just ignored him. He can't actually *force* me to live there and spend his money, after all.' He waited. 'Then I look at the children. It's not as if they want for anything, but there's so much I'd like to be able to give them. That school Hope goes to .... ' Picking up his pint only to put it down again, he went on, 'She's a pauper compared to most of the girls there. You should see some of the cars that roll up on Sports Day. The Jacksons *walk* to Sports Day.'

'What will you do?'

'Nothing.' He shrugged. 'It's just a bit unsettling, having to turn down thousands and thousands of pounds. It's *especially* unsettling for an accountant.' He sighed. 'They are not my thousands though – that's what I keep telling myself.'

They finished their drinks and talked about work and a little about his children, ordinary conversation as the pub became busier, the jukebox playing almost constantly, the air becoming thicker with cigarette smoke. All the time she imagined he was thinking about his strange friend and the huge amount of money he couldn't bring himself to accept. All the time he held her hand tightly and once, during a lull in their conversation, he lifted her hand to his mouth and kissed it, an act that was more intimate for its very absent-mindedness. And because she was tired she rested her head on his shoulder and they sat together in silence, watching the crowd of Teddy Boys and their girls drink and kiss and shuffle about to the music they chose. *We are companionable*, she thought, and this thought surprised her more than any other she had ever had. Paradoxically, it broke the companionable spell, and she sat up as suddenly as if he had shaken her awake.

'I should go home,' she said.

He walked her to her door. There, he pulled her into his arms and kissed her, a soft, undemanding kiss. He said, 'Thank you for tonight,' and kissed her again. She held her body stiffly from him, but this made her feel as though she was pretending to be someone else, that prick-teasing girl she had never had the heart to be. So she held him tightly and he groaned, holding her tighter still, lifting her off her feet. 'Oh God, Val, I think I might be too old for this.'

Setting her down, he held her at arms' length. Searching her face he said, 'Saturday night – the children are going to stay with their grandparents. I'll cook us supper.'

She nodded.

'Yes?' He cleared his throat. 'You sure? I just want to take you to bed . . . I love you.'

She wanted to tell him that he didn't have to say that, that it would be easier for her if he didn't lie to her. But if she did tell him, he would know without any doubt what kind of a woman she was. Anyway, why shouldn't he say it? Perhaps for a few seconds he even believed it.

Chapter 11

Standing at his upstairs office window, Harry watched his last client walk along the High Street towards a waiting taxi cab. She staggered a little as she fumbled in her handbag and pulled out a handkerchief. The lacy white square of Irish linen was sodden, he knew. For the last hour she had sat in this office and used the hanky to wipe her eyes and nose as she told him how really she shouldn't be there, that it would all blow over – all this silliness. She had laughed even as she wiped the tears away. 'He won't go through with it. He won't, of course not. But he says I should find my own solicitor . . . '

He'd stood up and walked around his desk, resting against it, close to her, so he would seem to be less intimidating, less like the official who was to take part in the ending of her marriage. She had been married twenty years. She'd smiled at him tearfully. 'We have two lovely children, but he says they're not children any more . . . that he doesn't have to stay any more . . . ' She wept and he waited silently for her to compose herself, except she didn't, not really, although she managed to smile at him again and apologise for the silly show she was making of herself. He could smell the gin on her breath.

He turned away from the window and the sight of this unhappy woman climbing half-drunk into the back of the cab. Going through to the outer office, he took a pile of letters typed ready for him to sign and read them quickly before scrawling his signature. His secretary Maureen came back carrying two cups of tea. She handed him one. 'I supposed you could do with this.'

'Thank you.'

'You've eaten all the biscuits.'

'Have I?' He glanced up at her from signing another letter. 'Stop bringing biscuits, Maureen. Make me diet.'

'*Make you*? Ha! That'll be the day.' Sitting down at her typewriter, she yanked out a finished letter and its carbons and held it out to him. 'Last one and then you can go home. After you've seen the rather peculiar man sitting in reception.'

He frowned at her. 'There's someone waiting?'

'Yes, but I thought you might need that cup of tea first, after your last client.' She sighed. 'Go and sit down; drink your tea. I'll send him in when you've caught your breath.'

Peter Wright said, 'I hope this isn't an inconvenient time, Mr Dunn.'

Harry got up, holding out his hand. 'No, of course not. Please, sit down.'

He sat, and Harry offered him a cigarette from the box he kept on his desk. Wright shook his head. 'I don't smoke, thank you. And I won't stay long. It was just that I was in town and I saw your office and I thought I would come in and let you know that I've spoken to Jack – Mr Jackson. He knows now that he's to inherit.'

He had been clutching a string shopping bag on his knee, tins of soup and baked beans bulging through its net, brown paper bags of apples, onions and carrots resting on top. Now he put the bag down, steadying it so that its contents didn't roll all over the floor. Maureen had said he looked peculiar, perhaps because the macintosh he wore was so old-fashioned and too tightly belted, each button fastened, or perhaps because of the shopping – damning evidence that he was a bachelor. Unmarried men were odd, in Maureen's eyes. There had to be a good reason why they couldn't find a wife to look after them. Maureen wouldn't have noticed Peter Wright's gentle manner. Perhaps she had; he imagined that gentleness wasn't something Maureen admired in a man.

Smiling at him, Wright said, 'So, that's what I wanted to tell you. I've told Jack.'

'How did he take it?'

'He was shocked, of course. And of course he insisted that he didn't want anything to do with it. I think I've persuaded him though. I told him that it's a wonderful house for the children – or it could be, once all our ugly old bits and pieces have been cleared out. I told him he'll need a few strong men with big vans.'

'And what about you?'

'Me? I've been looking at places to rent. Actually, I've found somewhere – a house on one of the terraces behind the High Street here. Just a two up, two down, but more than big enough for me. It's on Inkerman Terrace.'

Inkerman Terrace. Even hearing the name of the street where Val lived sent a shock of adrenalin through him. He saw himself in bed with her in that little house, her father's pigeons cooing on the roof above them as she lay sated and drowsy in his arms. Unable to sit still, he got up and went to the window, his hands clasped behind his back. On the street below, the market traders were dismantling their stalls; a tramp searched amongst the waste, finding a box of half-rotten fruit. He began sorting through the bruised apples and blackening bananas, stuffing them into the pockets of his Army greatcoat. Harry watched him blankly, his thoughts disorganised, unfocused. He closed his eyes and rested his forehead against the window and forgot about the man seated behind him, forgot everything but his own misery.

He felt a hand on his arm. 'Mr Dunn, why don't you sit down?'

Harry shrugged him off and immediately felt rude. Even so, he said impatiently, 'I'm all right. I'm fine.'

Wright said cautiously. 'Are you sure? You look rather pale.'

Harry shook his head. 'It's been a long day, that's all.' Managing to smile at him he said, 'Don't worry about me. I'm pleased you've found a decent place to live. They're good, solid little houses . . . ' He trailed off, unable to think about Inkerman Terrace without wanting to cry.

Wright went back to the chair he'd been sitting in and picked up his shopping bag. Hesitantly he said, 'Well, I'm sure I've kept you long enough. Good afternoon, Mr Dunn.'

Just as he had watched his last client walk along the High Street, Harry watched Wright make his way towards his car, a scarecrow of a man, one badly in need of someone to take care of him. As if he sensed he was being watched, Wright turned; looking up, he smiled and held up his hand in a brief wave. Harry found himself waving back, smiling too. As Wright got into his car and drove away, still Harry watched after him, touched by his gentleness, his concern. He thought that perhaps he could call on him at Inkerman Terrace, see how he was coping. If he was to bump into Val, well, he would have an excuse. Comforted by this plan, he turned from the window and prepared to go home.

In his kitchen, Harry found Esther sitting with Ava at the table. There was a jigsaw between them, half-completed, Windsor Castle suspended from blue sky, as yet unconnected with the ground. Esther stood up hastily, always slightly put out by him; her shyness gave him the impression that whenever he entered a room she immediately wanted to leave it. She was a rather mousy, sharp-featured girl, her hair tied up in a high ponytail. Dressed in slacks and an over-sized shirt cinched at the waist with a wide belt, she looked very young, too young for any kind of responsibility. As usual, Harry felt guilty that such a girl was taking care of Ava; he was afraid Esther might collapse in a fit of nervous exhaustion. She said, 'Oh,

Mr Dunn, you're home.' She glanced at the clock. 'I didn't realise the time.'

Harry kissed Ava's head. His wife ignored him and went on moving the pieces of stone-coloured jigsaw about the table. Smiling at Esther, he said, 'How have things been today?'

'All right.'

He nodded, never sure what to say to her, except that he was grateful, desperately, desperately grateful that she continued to stay; but he had to think of more ordinary things to say to her, an effort that too often defeated him. He thought of her little bedroom, with its adjoining door to Ava's room and its narrow, single bed covered in a pink candlewick bedspread; there was a wardrobe and a chest of drawers and a Lloyd Loom chair and there was a picture of kittens in a basket above the bed. The window looked over the garden, and it was a nice, sunny little room, except that it seemed rather characterless. He had an idea that Esther was homesick, and whenever she left her bedroom door ajar it was as if she was allowing him a glimpse of her unhappiness. Once he had seen her Sunday dress, the one she wore on her visits home to her mother, hanging limply from the wardrobe, and he had quickly closed the bedroom door, not wanting to be reminded that Esther had a mother.

Harry said too brightly, 'Shall I put the kettle on?'

His kitchen was large, its walls painted a pale primrose yellow so that the room seemed to capture and hold onto all of the sunlight that streamed through its large window. There was a smell of baking, a wire rack of small cakes cooling on the dresser beside a jug of pussy-willow. Next to the jug was an untidy pile of children's books and he imagined that a stranger would wonder where the children were because there was further evidence of them in a pair of tattered rag dolls sitting on an easy chair facing the kitchen's black-leaded range. The stray tabby cat Esther had befriended curled on the chair, too, the dolls smiling happily over its sleeping body. On the floor by the back door were two small pairs of muddy Wellington boots, Esther's and Ava's, both women's feet as tiny as children's. The door was propped open with a jar full of seashells, revealing the garden and its plundered willow tree. As the kettle boiled, the girl went to the door and closed it, placing the shells on the windowsill.

'When we bake it gets too warm,' she said. Then, 'Would you like a cake? They got a bit burned – I forgot about them.' She sat down, only to get up again as the kettle whistled shrilly. 'I'll make the tea,' she said.

She made tea in a big brown pot, quick, deft, anxious still. Gesturing at the cakes she said, 'We were going to make them into butterfly cakes. I don't think we shall, now.'

'Butterfly cakes?'

'It's silly. You cut out a little from the middle, top the hole with butter cream and make wings from the piece you cut out. It's something to do.'

Ava got up. Taking one of the rag dolls from the chair, she went out into the garden. Disturbed from sleep, the cat jumped down and followed her. The door hung open and Esther placed the shell-jar against it again. Standing in the doorway, she watched Ava cross the lawn before turning to him.

'The cakes got burned because Mrs Dunn was upset. I was trying to calm her down.' With a rare flash of assertiveness she said, 'Guy picked up one of her dolls.'

Harry sighed. 'I'll speak to him.'

'He didn't do anything really – just picked it up.'

'But he knows not to go near the dolls. It's all right, Esther, don't worry. I won't let him know you told me. Where is he now, do you know?'

'In his room, I think.'

The boy would be lying on his bed, Harry thought, smoking and listening to his music. He seemed to do little

112

else since he arrived home. He heard himself sigh again. A cup of tea was placed in front of him and he smiled at Esther to reassure her. 'I think I will have one of those cakes. They don't look too burned to me.'

Guy lay on his bed, fully clothed beneath the slippery silk of the eiderdown, his flies undone, his hand closed around his erection. He thought of Hope, and of Esther, the two of them naked and taking turns to suck his cock. Hope was the most eager, even though she looked so innocent, encouraging Esther, shy, timid Esther with her ratty, common little face. He would be less rough with Esther than he would be with Hope, who needed to be humbled, degraded even, because she was so coolly self-possessed. He would ruin Hope, make her filthy, he would make her perform the most perverted, indecent acts and he and Esther would watch. He groaned quietly, his hand moving faster around his cock. He came.

Lying very still, he stared at the ceiling and gradually, predictably, began to feel disgusted with himself. His hand was sticky. Groping blindly about the floor, his fingers searched out a discarded sock which he used to clean himself up. He thought of Esther, who was not ratty or common – these were descriptions that only occurred to him when he was wanking – but oddly pretty in a way he found difficult; he was constantly trying to work out why he found her so attractive. He suspected that she was attracted to him, although he could be wrong – there was absolutely no reason why she should be. If she was odd-looking, he was odder-looking still. His eye made him ridiculous. Hope had stared and stared at his eye, as if she wanted to shine a doctor's pencil-like torch into it.

Ava had told him never to mind if people stared. In her funny, accented English she'd said, 'Don't care! Why should you care what any silly person thinks? You are a handsome, handsome boy – like your dear daddy!' He had begged her to speak German, because her English made him squirm with embarrassment for her, although he would never, ever tell her this. They spoke German together and it was his secret, a secret that made him feel powerful and superior to all the other boys who acted out their war games in the playground. In those games, all Germans were Nazis, torturers and murderers and ultimately cowards. He thought such games were beneath him.

Guy tossed the soiled sock down and zipped up his fly. He reached for a cigarette and lit one and practised blowing smoke rings at the ceiling. His thoughts strayed to Esther, as they often did, as she was this afternoon, weighing flour and sugar for the cakes, gently directing Ava so that it seemed that his stepmother was actually helping rather than just getting in Esther's way. And Esther's delicate hand had cracked one egg and then another and another into the bowl, a bowl she cradled against her breast as she beat the mixture, as she chatted to him, as the sunlight streaming through the window made her mousy hair shine. The cake mixture that had filled the kitchen with the smell of vanilla essence was spooned into paper cases. Esther ran a finger around the empty bowl and licked it; he watched her bend over to place the cakes in the oven, her backside firm and delicious-looking in tight black ski-pants. He had been telling her about school, making her laugh with his impression of the masters and, forgetting, he had picked up Danny Doll, the male rag doll Ava so guarded. All hell had then broken loose.

Guy blew out cigarette smoke, remembering how at once Esther had become so much older than him, stern, authoritative. She had held onto Ava's arms and repeated that she should be quiet, be good. 'Hush now,' she'd said, and, 'What a to-do! There – see! Danny's fine.' She'd glared at him, as if to say '*See what you've done!*' But this rare flash of anger was quickly over with. As Ava cried and struggled against her, Esther had said quietly, 'You'd best

114

leave us alone.'

He'd gone to his room. He listened to Ava's shouts and cries and felt like burying his head beneath his pillows but had forced himself to listen, his body stiff with the effort of just lying there. Eventually she became quiet. And eventually, his thoughts turned to Esther's backside as she bent over the oven.

He heard his father arrive home and guessed that in a few minutes he would come upstairs, tap on his door and come in without waiting to be asked. He would ask him what he'd been doing all day, wearily, not really caring. He might even sit on his bed, in that slumped, defeated-looking way of his as if everything was really too much of an effort, sitting and sitting and not saying anything, sighing from time to time. When his father was in these moods of his, Ava used to tease him, reminding Guy of a bright, brave bird flitting around the teeth of a crocodile. But Harry never shouted or became impatient with Ava as he did with him. Ava wasn't ever scared of his father. 'Your daddy rescued me,' she always told him. 'Your daddy is the kindest, best, most generous man in the world.'

Obstinately, he'd said, 'I don't call him Daddy.'

She'd replied, 'Then we shall be very right and proper and call him *Vater*.'

All this said in German, that strict, stern language Ava made soft.

In German, softly, she told him about her brother Hans. 'He was my bright star,' she said. She showed him a photograph of a tall, blond boy in an SS uniform. 'This photo is our secret,' she whispered. 'You father would not like to know that it exists.'

He knew he shouldn't have found Hans glamorous, that he shouldn't have been so much on his side, but Ava made him heroic.

His father knocked on the door, opening it at once. He said, 'May I come in?'

115

Guy sat up; he crushed his cigarette out in the ashtray he'd commandeered from the living room and smiled at Harry brightly. 'Good evening, Father. How was your day?'

Wearily, Harry sat down on the chair in the corner of his room and gazed at him, his expression unreadable so that Guy decided it would be best to keep quiet. At last he said, 'Guy, Esther told me that Ava was upset earlier.'

'Yes.' He frowned. 'She didn't say it was my fault, did she?'

'Was it?'

'No! What did she say?'

'Only that you picked up one of the dolls.'

'I forgot, all right? I put it down again *straight away*! I can't believe she even told you!'

Harry looked different tonight. He looked crumpled; there was a grubbiness about him, an untidiness that was out of character. His trousers had ridden up so that between turn-ups and socks an inch of death-white skin was exposed, a few sparse, straggly black hairs. He needed to shave, to wash his hair that was combed, greasily, thinly over his scalp. He looked older than most fathers Guy knew. Older, fatter, sadder. Guy's anger dissipated into a kind of exasperated pity.

'I'm sorry,' Guy said. 'I'll stay out of her way in future.'

'You only have to be careful, that's all. I don't want you to stay out of her way, as such. Just . . . well, be kind to her.'

Guy was outraged; he wanted to say that he *was* kind, had always been kind, but he forced himself to suppress his outrage, to keep his expression neutral. Lighting a cigarette, he drew the smoke deep into his lungs, hoping it would help smother his anger.

'Guy?' Harry laughed slightly. 'You smoke like a hardened criminal. When did you start smoking, anyway?'

He glanced at him before tossing the spent match into

the ashtray. 'At school.'

After a while, Harry said, 'Have you thought any more about what we discussed last night?'

'Discussed' was the wrong word, Guy thought. His father had talked and he had listened, or pretended to. He had allowed the words to wash over him, only making the right noises from time to time. He had thought about Hope despairingly because he'd come to a realisation that she was too beautiful for him and that she must know this; he had an idea she would laugh at him when he arrived at her house to take her out. Laugh, or shut the door in his face, or both. He was just thinking how terrible it would be if he never got to see her naked when his father had said sharply, 'Guy, are you listening to a word I'm saying?'

Now Harry said cautiously, 'I know you're against the idea of going to university.'

'There's no point.'

'Of course there's every point! Your Headmaster thinks that if you only applied yourself –'

The boy made a derisive sound.

'Don't pretend you're not intelligent – that you're not brighter than most,' his father snapped. 'So, are you going to just sit around and wait until you're called up for National Service?'

'Actually, I thought I might enlist of my own free will.' Guy had been thinking about this vaguely and suddenly it seemed suddenly the right, proper thing to do – obvious, even. He smiled at his father's incredulous expression.

'Is that really what you want to do with your life?'

'Probably not my whole life, Dad.'

'For God's sake, boy! This is serious – can't you stop smirking for five minutes?'

Guy bowed his head, disturbed as he always had been as a child by his father's anger and contempt. As a child he'd suspected that his father blamed him for his mother's death; later, he was certain that he blamed him for the

117

accident.

The accident. No one ever referred to it; for years it had been just two capitalised, terrifying words that he knew had the power to stop his heart if they were ever spoken aloud. Except sometimes, rarely, when he was feeling particularly angry, he had an urge to ask his father if he really believed that he'd pushed Ava over that cliff; but then he would be standing on the cliff's edge, ground shifting beneath his feet, he would see the sudden, tumbling avalanche of rock that bounced and struck against the cliff face, rock that until a moment ago had been safe and solid as any pavement. And he and Ava, holding hands, were falling after the rocks, bouncing and striking in exactly the same way, two rag dolls like Danny and Martha, soft and helpless. He would see the two of them sprawled on the ledge that had broken their fall and saved them, spears of yellow gorse poking between their bodies, and his anger, his urge to confront his father over his shaming suspicions, would shrivel and die, overwhelmed by fear. He could no more talk about the accident than throw himself under a train – no matter how strong the urge.

He stood up, too agitated to sit enduring his father's gaze. He said, 'Did you want to speak to me about anything else? Because I'm going out tonight so I should get ready.'

'Oh?' Harry made an attempt to look interested. 'Where are you going?'

'To the cinema.'

'Who with?'

'No one.'

Harry gazed at him. At last he said, 'Guy, if you want to join the Army . . . well, all right. If you believe you'll be able to cope with the discipline, with taking orders – things you've never shown any respect for before . . . ' More gently he said, 'Look, please reconsider. I really don't think you're the type of boy –'

'Dad, I'm sorry, but I would like to change now.'

'Why change if you're going to the cinema alone?' When he didn't respond, Harry went on, 'So, are you seeing some girl?'

'I said I was going alone, didn't I?'

'All right. Have it your way. Be quiet when you come home, I'll be angry if you wake Ava.'

He left, and Guy listened to his heavy tread on the stairs, heard him say something to Esther. A moment later Esther shyly put her head round his door, her voice anxious as she said, 'He wasn't cross with you, was he?'

It was impossible to stay angry with someone who looked so timid, so remorseful. On impulse, Guy took her hand, leading her into the room before closing the door. Releasing her, he said, 'He's terribly angry. He's throwing me out, in fact, on the streets. I was just about to pack my bags.'

Nervously, she glanced over her shoulder at the closed door. Looking at him she said, 'That's not true, is it?'

He gazed at her, thinking that perhaps it was her timidity that attracted him, her servility; he imagined that he could order her to take her clothes off and she would do so, shaking and fearful, but unquestioning; she would lie still. Feeling the beginnings of an erection, he turned away and went to open the window, imagining that the room stank of his bloody wanking.

Trying to make her voice light, she said, 'He wasn't really angry, was he?'

'No.'

'Good. That's okay then.' She glanced around, and he realised that she had never been in his room before. Her eyes rested briefly on his unmade bed, then went back to the door again. 'I should go,' she said.

He nodded, although he would have liked to have stopped her, to take her hand and lead her to the bed, just to sit and talk with her, to gaze at her and try to make sense of her. After all, next to Hope she was a scrawny, common little thing. Suddenly, he wanted to lie on top of her and overpower her completely; he thought of Hans, who would no doubt do just that, without conscience to trouble him. Ashamed of his filthy urges he said, 'Were you really concerned about me?'

'Yes.' She met his gaze for a moment before turning away and letting herself out of the room.

Chapter 12

Hope fed her brothers a supper of Heinz tomato soup and sliced white bread which they tore up, floating the bits in the soup and calling them bread boats. She told them not to play with their food, to hurry up and finish it or they wouldn't get any pudding.

Stephen looked at her in surprise from sinking a boat with his spoon. 'Is there pudding?'

'Apples.'

'Bugger and pooh!'

'Stephen! If you say words like that again, I'll tell Dad.'

He gazed at her. 'Bugger, pooh, bugger, bugger.'

'You're horrible.'

'Bugger.'

'Stop it.'

From the kitchen doorway her father said, 'Yes, Stephen. Stop it, now.' He came in, put his briefcase down and went to stand behind Stephen's chair. Stephen hunched down, expecting the usual clip round the ear his father administered. Taking a slice of bread, Jack dipped it into Martin's soup and ate hungrily. 'Have you eaten, Hope?'

'No.'

'That's good, we'll eat together. I need to talk to you.'

Martin said, 'Talk to us, too!'

'It's grown-up talk.'

'She's not grown-up!' Martin was outraged. 'She's not! If she is, *I* am!'

'And I am, as well.' Stephen twisted in his seat to look

121

up at his father. 'I'm the second eldest, anyway.'

'By all of ten minutes. Tell you what, I'll speak to Hope and then we three men will have a special talk when you're in bed, all right? And if you're good and listen nicely, afterwards I'll read to you.'

Jack never read to them. The boys' eyes grew wide with anticipation. Martin said, 'Read one of Uncle Peter's books.'

'If you like.' Glancing at her, Jack said, 'Should I open another tin of soup?'

Hope expected him to talk about Val. She knew that his last date with her had gone well because, the morning after, she heard him singing in the bathroom as he shaved. To her surprise he sang 'Peggy Sue', although only the same couple of lines over and over. For the last few days he had been humming the Buddy Holly tune under his breath and she decided that it was good that he was happy. She hadn't told him yet that this evening she was going to the pictures with Guy; she had secretly decided it would be best to tell him at the last moment when he couldn't do much about it, knowing in her heart that this putting-off was only cowardice. Besides, she could barely imagine Guy turning up as he'd promised. The whole idea of Guy Dunn seemed too good to be true. Thinking of him, her stomach quickened with nerves so that she could barely swallow the sickly soup her father had heated and poured into Martin's emptied bowl so as to save on the washing-up. He took Stephen's bowl, having chased the twins off to their room. Sitting down opposite her, he said, 'How was school today?'

'Fine.'

He dipped a folded slice of bread into his soup. Swallowing a mouthful he said, 'Nothing worrying you, then? Everything's all right?'

She looked at him sharply, afraid he might have

guessed she was nervous and would want to know its cause. More firmly she repeated, 'Everything's fine.'

'Good. Excellent. And you know that if you need any help with your maths homework, you only have to ask.'

She would never dream of asking him; all the same she said, 'All right. Thank you.'

'Uncle Peter's house is closer to your school than here, isn't it? Not as far to walk.'

The mention of Peter's name had become enough to turn her stomach over. Suspiciously she asked, 'And so?'

'Do you like his house? I know it's a bit dark and dismal, but it's big, isn't it? And the garden's fantastic. The boys love it there – better than here. There's more room.' He paused, then said, 'Hope, I might as well just tell you straight. Uncle Peter's father has left me his house. And money. House, money – the lot.'

'Why?'

Jack laughed, bemused. 'I know, it's astonishing, isn't it? I keep asking myself why. And you know why I think he did it? Spite. He did it to spite Peter.' Reaching for another slice of bread only to put it down again, he said, 'I'm still not certain if I should take it or not. Peter wants me to.'

Trying not to sound as anxious as she felt, she said, 'If you do, would he live with us there?'

'No. He says he wouldn't want to do that. I suggested it, of course. But he said no.'

Hope tried to imagine living in that horrible house, its rooms so stuffed full with furniture, with the kind of ugly knick-knacks she only ever saw piled up in boxes outside junk shops. She remembered playing hide and seek there. Peter had found her easily because she had hidden in a blanket box but had been too scared of its musty darkness to close the lid completely. She had held it open an inch, her hand trembling against its weight. Peter had crouched down, his eyes smiling through the crack. 'Sprite, have you seen a little girl pass this way? Her name's Hope and I think

123

she wants to be found now.' Lifting the lid a little, he said, 'Oh, it *is* you!' As he opened the lid fully, she held up her arms for him to lift her out. She remembered that a moment earlier she had been thinking that she was too old to be playing this game; now she wanted only to be babied by him, to be cradled in his arms as he cradled Stephen and Martin, a feeling that came over her often in those days when Peter was around and the accident had taken her parents away.

Her father said, 'Hope? You're very quiet. I would like to know what you think about all this.'

She shrugged.

Jack pushed his empty bowl away and immediately lit a cigarette. 'Shall I tell you what I think?' He exhaled, cigarette smoke flaring his nostrils. 'Oh, I don't know. I hate the house, really. It's full of the old man – I feel I should have to ask Father O'Brien to exorcise the place. Or I could sell it, I suppose. Not that I'd get much for it, the state it's in.' Flicking ash into his soup bowl, he said, 'I know what your mother would say.'

He rarely mentioned her mother. Afraid that showing too much interest might silence him Hope asked lightly, 'What would she say?'

'That we shouldn't take Peter's home from him.'

'Then don't.'

'No. No, of course. You're right.' Jack pushed his hand through his hair. 'Well, I suppose that settles it,' he said dully.

She wished she had mentioned Guy earlier, when his mood was still lifted, because now he was gloomy, obviously preoccupied with what he had just decided to give up. If she mentioned Guy now he would be stern, too full of questions; he might, because of his own disappointment, decide not to let her go. But it couldn't be helped – Guy would be arriving in less than an hour.

Quickly she said, 'At that party on Sunday, Irene's

cousin asked me if I would go to the pictures with him.'
Because she thought he might approve of what they were
going to see, she added, quickly, 'He wants to see the film
about the Battle of Britain that's showing.'

'Oh, does he?' Jack grunted. 'Well, tell him not to
bother – it's rubbish.' Stubbing his cigarette out he said,
'How old is this boy?'

'Seventeen.'

Her father raised his eyebrows; he always knew when
she was lying. 'Seventeen?'

Blushing, she looked down at her half-finished soup
and heard her father sigh.

'How old is he, Hope?'

'Eighteen.'

'Eighteen?' He held her gaze. After a moment he said,
'Is he coming here? Then I want to meet him.'

'But I can go?'

'If you're back by ten o'clock.'

'I will be.' She smiled at him, relieved. 'You'll like
him.'

'Will I?' He shook his head. 'I very much doubt it.'

He was late. Hope waited at the window for him and after
fifteen minutes of waiting she went to the front gate and
looked up and down the street. She saw him then, walking
briskly; when he saw her, he quickened his pace, not quite
breaking into a run. He was too cool for that, she thought,
and didn't know whether to like him more or less because
of it. As he reached her he said, slightly breathlessly,
'Sorry. Are you ready to go?'

She looked back at the house. Her father was upstairs
reading to the boys as he'd promised, but he had repeated
that he wanted to meet Guy and she was afraid that if she
disobeyed him on this, he might not allow her to see him
again. Hesitantly she said, 'Would you come in for a
minute?'

'Why?'

Feeling childish she said, 'My father wants to meet you. Sorry.'

Guy laughed. 'That's all right. I'm good with parents.'

Hope remembered how he had been with Peter and how Peter had seemed unimpressed with the way he called him *sir* so often. She dismissed this thought at once. Peter was odd, he didn't behave like ordinary men. Her father would like Guy, despite what he'd said.

Leading Guy into the house, Hope called up the stairs. Her father appeared on the half landing; she was relieved that the twins were nowhere to be seen. As Jack came down, Hope told him, 'This is Guy.'

Guy held out his hand, his voice as bright as it had been when he met Peter. 'Hello, sir. Pleased to meet you.'

His outstretched hand was ignored. 'Have my daughter back here by ten, do you hear?'

'Yes, sir.'

Looking at her, Jack said, 'Ten o'clock, Hope. No later.'

Guy said, 'Do you want to go to the cinema?'

Hope looked at him uncertainly and he thought how shy she was, more timid than he remembered so that suddenly he felt angry that she wasn't the sexy girl he'd built up in his imagination. Too sharply he said, 'Let's do something else instead.'

'All right.'

She sounded wary of him and at once he was ashamed of his anger. After all, she was still the girl who had kissed him so surprisingly passionately. He thought about the party and the way she had looked at him as though he was special; no one had looked at him like that before. His fingers went to his eye. He said, 'I know somewhere – somewhere we can be alone. Would you mind being alone with me?'

She shook her head, making him smile because she looked so scared.

'Sure? All right. It's this way.'

The house had been uninhabited for years. When he was much younger he would go there, climb over the wall and play in the overgrown garden. He told no one about the house, this derelict, wild place he had discovered; each school holiday he would return, finding it subtly changed each time – a drainpipe fallen further from the wall, another windowpane broken. On one of his very first visits he had found a key hidden beneath a loose paving stone; it unlocked the back door. He had explored the house, empty but for a table and a few broken-backed chairs. In the summer, the rooms smelled of dust, a dry, inflammable smell. Dead flies and moths gathered on the window sills amongst the flakes of white paint; the floral patterned wallpaper peeled from the wall above the marble fireplace in the sitting room.

The house was kept secret by the trees growing in its garden, horse-chestnuts and sycamores, too-big trees Guy believed would one day destroy the foundations so that the house would fall in on itself, becoming nothing but a pile of bricks and timbers.

He hadn't thought of taking Hope to the house, not until he saw her and her shyness had made him feel so unexpectedly angry. All at once he couldn't be bothered with going to the cinema, with the crowds of people, the shuffling, infuriating queues for tickets, for ice cream – she would expect ice cream, he was sure. He especially couldn't be bothered with having to sit still watching a film about the war. The war was too close, there all the time in his house where it hung about his father like a bad smell, hanging about Ava, too, of course. He was sure Ava lived in 1945 in her head, an explanation for her sadness, and her preoccupation with the bloody dolls. The war was the last thing he wanted to watch; to waste his precious time with Hope in such a way had suddenly seemed unthinkable.

Outside the house, he said, 'This is it.' Feeling it would be easier to lie, he said, 'It belongs to my father, he just hasn't got round to selling it.' He pushed open the creaking gate and took her hand. 'We have to go round the back.'

He took the key from the new hiding place he had found for it beneath the kitchen's rotting windowsill, unlocked the door and picked up the torch he left just inside on the abandoned table, knowing it would be dark soon and that anyway the soft evening light would hardly penetrate the grimy windows. He turned to Hope. 'I've made a kind of den,' he said, and felt childish suddenly. Quickly he added, 'There's somewhere to sit, anyway.'

She smiled at him uncertainly. 'No one lives here?'

'Only the ghosts.' He took her hand again and squeezed it. 'Don't be scared. They've been dead so long they've forgotten they're supposed to be frightening.'

He had brought cushions from home and an old rug, laying them out in front of the fireplace where he had placed half a dozen candles. The candles stood securely in puddles of melted wax and Guy took out his matches and lit them, filling the room with shadows. Sitting down on the rug he held out his hand to her. 'It won't dirty your dress,' he said. 'The carpet's clean – from home.'

She sat down, a little way from him. 'You just took it? Won't your mother notice it's gone?'

He gazed at her, thinking how little she knew about him, how much he would have to tell her; or not tell her. He supposed he could go on lying, invent a whole family for himself; like his lie about the house, it might be easier than explaining the truth. Much easier, in fact. The truth sounded like a lie, so implausible, so preposterous – it set him apart from normal people like Hope. Then he remembered that Hope's mother had been killed, that her death had been the kind of tragedy people talked about, just as they talked about his family. He remembered the strange man who had collected her from Irene's party, someone she was so quick to disown, and thought that perhaps Hope wasn't as normal as she looked.

She was gazing around her and her eyes came to rest on the candle flames flickering in the draught from the chimney. He watched her, pleased that she didn't chatter as he suspected most girls would. Most girls would want to hide their embarrassment behind a stream of silly talk. Hope just sat quite still and he was content to look at her and say nothing, but it seemed that she sensed him watching.

'Why do you come here?' she asked.

Surprised at her bluntness, he shrugged. 'Because I can.'

'What do you do here?'

Obviously, she thought he was odd. At last he said, 'I don't do anything. It's just a place to be on my own.'

They sat at either end of the rug, a brightly coloured raft on a sea of paint-stained, splintered floorboards. The rug was Persian, expensive, its pile deep and soft. His father hadn't missed it – at least, he had never questioned its absence. The smell of this empty house clung to it; Guy wanted to lie down, hold out his arms to her, but thought she wouldn't want to lie on a carpet that smelled so musty. Perhaps she would think he was more than odd – weird, in fact, to bring her here. He took his cigarettes from his pocket and offered her one just for something to do.

Shyly she said, 'I don't smoke.'

Lighting a cigarette, he handed it to her. 'Try it.'

'Really, I'd rather not.'

'Go on.'

As if she didn't want to offend him, she took the cigarette and drew on it inexpertly. She coughed and handed it back. 'I don't think I'll ever smoke. It's horrible.'

'I thought so too, at first. But I *persevered*.' He grinned

129

at her. 'You didn't like Irene's champagne either, did you?'

She looked down at her hands. After a while she said, 'You think I'm too young.'

He laughed. 'Too young for what?'

'I don't know.' She seemed to force herself to meet his gaze. 'You like making fun of me, though.'

'I don't.' He moved closer to her. 'At that party I only wanted you to notice me. I'm sorry if I behaved like an idiot.' Edging closer still, he said, 'It was nice, wasn't it, being alone in the garden?'

She nodded, eyes cast down. Placing a finger under her chin, he tilted her head back a little. 'Have you thought about me much, since then?'

'Yes.'

He kissed her mouth lightly. Drawing back he said, 'I think about you all the time.'

'Really?'

She looked surprised and hopeful at the same time.

Kissing her again, he whispered, 'Really, truly.'

She placed a hand on his chest. 'We shouldn't be here.'

'Why not?'

Shuffling back from him she said, 'You know why not.'

Tossing his cigarette into the hearth he sat back on his heels. 'What should we do, then?'

'I don't know.'

'What would you *like* to do?'

She avoided his gaze, her silence going on and on until at last he said, 'Hope?'

'I suppose I just want to stay here with you for a while. But I don't want you to have the wrong impression.'

'Would you like me to sit on the other end of the carpet again?'

She giggled, despite herself. 'We could just talk, I suppose.' Brightly, she asked, 'Where did you go to school? It wasn't Thorp Grammar, was it?'

'No. I went to a boarding school near London. Before that, I went to one in Durham. Before that, one in Essex. Before that . . . ' He frowned. 'Oh, yes. Before that it was somewhere in Yorkshire. I wasn't there long. During the war I was evacuated to a school in Kent. It was OK there. I could have stayed there.'

She looked horrified. 'But you would have only been a baby . . . '

'Yes – it was a nursery school. I was sent there when I was four.'

'On your own?'

'Dad took me.' He remembered the train journey, Harry in his Army uniform so that he felt proud of this great big man holding his hand. The train had seemed full of soldiers, but none as smart as his father; he'd thought that Harry was a General, a General whose pockets were full of toffees.

Hope said, 'Did your mother go with you?'

For a moment he considered lying, but she was looking at him with such concern that he realised he wanted only to be honest with her, not to wreck this relationship as he wrecked everything else. He said, 'My mother died when I was a baby.'

'Oh. I'm sorry.'

'I didn't know her.' Suddenly, because it felt as though the truth should be hurried out, he said, 'Actually, she killed herself. After I was born she went a bit mad, apparently. I read up about it. It's not that uncommon for women to be suicidal after having a kid.'

'That's terrible,' Hope gasped.

He had a strong urge to kiss her, take advantage of her sympathy, but that seemed a dishonest thing to do and he wanted to behave properly with her. 'You go to Irene's school, don't you?' he asked in turn. 'Do you like it?'

'No.' She blushed. 'I'm a bit of a dunce, really.'

He grinned at her. 'Oh, me too!'

'Did you like your school?'

'*Schools.*' He laughed shortly. 'No. I kept getting myself expelled.'

'Really?'

Unable to resist, he reached out and hooked a strand of her hair behind her ear. 'Hope, could we lie down, do you think? I'd only hold you – I promise I won't do anything you don't want me to do.'

'I don't think we should.' Quickly she said, 'Did you really get expelled?'

He lit another cigarette. Exhaling, he said, 'Didn't Irene tell you how bad I am?'

'No – you know she didn't.'

A cushion lay at his side and he reached for it, putting it under his head as he lay down. He'd been thinking about her naked and his erection ached. Trying not to think of her hands around it, he said, 'I never saw the point of school. Once I could read and write . . . well, I suppose I thought I could find out what was worth knowing for myself.'

She seemed shocked; he liked the way her eyebrows went up, the way her lips parted a little as though she was about to say something but was too surprised to find the right words. She looked so sweetly innocent, so easily outraged. He wondered how she would react if he asked her to take her clothes off, amused at the idea of her reaction, even as his cock became even harder and he knew he could do nothing to relieve himself.

To his surprise, Hope lay down beside him, a hand's breadth away. To the ceiling she said, 'I've never been in trouble. I've always been good.'

Cautiously he said, 'You sound as though you regret that?'

'No.' After a moment she said, 'Maybe. Sometimes.' Turning her head to look at him, she went on, 'Everyone thinks I'm terribly sensible.'

He wanted to trace the outline of her mouth that was set

132

in a straight, serious line. 'Do you know I think you're the most beautiful girl I've ever seen?'

She turned away from him to gaze at the ceiling again. 'What's that got to do with anything? Besides, you're only saying it. It's only *talk,* something to say to get what you want.'

'What do I want?'

She kept silence, closing her eyes, and Guy turned on his side, propping himself up on his elbow to look down into her face. Her skin was flawless, her eyes, her nose, her mouth all in perfect proportion, perfectly conforming to accepted ideas of what was beautiful. He couldn't help comparing her to Esther, who was not perfect, whose puzzling oddness was so compelling. He could gaze at Esther for hours and still not understand why he was attracted to her. He looked at Hope and knew at once.

He kissed her, his lips barely brushing hers. He placed his hand on her waist, and she kept still, like a child pretending to be asleep so that she seemed even more alert, more aware of every move he made. He felt his heart quicken, his need for her become more urgent so that he could barely trust himself to speak. He trembled and she opened her eyes to look at him.

For some moments she held his gaze. At last she said, 'Would you be careful?'

He made to speak but his voice broke. He cleared his throat. 'Careful?'

'I don't want a baby.'

'Hope . . . ' He made to kiss her but she placed a hand on his chest, holding him back.

'I like you,' she said, 'more than like. I saw you and I knew you would be the one who . . . I've been thinking about it a lot. You don't have to say you love me or anything – no lies like that.' She closed her eyes again and he could sense her frustration. Quickly she went on, 'I just don't want to be *me* any more – good, sensible me.'

133

And then she opened her eyes and it was as though she wanted him even more than he wanted her, so that he drew back, astonished by her, intimidated, suddenly unsure of his ability to be who she thought he was. All the same, he ached for her; all the same, he felt unable to move, afraid of his own inexperience. He would be clumsy, he would make a fool of himself. If he began he would have no way of stopping, but he had no idea of how to begin. He groaned, stubbing out his cigarette too vigorously.

'Hope . . . '

Her hand brushed against his erection, lightly as though she had dared herself. He caught her wrist and held it. 'Hope.' He laughed painfully. 'Should we get undressed?'

She nodded. Sitting up, she pulled her sweater off. Static electricity caused her hair to fan around her head and he knelt in front of her and smoothed it down with both hands. Holding her head, he kissed her, drawing back to sit on his heels, watching as she began to unbutton her blouse. Her bra was white, with a pink rosebud sewn between her breasts; she put her hands behind her back and unhooked it. He saw how hard her nipples were.

'Lie down,' he said, and she did as she was told obediently, gasping with pleasure as his mouth closed around her breast.

Chapter 13

Harry dreamed. He was walking through the rubble of bombed buildings – stumbling, slipping and sliding on loose stones, holding out his arms to steady himself like a fat clown on a highwire. Behind him, Hans laughed. He shouted, 'You're walking on their graves, Major! Be careful now.'

Harry turned, saw the small figure of a boy who walked towards him and then became a grown-up Hans, his SS uniform immaculate, the death's head on his cap catching the sunlight. 'Help her,' Hans said. 'Please.' And they were back in the interrogation cell, and Hans's nose was dripping blood, his eyes swollen closed. Ava sat beside him, gazing down at the ragged doll on her lap. Hans took the doll and thrust it into his arms. 'There, Harry. Your child.'

Harry woke suddenly, thinking he was still in the office and that he had fallen asleep at his desk. Sitting up, the slow realisation came that he was in his own bed, that last night, despairing of everything in his life, he had drunk too much and had fallen asleep only half-undressed, unwashed. His mouth tasted foul.

Staring at his bedroom ceiling, he heard Esther and Ava in the bathroom. Esther would be washing his wife's face and hands then coaxing her to brush her teeth. He listened to Esther's sing-song voice encourage Ava and thought how he must get up, that he couldn't go on lying in bed when there was so much to do, so much relying on him. Except he didn't have the energy; his limbs felt weighted to the bed. Perhaps if he were to lie still for a while, perhaps if he only closed his eyes for a few minutes he would feel strong enough to face the day. But if he closed his eyes he might sleep again; the nightmares might come again. He truly didn't want to see Hans again or hear his voice so distinctly. There was no sense in remembering him, even in dreams.

On the landing outside his room, he heard Guy say good morning to Esther with his usual exaggerated, cheerful good manners. Harry thought of his meeting with his son's Headmaster just before he drove Guy home, how the man had seemed so sadly resigned to Guy's rebelliousness, his total lack of respect for anyone supposedly in authority over him. The Headmaster had even seemed rather admiring of the boy; that was the point when he'd told him how brilliant Guy was, that if he could only knuckle down . . . The man had sighed, becoming resigned again. He knew as well as Harry did that Guy would never *knuckle down*. The idea of Guy becoming a soldier was preposterous: his son couldn't possibly be serious.

Harry heard Esther explain to Ava that they were to go downstairs now and have breakfast, and that later, if the weather kept fine, they could go for a walk in the park and wouldn't that be nice? There was a desperate edge to her voice. He'd heard this edge more often lately, but in his present, useless state her desperation seemed worse, as though he had become as hyper-sensitive to the feelings of others as he was to his own.

This had been especially true yesterday, when his string of troubled clients had culminated with that woman whose husband wanted to divorce her, whose misery had felt suffocating. And then, when she had gone, and Peter Wright sat in his office, so pathetically brave and optimistic, after Wright had innocently conjured Val so that it seemed she was standing beside him, he had turned to the window and saw the scavenging tramp, a man who had suddenly become every human being he had ever seen suffer. How sentimental that feeling seemed now, and shamingly self-indulgent; he closed his eyes, despairing of himself, and heard Hans laugh.

He had known Hans for only a few weeks in Berlin during the spring of 1946. The morning they met he had noticed the thickening buds of a lilac tree growing in the garden of a bombed house and had been surprised that the season had changed. Berlin still felt in the grip of an icy winter, a dark, petrified city he couldn't wait to leave. All around him the ruins were a reminder that everything was futile, ending only in the grave. He could do no good, could change nothing; he could translate this prisoner's words, that Nazi document, and feel only corrupted, that by understanding their language he was somehow complicit. How weary he had been that spring, so sick to death. The ruins stank of coal fires extinguished by rain, of damp and musty, rat-infested cellars. And the dead were buried beneath it all, and the living made burrows from which starving children scrambled, filthy, stinking.

He had thought of the victims and felt himself grow even wearier. It wasn't even pity he felt, not even outrage or a righteous, burning desire for justice. He wanted to go home, to his own bed. He thought abstractly of the son he barely knew, safe in his boarding school in England, and daydreamed of being a proper father, making up for his absence during the last six years of war. Sometimes he could barely remember his son's face – and this only added to his sense of total exhaustion. He couldn't be a father; after this, he felt he couldn't be anyone much at all.

He passed the lilac tree growing in the rubble and turned the corner to the place where he worked. He was a Major in the British Army; he had important tasks to perform. There were prisoners to interrogate, reports to write, questions to find the answer to. Even though they were the victors, the questions seemed plaintive to him: he heard the voice in his head whining, *But why?* Pathetic, really, when the answer was so mundane.

137

In his office, he took off his Army greatcoat and cap and hung them from the hook on the door. He smoothed back his hair and sat down at his desk and wondered if this would be the day that they told him he could go home, duty done. Looking up from the piles of documents on his desk, he saw Sergeant Roberts standing in the doorway. The Sergeant smiled, used to his misery, indulgent of it. He said, 'Everything all right, sir?'

'Unless you're going to tell me otherwise, Sergeant.'

The man sighed. 'They've brought someone in they want you to interrogate. They want you now, sir. Downstairs. They said as soon as you came in , . . '

Harry wondered at the urgency, it stirred some spark of curiosity in him. He got up from his desk and Sergeant Roberts held the door open for him. 'Shall I fetch you a cup of coffee, sir?'

Downstairs was where the interrogation rooms were, where he had heard such stories, such excuses. The rooms were small and windowless, the stone walls painted two dull shades of green so that the air seemed colder, danker. He was directed into the first room, where a single bulb caged in a metal shade hung from the low ceiling and cast a brutish, ineffectual light; there was a wooden table, two chairs, a guard standing in the corner, and there was Hans. Hans sat at the table, he was handcuffed. He sat very straight, very still, and his expression didn't alter when Harry walked in but remained blank, as though he was looking at a dull picture in a doctor's waiting room. Prisoners weren't usually handcuffed, but this boy, or so Harry had been told, was a nasty piece of work, dangerous. He had killed his neighbour. 'Stuck a knife in his guts,' Lieutenant Brown had told him, and had laughed incredulously. 'You'd have thought they would have had enough of killing each other, wouldn't you, sir? Bloody barbarians.'

Hans's papers were forged.

138

Harry believed that killing his neighbour was Hans's way of giving himself up. This idea had made him despair, so that he found himself surprised at his ability to feel anything at all.

Much later, Hans told him that he had been tired of hiding, pretending to be a no one. 'Such cowardly, skulking behaviour! I am disgusted with myself. But at the time . . . well, sometimes one only wants to live. I am human, after all.' And he'd smiled, as though he believed Harry thought otherwise, his vanity as monstrous as his contempt.

Lying in his bed, Harry suddenly tossed the covers aside and got up: he had to get out of bed quickly or he'd stay there all day. He went to his bedroom window and lifted the curtains aside. Below him in the garden was Ava and he watched her walk back and forth across the lawn, seemingly without aim. She looked even more like her brother nowadays, like Hans when he retreated into himself, when it seemed he couldn't even be bothered with his own posturing any more. He would seem very young then, even younger than his years. Once, Hans had looked up from one of these reveries, frowning at Harry as if he didn't recognise him. 'My father was a good man,' he had said. 'There. I want you to know that.' This was the closest Hans ever came to admitting his own badness, and at once he'd returned to his silence, his face become blandly youthful again, just as Ava's was now, both closing themselves off from their bleak futures.

Harry went downstairs and into the kitchen where Guy sat at the table with Esther. At once, Esther stood up as though she believed it was wrong to be sitting down with his son, even sitting down at all. She said quickly, 'I'd better go and see what Mrs Dunn is doing.'

When she'd gone into the garden, Guy said, 'You know we talked about me joining the Army? Well, like it or not...' He picked up an envelope and held it out to him. 'Unless I fail the medical, which I won't.'

Harry took the envelope and, not needing to read its contents, placed it on the table.

Guy said insolently. 'Aren't you even going to say that at least it will make a man of me?'

'Why should I say such an absurd thing?' Harry sat down opposite him. 'Is it still what you want?'

The boy didn't answer, only took out his call-up papers from their envelope and gazed down at them, turning a page over as if he thought he might have missed some vital piece of information. At last, looking up at him, he said, quietly, 'Yes, it's what I want.'

'Then good.' Harry stood up, began to make tea and toast. He felt relieved that this one thing was settled; unless there was a war he could go back to worrying about Guy in the abstract and not have the real, living, breathing Guy hanging around being *Guy*, scornful, facetious, unknowable. *Unless there was a war*. He was struck by the terrifying idea of having to worry about his son in such an all-consuming way; he was sure he wouldn't be able to cope with such an enormity of worry. He wondered if this proved that he loved him. He hated how much he needed proof, even the kind of proof that would put his child in mortal danger.

Harry turned to Guy. Gently he said, 'Is there anything you'd like to ask me?'

'Such as?'

'Well – anything. I was in the Army for six years.'

'*War years*.'

'Still the Army.'

'It's all right, Dad,' Guy said airily. 'But if a question occurs to me, I'll be sure to ask.'

Harry gazed at him, wanting to remember a time when this handsome, intelligent boy had ever shown any sign of needing him. When he was a baby, perhaps, when he'd found him curled beside his mother's dead body. Guy had cried himself to sleep but had woken as soon as he lifted him from Julia's arms, his eyes startled, terrified so that he had started to cry again, a terrible, distressed crying unlike anything Harry had ever heard before. He'd had to put him down, desperate to see to his wife, unable to believe that she was dead, although it was obvious. Guy had cried and cried and reached up his arms to him; Harry remembered that he had ignored his cries, told himself it was because he was panicked, unable to think of anything but reviving Julia, his beautiful, wonderful girl. He remembered that Guy hauled himself up, holding on to the side of the bed, only just able to balance on his two feet, a few days away from his first steps. He cried for his mother and Harry had hushed him, not looking at him, just telling him to be quiet, to be good, a good quiet boy. Guy's nappy was soaked and soiled, weighting down his pyjama bottoms. He had been lying beside his mother all morning; Julia had carried him into bed with her after she had taken the pills. If Harry had not come home that lunchtime, he would have lain there all day. Later, thinking about this, Harry had clutched Guy to him and wept, saying how sorry he was, over and over again. Guy had struggled against this overwhelming embrace. He wanted his mother – only Julia could comfort him. Harry was no use to him at all.

Sitting down at the kitchen table again, Harry began, 'Guy . . . ' But he was unable to think of anything to say to him; often it felt like they were strangers, now more than ever. Suddenly desperate not to feel so alienated from his son, he blurted out, 'I love you.'

Guy laughed, surprised.

'Why is that funny?'

'I don't know – it isn't. Sorry.' Guy looked away, such a closed expression on his face that he looked almost pained. Eventually he repeated, 'Sorry.' Then he stood up, saying awkwardly, 'I need a shave.'

'Have you any plans for today?'

'Why?'

'I was only wondering. I suppose you should make the most of your time before you leave.'

'Yes.' Guy turned to him from the kitchen door. 'That's exactly what I intend to do.'

Harry ate his breakfast. Esther and Ava came in from the garden, went out again, came in again; Esther smiled at him despairingly. She sat his wife at the other end of the table from where he was and spilled the jar full of shells out on a tray. 'There,' she said, 'Find the prettiest for Mr Dunn.'

Ava began raking her hands through the shells, turning them over, peering at one before placing it down and searching out another. She seemed absorbed in this task, happy even. Even so, Harry found he couldn't bear to watch her. He got up, grateful that he had his work to go to.

Chapter 14

When I told Jack that my father had left him the house and all his money, he just stared at me. His mouth opened only to close on whatever it was he was about to say. He shook his head. At last, almost angrily, he said, 'That's mad. I can't believe he'd do such a thing. He's left me *everything*?'

I nodded.

'But what about you?'

'What about me?' I smiled, quite enjoying his reaction. I had his full, astonished attention, after all. 'I'll be all right.'

'How? How will you be all right?' Again he shook his head. Then: 'No, this is nonsense. I'm not going to take your house – your home, your money. I couldn't be your friend and do such a thing!'

'I want you to have it.'

'No.'

I laughed out loud. 'What do you mean, *no*?'

'I mean I refuse to take it. Listen, forget all about it.'

'The house is yours, Jack. I've already found somewhere else to live.'

He sat down, indicating that I should sit down too. We were in the front room of his house, a house he believed Carol had never thought good enough for her; it was too small, the rooms too poky, the patch of garden too over-looked by all the other, identical houses crowded round it. I sat on the sofa he and Carol had bought together, part of a suite that, like everything in this house since her death, had become shabby. I noticed how worn the carpet was – the boys took their toll on everything and Jack had long ago given up trying to keep the house up to the standards Carol had maintained. The dust was thick on the sideboard where Carol smiled from her wedding photograph, her arm linked through Jack's. I looked at it, and for a moment imagined that I had been there that day because the photo was so familiar.

Jack said, 'Why did he leave me everything?'

I said simply, 'I don't know.'

'Did you know he was going to?'

'I knew he wasn't going to leave me anything. He told me often enough.'

'Christ.' Jack stared into space. Softly he repeated, '*Christ*.'

'Jack, I'm not unhappy about this,' I reassured him.

He laughed that dismissive laugh of his. Looking at me, he said, '*I'm* unhappy, Peter. Actually, I find it disturbing. I don't want anything to do with it.'

The boys ran in from the garden, excited when they saw me, demanding that I play with them. I would have been happy to do so, but Jack told them to leave us alone, his voice becoming angry when they didn't do as they were told at once. When they'd gone, I said, 'Think of the space the boys would have, Jack. They could have a bedroom each, and Hope wouldn't have to sleep in the box room.'

He looked at me sharply. 'It's not a *box room*. And the boys don't need a room each. Look, Peter, it's out of the question.'

'Why?'

'Why? Because it's *yours*! Listen, we both know why he did this, and I don't want any part of it.'

'Why did he do it?'

Fumbling in his pocket for his cigarettes, Jack lit one. At last he said, 'Because he was a spiteful old bastard. Jesus, he even found a way to get at you from beyond the grave.'

'I don't want the house, Jack.'

'No?' He shook his head. 'Nor do I.'

'Then give it to the children. Sell it; keep the money in a trust for them.'

I could see him struggling with this idea and gave him time to think about it. From the photograph on the sideboard, Carol smiled at me. I gazed back at her, noticing as I always noticed the way she held her bridal bouquet in front of her, shielding the small bump that was Hope. I looked away, no longer caring what Jack did; I was going to leave that house whether he wanted it or not, and it would be like being relieved of a heavy burden.

I went into town when I left Jack, did my shopping, and called in to see Harry Dunn, who looked at me just as Jack had – as though I was too unworldly to be out on my own.

Carol used to interpret this unworldliness as kindness; she would say that I was the kindest man she'd ever known. Whenever I looked after her children, whenever I invited all of them to Sunday tea or bought the children presents, she would tell me how kind I was, as though my kindness dismayed her. Part of me relished her mild dismay and the momentary twinges of guilt that showed on her face. I liked to hear her protestations of *you really shouldn't have* when I gave Hope some small gift. There was always something in her eyes at those moments that told me she hadn't forgotten how badly she had let me down.

There was a time, soon after my return, when I had expected an apology, a tender moment alone during which she would say how sorry she was. I imagined her weeping; I imagined being cruel to her in some smart, cutting way. But of course that moment never came. I went on pretending to be kind, mercifully as it turned out; my regrets are hard enough without the burden of knowing I could be so pointlessly vindictive.

After that Japanese officer had broken my ribs, we were marched off through the jungle. A Sergeant supported me, a man named Arthur Graham. The pain in my chest grew worse with each step I took, and although Arthur encouraged me with kind words I felt that it would be best for everyone if I lay down and died. Some men did just that. We walked for days, and sometimes villagers would try to help us, sometimes succeeding in giving us a little rice. I remember how beautiful their tiny children were, their eyes big with wonder, as afraid of us as they would be of ghosts.

We walked until we came to a railway line and were put into cattle trucks. I lay down on the truck's wooden planks, curled small because there was so little space, watching the ground flash beneath us through the gaps, concentrating on this, wanting to be mesmerised, but drifting in and out of restless, dream-filled sleep. I dreamed of Carol standing on a railway station platform, and she called to me and called to me but I couldn't hear what she was saying. I called back to her that I loved her and woke, startled, distraught because the train had left her behind. Then I realised where I was, my cheek resting against splintered wood, the hot stench of so many sick, unwashed men all around me and the pain concentrated around my heart. I watched the ground speeding away only inches from my face and it was as though my strength was being poured through the boards' cracks like sand; soon there would be nothing left of me. I closed my eyes. So this was dying, then – this slow emptying of self. I would not accept it. I forced myself to sit up. Carol had been left behind but it didn't mean that I wouldn't see her again. I told myself I would go home and she would be my wife. I made a promise that I wouldn't die because I was precious to her and that she would be waiting.

The day before I left her we had walked in the park where we first met and she was quiet, so quiet for such a long time that I was afraid – but then she told me that her parents had gone away and we could go back to her house and there would be no one there. We went in through the back door, afraid of being seen, being heard, although we didn't speak. Nervousness stopped my voice, just as I believe it stopped hers. She led me upstairs, to her room at the back of the house, a room full of her childhood: a dolls' house, a rocking horse, stuffed creatures that stared out at me from the window seat. Because her bed was narrow as a child's, she spread an eiderdown on the floor, a soft square of pale pink that smelled of her. She smelled of roses, such a faint, elusive scent; I pressed my face against her neck and inhaled deeply, feeling her fingers curl into my hair.

We didn't undress, I wish more than anything that we had undressed and I had felt her skin against mine, seen her breasts, her thighs, her cunt. I only moved my hand beneath her skirt, her knickers, felt her tenseness, her dryness so that I wet my fingers in my mouth and pushed them breathlessly inside her. I felt sure she could hear my heart beating: my desperation seemed loud to me, a vibrating pulse that filled the whole room with noise. I couldn't wait, couldn't take my time caressing her and kissing her, reassuring her. The noise drove me on, deafening, isolating so that I might just as well have been alone, her body only a maddening object to be broken into before I could find release. She cried out when I entered her; I know I caused her pain. She turned her face away from me afterwards and her skin was white, her lips quite bloodless. I thanked her and smoothed down her skirt. After a little while I helped her to her feet and saw that we had left a stain on the pink eiderdown, a dark patch of blood and semen.

Mostly though, I didn't think of this in the camps. In the camps at night I made love to her so gently, so carefully, undressing her so that only a little of her was exposed at a time so that finally she felt easy in her nakedness.

Mostly though I didn't have the strength even for

imagining this slowness; malaria would too often have me in its clutches, hunger always cramping my guts which constantly leaked diarrhoea until I thought I would shit my life away. Why not die like that, after all, when so many others had died such disgusting, demeaning deaths? But somehow my heart kept up, dogged and unfailing whilst the rest of me rotted and stank and became grotesque. My ribs showed through my stretched-tight skin and could be counted at a glance; I could feel the places where the breaks had mended, imagined that others could see my heart, my one unbeaten organ, pumping away behind its flimsy cage.

If I said that thoughts of Carol kept me alive, then I think I would be lying. On that train, at the beginning of my journey, she did save me. Later, I think it was only some trick of my heart, a strength it has that no one – least of all me – could have suspected. And there were days when I forgot her, and days when I would have exchanged my life for hers because I was so desperately afraid of dying.

But I didn't die. Despite sometimes believing that fear alone would kill me, I came home. I came home and saw Carol by chance as she walked along the street. And I've already written that she looked so shocked to see me, so surprised that I wasn't killed by the Japanese, although they'd done their very best to grant her wish. Because of course she wished that I'd died, just as I wished she'd never existed. My death would have saved her so much awkwardness.

When I left Jack today I had the feeling that our friendship – which has lately seemed so frail – will not survive my father's legacy. I would not mind so much if it wasn't for the twins and Hope. Especially Hope. I try to imagine ways of keeping her close to me, and perhaps if she was still a child it would be easy. But she is neither child nor adult; she can't love me as she once did, nor can she bring herself to be polite. We have been too intimate and she is too young for such chilly self-control. So, I am rather at a loss. I remember the fairy stories I used to tell her, in which impossible tasks were set and only sorcery and magic gained the hero the princess's love. I would not need magic, only the right words, said carefully, and a mirror, I think, one large enough for us both to stand side by side, facing our reflections, the truth staring her in the face.

I packed a small suitcase of clothes to take to the house on Inkerman Terrace, and another case containing my materials. My new home is furnished sparsely with plain, utility pieces that are as solid as they are dull, although there is a large, iron bedstead that is terribly ornate and takes up much of the space in the bedroom. I have never slept in such a bed before, the kind of bed in which babies are conceived, in which those babies are born and the old die. When I saw the bed it occurred to me that when my new neighbours discover I'm not married, they might believe I'm odd, even – whisper it – *homosexual*. After all, I make my living as an artist and so the evidence mounts, although queer men have never mistaken me as one of their own. I am much too charmlessly gauche and inept.

I decided that I'll go back later to collect my few remaining possessions I've left in the house. But I can't stay there another night. I must be free of the place now – I've delayed too long. Besides, leaving the house is the best way of convincing Jack that I am happy for him to take it. And if he decides not to move in, then at least I have escaped from the place and its memories.

Chapter 15

'We've got a new neighbour,' Matthew said. He was peeling potatoes at the sink and he glanced over his shoulder at her. 'Proper gent, he is. Real la-di-da.'

Val looked up from flicking through the evening paper. 'Oh? What's he doing living round here, then?'

'There's nowt wrong with living here.' Plopping a potato into a pan he added, 'But aye – I think he must be down on his luck. He has a car, though. You'd have seen it parked up outside, did you?'

She had, and had thought that the doctor was visiting next door but one, where a young woman was expecting her first baby. No one on Inkerman Terrace owned a car. Curious now, she said, 'What's he like?'

'I've just told you!' Another potato went into the pan and Matt began to peel one more, frowning as though deep in thought. At last he said, 'Your mam would have said that he had an old soul.'

Val remembered how her mother used to talk about some people as having been *here before*; these people were always slightly eccentric, and as a child she had been a little afraid of those her mother gave such a label to. Val glanced towards the wall dividing their house from their new neighbour's. She hoped he wasn't too strange, too creepy, as were most of the few single men who had at one time or another lived in the Terrace. When she was a child, some of these men would take too much interest in her and her friends, watching them play in the street, offering them sweets, inviting them into their untidy, smelly houses. She and her friends would laugh at these men, knowing exactly what they were after, but if she ever found herself alone with one of them she was afraid. It didn't help that sometimes her father thought they were harmless; sometimes even good men couldn't see who the rapists were amongst them. This new neighbour could easily have taken her father in.

She folded the newspaper and tossed it down. 'I'm going out with Jack tonight.'

'Aye?' He glanced at her. 'Second time in a week, eh?'

'So?'

He shrugged. Putting the potatoes on to boil he said, 'Well, if you want any tea it'll be ready in half an hour. You've time to go next door and introduce yourself.'

'Why would I want to do that?'

Matt smiled, a rare, teasing smile. 'He's a nice lad. Wouldn't do you any harm to keep one like that in reserve. Go on.' He opened the oven and took out a small meat pie. 'I made this for him. You take it round there – it'll be a neighbourly gesture.'

She hesitated, for a moment becoming that little girl again who was scared of strangers. But then her curiosity got the better of her. 'All right,' she grinned. 'At least I can judge for myself whether he's a *nice lad* or not.'

'My dad made it,' Val explained. 'It's a pie, probably corned beef and potato.'

The man who had answered her knock on the door smiled down at the tea-towel-wrapped pie in her hands, then he smiled at her – and she felt her insides contract. He was extraordinary, tall and very slim, his cheekbones sharply defined, his nose straight above a soft, full mouth. His eyes were the bluest she had ever seen, his pale blond hair pushed back from his forehead; there was the faintest shadow of a beard. He was like the Jesus in the pictures that had hung on the walls of her childhood Sunday school. She

151

found herself staring at him stupidly, wondering if she had ever seen anyone more angelically beautiful.

He said, 'Won't you come in?' He held the door open. 'Come through into the kitchen.'

Leading her along the passageway, he turned to her. 'This is very kind of him. Awfully kind. I was just about to go out and find a fish and chip shop, and now I won't have to.' In the kitchen he placed the pie down on the table and held out his hand. 'I haven't introduced myself – Peter Wright.'

'Val Campbell.'

As she shook his hand he said, 'Would you like a cup of tea, Miss Campbell?'

'No, thank you – really. I should go.' She glanced towards the door, suddenly shy of this man as she might be of a priest. There was a calmness about him, a gentleness that made her feel that he could see through to her soul. She imagined making her confession to him, that she had been an adulterer – was still, in her heart, an adulterer. She imagined him listening behind the confessional's screen, his head bowed, intent on her words. It would be best that she couldn't see him, only his shadowy outline in the darkness; he would be too distracting – she would think how grubby everything was, compared to such a man.

She made herself meet his gaze, wanting to see that he was ordinary, really, but he smiled, disarming her, so that she found herself asking, 'What made you come to live here?'

He laughed, surprised. 'It happened to be immediately available.'

'Do you come from Thorp?'

'Yes.' After a moment he added, 'From Oxhill, near the park.'

'It's really nice there.'

'Yes, it is.'

She wanted to ask him why he had left, but instead

blurted out, 'We used to go and play in the park when we were kids. There was this big house on the corner, opposite the cemetery. I was scared to walk past it because it looked like something out of a ghost story.'

'That's Doctor Walker's house,' he told her, 'And yes, it's quite a horror, isn't it? I lived a few doors away, nowhere near as grand.'

She glanced around the bare little kitchen he had yet to make any mark on. This had been Mrs Granger's house and she had lived here for as long as Val could remember, a quiet old lady who went to church twice every Sunday and had died peacefully in her bed. Matthew, checking on her as he did every day, had found her. 'I hope to God I go like that,' he'd told Val that evening. 'God keep me from hospitals – I've had enough of them.'

Mrs Granger had kept the kitchen table in the centre of the floor, but he had moved it so that it stood beneath the window. Beside the meat pie, she noticed a sketch-pad open on a drawing of a sparrow. She stepped towards it, to look more closely. The drawing was life-sized, the little bird's head cocked, its eye bright, so exquisitely detailed it looked as if it might fly off the page. She turned to him.

'It's lovely.'

'Thank you.'

She looked down at the drawing again, compelled to reach out and touch the bird's wing. 'You haven't finished it.'

'No.' He came to stand beside her. 'I was idling really; he flew down onto the windowsill.'

'*Idling*?' Astonished, she said, 'I wish I could *idle* like that.' Turning to him, she said, 'I would love to be able to draw.'

'I give lessons,' he smiled. 'Special rates for neighbours.'

'Really?'

He grinned and confided. 'I used to teach, but found I

153

wasn't very good at it. But here,' he tore the drawing of the sparrow from the pad. 'Have this, if you like it. A thank-you for the pie.'

'Are you sure?'

'Of course.'

She smiled shyly at him. 'Sign it.'

He laughed but did as she asked. As he handed it to her he said, 'There, a genuine Peter Wright. Worth exactly as much as the paper it's drawn on.'

She looked down at the picture, saw that his signature was a tiny, indecipherable scrawl, the date in slightly larger letters below it, and she thought how modest he was, how unlike anyone she had ever met before. She had an urge to say something that would make a connection with this astonishing man, but could think of nothing except, 'Thank you.'

Reluctantly she added, 'I should go, Dad will wonder where I've got to.'

As he showed her out, Peter said, 'Perhaps you and your father would care to have supper with me one evening?'

Stepping on to the street, she was about to make an excuse because she knew her father would think it daft to go and eat in a neighbour's house – especially a neighbour he barely knew. Even the word *supper* set him apart from them. They had *tea* at six o'clock; she imagined what Matthew would say to *supper*. All the same, she said, 'That would be lovely, thank you.'

He glanced past her to the girls playing a skipping game in the street, his eyes lingering on a girl of about twelve who ran into the turning rope, her blonde ponytail catching the evening sunlight, her buds of breasts bobbing unrestrained as she began to skip. For a moment Val watched him watching this girl, saw how suddenly distant he looked, as though some terrible sadness preoccupied him. But there was also longing in his eyes and she felt cold suddenly; perhaps she had been taken in, perhaps he was like those other odd bachelors after all, one of her childhood bogeymen.

Quickly she said, 'Goodbye, Mr Wright.'

He seemed to come to his senses then, turning that beautiful smile on her so that she wondered how she could have had such disgusting thoughts about him. 'Peter,' he said. 'Please call me Peter.'

As she reached her own front door she looked back to see if he was still watching the girls. To her relief he had gone inside.

She thought about Peter Wright that night as she lay sleepless in bed, wondering what it would be like to have him as a friend. She imagined going to him, sitting at his kitchen table and saying, 'Jack proposed to me this evening. He wants me to marry him and be a mother to his children, he wants me to give up work, to stay at home and cook and clean and shop for him. He wants regular sex again, the ordinary sex married couples have. This is what drives him most. He wants to have sex with me and not feel ashamed or guilty afterwards, even if this means giving up excitement. He's decided, reluctantly I think, that regularity outweighs illicit thrills. His proposal comes down to this: he would like me as a mistress but can't find a wife.'

And perhaps Peter Wright, who looked like Christ about to give His list of those most blessed, would ask, 'Do you love him?'

Val rolled on to her side and her single bed creaked and rocked a little because its metal joints were loosening. She had slept in this bed all her life and had spent only a few nights away from it – short holidays with her parents before the war, weekends with Harry in the hotel by the sea. Those weekends when it seemed that they would hardly leave their big bed except once to walk on the sands, make-believing a future – castaways imagining the luxuries that would be theirs once rescued. Harry had stopped to skim a stone across the still water. They had been silent for a while, the kind of pensive silence that follows wishing games, when suddenly he'd said, 'I should never have asked you to dance.' He turned to her. 'I should have kept my vow.'

He meant the vow of chastity he had made to himself, that challenge he had set to prove he was strong enough to do anything, even subjugate his own true self. Because Harry loved sex like he loved food and drink – he was a greedy connoisseur and there had been lots of women before his marriage, before his vow. On the beach that day, alone with her, he had said, 'I wish things were different,' such a vague wish, unlike the wishes that had gone before it. He should have wished only that he wasn't married, but he couldn't bring himself to, couldn't disown his marriage despite the pain it caused him.

He spoke of his wife once, relating her story as though it was a fairytale, full of wickedness and misfortune, of impossible tasks and challenges. 'There's no happy ending,' he'd said, 'except that she is safe. It's a kind of safety, I suppose, even if she is frightened all the time.'

Once, late in their relationship, too late for his answer to make any difference, she had asked him, 'Do you love her?'

'I love *you*,' he said, and he'd covered his face with his hands as though appalled with himself.

Her bed protested as she turned on to her back. She wondered if her new next-door neighbour could hear her restlessness through the thin wall. Of course, she couldn't talk to Peter Wright as a friend – men and women were never friends. She couldn't confide in him, she couldn't confide in anyone. Somehow she had managed to become friendless – the fate of a single woman of a certain age unable to find another unmarried woman to share her scorn at the rest of the world.

They had been sitting in his front room, the children –

even Hope – sent to their grandmother's house for the night, and Jack had taken her hand, kissed it and said, 'Val, I think you're wonderful. I can't tell you how much my life has changed since you and I . . . Well, since you and I began to be serious about each other.'

He was too fastidious to mention the word sex, to say that he couldn't bear to give up fucking her now that he'd got a taste for her body. When they were still exchanging mildly flirtatious remarks in the works canteen, she had believed that Jack Jackson was the kind of man who would want a neat, slim woman in his bed, a woman who didn't ever initiate sex but would oblige decorously whenever he guided her hand towards his erection. She'd guessed that his wife had been the kind of woman who would lie still and quiet beneath him, neither expecting nor receiving very much except the sly satisfaction of witnessing his brief abandonment of his stern self-control.

She thought now that she had been a bitch to think of his wife like this, especially when in her heart she didn't really believe such women existed. But she had been jealous of married women, and to take the sting from her jealousy she had mocked them. Yet she had still believed that Jack wouldn't fancy her: she wasn't slim and she dressed too fashionably, too smartly to be considered anything as lame as neat. In truth, she had thought that she was too sexy for him; that he would want more tender meat. She supposed that had been just inverted naivety. He wanted her as much as any man she had ever been with – more, perhaps. She excited him; he made her feel powerful.

She had told Jack that she would think about marrying him.

She thought about life in his house, with his children, and pictured herself with a child of her own. This was the thought she held close. Like a gold coin found on a crowded street, she was full of the furtive, thrilling pleasure it gave her. Jack, she suspected, didn't want any more

157

children, but accidents happened. He wasn't the kind of man who was as careful as Harry had been.

Rolling on to her side, she stared at the wall and tried to imagine the face of the baby she might have. She sighed. Of course she would marry Jack; there was no other way of getting that child, the baby of her own that she most wanted in the world.

Chapter 16

Three months later

I went back to my father's house today, just to make sure – although of what I don't know. I suppose I was afraid that it might have been broken into, or that the recent high summer winds might have blown tiles from the roof, allowing the rain to get in. But everything was fine. Only the dust had settled more thickly, making the place smell of its airless neglect.

The garden has become overgrown, of course and the tree-house looks forlorn. It is missing the boys, just as I miss them. I see them less often these days; Inkerman Terrace becomes altogether too tiny when the twins visit and they soon become bored with no garden to play in. They could play out on the street, but Jack won't allow it; he thinks the local children who play football on the road outside my window are much too rough for his boys to mix with. Bored, Stephen and Martin ask me why I'm living here. Stephen called it 'a horrid little house', and Jack told him off at once, embarrassed as he always is in my company these days. He thinks it's idiotic that I should have left my father's house, that it now stands empty. Sometimes, uncharitably, I believe he would rather have me living there looking after it for him, a caretaker whilst he makes up his mind about what is the *done thing*. Of course, he doesn't think of how humiliating that would be.

Val tells me that she believes Jack would like to sell the house, but that he thinks it's somehow not done. She looked at me as though I have the power to put an end to Jack's discomfort, as though I was holding back some vital piece of information that would make Jack content. It seems to me that all she wants is Jack's contentment; if he is content, well then, the ship can be gently steered in the direction she wants it to take. Sitting at my kitchen table, she asked me if I would speak to Jack again, tell him again that I won't contest my father's will, and am happy not to, happy that everything is his.

'Do you think I'm happy about it?' I asked her in return.

She frowned at me. 'Aren't you? If not happy, then at least you don't mind.'

'No, you're right. I don't mind that I've lost a fortune.'

Flatly she said, 'You do mind. I'm sorry – it's just that you seem happy.'

I was happy because she was sitting in my kitchen, because we had just finished a good supper and a bottle of beer, and because until a few moments earlier I had managed to forget all about Jack and the fact that she was his fiancée. Since she'd reminded me, I could hardly bring myself to look at her. I got up and began clearing away the supper plates.

She got up too, and we washed the dishes in silence. We are often quiet together but that evening, the silence was awkward. After a while, as I handed her a plate to dry, she said, 'Are you happy – generally, I mean?'

She looked so concerned that I wanted only to reassure her. 'Yes, I'm happy.'

She smiled, relieved.

We don't tell Jack that we have supper together each Wednesday evening when Matthew goes to see his sister; it's an unspoken agreement between us that we should keep our relationship secret. She tells me I'm her best friend; she thinks I'm a Bohemian and Bohemian men can be friends with women in a way work-a-day men like Jack cannot. If I

160

asked her to pose for me naked I'm almost certain that she would because I am an artist with pure, artistic motivations; she can't see how much I want her. I've become too adapt at hiding desire.

When Jack first introduced me to her one Saturday evening in the Grand Hotel's bar, she laughed, astonished. 'We've already met – Peter has just moved in next door to us.'

Jack was only mildly surprised, mildly put out. He said, 'Well, it's a small world,' and then he put his arm around her waist, drawing her close to him, gazing at me with just a hint of warning in his eyes. He doesn't really believe I could take a woman from him; besides, he thinks a woman like Val wouldn't look twice at me. So he laughed, patting her bottom as he said, 'Shall we sit down?' Val glanced at me, embarrassed I think, by Jack's behaviour. It's all he can do to keep his hands off her. He calls her 'sweetheart' and 'darling', I don't think I've ever heard him speak her name, except to me, when we're alone. The day before we met in the hotel he said, 'I've asked Val to marry me. She said yes. I'd like you to meet her.' He hesitated, then in a rush said, 'I'd value your opinion.'

In his heart, he thinks Val is common; it's quite obvious in the way he speaks about her, his way of being around her. He wanted me to tell him that she's not. I asked him what my opinion mattered anyway, since they'd already agreed to marry, and he said crudely, 'I just hope I haven't allowed my dick to rule my head.'

Val and I talk during our Wednesday suppers. She tells me about her job, that she has the fastest typing and shorthand speed of anyone in the office, and that these were skills that seemed to take very little effort on her part, but came as naturally as talking does to an infant. She told me she *rose through the ranks* at Davies & Sons, but that she has gone as far as she can go and is bored. She looked pensive then, her gaze fixed on the circles she was tracing on the table with a teaspoon. 'If there was anything special about me – if I had a talent like yours . . . ' She smiled at me then, only to lower her eyes again.

More than anything, I want not to be in love with her, not to feel my stupid, dogged heart ache whenever she mentions Jack. She doesn't love him, I'm certain. She loves someone else, I'm certain of that, too – a man who broke her heart. She pretends that it was all a long time ago, but I can see that it wasn't; the pain in her eyes is too fresh.

Walking back from my father's house, I called in on Jack because seeing the tree-house had made me long to see the boys, to be mobbed by them, flattered by their excitement at seeing me. I thought I might take them to the park, perhaps even ask Hope along too. I imagined the four of us as happy together as we always were before Hope grew up, and it was these memories that made me optimistic as I approached Jack's house. He was mowing the front lawn, something he always does on a summer Sunday afternoon, the boys sitting on the low garden wall eating ice creams from the van that had just driven away, its chimes sounding 'Green Sleeves' down the street full of children playing, of mothers and fathers working in their gardens or chatting over the privet hedges.

Stephen jumped from the wall and ran to me. 'Give me a piggy-back!'

I took his hand. 'Later.'

Jack stopped pushing the lawn-mower, wiping the sweat from his face with his forearm. 'Oh good – just the man!'

'Am I? Why?'

Martin had jumped from the wall too and I lifted him into my arms, taking a lick from his ice cream. Raising his voice to be heard over Martin's squeals of outrage, Jack said, 'I thought you wouldn't mind looking after the boys for me – just while I go and see Val. *Do* you mind?'

'You don't mind, do you, Uncle Peter?'

I set Martin down. 'No, Martin, why should I mind? We'll go to the park, eh? Where's Hope? Go and ask her if she'd like to come with us.'

The twins giggled, hands over their mouths, and Jack grunted. 'All right boys, behave yourselves.' He looked at me. 'Stephen and Martin think it's a huge joke, but Hope's got a visitor.' Crouching down to unhook the grass box from the mower, he said, 'The boy she met at that party you drove her to?' He glanced at me then returned his attention to the box. '*Guy.*' Laughing dismissively, he added, 'I think he's a little s-h-i-t, but then I suppose I would.'

'We know you said shit, Daddy.'

Jack sighed; straightening up he said, 'Go and wash your hands and faces – you're covered in ice cream.'

When they'd gone inside the house, Jack took his cigarettes out and lit one, exhaling smoke wearily. At last he said, 'You look surprised, Pete. Even a bit shocked. We knew it would come, didn't we – that she'd start *courting*, that she wouldn't be our little girl any more.' He looked at me from gazing at the tip of his cigarette. 'Don't worry, I'm making sure the boys don't give them any peace or any amount of time alone.

He turned towards the bay-windowed sitting room, screened from the street by the lace curtains Carol had bought. Drawing heavily on the cigarette, he turned back to me. 'Go and introduce yourself – you can tell me what you think of him.'

'I met him at that party.'

'Oh? So, what did you think? Because *I* think he's a cocky little bugger. Well, he'll get all that nonsense knocked out of him soon enough. He's off to do his National Service soon. Thank Christ.'

The boys came out of the house, unwashed. Behind them came Hope, her face flushed and angry. She didn't look in my direction but deliberately ignored me as she said to Jack, 'They're saying I have to go to the park with them.

163

I don't want to, you can't make me.'

Stepping round Hope, the boy I'd met at the party smiled at me. 'Hello again, sir.'

He seemed older than I remembered – more confident, if that were possible. I thought of myself at his age, a child in comparison, unsure of everything and everyone. He looked supremely sure; it occurred to me that his parents must have indulged him since the day he was born to have turned out a boy like this one.

Sardonically, Jack said, 'Oh, Hope – it's such a lovely day! Of course you and Guy should go to the park with the boys and Uncle Peter. I don't want you cooped up in the house on a day like this. What kind of a father would that make me, eh, not seeing that his growing girl gets her vitamin D?'

'We can sit in the garden.'

Jack shook his head, his voice ordinary again as he said, 'No, Hope. You either go out with Peter and your brothers or Guy goes home.' He glanced at Guy, only to turn to Hope again. 'It's up to you.'

Guy said, 'I'd like to go to the park, actually.'

'There you are.' Jack began to roll the mower towards the back of the house and the garden shed. Over his shoulder he said, 'I'll be back around eight, Peter. You don't mind giving the kids their supper, do you?'

Hope and Guy walked ahead of us, holding hands but keeping a decorous distance from each other so that their arms and entwined fingers formed a deep v between them. I carried Stephen on my shoulders; very soon both boys will be too big to be carried, to want to be carried. They will be seven in a few weeks; they barely remember Carol at all.

Holding Martin's hand, I said lightly. 'Do you like Guy?'

'He gave us money to leave him and Hope alone.'

'Did he now?'

'Sixpence each. We took it but we didn't leave them alone, Daddy didn't want us to.' Martin looked up at me. 'Can we go in the café?'

'Maybe. Do you still have your sixpences?'

'Yes.'

'You know it was wrong to take Guy's money then not keep up your part of the bargain, don't you?'

'He's not allowed to kiss Hope.'

'No, but I think you should give him his money back. It's the honourable thing to do.' I stopped and lifted Stephen down. 'Show me the money.'

They reached into the pockets of their shorts and reluctantly held out the silver coins on the palms of their hands. 'All right. Go and give them back to Guy. Say sorry.'

'But he was wrong too!'

'Go on.'

Hope and Guy had stopped, Hope continuing to ignore me so pointedly that it obviously embarrassed Guy. As the boys ran up to him and pressed the sixpences into his hand he looked at me in surprise. At once he didn't look confident at all, only rather sheepish. At least he had the grace to smile. Recovering himself a little he said, 'Thank you. Now I can buy us all an ice cream.'

'I think they've had enough for now, Guy,' I said. 'We'll go to the swings first.'

Sulkily, Hope said, 'We're not coming.'

Guy laughed. 'Why not?' To the twins he said, 'Come on, you two. I'll race you!'

And he ran off, pursued by the boys. At once Hope followed them, almost breaking into a run in her haste to get away from me.

Chapter 17

Guy sat on the grass, watching Hope on the swing, the desultory way she moved back and forth, keeping her feet half on the ground. He had sat down to catch his breath, although her brothers were still running around like devils with their backsides on fire, as was that friend of their father's, Peter Wright. Suddenly one of the boys – he could barely tell one from the other – jumped on his back, shouting, 'Get up!'

Wright stood over him. 'Martin, leave Guy alone now. Go and see Hope, ask her to push you on the swings.'

Martin went, Stephen hard on his heels. Sitting down next to him, Wright said, 'Tag with those two isn't a game for the faint-hearted.' He smiled. 'With a bit of luck Hope will keep them occupied for five minutes whilst I get my breath back.'

He didn't sound breathless at all, and despite the fact that he looked thin enough for a light breeze to blow him away, he'd swung the boys about as though they were no heavier than Ava's rag dolls. He couldn't understand why Hope disliked him so much. At least he wasn't a sarcastic, angry bastard like her father, Jack. Wright seemed decent – kind, even. Her brothers obviously adored him; they even seemed like nicer children when he was around, as though they wanted to behave well for this man who treated them with so much warmth and fairness. Guy remembered the sixpences that had been returned to him and looked away, not wanting to catch Peter's eye, knowing that he would look guilty as sin.

Wright said, 'Hope's father tells me you've been called up?'

Guy plucked a blade of grass; running his thumbnail down it, he said, 'Yes.'

'Do you have any preference?'

'Army.' Guy managed to look at him. 'I get sea sick and I'm not keen on flying.'

Wright laughed. 'Sometimes even soldiers have to travel abroad.'

'But I'm hoping we'll spend most of the time on dry land.'

'Well, no harm in hoping.'

Curious, Guy asked, 'Were you in the Army, sir?'

Peter smiled at him. 'You don't have to call me sir. Peter will do.' After a moment he said, 'I was a Captain in the West Yorkshire Regiment.'

Wright was quiet for a while, watching Hope push the boys on the swings, alternating between the two of them. Finally he turned to him. 'Off you go with Hope. See she gets home safely.'

They went to the empty house and sat in the garden where the remnants of the flowerbeds, lupins and hollyhocks and delphiniums, struggled against the weeds. The long grass was warm and Hope lay down, closing her eyes against the sun. Guy gazed down at her, at her beautiful, familiar face, and for a moment hoped that she would sleep so that he could go on watching her in this peaceful quiet. Earlier, at her house, she had cried because he was going away, becoming angry when he promised that he would always come back to her, no matter what. 'You say that,' she wiped her eyes impatiently and glared at him. 'But people change when they go away.'

'I won't, I swear.'

The twins had rushed in then and ran round and round the sofa where they were sitting, whooping and hollering because they were Red Indian braves. He had bribed them to go away because once they had noticed that Hope was crying they had stared at her in astonishment, nagging at her to tell them why. But Hope's brothers were spoiled little monkeys and only left them alone once they heard the chimes of the ice-cream van. Attempting to smile after them, Hope said, 'They've never seen me cry before. I think they were a bit scared.'

He too had been scared, scared of the depth of her feeling. Yet he had been in awe of her since that moment weeks ago when she had lain down on the rug and unbuttoned her blouse. What Hope did was beyond his wildest fantasies; he still felt shocked by her. At times, when he was away from her, he convinced himself that she was mad. She had allowed him to have sex with her on their first date. More than allowed – she had responded with a passion that had left him breathless. Alone, remembering, sometimes he would laugh at the unexpected sheer bloody joy of it. But there was always the suspicion that she wasn't quite right in the head, and his laughter made him feel as though he was as crazy as she was. He tried to imagine Irene, or any of the sisters of boys he'd known at school, behaving like Hope, and couldn't. Perhaps it was because she didn't have a mother, not even an aunt, no one to instil in her that lying down with boys was wrong. Her father, he guessed, was useless.

Guy lay down beside her now. Above them, in the sycamore tree, a blackbird sang *teacher teacher teacher*. It flew down to land a few feet from them and he watched its stop-start search for insects. In a neighbouring garden, children were playing cricket with their father, who shouted, 'How's that!' Lazily, Guy turned on his side and kissed Hope's mouth. He whispered, 'Are you sleeping?'

'No.' She opened her eyes to look at him. 'I'm sorry I cried.'

'Don't be.'

'I never cry. Never ever. I hope the boys don't tell Dad – he'll know then.'

'Know what?'

She sighed. 'You *know* what. Can I have a cigarette?'

He lit two cigarettes at once, and handed her one. She smoked steadily, having long mastered the knack of inhaling. Nowadays, she seemed to need cigarettes more than he did. He left the open packet and box of matches beside her and got up, wandering the garden's perimeter restlessly, unable to stay still any longer. He hadn't slept for nights. Although he was used to going away, to leaving home – such as it was – for unknown places full of unknown boys, this felt different. He tried to tell himself that the camp they were sending him to for his basic training would be just like one of his schools, most of which had a brigade with uniforms and rifles, but he had never felt like this before, so desperate not to go. Before Hope he didn't care, had been content to go with whatever the unknown powers that governed his life had in store for him next. Since Hope he could only think of how much he would miss her. But there was something more, a tiny part of him that suspected she would soon find someone else, would throw herself at him, wrapping her legs around his waist and crying out his name just as she did with him. He loathed himself for suspecting this – but if she had slept with him, why not with others?

He stood at the end of the garden and looked back at her. She had sat up and was plucking at the grass listlessly. Often she seemed sad like this and hardly spoke, wanting only to make love. *Make love*! Such a hugely adult expression! He had set out with the intention of trying only to get his hand inside her knickers, expecting her to stop him with at least a show of outrage; yet now they were lovers. And she seemed older than him at times, and at other times young and very vulnerable – those times when he held her afterwards, her head against his heart. *Oh*

Christ, he thought. Sweet Jesus Christ.

She looked up and caught him watching and he went back to her and took her hand.

Looking towards the house, she said, 'We'll go inside, soon.'

'Yes,' he smiled. 'If you want.'

'If I *want*.' She laughed shortly. More softly she said, 'I want and want and want.'

'Yes.' He kissed her, aroused by her strangeness. 'So do I.'

Drawing back from him she asked, 'What were you and Peter talking about in the park?'

'Nothing much.'

'It didn't look like nothing much. You looked all serious.' Stubbing out her cigarette in the grass she said, 'He's creepy, isn't he?'

Guy laughed in surprise. 'No! I should introduce you to some of my ex-house masters, *then* you'd know what creepy is.'

'But he's really odd.'

He frowned at her, puzzled by the vehemence in her voice. 'Then why do Martin and Stephen like him so much?'

'Because they're just little kids!'

'Your father likes him.'

She grimaced. 'Does he? And even if he does, even if he doesn't just use him so he can palm us off on to him whenever he wants to sneak out . . . ' Suddenly she said, 'Peter looks at me. Looks and looks.'

'Oh.' Guy thought how easy it would be for any man to look and look at her. 'Oh well. Look back. Stick your tongue out or something.'

'I'm not ten!'

He grinned, unable to help himself because in fact she was behaving like a ten-year-old, completely out of character. 'No,' he said. 'If you were, he wouldn't look.'

170

'He's *always* looked at me!' Her cheeks flushed. Angrily she said, 'You don't understand – I knew you wouldn't. You're just like Dad.'

'I'm not like him. It's just . . . Hope, you're beautiful. Men will look at you.' He despaired at this bald, uncomfortable truth. Flatly he said, 'Ignore him.'

'I do!'

'Yes, I noticed.'

'Oh – so you noticed. You should thump him!'

He gazed at her; she was close to tears again and he couldn't believe it was all because of Wright. Hesitantly, because he had been dreading asking her all afternoon, he said, 'Hope, is there something wrong? I mean, apart from me going away.'

'No. I just don't want you liking Peter, that's all.'

'Then I won't.'

'He's a creep! I can't stand him!'

'All *right*.' He put his arm around her. 'Calm down.'

Shoving him away she said, 'What did he say to you? Was it about me?'

'No! For God's sake, we hardly said anything anyway, just a bit about me joining the Army, that's all.'

'He was captured by the Japanese – I bet he didn't tell you that. I bet he just laid his gun down as soon as he came within a mile of them,' Hope said spitefully.

'That's a terrible thing to say.' Guy thought of the photographs he had seen of men who had been held prisoner in the Far East. Somehow it was hard to believe that men who had suffered so much could ever have been cowards. Feeling only pity for Peter Wright, he said gently, 'Let's forget about him, eh? Let's go inside.'

Sulkily she said, 'It's horrible in there.'

'But it's private.' He ducked his head to look into her downcast face. Then he whispered, 'And you've never complained before.'

'But I'm complaining now!'

171

'Well, there's not much I can do.'

She bowed her head and began plucking at the grass again. After a while she muttered, 'There's somewhere else we could go.'

'Oh?'

'Don't look at me like that, as though I'm making things up! There *is* somewhere – you're not the only one who knows places.'

'Okay. Where?'

Quickly she said, 'If we go there, you're to keep it secret. I know you will, but promise me.'

'I promise.'

She stood up. 'All right. We'll go now.'

Hope felt as though she was about to walk out onto a stage to act in a play she hadn't rehearsed. She had felt like this for weeks now, ever since she had first placed Guy's hand on her breast and heard him gasp. He had been a virgin like her, and this had surprised her because he had seemed sophisticated and bold. But Guy was a good actor; she believed she knew him well enough now to know that he was just as strange as her. She realised that this was why she had been attracted to him when everything else – his good looks, his charm – was stripped away. They were two oddities, her and Guy.

She had decided to embrace her oddness; to know that she was out of step made her feel strong and she had noticed the other girls at school, even the teachers, looking at her as though they suspected her of keeping a secret. She was beyond them; she realised she always had been, but had been too timid to be herself. And having sex with Guy had done most to make her understand how powerful she was. That gasp when he touched her breast was thrilling; she would never have imagined he could be so much in awe of her. She relished being so bad, knowing her father had no idea, that he was still afraid that Guy would kiss her when

172

his back was turned.

Only Peter had seemed to understand how she had changed; she had seen the look of painful recognition on his face that she wasn't his any more. Seeing that look a few days after she had first been with Guy had made her want to flaunt herself in front of him Rather than stick her tongue out as Guy had suggested, she'd had an urge to flash her knickers. But that angry defiance hadn't lasted. This afternoon she was back to being her timid self again, despite Guy's presence. Guy was going away. She didn't know how she could carry on without him. Seeing Peter had only added to her misery: he looked as though he understood everything. She had wanted to scream and rage at him in frustration for knowing so much.

They had reached Peter's house. Outside the gate that opened onto the path leading to the back garden, Hope hesitated, unable to find even a little of the courage she had thought she had so much of until today. 'Perhaps we shouldn't.'

'Is this the place?'

'Yes, but I don't think we should go in.'

Guy looked up at the house. 'Who does it belong to?'

'Peter.'

'And because he's at your house with the twins, you thought we could sneak in? What if he catches us?'

'He doesn't live here. It's not Peter's any more, not really. It's Dad's – ours.'

'I don't understand.'

Impatiently she said, 'It doesn't matter! All you need to know is that he doesn't live here any more and that there's a key he keeps outside the back door. Do you want to go in or not?'

Guy bit his lip. 'I don't know.'

'Coward!'

'It's not that,' he said. 'It just feels wrong.'

Unwittingly, he had said the right thing: his weakness

173

made her bold. 'Come on. No one will know.' When he hesitated still, she said, 'There's a bed. A great big soft bed. You can do anything you want to me on a bed like that.'

'All right,' he said, aroused. 'But let's go in quickly, before the neighbours see us.'

Hope had been afraid that the key wouldn't be beneath the flower pot and that they would have wasted their precious time in going to Peter's house only to have to return to the place she thought of as Guy's den. But the key was there, and it turned in the lock easily.

Inside, the house was cold, insulated from the sun's heat. When her eyes had adjusted to the sudden change from bright sunlight to what seemed like the semi-darkness of the kitchen, she saw that everything was as it always had been. There was the battered kettle on the stove, the tea towels folded neatly on the rail by the sink, the shelves with the rows of brightly coloured mugs and plates that Peter had kept especially for her and the twins when they came to visit. When she was younger, he would sometimes set the kitchen table as though for the Mad Hatter's tea party and an elaborate make-believe game would follow; at other times, all the many dolls and stuffed toys that Peter kept for them in a room upstairs would be brought down and they would have a teddy bears' picnic on the lawn. He would solemnly ask the bears and dolls how they took their tea, allowing them time to answer, talking back to them as if they had.

Lately she told herself that she had been embarrassed by these antics of his, that even as a little girl she had thought how silly and odd Peter was. But in her heart she knew that she had been captivated by him; she had believed he was a magician – that if anyone could make her doll Katie speak it would be Uncle Peter. She knew too that she had loved him more than anyone – even more than her own father, who never had time for such games and even if he had, would have somehow made them less fun. Standing in his kitchen that still smelled of those times, that was so full of her childhood, she told herself angrily that if she had loved him then, she didn't love him now. Peter was nothing but a dirty old man. He made her squirm when he looked at her.

She turned to Guy. Still angry, she said, 'I'll give you the guided tour.'

He glanced back at the door. 'Hope, we shouldn't. He's your father's friend, he trusted me.'

'Trusted you? So you did talk about me!'

'No!' Guy sighed, exasperated. 'But he let us go off together, didn't he? Which is more than your father did. I think we should go back to your house – he'll still be at the park with your brothers.'

Although she knew he would stay with Val until late tonight, she said, 'Jack might come home.'

'Jack! Why do you call your father by his Christian name? Jack!' Guy shook his head and she could see he was becoming as angry as her. 'Honestly, Hope – you don't have to be so bloody weird all the time.'

'Weird?' She laughed harshly. 'I'll show you weird.'

'Will you now? How?' He was smiling infuriatingly, making fun of her.

Turning away from him, she walked out of the kitchen into the even darker hallway, not caring if he followed her or not.

He did follow her, after a moment's hesitation. He followed her upstairs and into the bedroom at the back of the house where Peter kept all the toys and games he had bought for them over the years. There was a Wendy house in one corner, a doll's crib beside it, and a rocking horse beneath the window that looked out over the garden. Piled on shelves in the fireplace alcoves were books and games and jigsaws, and the stuffed animals and bears that had so often sat on the lawn where the dolls' tea-set would be laid out in front of them. Katie, the blonde, curly-haired baby doll she had once adored, sat in a wicker chair, the skirt of her beautiful pink satin dress spread out around her, her arms sticking straight out in the stiff pose that had always made Hope want to pick her up, feeling guilty that she had left her alone in Peter's house. She remembered how she would make Peter promise to look after her and he would say that she could take Katie home if she wished. But her father wouldn't allow it. 'She has enough stuff at home,' he would say. 'More than enough.'

Guy went straight to the train-set on the table where a bed should have been. He exclaimed, all his irritation with her seemingly forgotten as he flicked a switch and the engine began to speed round the track. 'I always wanted a set like this. Look – it has a station and everything. Even a little model guard – and passengers!'

She went to stand beside him. 'He bought it when the twins were born.'

Guy glanced at her, beaming, happy as a little boy in a toy shop. 'It's fantastic. He's taken so much care with it – everything to scale . . . '

She tossed her head and he frowned at her. 'Come on, Hope, you must admit it's great. Well, maybe not to a girl.'

'I didn't want to show you that.'

'No?' He looked at her briefly, only to return his attention to the train-set, picking up one of the other engines and turning it over to look at the workings underneath.

'Put that down and come over here.'

Above the fireplace was one of Peter's drawings.

Peter had presented her with the picture on her thirteenth birthday. He'd had a party for her, just her and the twins and Jack – she'd already had a party with her schoolfriends at home. After she had blown out the candles on the cake Peter had bought for her, he had brought out her present.

Laughing and groaning at the same time, her father had said, 'Pete, you've already given her a present. You don't have to spend your money like this.'

'I didn't spend any money.' Peter had smiled at her. 'Open it. You can probably tell what it is, anyway.'

From the shape of it she knew that it was a picture, a boring present compared to the roller skates she had asked for and he had duly bought. Smiling so as not to hurt his feelings – she had still desperately cared about his feelings in those days – she had made a show of being excited as she tore off the cheap wrapping paper. There, in astonishing, colourful detail, was the prince from *Sleeping Beauty*, the story she most loved of all the fairytales he read to her.

In the picture, as if about to step from it, the prince led his white horse through dense, dark woods, his eyes watchful, afraid even. He wore a blue and gold brocade coat, a matching cap with a gaudy feather that shimmered in the single stream of sunlight breaking through the trees. The horse's mane had ivy leaves woven through it, each leaf finely veined. Its eyes were as wary as the prince's, its nostrils flared; it seemed to be picking its way carefully, as though the ground beneath its hooves was treacherous.

But you had to look carefully to see what the picture was really about. There, in the undergrowth almost out of sight, was a goblin-like creature, peeping from behind a tree trunk. The creature smirked from its hiding place, such a look of up-to-no-good on its ageless face. At first she hadn't noticed the goblin at all – she had eyes only for the handsome boy leading his horse so nervously – until her father pointed him out to her.

Hope had come to believe that Peter had meant the goblin to be a surprise, that he hadn't wanted her to see it that first time, had wanted her to believe that the creature had crept into the picture when her back was turned, that there was still magic in the world even for a girl who worried so much about her father and brothers, about

177

everything, in fact. Looking at the picture as she did often, her eye was drawn to that corner where he lurked, where the mischief was. Finally, she had asked Peter about the goblin, curious because there were no such creatures in *Sleeping Beauty*.

'I didn't draw any goblin,' he protested.

'I know you did!'

He'd smiled. Then, more serious than he ever normally was when they were alone together, he said, 'I suppose he's there to remind you to be careful.'

Standing beside her in front of the picture, Guy said, 'Is this what I'm supposed to be looking at?'

'He drew it.'

'Who?' Stepping closer to the picture, Guy peered at it. 'Peter Wright.' He touched the signature in the bottom left-hand corner. 'Peter who lives here?'

'Yes.'

He whistled through his teeth. 'It's good, isn't it?' Still peering at it, he smiled and she knew he had caught sight of the goblin. 'What's this? It looks like a devil climbing out of hell. I suppose if he thought of putting something as scary as that in a kid's picture, maybe he is a bit weird.'

Looking at the picture, Hope said, 'It's meant to be a warning.'

'Of what?' Guy turned to her, ready to tease. 'You know there are no such things as fairies, don't you? I think he might believe in them, though.'

'I think it's a warning about boys . . . sex.'

He laughed. 'Yeah? Well, you should have taken more notice of it, shouldn't you?' He turned away from the picture and looked around the room. 'Why does he keep so many toys in his house?'

'They're ours. We were always here. Dad could never be bothered with us.'

Guy sighed. Drawing her into his arms, he kissed her head. 'Do you think all fathers are bastards, or just ours?'

Hope wrapped her arms around his waist, holding him closely so that he might go on holding her; there was a strength, a solidness about him that she couldn't get enough of. She thought of him leaving, abandoning her, and wanted to cry.

Softly he said, 'Hope . . . ' He laughed brokenly, stepping back from her. 'Hope, I don't know if I should say this . . . '

Alarmed, she said, 'What? Say what?'

He gazed at her. Brushing a strand of her hair from her eyes, he said, 'That I love you.'

She looked away from him, feeling her face flush.

'Sorry,' he said immediately. 'I'm really sorry.'

'No, it's all right.'

He smacked his brow. 'Damn! I've made things awkward now.'

'No!' She touched his hand. 'I think I love you, too.'

'You think?' He smiled crookedly. 'I suppose that will have to do, then.'

After a moment he turned to the drawing. 'That bloody creature's watching us,' he said huskily. 'Come on – you said you were going to give me the tour.'

Chapter 18

Harry walked in the park with Ava and Esther. Ava held Esther's hand, Ava's other hand holding onto his arm so that they took up the whole of the path leading to the bandstand and others had to walk around them. Some of the children, even some of the adults, turned to take a second look; they did appear to be odd, Harry supposed. Esther carried the rag dolls because Ava kept dropping them, causing Esther to appear almost as eerily childlike as his wife. And the way she held the dolls didn't help; she clutched them both to her breast, Danny's head lolling because the stuffing in his neck had drifted. Harry smiled at Esther after yet another ill-mannered child had turned to gawp.

'Maybe Danny should see a doctor.'

Esther smiled shyly and touched the doll's black wool hair. 'Maybe. Or maybe I'll just put a few stitches in him when Mrs Dunn has gone to bed.'

'Perhaps I should buy a pram for them. Do you think Ava would like to push a pram?'

'I don't know.' Her face became closed, as though she thought that actually this was a very bad idea, crass and insensitive. Because it was, of course. Harry sighed, wishing he hadn't volunteered to accompany them here. He hated parks; he hated the way people looked at Ava. He hated most of all the fact that he had nothing whatsoever to say to this timid girl who took such great care of his wife. But the sun was shining and he had no work to do and he had thought it might be pleasant to be out in the fresh air.

He'd had an idea that he would start up a conversation with Esther, questioning her about her family, her childhood. Now, in the face of her stoic quietness, such questions seemed impertinent.

Then, her voice brighter than he had ever known it to be, Esther said, 'Look, there's Guy!'

Sure enough, he saw his son walking towards the park's main gates, too far away to be hailed. He was hand-in-hand with a girl, a blonde who was almost the same height as him, her shapely figure emphasised in a tightly-belted, full-skirted dress. They reached the gates and disappeared from sight, and Esther turned to him, laughing a little to hide her obvious, surprising disappointment.

'We won't catch them up.'

'No.' Harry imagined that being caught up by them was the very last thing his son would want. He would have to explain this odd threesome to his girl. Wildly, Harry imagined only speaking German as he was introduced, forcing Guy to translate for the benefit of his friend. Esther, understanding every word, would be embarrassed, of course, but all the same it would be interesting to see Guy's reaction. At the very least it would teach him not to be so secretive about what went on in his life.

Turning to Esther he said, 'Would you like a cup of tea?'

'That would be very nice, thank you.' Sotto voce, she added, 'And I think Mrs Dunn needs to go to the toilet.'

He smiled bleakly, wondering why he should care that she said toilet instead of lavatory. Perhaps if he sat down and thought about it for long enough he wouldn't care at all; perhaps his snobbishness was all surface and knee-jerk.

'Tea then,' he said, hating the teeth-grinding cheeriness in his voice. 'Tea and cake, I think.'

The park's café was a bottle-green, half-timbered chalet looking out over the boating lake. There was a long counter the length of one wall with glass cases displaying slices of fruit cake and scones, and ham or cheese sandwiches made of very thin white bread cut corner to corner. A box of Blue Ribbon chocolate biscuits stood beside the tea urn that lent the place its peculiarly war-time smell, a smell of over-boiled water Harry associated with train stations and sturdy women in Red Cross armbands. Minus their armbands, the same breed of women manned the café's urn and were rushed and flustered because the sun had brought everyone out, everyone wanting tea and a sit-down at the same time. With no unoccupied tables, customers were carrying out trays of tea and sitting down on the grass verge surrounding the lake.

Joining the end of the queue that snaked outside the café's double doors, Harry smiled encouragingly at Esther and his wife. Quietly he said, 'Esther, do you want to take Ava if you think she needs to go to the lavatory?'

'Will you hold on to these?'

She thrust the two dolls at him. He and Esther were the only people allowed to touch them, but all the same he turned to Ava. 'Is it all right if I take care of Danny and Martha?'

She gazed at him and he reached out to touch her cheek. 'Go with Esther,' he said softly. 'When you come back we'll have some tea.'

He watched Esther lead Ava towards the back of the crowded café, heard her repeated, shy *excuse me*. Her accent wasn't anywhere near as broad as some in Thorp, although she had been born and brought up in the town; in fact, it was quite difficult to assess where Esther came from by her voice, even which class she belonged to – which rather disconcerted the few people he knew who had met her. If he had taken the trouble to explain to them that both of her parents were Austrian Jews, he was sure that a look of smug knowingness would cross their faces, a look that came with the reassuring pleasure of having their

182

snobberies left unchallenged.

Esther had been the answer to a prayer he hadn't prayed simply because it had never occurred to him that he could ever find a German-speaking woman who would be willing to do what was required. Preparing for Ava to come home from her last nursing home, he had set out only to find a kind, competent woman to be Ava's nursemaid – the most accurate job description he could come up with; even if he found the description demeaning, at least it was accurate.

He had advertised the position in *The Lady* magazine and of the few replies he received, none of the women he interviewed seemed to him to be right, being too old and either too timid or too domineering. Then one day Esther applied for the job of secretary in his office and during the interview he had asked about her Germanic surname. Nervous with hope, he had asked if she spoke her parents' language. Then he had told her about Ava, a little at least, as much as she needed to know. He told her that he would pay her three times the amount he was offering for the position of secretary, and that she would have free board and lodging – her own lovely room, the run of his large house, a beautiful garden she could sit in whenever she wanted to – everything he could think of to entice her. And it did feel as though he was enticing her, baiting his trap so she might be coaxed into leaving her beloved parents.

He knew that she loved them; they most certainly loved her. He knew because he had invited Esther and her parents to tea the following Sunday afternoon in order that they might meet him and see for themselves his impressive, well-managed home, the light and spacious room that might be their daughter's if she would only come and work for him. He thought it expedient not to mention Guy, who at any rate was away at school for most of the year, and tried to impress on this wary couple that Esther would be happy in his peaceful home, even though it was obvious that the job wasn't what they wanted for her. Her father had told him that Esther had been the best student in her year at secretarial college, the brightest of the bright girls. 'And she speaks German, Mr Dunn,' her father said, 'and French. She is not a maid, not at all.' Her mother, sitting on the edge of his sofa, her tea-cup and saucer rattling slightly in her hands, had managed to overcome her nervousness to ask, 'How poorly *is* your wife, Mr Dunn?' Coming straight to the point was, Harry conceded, her duty as the girl's mother.

Finally though, it was Esther's decision. While he tried to convince her parents, she had taken Ava out into the garden and he had become distracted from explaining Ava's condition as he caught glimpses of Esther pointing out a robin to his wife. He heard her laugh, heard her say in German, 'See – he's flown into that tree up there? Perhaps he'll come down again if we're quiet.' Harry stopped talking to watch surreptitiously for the bird, telling himself that if it flew down, Esther would stay. He held his breath. The robin landed in a flash of red a few yards from the two women.

The queue for tea shuffled forward and Harry became aware of two small boys staring up at him; he smiled at them awkwardly, never comfortable with children, hoping that this response would snap the pair out of their staring and they would go away. But they only smiled back at him in uncanny unison. One of them reached up and touched Danny's dangling leg.

'Why have you got *two* rag dolls?'

The other boy said, 'Are they twins? We're twins.'

Harry sighed. 'Are you?'

'Most people can tell.' Just as his brother had, he touched Danny's leg. 'Can we see? They're very odd.'

'Boys!'

Harry turned to see Peter Wright stand up and edge hastily through the packed café to reach him. Smiling

184

apologetically, a hand on each of the boys' shoulders, Wright said, 'Mr Dunn – hello. The boys were curious, I hope you don't mind. Martin, Stephen, this is Mr Dunn. He helped me when my father died.'

The boy called Martin looked up at Wright. 'How did he help?'

'He told me what I had to do with all the things my father owned.'

It was hard to tell whether the child was satisfied with his answer or merely utterly bored by it. The explanation seemed unnecessary to Harry; he had always believed that children should be ignored, on the whole. To him the boy said, 'They are very ugly, your dolls. Why are you carrying them about?'

'Martin, I don't think that's any of our business.' Wright glanced back at the table he had just vacated and saw that it had been taken. 'Oh, I should have saved it for you. I'm sorry.'

'It's all right, I was thinking of sitting outside.'

'Well, it is a lovely day.' Wright smiled suddenly. 'And they do very good teas here. Once again I can recommend the fruit cake, if you ever reach the front of the queue.'

Harry thought how much he seemed to have changed in the months since he'd last seen him, as though he had lost ten years. Because he wasn't quite as gaunt, Wright looked less like a scarecrow – even almost ordinary in a short-sleeved shirt that showed off his tanned, surprisingly muscular forearms. His hair was neatly cut, his trousers pressed, shoes polished. It struck Harry that no matter how much he tried to impersonate a run-of-the-mill ex-Army officer, he still looked like one of the angels ordered back to earth to check up on the struggling mortals. And the twin boys were his small apprentices, by the looks of it. Knowing that Wright had no brothers or sisters, Harry asked too jovially, 'And who do these two boys belong to?'

Wright squeezed the children's shoulders as though

claiming them. 'They're my godsons.'

Esther returned from the ladies' lavatories, leading Ava by the hand. Flustered, not noticing Wright or the children, she said, 'There was such a long queue and she wouldn't wait nicely – but now I'm not sure how long she can hold on . . . ' She glanced at Wright and her face flushed darkly. 'Oh, I'm sorry.'

Harry smiled at her to try to lessen her embarrassment. 'Mr Wright, this is Esther, my wife's companion. And this is my wife, Ava.'

'How do you do, Mrs Dunn, Esther.'

One of the boys said loudly, 'What's wrong with that lady, Uncle Peter?'

Wright took the boy's hand. 'Perhaps Mrs Dunn is feeling unwell, Stephen.'

The boys began to giggle, hands over their mouths, and Harry saw Esther look down, horrified. Ava had urinated on the floor.

Holding their noses the boys said, 'Phew! Look what's she's done! How stinky.'

'Be quiet, boys.' Wright frowned at Harry sympathetically. 'Why don't you take your wife outside, Mr Dunn? I'll let the staff know there's been an accident.'

Outside the café, in the bright, blinding sun, Harry thought how wonderful it would be if he could run away. Run and run to a place where no one knew him, where he couldn't be found. He would start again. There were other lives he could live, he was sure, other far less complicated lives, the kind that other men lived, with sweet, contented wives and untroubled children. He closed his eyes against the disorientating brightness, saw the dark spots on his eyelids explode and burn out. Esther went on apologising. Wearily he said, 'It's not your fault Esther, please – don't say any more.'

The twin boys ran around; it seemed they found it

186

impossible to stand still to wait for their godfather. Brats, Harry thought. He could never remember Guy behaving so badly. In his memory, Guy as a small child was always a model of good, quiet behaviour. He sighed, profoundly miserable, and tried to imagine how Wright could possibly be explaining the fact that a woman had pissed on the café's floor. But he had faith in him; he would know how to deal with such an event. Wasn't he an angel, after all? Harry smiled, despite himself. He turned his smile on Esther and said, 'It will be all right. Everything is going to be all right.'

Just then, Wright came out of the café. He said, 'There, no harm done. Listen, my house – my father's house – is just the other side of those gates. The car's parked in the garage. If you wish, we could all go there and I could drive Esther and Mrs Dunn home – if you wouldn't mind looking after the boys until I get back.'

Harry thought just how long and miserable the walk back to his own home would be, and how uncomfortable for Ava in her soaked skirt and underclothes. Gratefully he said, 'That would be very kind of you.'

Wright smiled and touched his arm lightly. 'Not at all.' To the boys he called, 'Come on, you two. We're going to the old house. Run on ahead – you can be my reconnaissance party.'

Chapter 19

Harry sat in Wright's garden. The boys he was supposed to be minding were up in a tree-house and at least were being quiet, perhaps worryingly quiet, although he wasn't inclined to get up from the garden bench to investigate. A few minutes ago, they had run out from the house where they'd been for some time. He noticed when they ran past him that their clothes were dusty and that old cobwebs clung to their backs.

Harry was smoking a cigar, for consolation he supposed, indulging his unhappiness. He rested his head back, savouring the taste of the fine tobacco, and, now that he was alone, he allowed himself to think about Val. Today was her birthday, her thirty-first.

A year ago today he had driven her to the Lake District, to a hotel he knew on the banks of Ullswater where they'd had lunch on the terrace looking out over a garden that sloped down to the still water. He had ordered champagne to be waiting on ice by their bed, along with two dozen red roses, and he had bought her a gift, secret in its velvet box in his pocket, his fingers returning to it time and again, worrying its soft pile so that he was afraid when he finally presented it to her that it would be sweat-stained and shabby-looking. When she was in the bathroom, he placed it on her pillow and the box only looked dark and expensive, impressive against the white counterpane just as it had in the jeweller's shop. He moved it a little to the left so that it was more central, only to snatch it up and return it to his pocket as she came out from the bathroom. She was wearing the black silk negligée he had bought her; it clung to her hips, her thighs; her breasts spilled pale as milk from the low-cut bodice.

She'd teased him. 'I thought you'd be in bed by now. You haven't even taken your tie off.'

'You look beautiful.' He stepped towards her. Holding her face between his hands he kissed her tenderly, tasting the port they'd drunk after lunch. 'I love you.'

She frowned. 'What's the matter?'

'Nothing! What could possibly be the matter when I'm with you?'

But his tone was too vehement and he was sweating, a film of perspiration on his face caused by the rich food and wine, the midsummer heat, the idea that he might be about to change his life for ever, one way or the other. She searched his face, concerned: he was perfect heart-attack material, after all, and she made his heart work too hard, she knew that. Touching his cheek she said, 'Lie down. I'll undress you.'

The jeweller's plush box stayed in his pocket; Val thought that the roses, the champagne, the weekend in the hotel with its expensive smell of polish and pot-pourri were her birthday present. He didn't propose to her until months later. He thanked God for those months, the extra time he wouldn't have had if he'd kept his nerve in that hotel room.

The twin boys dropped from the tree-house's rope ladder and ran towards him. He steeled himself, sitting up straighter, having an idea that they might climb all over him. But they stood a few feet away, looking at him as though he was an exhibition in a museum; he half-expected them to begin talking about him as if he was a not very realistic waxwork. He thought how beautiful they were. He thought too of how Ava would have adored them; she would have laughed at his idea that they were too naughty to be loveable, she would have told him that he had a cold, wicked heart, that all children were easy to love. She had

189

loved Guy, after all, but Guy was supremely normal compared to these peculiar little boys.

Smiling at them, in the faux enthusiastic voice he seemed to use on all children nowadays, he said, 'That's a fine tree-house.'

'Uncle Peter built it.'

'We helped.'

'I'm sure you did.'

'Where are the funny dolls?'

'They've gone home.'

'See?' Martin turned to his brother. 'I told you they weren't *his*! That would be just stupid.' He looked at Harry as though he expected him to agree.

Stephen said angrily, 'Whose were they then?'

Harry sighed. 'They belonged to the lady I was with.' At once he was ashamed that he couldn't bring himself to tell these children that Ava was his wife. When Martin asked if he meant the lady who had wet her pants, he said too sharply, 'Run along, now. Go and play.'

Behind him, Peter Wright said, 'Yes, boys. Go on, off you go. No more questions.'

He sat down beside Harry. Watching the boys run back across the lawn, he said, 'I'm sorry, they can be quite brutal.'

Harry laughed shortly. 'Quite.' Turning to Wright he said, 'You got Ava home all right?'

'Yes.' He smiled. 'Esther even stopped apologising – but then she started thanking me instead.'

'She believes everything is her responsibility – her fault.' After a moment he said awkwardly, 'Ava didn't ruin the car's upholstery, I hope?'

'No. There was an old blanket in the boot. Esther folded that . . . ' He trailed off, and Harry suspected he was as embarrassed as he was, but it seemed he was merely frowning at the boys who were swinging perilously on the rope ladder. When they jumped to the ground he said,

'Anyway, they're home now, safe and sound.'

Stiffly Harry said, 'Thank you.' He glanced at him, feeling he ought to say more, offer some explanation, but he felt too weary.

Wright caught his eye. Gently, as though he was a survivor of some catastrophe, he said, 'Mr Dunn, would you like a drink? I have a bottle of Scotch in the house.'

He went inside and came back with two tumblers. He handed the glass with the larger measure to Harry and sat down, squinting a little against the sun as he looked out over the garden. Harry was wondering if he missed the place when Wright said, 'I should mow the lawn.'

'Leave it. It's not your problem any more.' Carefully Harry asked, 'Is Mr Jackson going to move in?'

Wright sipped his drink. After a while he said, 'He wants to. And I think he will – soon, actually. He's just about finished convincing himself that it's a waste for a house like this to stand empty.' Taking another sip of the Scotch, he went on, 'Jack's getting married again. He'll want to bring his new wife here, away from the home he shared with his first wife.'

'And what about you? Are you settled in your new home?'

'Yes, thank you.'

Thinking of Val, Harry asked, 'How are you getting along with your neighbours on Inkerman Terrace?'

Watching the boys, Wright said, 'It's rather a coincidence, but Jack's marrying my next-door neighbour.'

Harry felt his heart lurch, some inkling of what Wright was going to tell him making him brace himself in order to withstand the blow. As evenly as he could, he asked, 'Oh? What's her name?'

'Val Campbell. She works with Jack at Davies and Sons.'

The twins ran to Wright, tugging at him. 'Play with us! Play with us now!'

'Soon. Go into the house and find the best hiding-place – somewhere you think I won't find you.'

When they'd run shouting into the house, Wright turned to him. 'You look unwell, Mr Dunn. Would you like me to drive you home?'

Harry got to his feet. His legs were shaking and he staggered.

Wright stood up, too. He caught Harry's elbow, steadying him. 'Sit down, finish your drink in peace whilst I go and find the boys. Then I'll drive us all home.'

I imagined the boys would find Hope upstairs; I imagined that she and Guy would be standing shamefaced in the hallway as Martin and Stephen jumped around them. But of course, they must have run out of the house as soon as they thought they could without being seen. For the first time I felt ashamed of her; I never would have believed she could behave so badly.

When I arrived at the house with Dunn and his poor creature of a wife, I had an idea that Hope was inside. The key from beneath the plant pot that Hope had always known about was in the back door and the door was ajar. The boys had run straight to the cellar – they have always been attracted to its damp scariness. Dunn, his wife and the girl who looks after her, waited in the garden and I said nothing to them about my anxiety as I went inside to fetch the car keys. I walked as quietly as I could into the hall, holding my breath. From upstairs I heard a panicked scrambling and I stood still, straining to hear, half-hoping that it was burglars even as I berated myself for leaving the key in such an obvious hiding-place. But in my heart I knew it was Hope and Guy. It was so obvious that they should come here. She was just like her mother, just as bold and defiant, just as heedless of the feelings of others.

Standing so still and quiet, they must have believed I'd gone, because after a moment I heard their frantic whispering, first the boy and then Hope, indisputably Hope. They were in my father's bedroom and I was so angry I almost went upstairs to confront them. But if she was naked, if they were lying together naked on that bare mattress, I was afraid I would completely lose my head. And outside the children were playing, and that poor woman and her timid nurse were waiting for me to drive them home; and then there was Dunn himself, of course, who looks at me in such a patronising, insufferable manner, who was slumped on the garden bench as if he hated to be beholden to someone like me. I couldn't cause a scene in front of any of them. I'm used to controlling my anger, after all, used to keeping it tightly contained within myself and behaving as if nothing is wrong. I even managed to smile as I came out of the house with the car keys, to be pleasant as I drove the two women home. I felt sick to my stomach; if Guy had appeared in front of the car I think I would have run him down.

I knew the twins would be in their usual hiding-place – the place that half-scares them to death, which is why they like it so much. At the top of the cellar steps I turned on the single, unshaded bulb that casts its poor light in the low, dank room dug beneath the kitchen. There is nothing much down there; the boys were hiding in the old coal store and I went straight to them, hearing their stifled giggles, thinking of Hope, how she must have held her breath as she anticipated being found.

'Come on, you two. I'm taking you home.'

'We don't want to go home!'

'Do you want me to leave you down here with the mice and spiders? Come on, quickly now.'

I followed them up the stairs. As we walked out into the garden and as I locked the door behind me, pocketing the key, Stephen said, 'We found some bones down there.'

I wasn't in the mood for their stories. Sharply I said, 'That's enough.'

193

'We did! We found them ages ago and we just didn't tell you!'

Dunn had stood up. He looked pale and was sweating, wiping his brow with a big white handkerchief when he saw me, attempting to smile which only caused him to appear sicklier. Despite the fact that he seemed so ill, I felt no sympathy. He's too fat, no doubt he smokes and drinks too much, indulging himself without a thought for anyone. Calling to the boys, I walked to the car. Dunn followed me, meek as a lamb.

Chapter 20

Matthew had gone fishing. He'd said, 'Sure you don't mind me leaving you alone on your birthday?'

Val had laughed. 'Go, Dad. I don't care about birthdays at my age.'

'*Your age*!' He snorted, packing a box of maggots into his haversack. 'I wish I were your age. You're nowt but a bairn.'

A bairn, a child, young. She wasn't young, although she lived more or less the same life she had lived when she was sixteen. All the girls she had been at school with were married and had children; one girl, Dorothy Hedges, had a daughter of fifteen – no doubt, soon enough, Dorothy would be a grandmother. Val was the only one who was just starting out, about to be married, leaving her father at last.

When she'd told Matthew that she was going to marry Jack, he had exhaled sharply as though he had been holding his breath all these years she had been unmarried. He'd nodded. 'Well, if you're sure about him.' After a moment, unnecessarily, he added, 'I'm pleased. He's a grand lad.'

Jack was a grand lad because he had a good job – a career – and his own home. He could talk easily about cricket and Middlesbrough FC; he was straightforward and pleasant. Most of all, he had been an officer in the RAF, and although Matthew's lip curled when on rare occasions he mentioned the officers he'd served under in 1916, Jack escaped his contempt because, she supposed, flying a bomber wasn't a bit like ordering young lads over the side of a trench into machine-gun fire. Her father liked Jack, although he had seemed to have forgotten that he had children. Sometimes she wished she could forget. Forget Hope, especially, who seemed to be colder towards her with each meeting.

Jack was sleeping, lying on his side, his nose almost touching hers because her bed was so narrow. They hadn't intended to go to bed, only to spend some time discussing wedding plans. But after all there seemed little to discuss: they were to marry in a register office, with only the children, her father and Peter as witnesses; then they would go to the Grand Hotel for lunch before she and Jack left for their honeymoon in Filey. Peter was going to take care of the children. Jack had sighed over this. 'Hope will kick up a fuss – she can't stand being in the same room as him nowadays. God knows what's got into her. Ever since she met this damn boy . . . '

Val remembered what she had been like at Hope's age, when boys were the most important creatures on earth and adult men – her father, her teachers – were just laughable or cringe-making and usually both, too much a part of the childhood she so desperately wanted to escape from. She could well imagine why Hope wouldn't want to be around Peter.

Not wanting to think about Hope, Val brushed her nose against Jack's. 'Jack, wake up.'

He blinked his eyes open, confused for a moment. 'I wasn't snoring, was I?'

'No. But we should get up, in case Dad gets back early.'

'I was dreaming we were already married.'

'We will be, soon.'

He was gazing at her. At last he said, 'It *is* what you want, isn't it?'

'Of course!'

'Only sometimes . . . ' He sighed. 'You seem sad, that's all. Sometimes you seem very sad.'

'I'm not.'

'I do love you, you know. It isn't just about me wanting a wife . . . '

'I know,' Val said. 'And I love you.'

'Do you? Honestly?'

'Jack – of course! What's this about?'

'Nothing. Only . . . if you have any doubts, any doubts at all . . . ' He pulled himself together. 'Christ. All right, I'll tell you what it's about. I overheard some talk in the office. I got the impression that they thought you were on the rebound.'

She felt herself go cold. 'I'm not.'

'No? All right.' After a moment he repeated, 'All right.'

She got up and began to dress and all the time she sensed him watching her. She kept her back to him, thinking that he would be able to see from her face that she was lying, that perhaps he could even tell from the way she put on her clothes – quickly, shyly – as though he had never seen her naked before, as though she would rather be with someone else. She thought of Harry, who had wanted to marry her, who had come up with a plan he had only half-thought through, the half that concerned only him, his own happiness.

Quietly, Jack asked her, 'Will you forget I said anything? We're together – that's all that matters to me. The past is past.'

She knew he was thinking about his wife; he thought of her all the time, after all, and sometimes he had to close his mouth on some story about her. Her name had become a sentence with all the other words cut off, all the memories, all the anecdotes falling away from those two syllables. He would shut his mouth on them and avoid her eye. But that was all right, she didn't want to hear about his dead wife, just as he wouldn't want to hear about Harry. This mutual discretion was for the best, and was kinder and more considerate than a messy unburdening of grief.

She turned to Jack. He was lying on his side in her childhood bed, his head propped on his elbow, his eyes on her as if he wanted to search into her soul, to discover secretly what she was feeling without any painful discussion. He looked vulnerable and therefore young, like the man Carol would have known when they first met. A moment ago, Val had told him she loved him; she hadn't told him this very often, not quite believing it, only wanting to. After all, she would love the child they would have together and that love would spill over onto him, she had no doubt about this.

Going to him, she knelt by the bed. She had been about to tell him again that she loved him, stressing the words, making him believe it; her conscience stopped her and she only kissed his mouth. 'Get dressed,' she said softly. 'I'll make you a cup of tea.'

Harry sat in Wright's car and thought that he might be having a heart-attack. He tried to hold himself very still, stiffening himself against the pain; he rested his head back and closed his eyes and didn't care what Wright thought of him. He didn't care what anyone thought any more. If this was dying, he was terribly afraid. It was as though he was entombed; there seemed no way out to the ordinary world Wright and the children inhabited. He whimpered and he wasn't even ashamed, and then he heard Wright say, 'Mr Dunn? Are you all right?'

He sounded alarmed and also distant, as though he was speaking to him through the wood and silk lining of his coffin. Harry felt the world begin to slow, heard Wright's voice nearer now, calmer, felt his arm around his shoulders. 'You're home now, let's get you inside.'

He was led into his house. He thought how strong Wright was, how reassuring his voice as Peter said, 'Try to breathe deeply, Mr Dunn, try to be calm. You're quite safe;

everything is going to be all right.'

He wanted to believe him. He felt himself lowered onto the couch in his sitting room and opened his eyes; Wright crouched beside him, his kind, concerned angel, and Harry made a great attempt to smile at him.

Wright said, 'That's right, breathe deeply now. You're safe at home, all's well.'

'I thought I was dying.'

'I know. But you're not. You're not. You're fine.' He said gently. 'I know what it's like – you feel as though you're never going to be able to breathe normally again . . . But there now – you're all right.'

Wright glanced over his shoulder to where the two little boys stood anxiously in the doorway. 'Go and wait in the car as I told you to.' Turning back to Harry, he said, 'I'll go and fetch you a glass of water.'

When he came back, he said, 'Esther and your wife are in the garden. I thought it best not to disturb them.'

Taking the glass of water from him, Harry took a sip, avoiding his eye, ashamed of himself now he was calmer. He wanted Wright to go, he wanted to be left alone in his misery; he would shut himself in his bedroom and think about Val marrying another man – this man's friend, if they were still friends after that business of the will. Perhaps Wright hated Jackson as much as he did. All at once he was curious about Jackson – best to know one's enemy, after all. Looking up at Wright, he said, 'Why don't you sit down?'

'I should go, the boys –'

'Tell them to go and play in the garden. Esther will keep an eye on them.'

'I think it would be best if I took them home. And you should rest. Goodbye, Mr Dunn.'

'Wait.' He sighed. 'Listen, perhaps I could buy you a drink sometime, as a way of thanks.'

'There's no need to thank me.'

He left, closing the living-room door softly behind him.

Harry heard him call out to the boys to get in the car and do as they were told for once in their lives. He sounded angry, but also as though anger didn't come naturally to him. Obviously something had upset this gentle man very much indeed.

Still feeling shaky, Harry got up. He went to the window and watched Wright drive away. It seemed that Wright had known he wasn't – as he himself had believed – having a heart-attack, but merely some kind of crisis of nerve. Wright had recognised that he wasn't dying and had reassured him, as if he too had suffered such a crisis. No doubt he had, given his war-time experiences.

Harry snorted. They'd all had *war-time experiences*, all unique, all just as bloody ghastly. Wright was just one of thousands, in no way special – he shouldn't persist in thinking of him as somehow special. He rested his aching head against the cool window pane. Wright lived next door to Val, and in Harry's present, hysterical state, Wright's link to her made him special enough. He had a vision of himself going to Wright's house, and on some pretext, going upstairs to drill a hole from Wright's bedroom into Val's so that he might spy on her. He would watch her undressing, he would watch her climb naked into bed and, holding his breath, he would go on watching as she began to masturbate – an act she had once confessed to. When she came he would come too, groaning in ecstasy and despair, and she would hear him and know that he was there, that he would always be there, that he would love her no matter what bastard she was married to.

Harry slumped down on a chair. He heard Esther and his wife come in from the garden and hoped that they wouldn't come looking for him. He couldn't face Ava in the state he was in. Even if she had no idea of his adultery, he felt that simply being in the same room as his wife sullied her. And she had been the kindest, most honest woman he had ever met and she would have tried to understand. She would have forgiven him, just as she forgave Hans.

He had asked Hans why he had murdered his neighbour.

'I don't have to tell you why.'

'You do, if you want me to defend you properly.'

'*Properly*!' Hans had laughed as though delighted. 'Will they hang me any more properly?'

Harry remembered sighing, he sighed often around him as though Hans was a naughty seven-year-old, exasperating but also beguiling in his way. He had to keep reminding himself that Hans was a grown man, one who was unrepentant of all the crimes he had committed, of which sticking a knife in his neighbour was only one. It was also the most mysterious one. The neighbour had been a good Nazi, after all, a member of the Party. Harry didn't want to be intrigued, but he was, although he couldn't allow Hans to sense his curiosity.

Trying a different approach he said, 'Your sister's been here, asking if she can see you.'

Hans snorted, glancing away.

'She's very concerned about you, apparently.'

'Apparently?' Hans frowned at him. 'Didn't you see her?'

Gazing at him, Harry said, 'I'm going to call her in, question her.'

'Why, when I've confessed? Have you nothing better to do?'

'Don't you think she could help your defence?'

He was silent and Harry repeated his question.

Hans bowed his head. Softly, he began to sing the anthem of the SS. The guard stepped forward. Grasping a handful of Hans's hair, he jerked his head back.

'Answer the Major.'

His eyes contemptuous, Hans said, 'You must do only what you think is right, Major Dunn, sir.'

Doing not what he thought was right, but what he

thought would satisfy his curiosity, he had Ava brought in.

She had sat opposite him in one of the less forbidding interrogation rooms, her back very straight, her hands held together on her lap. Harry noticed how thin she was and pale; he guessed at how poor her diet was. Believing that she was no more than twenty, he saw from her papers that she was twenty-nine. She had worked during the war in a paper mill; two brothers had been killed on the Eastern front, her parents in an air raid late in 1944. Hans was her only relative, her little brother, and she looked like him; she had the same green eyes, the same soft, full mouth. Just as Hans was handsome – a poster-boy for Teutonic manhood – Ava was beautiful, although she was too slight, too delicately fine to advertise Fatherland and Motherhood. When he smiled at her and told her she had nothing to worry about, she bowed her head shyly and explained that he didn't need to speak German; her English was quite good.

Quite good, such a typical expression of Ava's. She understated everything – her ability to speak his language, her ill-health, her love for her brother – this last most of all. Although she had seen, as he had, the film of the bodies being bulldozed into the pits at Belsen, she refused to believe Hans had had anything to do with it. About the neighbour he had all but eviscerated, Ava had nothing to say – only that the neighbour was very wicked.

Harry had laughed at this, a lapse in self-control for which he forgave himself because he was so weary of the excuses, the blame these people cast at each other. Studying her, he said, 'Tell me what he did that was wicked.'

She only shook her head, her lovely mouth turned down as if her answer would be of no importance.

For some time he gazed at her, intending at first to discomfort this composed and dignified woman. But then he found himself only wanting to look at her for her own sake; she was the most exquisite woman he had ever seen.

Even in this cell-like room with its harsh, unforgiving light, she was radiant. Then, remembering who and where and what he was, he cleared his throat. 'Is there anything you could tell me that might help your brother?'

'No.'

'You know that he will hang?'

'Yes. He isn't afraid.'

'How do you know?'

'I know him.'

Harry sighed. He thought how little he cared that he couldn't help Hans escape the gallows; he richly deserved such an end, after all. But still his curiosity nagged – and there was one simple trick he could play. Leaning towards her, he said, 'Your brother told me what your neighbour did to you.'

Her hand went to her throat and he saw that her eyes were full of tears. He felt like a bastard. It hardly seemed to matter that he had been vindicated, that what he had suspected all along was right: that Hans had been defending his sister's honour.

At last Ava looked up. Her voice hard, her eyes glittering with hatred, she said, 'I should never have told him. It was nothing to me, nothing that hadn't happened before when the Russians came. Just men, being dirty men – no better than children, I think. Wicked, nasty children!'

Later, Hans had said, 'You should apologise to her.'

Later still, the day before his execution, Hans had begged to be allowed to speak to him.

Standing in the doorway of his cell, it seemed to Harry that the boy had aged a hundred years since he last saw him a few days earlier. Hans had stood to attention but rather than meet his eyes as he always had, instead he lowered his gaze, his voice quiet as he said, 'Would you please give this to Ava?' He held out an envelope. 'Please take it to her yourself – I cannot trust anyone else.' He had smiled then, an odd, wry grimace that gave a glimpse of the man this boy might have been if not for the times he'd lived through.

As Harry made to take the envelope from him, Hans drew it back a little. 'You will take care of her, won't you? Now that she has no one?'

Sitting in his study, Harry heard Esther take his wife upstairs. He thought of Ava on their wedding day, in that terrible dress, those men's shoes. He remembered how he had found it so hard to believe that she was marrying him, that his life could suddenly be so altered. All the same he had felt joyful. She was beautiful, he loved her; he had repeated these statements like a mantra to ward off his disbelief in the wild turn his life had taken.

Harry stood up from his desk and went out into the hall. Calling up the stairs to Esther that he was going out for a while, he left the house and began to walk towards Inkerman Terrace.

Chapter 21

Hope listened, ears straining for every sound, as Peter put the boys to bed. She heard his voice, a low murmur as he read to them; once she heard him laugh. Lying on her side on her bed, she listened and felt sad and nostalgic and had to fight the urge to go into her brothers' bedroom, demanding that they make room for her to snuggle in beside Peter, too. She remembered that he always smelled of soap – never of cigarettes as her father did, but clean, like fresh laundry, and also of something more subtle – a warm, elusive scent that would have her pressing her face against him, making him chuckle and push her away. 'Little puppy,' he would say. 'Little sniffle pup!' He would tweak her nose, and his eyes would have that look in them, sad and happy all at once.

At those times she believed that she would marry him.

That afternoon, she had led Guy from the room full of toys along the hall to the other bedrooms. She had never been allowed in these rooms; there had been an unspoken rule that these were private places, and while the children might run around the rest of the house, Peter's bedroom and that of his father were out of bounds. She had never wanted to go into his father's bedroom. The old man disgusted her with his smells and his grunts, his fleshy, dribbling lips and vast red, pock-marked nose. He scared her, too; although he was very ancient and slow, she had a feeling, that when no one was looking, he would be fast and powerful, pouncing and swiping like a bear. Once she had peeped around his door and saw that his room was chaotic, his bedside table littered with medicine bottles and tumblers, the floor heaped with clothes. This was before he became bedridden, when the room became neat and clean under Peter's control.

A few weeks before his death, the old man had asked to see her.

Peter had said, 'Would you mind very much, Hope? He wants to say goodbye. I'll go up there with you, if you would feel more comfortable.'

But she had decided to see him alone; it would be a good test of the feeling that she had about herself – that she was an adult now. So she had left Peter in the kitchen and climbed the dark staircase, with each step becoming more anxious, more ready to turn around. The man was dying and she had never seen anyone so ill before; she wondered what she would say to him, even if she might cry with the scariness of it all. At his bedroom door she had hesitated; she could hear Peter's wireless, tinny voices and laughter. Drawing breath, she knocked timidly only to think the old man might not have heard, so she knocked again more loudly and he called out that she should come in.

The room was dark, the curtains drawn against the late-winter sunshine, a lamp struggling to cast much light through its dark red shade. There was a smell of sleep-fugged, unchanged air, thick and stifling. As she stepped closer to the bed where Peter's father was attempting to sit up, she caught a sweeter scent, like gas at the dentist's. She held her breath, wanting to put her hand over her mouth and nose.

The old man gazed at her, his eyes narrowed and watery. After a moment he said, 'You're very like your mother. I suppose he tells you that – my son; he tells you you're like her, I imagine?'

She felt wrong-footed; she had expected feebleness and self-pity, but his tone was strong, even mocking. He went on gazing at her. 'Doesn't he say, *Oh, you're so like Carol when she was your age!*?' He laughed, and this noise was feeble, quickly becoming a cough that went on and on. At last, slumping back against his pillows, he said, 'I'll be dead soon and he'll rejoice. You watch. See he doesn't have a sneaky little dance on my grave.' There was a handkerchief clutched in his fist and he wiped his mouth. Closing his eyes, he breathed out as though he'd been storing breath he found he had no need of any more.

'Keep away from him.' He opened his eyes and his gaze was cold, powerful; she thought of the bear she had imagined him to be, chained to a post but still able to kill. 'Keep away from my son,' he repeated. 'Unless you want his fingers inside your knickers, unless you *want* him to fuck that pretty little cunt of yours.'

For a moment it was as though she couldn't make sense of what he'd said, unable to believe that he could use such words. She felt her insides soften, that familiar loosening that came with humiliation but was so close to the pleasurable sensations she could arouse in herself. The old man went on gazing at her; she felt unable to move, to do or say anything, so thoroughly had he degraded her. Eventually he waved his hand weakly, dismissing her as though she was nothing and the vile things he had said were no more than a comment on the weather.

She had left the room, walking normally she supposed, although her legs were shaking. She had even closed the door softly because he was old and very ill, still a part of her thinking that perhaps she had misheard him. She remembered that she felt numb; later, when she was alone in her bedroom, she felt as if he had stripped her naked and put his hands all over her body, prodding and poking, invading her, except it was Peter's hands she imagined, Peter pushing himself inside her.

Listening to Peter reading to her brothers in the next room, Hope remembered how she had run out of that house, brushing past Peter who had come out of the kitchen, unable to look at him. His father had changed everything between them with only a few utterly shaming words. Whenever she saw Peter she thought about his father and that f-word, that c-word, and she thought how stupid and blind she must have been not to have seen what was so obvious – obvious in the way Peter looked at her, the way that he could hardly take his eyes off her, such soft, smiling, *wanting* looks. He made her feel exposed and defiled; she believed that when he looked at her, he was seeing nothing but the *c* place between her legs.

Walking into the old man's bedroom with Guy, she had experienced again that degrading humiliation, even though the room was quite different, stripped of all his possessions, the sun streaming though the window. The bed was stripped too, down to its striped, stained mattress, its metal frame stark against the faded, flowered wallpaper. She had felt for Guy's hand, needing his support. He had turned to her, smiling, unknowing.

'Well, well – a double bed.'

'It's filthy.'

'Maybe there's some bedding.' He glanced around and stepped towards a chest of drawers. 'Just a sheet or a blanket is all we need.'

'No, Guy. Let's go downstairs.'

He spun round, laughing in disbelief. 'It's a *bed*, Hope – you said yourself, a great big bed.'

'Not this bed. He died in this bed.'

'Who?'

'Peter's father.'

Guy laughed again. 'Really? Christ. Maybe he's still here – a ghost, hanging around, wanting to watch . . . '

'Don't! Don't be so disgusting. We shouldn't be here anyway.'

'No. But who cares?' He stroked her face. 'Are you going all prudish on me now? Has seeing all those toys again turned you into Irene or one of her friends? Goody-two-shoes virgins.' He grinned. 'I thought you were like them – until you stuck your tongue down my throat at that party.'

'I did not stick my tongue down your throat!'

He sighed. 'Come on, Hope, don't be like this – it's boring. And it's a waste of time. Peter will expect you back at your house when he takes the twins home.'

'I don't care what he expects. I hate him!'

'Yeah, well – I think we've established that. Christ knows why, though. I think he's pretty decent.'

'Yeah, well – I think we've established that, too. You've no idea, have you?'

'Of what?'

She hesitated then said quickly, 'He wants to have sex with me.'

Guy laughed shortly. 'So what if he does? Hope, most men want to *have sex* with young girls. Can't we just forget about him for once?' Gesturing at the bed, he said, 'You're right about the mattress, and if someone died on it . . . Do you want to go home?'

She hadn't wanted to go home. She had wanted him to say again that he loved her, that he didn't think she was odd – the kind of sex-crazed girl he imagined her to be. She wanted Guy to hate Peter as much as she did and stop pretending he understood everything about her. But ever since the moment the old man had unleashed those filthy words on her, she had barely understood herself, only that she somehow wanted to make herself strong, to make her body hers again and take away some of the disgust she felt about herself. Sex with Guy made her feel as though she was a proper, grown-up woman and that she could refuse to look at Peter if she chose to.

They would have stayed; she would have led Guy into another bedroom and they would have made love because when all was said and done she adored him, his body, the way she felt when he came inside her, when he groaned and cried out her name and was annihilated by her. But at that

209

moment they heard Martin and Stephen shouting out to each other in the garden below the window, heard Peter and another man talking. She had turned to Guy in horror, so afraid of being found – just like a child caught out in a naughty game.

Guy had pressed his fingers to her lips and the two of them had stood very still, hardly daring to breathe until finally they made a dash downstairs to the front door. Halfway down the street, Guy stopped running, catching her hand so that she stopped too. Breathlessly he said, 'Shall we just keep going – run way from all of them for good?'

'Yes!'

He laughed, gazing at her. 'If only.'

'Why not?'

'Because I think that would make me a deserter or something.'

She had forgotten that he was leaving. They walked back to her house in silence and she could feel him withdrawing from her, thinking about going away. She knew such thoughts didn't hurt him as much as they hurt her.

Later, Peter and the boys had come home, and she had hidden away in her room, and now she listened as Peter said good night to her brothers, as he closed their bedroom door quietly behind him. Once again Hope found herself holding her breath as Peter walked along the passage and knocked on her door.

I took the boys home to Jack's house. I fed them – fish-paste sandwiches, a shop-bought cake – and then read them a story, one they insisted on because I had illustrated it. They were quiet, sleepy, and I hugged them to me, one little boy under each arm, feeling their heads heavy against my chest, breathing in the familiar scent of their hair. There are times that I am so overwhelmed with love for them that I hug them too hard and they squirm away from me, sensing my distress, and I tell them I love them, but smiling, making light of my passion. Soon, because they are growing up, they will stop answering that they love me too, just as Hope has stopped. Thinking of Hope, as I'd thought of her all evening, I felt my anger tighten my chest. The moment I'd brought her brothers home she had retreated to her room and kept her door firmly closed. The house was charged with her defiance.

I closed the storybook. Briskly I said, 'Sleep time.'

'We want to wait for Daddy.'

'No, he'll be cross if he finds that you're still awake past your bedtime.'

'No, he won't!'

I couldn't argue, knowing that they were right. Jack was bad at routines and bedtime was only a vague idea in this house. Jack is at turns too stern and too lax, shouting at the boys only to ignore them if they are quiet, forgetting about them if they are out of sight or earshot. As for Hope, almost from the time Carol was killed he has treated her more or less as his equal, and as a surrogate mother for the twins. He made her grow up too quickly so that now she believes she may do exactly what she wants. I should have stepped in sooner, and much of my anger stems from the fact that I did not. I always thought it best not to interfere with Jack's parenting. Best! I suppose I mean easier. But I was always so afraid of losing contact with them that I couldn't risk giving Jack an excuse to end our friendship.

When I'd read the boys one more story and they could barely keep their eyes open a moment longer, I went along the passage and tapped on Hope's door. I heard her bedsprings creak and after a moment's hesitation, I knocked again, saying, 'Hope, may I come in?'

At once she opened the door, holding it in such a way that I was barred entry. Sullenly, she said, 'I'm tired, I was about to go to sleep.'

'It's only eight o'clock.'

'So? I'm tired.'

'Have you had any supper?'

'I'm not hungry.' She couldn't meet my eye, her guilt so palpable that I found myself touched by her childish inability to hide it. She tried to shut the door in my face as she said, 'You can go home now.'

'I'm not going anywhere.' I caught hold of the door. 'We need to talk about what happened at my father's house this afternoon.'

'I don't know what you mean.'

'I know you were there.' I sighed. 'Hope, I heard you.'

She turned abruptly and walked into her room, to the window, the furthest point from the door, from me. She was wearing a dressing-gown, buttoned and tightly belted with a cord, her feet were bare and her hair was down around her shoulders. I couldn't help but think of all the times I had put her to bed, the tenderness there had always been between us until so recently. Unsure what to say, I faltered, 'You must promise me you won't go there with him again.'

Without any note of contrition she said, 'I promise.' Quickly she asked, 'Are you going to tell my father?'

'I don't know.'

'Don't. Please don't tell him.' Hesitantly she took a step towards me. 'Please, Peter.'

She had never called me Peter before, only Uncle Peter. Lately she hasn't called me anything at all, has avoided addressing me altogether. But the way she said my name now, with such pleading, such adult, knowing inflection, made my heart contract. She stepped closer.

I saw that there was a mark on her neck, a dark, ugly bruise of a kiss. Her eyes flickered, her hand going to the mark, and for a moment she looked like a child again, but then she met my gaze. She stepped closer still so that I could smell her, feel the warmth radiating from her. I could see that she was trembling. Her fingers brushed mine. 'Peter, I'll do whatever you want . . . '

212

'Hope . . . ' I made a noise between a sob and a laugh. The child whose nose I had wiped, the little girl I had bathed and watched over as she brushed her teeth, read to until she slept, who had always loved me so easily and innocently, looked at me now as though she believed all I wanted from her was what any man could get from any whore. And I laughed because it was horribly absurd, as though my sweet three-year-old had covered her face with rouge and smudged her mouth with lipstick and tried to dance in her mother's high-heels. And I also knew for certain what I had been trying to ignore until then – that we could never be close again, the distance between us growing only more impassable with each boy who kissed her. I had lost her, and the pain was made worse by her suspicions, laughable as they were.

I stepped back from her. 'Hope, all I want is that you respect yourself.'

I lied. I wanted her to be ten again, and interested only in childish things. I tried to think of the right words to express what I felt for her, but the lie between us was too fundamental. Everything I said to her would be interpreted by her naïve suspicions into the language of a seducer. I wanted to hold her because she was trembling still; impossible now, although I ached to, although it took all my strength to turn away.

'I won't say anything to Jack,' I said. Closing her bedroom door behind me I ran downstairs and out of the house.

Chapter 22

Harry said, 'Please don't marry him.'

Val reached across the table. She touched his hand, only to draw away again as though she didn't want to seem to encourage him. 'I want kids, Harry. A proper family.'

'*I* could give you children! We could be a proper family!'

'No. You know that's not true. I want to be respectable . . . to have what other women have.'

'What do they have? Nothing! Nothing that's worth marrying a man you don't love!'

'I do love him.' Suddenly exasperated, she said, 'What makes you think you know anything about it?'

'Because you love me – just as I love you. Nothing has changed – nothing!'

'Exactly, Harry. Nothing has changed. You're still married.'

'I'm getting a divorce.'

For a moment it seemed she believed him. Something in her expression softened, something like hope troubled her eyes. Encouraged, allowing himself to hope, Harry leaned across the table towards her and grasped her hands. 'I'll divorce Ava, and I've found a decent home for her – a good place, run by nuns.'

She pulled her hands away. 'Nuns?' She laughed shortly. 'Oh Harry, I almost believed you.'

'It's true.'

'You would never do that to her.'

'She'd be better off.' He thought about the incident in

the park's café that afternoon. 'She's worse; lately she's become worse – since Guy came home, I think.'

Val stood up. The back door was open, Harry could see the tubs of geraniums her father had planted, a cat sunning itself on the outhouse roof; there was a smell of warm tar, mixed with the curious, garlicky scent of the flowers. In the alley beyond the yard gate, children were playing; a football slammed against the cobbles. Val stood in the open doorway, fumbling in the pocket of her slacks for her cigarettes. She rarely smoked, but when she did it seemed she needed the nicotine more desperately than most.

Blowing smoke out into the yard, she said, 'You won't divorce her, Harry.' She glanced at him. 'You won't put her in a home.'

'Val . . . ' He got up, standing a little way from her. 'I love you.'

'Do you?' She spun round to face him, tears of anger in her eyes. 'I know you love *her*. And if you do love me, you love her more purely. Maybe with me it's just sex!'

'No, that's not true! How can you say that? The times we've had together –'

'The *sex* we've had together! Was there ever a time when we didn't go straight to bed? Did you ever take me to the pictures, to the theatre, to dinner in a place that didn't have a bedroom waiting upstairs?'

'I loved you! It wasn't just sex. It wasn't like that at all,' He sat down heavily; he felt drained – it had taken all his courage to come here, knowing that this was his last chance. After today, if she couldn't be made to see how much they were meant to be together, he would have nothing left, not even the hope that had barely sustained him these last few months. He gazed at her; she was so sexy, perfect. It was unthinkable that she wanted to be with another man. Heatedly, he said, 'Listen, you can come with me to my solicitor. I'll prove to you that I'm getting a divorce.'

'No.' She tossed her cigarette down and crushed it beneath her foot. 'It's too late. I'm going to marry Jack, I promised him.'

'He doesn't matter – can't you see that? So what if you promised him?'

'Go home, Harry.'

'No! Not until you see sense!'

At that moment, Matthew came in through the backyard gate. Putting his fishing tackle down, he said, 'Well, I've had a grand day,' then caught sight of Harry and frowned. 'What's *he* doing here?'

'He's just leaving, Dad.'

'Aye? Good. He knows where he's not wanted, at least.'

Harry groaned. 'Matthew – you know she doesn't really want to marry this other man.'

'Oh? Why doesn't she?' Matthew demanded. 'Do you think he's too good for her, being single and that?'

'I know he's the kind of man who would take his friend's home away from him. Do you know about that? *Do* you?'

Val sighed. 'He hasn't taken it.'

'As good as. What kind of bastard would do that?'

'What kind of bastard wants to live in sin with my daughter whilst his sick wife is shut away?'

Harry wanted to weep in frustration. 'Please don't marry him!'

Matthew took his arm. 'Come on you, out. You've had your chance.'

Shaking him off, Harry turned to Val. 'You know I love you more than he does. Remember that. Remember when you look at him that I love you far more.'

Harry went home. He thought that he would write Val a letter, a long letter reminding her of everything they had ever done together, and it wouldn't be just about sex – they had made love often but that wasn't everything, not all they had together. She was wrong about that. He would show her how wrong she was – how she had twisted her memories so she could convince herself he hadn't loved her enough, that it would be all right to marry someone else. He began to compose the letter as he walked home; it helped to calm him a little, but only a little. The words were too slow in coming because he still felt so angry – so full of rage at her, at this other man, this *Jack Jackson* – that he could barely contain himself. He wanted to smash his fists into walls, to kick and bellow and tear about like a lunatic.

At his front door he thrust his key into the lock. Slamming the door behind him, he went straight to his study and poured himself a large Scotch. The window was open, letting in the wallflower-scented air, the birdsong, and he banged it shut, cursing at nothing, or perhaps at the sun that made everywhere look so bright, so cheerful. The world should be dark; the sun should respect his terrible loss.

As he sat down at his desk and began to search through the drawers for writing paper, there was a knock on the study door. He looked up. 'Yes? What is it?'

Esther came in. She stood just inside the door. Timidly, she said, 'Mr Dunn, please may I talk to you?'

'What is it, Esther? Can't it wait?'

'No, I'm sorry.' She took a step towards the desk. 'It's important.'

He motioned that she should sit down, trying to suppress his impatience. As usual, she avoided his eye, but she looked more anxious than ever and despite his anger Harry had a dreadful premonition. He tried to laugh. 'Esther, you look so worried that you're making *me* worried.'

'I'm sorry, Mr Dunn.'

'What about?'

She managed to look at him. Quickly she said, 'I've

217

been offered another job.'

Oh, how clever he was to have guessed! He almost laughed, and it would have been a harsh, deranged noise; he would scare this little mouse of a girl to death. As evenly as he could, he said, 'Have you accepted this other job?'

She looked down at her hands again. 'No. Not yet.'

'Would it help your decision if I offered you more money?'

Jerking her head up to look at him, she said immediately. 'It's not about money.'

'No? I find most things usually are.' Money or sex, he thought. He stood up, too agitated to keep still. He thought of the Home he had found but never truly considered. Val had been right – the nuns could just as well have been angels, he still couldn't bring himself to shut Ava away with them. The guilt he'd never been able to escape when she lived in that last Home had been too great. He swung round to face the girl. 'Esther, I know today was rather difficult . . . '

'It wasn't just today.' After a moment she repeated, 'Not just today.'

'Then what is it? What's made you want to leave us?'

She was silent for a while. Eventually, shifting in her seat, she said, 'I'm too young, I think.'

He thought how delicate she was, small and plain as a wren, and young, very young. He had hardly thought of this since she'd consented to work for him because she was so quiet and capable, and in truth he didn't think about her much at all, just left her to get on with the things he least wanted to do. All his anger, all that rage that had puffed up his pride so preposterously and made him feel he could change Val's mind with no more than a letter, left him. He sat down again. He covered his face with his hands.

'Mr Dunn?' She sounded frightened.

Harry dropped his hands. Painfully he said, 'You're right, Esther. Of course you're too young to be stuck in this house day after day, night after night. Do you need a reference from me? I shall give you one, of course.'

'I am sorry, Mr Dunn.'

'Don't be.'

She went on sitting there, and he wondered if she was waiting for him to say something, but there seemed nothing more to say: she wanted to leave, he couldn't blame her, goodbye and thank you. Although he did feel like weeping in despair, now all that boiling anger had gone so suddenly cold. He smiled at her, the kind of smile he used to bring meetings to a close, but Esther remained sitting where she was.

Finally, looking up at him, she said, 'May I say something?'

'Yes, of course.'

She hesitated, then in a rush said, 'I think that if you spent more time with Mrs Dunn, talking to her, just being with her, I think maybe she wouldn't be as . . . *unhappy* as she is now.' She looked down. 'Sorry. It's none of my business, really.'

Harry stood up. He walked to the door and held it open. 'I think in your contract we agreed on two weeks' notice. Two weeks from today then. Thank you, Esther. I think it's Mrs Dunn's supper-time now, isn't it?'

At the door, Esther stopped. 'She misses you,' she said, and her face coloured. 'That's what I think, anyway. Ava misses you.'

Harry closed the door softly behind her. He went to his desk and picked up his Scotch, only to put it down again, untasted. He shut his eyes tight, squeezing out the bloody tears; the pain was no more than guilt and he had no right to cry, no right at all.

Ava had said, 'He's dead, isn't he?'

He had nodded, taking off his cap, holding it in his hands in front of his body like a true mourner as this pale,

219

stricken young woman turned away and led him down a narrow corridor into her little room. Standing at an upturned crate that served as a table, she had seemed to regain most of her composure. 'Is it all right for you to visit me, Major Dunn? Is it allowed?'

'Yes, of course.'

'I thought perhaps there were rules about fraternising with German women?'

'Rules have become slack.'

She looked away. 'Not slack enough.'

Holding out Hans's letter, he said, 'Your brother wanted me to give you this. It's why I'm here – he wanted me to deliver it personally.'

'And you always do what your condemned prisoners want, of course.' She took the letter and thrust it into the pocket of the men's trousers she was wearing. The trousers were loose on her, gathered at the waist with a belt; they made her appear even thinner than she was. For the whole time he was with her, her hand kept returning to the trouser pocket and her brother's letter; he knew she ached to read it, that she couldn't wait for him to be gone so that she could, but he couldn't bring himself to leave. He wanted to understand her and her brother – the whole German people, in fact. The newsreels were still too fresh in his memory, those horrors he had seen with his own eyes fresher still. Impossible to understand a whole race, these two would be its representatives.

He sat down on the only chair. Ava sat on the narrow bed which was pushed up against the wall lengthways to take up less space. The room was part of a building damaged by bombs and fire, somehow shored up; from the rubble-strewn street it was hard to believe that anyone lived here at all, but the place seemed teeming with life. He could hear a baby screaming, two women shouting – there were few German men left in Berlin; the building creaked alarmingly and he glanced up at the cracked ceiling, half-expecting it to fall down on him. He sensed Ava watching him and turned to her.

She said, 'I shan't be staying here much longer. There's no reason for me to stay now.'

'Where will you go?'

'Home.'

'Where's that?'

'Hanau, in central Germany. It's where the Grimm Brothers were born. Have you heard of them, Major Dunn?'

'Yes, of course.'

'I have been thinking about their stories a good deal, how they were so full of cruelties. I wonder why we ever needed such stories. We won't any longer, I think.' Glancing towards the sound of the baby crying, she said, 'My mother read the fairytales to us – she was very proud of our connection to the Brothers – distant cousins, she believed. Hans would have bad dreams, sometimes, after the story of Snow White and the witch dancing herself to death in her red-hot shoes. I'd go to him, climb into his bed to comfort him. He was a very gentle little boy – I suppose you find that difficult to believe?'

He shrugged, not wanting to say anything that might silence her.

She smiled slightly. 'I've never met an Englishman before, Major. Where do you live in England?'

'The north. A town called Thorp. No one's heard of it.'

The baby stopped crying. With a final burst of expletives the women became quiet, too. Ava went on regarding him coolly, this specimen of unfamiliar English manhood. Harry found himself sitting up a little straighter in his hard, wobbly chair. A joist creaked and he laughed uncomfortably. 'I think you should leave sooner rather than later – before this place collapses on you.'

'I'm going soon enough.'

At once he regretted his words. He didn't want her to leave at all; he realised he felt something change in him

221

when he was with her. There was something about her calmness, her direct gaze, that made him feel easier. He thought how strong she must be to have survived so much, and his heart softened towards her, although he had determined to be hard, to hand over Hans's letter and leave. Hadn't everyone in the world survived so much over the last six years? Everyone but him, Harry Dunn, the onlooker, the listener, the sifter and repeater of other men's words, making enemies intelligible to each other. He sometimes wondered whose side he was on.

Ava said, 'Major Dunn?'

He made himself smile at her. 'I was miles away.'

'Home?'

'Yes,' he lied.

'With your wife and family.'

'My wife is dead.'

'I'm sorry.'

Because he wanted to sound cheerful for her, he said lightly, 'I have a son, Guy – he's five.'

'Oh, you must miss him,' she said. 'And five is such a nice age.'

He knew nothing about that. He said, 'Yes, it is,' thinking of Guy, whose face he could barely remember.

A rat climbed through a hole in the floorboards in the corner of the room. It scuttled along the edge of the wall and slipped through another hole beneath the bed. Ava had followed his gaze. As the rat's scaly tail disappeared, she said, 'There are so many of them, everywhere. My neighbour found one in her baby's crib.'

He hated rats – he remembered too well the tales his father had told about them, how they infested the trenches, making the misery of the Somme that bit worse. He stood up and went to the hole in the floor from where the rat had appeared. He squatted down. 'Perhaps I could block this up somehow.'

'There are lots of holes, Major Dunn. And nothing to

mend them with. Please, don't worry. They don't harm me.'

Standing up straight, he turned to her. 'I would like to help.'

'Thank you. But there's nothing you can do.' She glanced away. It occurred to him that she was ashamed; her expression had become closed again.

Because he was sure she was about to dismiss him, he said hastily, 'When I write to Guy I'll tell him I've met you – a distant cousin of the Brothers Grimm.'

Her face softened a little. 'Does he like their stories?'

He nodded, having no idea. 'Of course.'

'Hans . . . ' Her fingers went to her mouth as if to stop the words. After a moment she let her hand fall as though she had realised that it no longer mattered what she said. 'Hans . . . '

She buried her face in her hands and wept.

Harry picked up the glass of Scotch from his desk and downed it in one. He thought how it was that the first time he had touched Ava – when he had sat down next to her on her bed in that slum and put his arm around her shoulders – it was to comfort her over the loss of her brother, to try to ease the pain of this one woman in a world full of pain. He spoke softly, the German endearments coming naturally to him, *There, there, my dear, there, there.* He told her that her brother had been brave, that he had great dignity, and all the time he thought, *But he was a murderer, and so wicked – the cruellest man I've ever met.* And there was another voice in his head, repeating, *Whose side are you on?*– the film of the concentration camps playing before his eyes.

But he told himself that Ava, this woman with whom he had so quickly fallen in love, had nothing to do with her brother's crimes. This was reasonable, rational – an idea that fitted in with the new mood of the times. The German people shouldn't be blamed, as they had been blamed so disastrously after the last war; their country should be rebuilt, friendship should be fostered between the victors and the defeated.

He went back to Ava time and again, taking her tins of bully beef, chocolate when he could get it. She joked, said that had he been American, she would now be living off the fat of the land – or at least, tinned peaches and cream. Then she had touched his face as though she believed she had offended him. 'Thank you, Harry,' she said, and her voice was so tender, her touch sending shivers of longing through him. They made love on her narrow bed, the rats scrabbling beneath the floor, and he tried not to think about Hans, and how she looked like him when she smiled.

In his study, Harry slumped down at his desk. He remembered how he had brought his German bride home, that when he introduced her to Guy, the little boy had been shy of her, at first. But Ava loved children; she could enter his son's world so completely he often felt excluded. Ava taught Guy her language. He suspected that she also taught him about Hans, who had become – had always been in Ava's mind – a great hero, a dazzling prince riding out from the pages of the fairytales she loved so much. And Guy, who didn't remember his first mother, loved Ava. In time, strangers presumed his son was German as he spoke the language so well, so fluently, and this made Guy seem even less his, the bond between them becoming still weaker.

'He's a wonderful boy. He understands so much,' Ava told him.

There were secrets between his son and Ava, not just about Hans, but childhood memories she never shared with him, only with Guy. She and Guy talked and laughed a great deal together and Harry should have been pleased and not so childishly, shamefully jealous as he was. And one day, the two of them went walking together, from the holiday cottage he had rented on the Dorset coast, where he had left them, needing to work – there was always so much work to keep up with, so many divorces to arrange. The two of them went walking and the land gave way beneath their feet. The land gave way beneath their feet and they had fallen. He could hardly believe this, the appalling unlikeliness of solid rock becoming rubble and air. He found he couldn't bring himself to look at Guy, who sat up in his hospital bed, pale as the cast on his broken arm; there were too many suspicions in his heart. It seemed to him that Guy killed his mothers, one way or the other, because Ava might just as well have died; she was gone from him just as surely.

Harry got up from his desk and went into the kitchen where Esther was clearing Ava's half-eaten supper away. He said, 'I'll put Mrs Dunn to bed this evening, Esther.'

Taking Ava's hand, he led her upstairs to her room.

Chapter 23

I walked home through the park. The late evening was warm and the light soft, the sky darkening to purple edged with pink, colours I would be wary of using in my illustrations for their gaudiness. Young couples strolled arm-in-arm, leaning in towards each other, smiling, whispering. Some of them looked at me sideways, a lone man walking in the park at night. Of course I must be suspicious, an outsider.

I was flown home in 1945. The Army had graded us – I remember being weighed, the grave face of the doctor as he made his decision that I was to be amongst those worst cases that were sent home by plane. My first experience of England after so long away was of a bumpy ride in an Army ambulance to the hospital in London where we special cases would be treated. I was travel sick all over the shoes of the first doctor who saw me. He laughed, told me I would have to learn to keep my food down if I was going to get better. That doctor, I discovered later, had put long odds on my chances of surviving the week. My companion in the ambulance died the next day as though that last leg of our journey had been the final straw.

We were frail, lethargic creatures. I too wanted to close my eyes and not wake up, if only because I just couldn't be bothered any more. I was home – I had achieved my goal. Only a certain amount of curiosity kept me going, wondering what they would do with me next. On that first day in hospital in England, a nurse helped me to bathe. She said she could play chop-sticks on my ribs. I overheard her tell a colleague that we were like those poor Jews they'd filmed in the Nazi camps and wasn't it disgusting – didn't the buggers deserve the Atom Bomb? I'd heard what had been done to Hiroshima and Nagasaki, how my life had been saved.

I grew stronger, strong enough to be given my demob suit and a train ticket home. Not strong enough to stand up to my father, or to Carol or Jack. Just strong enough to breathe, to eat, to tentatively pick up a pencil again. The man in my ambulance had been called Michael Andrews. For years I dreamed about him. I dreamed that he had got on the train home with me, his head resting on my shoulder because he was so tired. In the dream he followed me to my father's house and I didn't mind, I was glad of the company, only there was no flesh on him, none at all, and when we reached our front door he collapsed, nothing but a skeleton, a pile of bones I had to hide from my father. I was so frantic in that dream – so desperate to find a hiding-place for Michael. I wept with the panic, the guilt of it all, because I knew I should have left him in the hospital. I would wake up weeping, the guilt like a mountain of stones pinning me to the bed.

After the dream, I would be jumpy for days and Carol would sometimes notice and go out of her way to be especially cheerful during her visits, especially talkative, not giving me a chance to get a word in sideways, as though she was terrified I would want to unburden myself, to talk about all that had happened.

Carol didn't know me very well. I sometimes think that she was rather stupid. But her mother and father had brought her up to believe her only role in life was as a wife and mother and she accepted this without question, so perhaps she was merely lazy. Her father adored her – he called her his princess; she was proud of being Daddy's girl, she wanted to make him proud and so of course he had to be proud of the man she chose to marry. Jack fitted the

227

bill perfectly: a hero, one who had never surrendered, never besmirched the idea of England her father carried home from his war in 1918, spent in Whitehall, safe behind a desk. I know how bitter I sound. I know there is too much luck in the world for any of us to judge one another.

She married Jack and she held her bridal bouquet in front of her pregnant belly like a shield. She thought about me. Jack, knowing that he might die any day, didn't think about anything at all except making love to his new wife, their hotel bedroom door shut fast on the world. Perhaps when it was over, when he had spent himself, he felt some twinge – as though he had caught his wife's guilt like a kind of sexually transmitted disease. No, of course, probably not. No doubt he slept, exhausted. He slept and Carol lay awake beside him and I know that she thought about me. She told me years later, when she judged me strong enough to hear, that all through her wedding day and night she thought about me, hating me because I hadn't written.

'I wrote! Of course I did!'

'But I never received your letters!'

'But I wrote to you.'

I held her because she was crying; her tears made a dark patch on my shirt. I held her, and felt only exasperation, bemusement that she should be telling me this now, after so many years when I was beginning to accept that she was married to Jack, beginning to imagine my life with someone else, if only I could find this someone. I held her and thought, *I don't love you any more*, and it was a revelation; I felt my spirits lift a little, free of the weight of regret that had held them down. I stepped away from her, holding her at arms' length.

'Carol, none of this matters now. You have Jack, and Hope –'

'Hope!' She laughed hysterically, wiping her eyes; I remember that she stamped her foot in an agony of frustration. 'Why can't you *see*? Why can't you *recognise*

228

her? Your father did – he saw it!'

The hairs on my arms rose. Hope was playing in the garden, from time to time I could see her as she ran in and out of the Wendy house I'd built; she had made a daisy chain and placed it on her head, the white flowers almost invisible against her pale blonde hair. Pale blonde like my own. When the realisation came, I felt so cold, as though a ghost had walked through me. Carol tried to hold me, but I couldn't stand to be touched.

'Jack doesn't know,' she said dully. 'He's as blind as you. But your father knows – he knew from the moment he saw her in her pram. I thought he might tell you. I kept hoping that he'd tell you.'

I sat down, unable to trust my legs. 'No,' I said, 'he wouldn't tell me.'

'Peter.' She knelt, taking my hands. 'Peter, I had to marry Jack, you must see that now. You must understand that now and forgive me. You have always been such a good man, and you love Hope, don't you? I know you love her! And she loves you . . . '

She was crying again and I wondered if perhaps she was going mad because there seemed no reason for her to have told me when she – and my father – had kept the secret for so long. I thought of Hope outside in the garden and was afraid she might come inside to find her mother in such a state; this was all I could think of, protecting Hope. Nothing else had any meaning.

I said, 'Get up, Carol, you shouldn't be on your knees to me.'

'But I should! Because I need you to help me . . . *Help me*!' She laughed, that same hysterical noise. 'I can't even think of the proper way to ask you.'

It took a long time for her to explain; the words wouldn't come, and each word when it did come was a betrayal of Jack. She called him *inadequate – not a real man*, because she was so desperate. Her desperation was

229

such it seemed that Jack hardly mattered; only her own longing was important, her own all-consuming need. I've mentioned before that Carol was selfish, but I should have said that I am too. How else would I have agreed to her scheme?

After my father had killed her, after the police had begun their clumsy, ultimately useless investigation, when Jack was still in hospital and thought unlikely to survive what my father had done, I went with her father to identify Carol's body. He had asked that I go with him; and at the time, I believed he was afraid that, at the last moment, he wouldn't be able to look as the policeman turned down the sheet covering his daughter's face. As it was, he couldn't take his eyes from her, his face full of a kind of wonder and surprise, as if he was witnessing the accident that had killed her. I was the one who could barely look; I only took a glimpse, enough to prove to myself that she was dead, that there hadn't, as I half believed, been a mistake. In that glimpse she was like every other corpse I've ever seen – a shell that gives only the most pallid impression of the life it once contained.

I took her father's arm and led him away.

Outside the silent, freezing place where we had left her, he jerked away from me. He said, 'I don't need you. I wish you weren't here.' He looked at me and the hatred in his eyes made me step back from him. 'If Jack dies,' he said, 'if he dies, we'll take the children. Don't imagine you'll ever see them again.'

I realised then that he had wanted me there to tell me this, away from the possibility of being overheard. Perhaps he imagined Carol would hear and know at last that he had guessed our secret.

Chapter 24

Matthew had gone to the Castle and Anchor, telling Val that he needed a drink after all that bloody nonsense with fella-me-lad. Her father found it impossible to speak Harry's name nowadays. But at least he didn't go on about what a lousy bastard he was, as he often did. At least he didn't try to lecture her again about how she had made the right decision. Val thought that perhaps this was because he had suddenly felt sorry for Harry – such a great big man who was once so confident, so full of life and spirit and sheer, joyous generosity – reduced to someone so unsavoury, a sweaty fatty in a crumpled suit, his bloodshot eyes watery with tears.

Val had carried one of the kitchen chairs out into the yard. She sat beside the geranium tubs, her fingers worrying the flowers' soft leaves, releasing the pungent scent. In their loft her father's pigeons cooed, settling for the night even as the warmth of the day still hung around the yard, trapped within the crumbling redbrick walls. She smoked steadily, concentrating on inhaling and exhaling, not wanting to think. She had made the right decision; she hadn't needed her father to tell her this even if he had been so inclined. Jack was a good man, reliable, hardworking. And beneath all that there was still a trace of the devil-may-care, of the man who had learned to fly for the hell of it when, at least in England, war was still an evil to be busily negotiated against. The RAF had given him Lancasters to fly, seeing something in him that suited a bomber's dogged determination rather than the breathtaking glamour of

231

Spitfires.

Jack was steady, then. Jack was also a considerate lover now that he was used to her, now that he was no longer so starved as to be desperate. He kissed her, his tongue, his lips, his hands, working their way down her body discovering what she liked best, what would most make her squirm or cry out. And he would look up and smile at her, although his eyes revealed how serious sex was to him. He was not like Harry, who was never truly serious in bed. And Jack was fitter, bigger, his size made her gasp, made her sore, he hurt her if he wasn't careful, as he had hurt her in that alley, the first time. Even then she had thought that this was all there should be to a man, this girth, this virile power forcing itself deep inside her, such a dirty thought, pornographic, degrading to them both, but helping her come, nonetheless.

Val flicked ash onto the ground. Sometimes she believed she was a slut; other times she knew how ordinary she was.

Today had been her birthday and there was still, even at her age, a different feel to this day, a sense of anticipation – excitement even. She had told Peter this when he had visited her this morning, bringing her a neatly wrapped gift. 'It's really nothing,' he said, and smiled that heartbreaking smile of his, his startlingly blue eyes teasing. 'Nothing to become excited over, anyway.'

Her gift was the drawing he had made of her one Wednesday evening after supper. He had made her look more beautiful than she believed herself to be, calmer and more certain of herself. He had seen something in her she hadn't recognised until then.

'Thank you.' She turned to him from gazing at this likeness he had created and laughed awkwardly. 'You've made me look like a grown-up. You know – that person we don't feel ourselves to be . . .'

'Don't want to be?'

'No. No, it's not that.' She looked down at the portrait again. He had been barely inside the door and now he came to stand beside her. As always when he was close by, she felt her skin tingle, a kind of nervousness as though she was daring herself to stand even closer to him but wasn't nearly brave enough. If she moved her fingers they would brush against his; he would turn to her and his angelic face would frown, questioning, gentle. He would say softly, 'Is this what you really want?' She had shuddered then, wondering if there were any other women as shockingly bad as her, wanting a man merely because he was beautiful enough to stop her heart. *Merely*! Sometimes she thought Peter's beauty was all that mattered, that she would sacrifice everything for a night in his bed. But she thought this only when he was with her. When he was gone, she was only relieved that she hadn't made such a fool of herself as to act on her lust. When he wasn't with her, she found she couldn't quite picture his face.

The alley beyond the yard gate was quiet now since the children had been called inside. Lately she noticed children more, found herself looking at babies in their prams; lately her job seemed to be a poor substitute for one of these alien little creatures she would be half-afraid to hold. Work had become something she was filling in time with until Jack made her pregnant. Becoming pregnant, to be so unimaginably transformed, so excitingly expectant, was all she thought about, and it was only since Jack that this had happened; she thought that there must be something about Jack that her body recognised as a good father. She sighed, flicking ash, thinking how she might sabotage the johnnies he was always so careful to use.

Harry had said that he would give her children, and something inside her had leaped at this, but it was that part of her that was too wild and careless, that didn't think of consequences, the same part that had climbed into Harry's bed in the first place. She had to tell herself again – *again* –

that Harry was a married man. Also, she told herself that Harry had never been a good father; it had been weeks before he told her he even had a son, although he'd told her he had a wife – would have told her even if she hadn't already known.

'I should tell you about my wife,' Harry had said.

She had heard that his wife was an invalid, a mental case, retarded, that there had been some kind of accident; no one knew the full story and lack of facts made them cruel, not least because she was known to be German.

They had been in Harry's car that smelled of expensive good times and he was driving her home from the Christmas party where they had met. Outside her house he pulled on the handbrake and turned in his seat to face her. He said, 'My wife is the most precious thing in the world to me, but precious in the sense only that I must keep her safe from harm. I can't stop caring for her because if I did, I would be the kind of man who ought not to be alive . . . ' He'd laughed shortly. 'God help me, I'm a pompous bastard.' But she knew that he meant what he said, he could just never honestly admit to the seriousness in his heart.

She had often wished that his wife had died in that accident.

'I'm wicked,' she said aloud. 'The wicked get what they deserve.'

'Val?'

His voice came from beyond the yard wall. She found herself sitting up straighter, stubbing out her cigarette beneath her foot as Peter opened the gate hesitantly. 'Val… I thought I heard you.'

Oh, but he was beautiful – not handsome, not even sexy, but so beautiful that if she slept with him it would be excusable and not unfaithfulness at all because he was so extraordinary. It would be like taking a fantasy to bed, the man she had invented as a twelve-year-old when she had first allowed her hand to slip between her legs.

234

What rubbish, she thought, and made herself smile at him, a cheerful, ordinary smile to hide behind.

'It's too warm to sit inside,' she said.

He stepped into the yard, leaving the gate open although she wished that he would close it so that it would be just the two of them, safe behind the high walls. He said, 'It's a lovely evening.'

She stood up. 'Stay – I'll fetch a chair.'

'Allow me.'

He went inside and came back with another of the kitchen chairs. Placing it beside hers, he sat down. Looking up at the sky he said suddenly, '"Look towards heaven, and number the stars, if you are able to number them".' He glanced at her 'Genesis'.

She laughed, surprised. 'Do you know the Bible off by heart?'

'There are passages I remember, that's all.' After a moment he said, 'I was a prisoner of war, in Burma. One of the very few possessions I managed to keep was a tiny Old Testament. It was confiscated eventually, but not before I'd memorised most of Genesis.'

She imagined him in the wet heat of the jungle, turning the fragile pages before a Japanese guard snatched the book from his hands. He had never spoken of his war before, and she had never asked. In her heart she had pictured him as a conscientious objector – bravely committed to the cause of peace; her heart often presumed too much, more often lately, since she had met him. Even now she couldn't imagine him carrying a rifle. She thought of all the raggedy, loin-clothed men filmed as the camps were liberated, and realised it was easier to picture him like this, stripped and vulnerable, but dignified still. Moved by this idea of him, she reached out and took his hand.

He gazed at her. At last he said, 'You're not wicked, Val. And you deserve everything your heart desires.'

She drew her hand from his, embarrassed that he had

heard her – that he had admitted to hearing her. She laughed brokenly; to her horror she realised she was close to tears. 'Everything my heart desires? You don't know me well enough to say that.'

'Tell me what you want most in the world.'

She laughed again, swiping at the shaming tears in her eyes. 'Why?'

'Because sometimes we should speak our hopes aloud. And look,' he smiled, glancing at the sky before turning to her again, 'the countless stars are listening.' More softly he said, 'And you need to chase away what you said just now, when you thought there was no one to hear. Break the spell.'

'I think you've illustrated too many fairy stories.' All the same, she looked up at the stars. Quickly she said, 'A baby.' She glanced at him, feeling herself colour, recognising that this was the most intimate conversation she had ever had. 'I want a baby.'

He held her gaze, his eyes searching hers. At last he said, 'Is that why you're marrying Jack?'

'Not the only reason.'

'You love him?'

'Yes!'

He breathed out heavily. 'I'm sorry. It's really none of my business.'

'Except that you're his closest friend.'

He laughed emptily. 'We're more like family now – not friends at all. The children . . . ' He trailed off. As if he hadn't realised it before, he said, 'You'll be their stepmother.'

'A wicked stepmother!'

'Don't say that.' He frowned at her. And then, as though he was about to break bad news, he said, 'What if Jack doesn't want any more children? Would Hope and the boys be enough?'

Val turned away from him, keeping her gaze on the

clouds scuttling across the bright face of the moon. She thought of Hope who had become even colder and more disdainful since Jack had announced their plans, of the boys who were so unruly, so desperately naughty whenever she met them. So far, it seemed Jack thought it best mostly to keep her and his children apart, and she had accepted this with guilty relief.

Lighting a cigarette, she said, 'Jack will want children because I do.'

'But what if he doesn't?'

'You remember what you said just now, about it being none of your business?' She stood up. 'It's getting chilly – I think I'll go inside. Good night.'

He stood up, too. 'Val, wait.' Catching hold of her hand, he repeated, 'Wait.'

'No, I should go in.'

He took the cigarette from her fingers and threw it to the ground. They stood facing each other, his fingers tight around hers. She saw how dark his eyes were, frowning with concern for her. No one had ever looked at her like that before, with so much compassion, and she gazed back at him, thinking that of all the times they had shared together she was the one who had talked and he had only listened. The most he had ever told her about himself was a moment ago and she had been filled with a pity that had felt like love; the feeling remained, a confusion of sympathy and desire: he was so beautiful, after all. She thought that if he kissed her, she would respond and allow him to lead her into his house and up his stairs to his room. They would make love and she wouldn't speak, just as she knew he wouldn't, keeping silent so that their betrayal would be nullified. She imagined how gentle he would be, and slow, gentle and slow and strong as her want for him. She stepped closer, reaching up to touch his face and he turned, kissing her palm.

'Val . . . Oh Christ . . . '

She touched his mouth. 'It's all right.'

'You shouldn't marry Jack. It would be wrong –'

She stepped back from him, ashamed now that he had broken the silence so resoundingly. Still feeling his eyes on her, hating the glibness in her voice, she said, 'I must have got carried away with all your talk about stars, eh?'

'Val . . . ' He held her by the shoulders, forced her to look at him. 'Please think about whether you really love Jack, whether you really want to marry him.'

She was angry now because it seemed he had encouraged her to behave as she had; it crossed her mind that all his soft looks and words were a test for her to pass or fail. Perhaps Jack had put him up to it. But then surely he would look triumphant or at least self-righteous; he only looked sad, afraid of the hurt he might have caused. Wearily she said, 'You'd best go home. Good night, Peter.'

As she turned to go inside he said quickly, 'Would you marry me, instead?'

She laughed, astonished.

'Is it so funny?'

'No . . . ' More gently, she said, 'No. But I love Jack.'

'What if he can't give you what you want most in the world?'

There was something unnerving about his intensity; she thought how jealous he must be, and how lonely. She should have been more careful of him; his strength was no more than an illusion. She wished now that she hadn't opened her heart to him, that she had realised how vulnerable he was. Jack had warned her about him, after all. She hadn't believed him when he'd told her how strange Peter could be, thinking only that he was jealous.

She heard the back gate close, heard her father singing softly, a little drunkenly, under his breath. Relieved, she said, 'It's Dad – he's been to the pub.'

Peter turned away; ignoring her father's greeting, he let himself out into the alley.

Chapter 25

Esther had known about Hans from the first week she had gone to work at the Dunns'. Not that she had meant to pry; she had only been putting away Mrs Dunn's underwear when she came across the diary in her drawer. She had lifted it out, thinking that it would be better taking up space somewhere else, when a photograph fell from between its pages. An SS officer gazed at her from the floor. Quickly, she had picked up the photo and put it back inside the diary, her hands shaking a little with the shock of seeing that uniform. For days she tried not to think about the diary or the photograph. But the next time she was putting laundry away her hand strayed against it. She had lifted it out, opening it at random. Unable to stop, her heart beating furiously, she had begun to read.

The diary was kept safe in her own drawer now. She sometimes thought that she should throw it away, bury it in the bin beneath the potato peel and newspapers and ashes from the fire. Or burn it perhaps, although she thought that would take too long; the cover was thick card, and it had a tiny silver lock – broken before she found it. Metal and card would be difficult to dispose of in the grate and she dreaded Mr Dunn or Guy finding her at such a task. Guy especially would ask too many questions, smiling and teasing but determined to get to the truth as always.

Guy. She wondered if he knew how his stepmother had adored him, how much she'd compared him to her beloved brother Hans the SS officer whose picture she kept in her diary, the man who had stormed through Poland and Russia, stopping only to force Jews to dig their own graves. On the back of his photograph were written the words, *To my darling sister Ava – take care of Rudi for me!* Rudi was a dog, an Alsatian like Hitler's. Ava had written about this dog in the diary, how he had been killed by British bombs alongside her parents.

The diary lay on Esther's bed now. She was packing, having decided that she wouldn't stay here another two weeks, even if it was in her contract. Mr Dunn could deduct money from her wages if he liked but she wouldn't stay, not after today. Today she realised she couldn't go on ignoring the idea she had that, in her mind, Mrs Dunn still lived with her brother in Berlin, that she still worshipped him despite everything she knew, that she would protect him no matter what.

Today Mrs Dunn had set upon that stranger who had driven them home from that humiliating outing, flinging her arms around him as he helped her out of his car. 'Hans,' she'd said. 'Hans.' She had begun to cry, silently, and the stranger who was kind and gentle had allowed her to hold him, had even put his arms around her, holding her quite close, although she stank of pee, was soaked in it. He had caught her eye over Mrs Dunn's shoulder, had smiled sadly. 'Let's get her inside, shall we?'

The stranger had looked like Hans; she could understand why Mrs Dunn had believed it was him. He had the same blue eyes and blond hair, the same perfect, symmetrical features. She had felt embarrassed for him, not that he seemed in any way perturbed; he had behaved as if that kind of thing happened to him every day.

Esther picked up the diary from her bed. It was from the year 1946, an eventful year for Mrs Dunn, the year she met Mr Dunn, the year she married him and came to England and fell in love with Guy – because it was like a falling in love, the way she described it, writing with far more joy and excitement than she ever wrote about her new husband. Meeting Guy, loving him, seemed to help with all the grief she felt over the loss of her brother, although sometimes it seemed Guy only helped a little. Some of the diary's entries were only about Hans, the childhood they'd spent together that was so idyllic, so full of picnics in summer and sleigh rides in winter. There was only a year's difference in their ages – they could have been twins, wished that they were. Ava missed him terribly; she dreamed of him at night. She tried to imagine what it would have been like for him when the executioner – one of his English murderers – had put the noose around his neck.

There was a knock on her door and Esther put the diary down, quickly hiding it beneath one of her sweaters. Guy poked his head around the door.

'Hello. I couldn't find you – or Ava. Is she in bed already?'

'Your father's seeing to her tonight.'

'Is he?' He raised his eyebrows in surprise, making her blink because sometimes she couldn't bear to see how handsome he was, how unattainable. She heard him close the door. 'What are you doing?'

'Packing.'

'Yes – I can tell that much.' He ducked his head to frown at her. 'Esther? What's going on?'

She managed to look at him. 'I've decided to leave.'

'Why?' He sounded horrified. 'You can't! We can't manage without you.'

'Yes, you can.' She brushed past him to fetch the few items of clothing left in the wardrobe.

'Does Dad know?'

'Yes.'

'And he's just letting you go?'

'Yes.'

'Didn't he offer you more money? He will – he was probably too shocked to think straight.'

'He did offer. But I've got another job.' She took her

241

winter coat from its hanger, realising that it was too bulky to be packed and that she would have to carry it home over her arm. Home. She could almost cry at the thought of her parents' welcome. Her father would be so pleased that she had left this place and its German woman. As she put her coat on the bed, Guy caught her arm.

'Esther, come downstairs. I'll make you some cocoa – you like my cocoa – and we can talk.'

'There's nothing to talk about.' She shrugged off his hand even as she wished he would hold her as that stranger had held Mrs Dunn today, tenderly. But she had seen him in the park this afternoon with that blonde girl, that beautiful, tall, princess of a girl. Few girls could compete with that – especially not someone like her.

Desperately Guy said, 'Please, Esther. Please don't leave.'

She frowned at him. Surprising herself with the harshness of her voice, she said, 'Why do you care so much? Your father will find someone else to do your dirty work.'

'Dirty work? Is that how you see it?'

He looked so hurt, as though she had slapped him. Immediately she said, 'I didn't mean it like that.'

'I thought you liked Ava.'

She snorted, not really meaning to but unable to conceal the scorn she felt so suddenly. '*Liked?*'

Stiffly Guy said, 'Cared for, then. I thought you cared for her.'

She thought of Ava, how she had bathed her and dressed her and coaxed her into eating, how she would sometimes sit and brush her hair for ages because it seemed to soothe her. And sometimes Ava would look at her as though she had just woken from a deep sleep and couldn't understand who this stranger was who was talking to her as if she was a child. At first Esther had been excited by these apparent awakenings; she would begin to ask Ava if she

242

knew where she was, if she remembered her name. Soon enough she realised that the looks were nothing, no more than an imitation of life.

The only thing left to pack was the sweater that lay on the bed, hiding the diary. She said, 'I'd like to get on now.'

'Esther . . . ' Guy sighed. 'Stay, at least until we find someone else.'

'I can't.'

'Why not?'

Because of Hans, she thought. She didn't even know his surname, enforcing the feeling the diary had given her that she was far more intimate with him than she would ever have wanted to be. She sat down on the bed wearily. 'I miss my family.'

This at least was true enough. Looking up at Guy she said, 'My father never wanted me to come here.'

Guy shifted, obviously uncomfortable. He knew her family's history, how her parents had only just escaped Vienna with their lives, leaving behind their own parents, their brothers and sisters, aunts and uncles and cousins. They never saw any of them again. He knew because she had told him, one sunny afternoon a few weeks ago when he had offered to help her peel potatoes for supper and he had asked how it was she spoke German so well. She had wondered then if he knew about Hans, believing that Ava would have found it impossible not to talk about him to this boy she loved so much. Looking at Guy now she was more certain than ever that he knew all about his stepmother's brother.

He sat on the bed beside her. 'I suppose we should thank you for staying as long as you have.' Turning to face her he said suddenly, 'I'll miss you.'

'No you won't.'

'I will.' He searched her face. Softly he said, 'I think you're lovely – you know that, don't you?'

She stood up, outraged that he should pretend like that

just to try to make her stay. The suddenness of her move
sent the diary slipping from the bed to land at his feet.

To her shame, Guy picked it up. He opened it, closed it
again. He laughed harshly. 'You've read this?'

'No.'

'What's it doing in your room?'

She felt herself colour darkly.

'You've read it.' He shook his head, gave that same
ugly laugh. 'Well, I suppose I can't say anything. After all,
I've read it. All *Hans this* and *Hans that*.' Holding the diary
by its spine, he shook it so that its pages fanned out. He
looked up at her. 'Where's his photo? I left it between the
last week of June, the first of July. Her birthday week.'

Unable to look at him she said, 'I left it in her drawer.'

'This is why you're leaving, isn't it?'

She nodded.

Gazing at her, he said, 'She used to tell me that he was
the best brother anyone could have – the kindest, the most
loyal. When everyone else had left her alone he came back
to find her, to take care of her. That's how he was caught;
he could have escaped like so many others, but he cared
about her too much.'

He stood up. 'I'll leave you to finish your packing.
Goodbye, Esther, good luck in your new job.'

Ava had said, 'I wish you could have known him, my
darling. You would have loved him so. Everyone did. He
was so handsome, so full of life.' She sighed wistfully.
Gazing out of the cottage window at the sodden English
countryside she said, 'Perhaps you and I should escape – go
home to Germany. I'll show you where we were born,
where we had so many happy times . . . '

It had rained for three days. Alone in the cottage his
father had rented for the month, Guy and Ava played the
card games she had taught him and Ava talked about her
childhood, halcyon pre-war days when the sun always

shone, bleaching Hans's hair still blonder and burnishing his skin to gold. Guy hadn't wanted to think about Hans, not really. He was the enemy, after all, and not just an ordinary enemy, like the dull-witted German soldiers depicted as such buffoons in his comics, but an SS officer, one of those men who despised fair-play and decency and the proper rules of war. But the more Ava told him about her brother, the more human Hans became, no longer a cartoon version of evil, but someone he could empathise with when Ava told him of the arctic conditions he'd endured in Russia. He forgot for the moment that the Russians had been on their side.

That rainy afternoon though, it seemed that Ava was determined not to be sad, allowing herself only that one sigh before turning to him, becoming bright and brisk as she said, 'We'll go for a walk. We shall put on our Wellington boots and take our umbrellas and the English rain shall not defeat us.'

Perhaps the rain had loosened the stones.

In the garden, Guy stopped his angry pacing and looked back at the house that had never truly been his home. His father had bought the place when he came home from Germany – a house to impress Ava, to make her love him; Guy had always suspected that his father believed Ava didn't love him as much as he wanted her to. But the house was just a house to Ava and couldn't replace all that she'd lost; not even he could do that. It was his role just to listen, to be the one to whom Ava could relate her tales of Hans and in telling those tales, make her brother live again.

He saw his father at Ava's bedroom window. Harry blamed him for the accident – of course he did – just as he blamed him for his mother's death. If he hadn't been born, his mother wouldn't have become ill with post-natal depression; if he had been good like other children – not being constantly expelled – he would have been at school that June, and Ava wouldn't have volunteered to take him away on holiday. His mother would still be alive; Ava would still be herself, if not for him.

Looking up at the bedroom window, he held his father's gaze. At last Harry drew the curtains without acknowledging that he'd seen him.

Guy went on gazing at the window, rage building inside him. Suddenly, he turned and ran through the garden and out onto the quiet street.

Chapter 26

Guy wandered the streets, his rage gradually subsiding: he could never be angry for long, it seemed too much of a waste of energy to him. Still, he couldn't bring himself to go home. Home was too full of Ava.

He walked until the storm came, the thunder so loud, the lightning striking down so fiercely after the heat of the day, so close; he knew how dangerous it was. He was only a few yards from the house, the place that Hope had shown him, the place he had probably been heading for all along. The key was no longer in its hiding-place so Guy smashed a pane of glass in the door and released the catch from the inside. He went upstairs, the lightning violently, briefly, illuminating the dark passageway. This house was full of ghosts; he'd sensed them that afternoon as Hope led him from room to room. He had wanted to explore the house alone. Only then they had heard the voices outside, and the panic had begun.

He went first into the room full of toys, where the picture of the prince hung above the fireplace. The picture had its own ghost, of course, its very own horror lurking to surprise the unwary. A warning, Peter Wright had called the goblin, at least according to Hope. A warning against sex with boys like him. He went to the picture and touched the goblin's leering mouth. Hope thought Peter Wright was a pervert. She didn't realise that most men were, beneath their earnestness or pompousness or stern aloofness or any of the other disguises used to make mothers and fathers believe their children were safe with them.

He had been six when a master first fondled him. He had been eight when he was first buggered. Buggered! What a fat, horrible word that was, disgusting and preposterous at once. He knew that most boys made more of a fuss about it than he did – that they cried more, at least; he didn't cry at all. He pretended to be someone else entirely when they touched him, not Guy Dunn at all but a boy called Dan who didn't care for anyone or anything. And when it all got a bit too much even for Dan, he simply ran away. He knew he wasn't like other boys, he had some crucial bit missing, some bit that was to do with pride and self-respect and taking yourself oh so bloody seriously. Most boys – most men – were stupid bastards, both the bullies *and* the weaklings. He had learned that from his first day at his first school. So far he hadn't met anyone to change his mind.

The prince in Wright's drawing had a very beautiful face, like Wright himself. When he saw this picture, Guy had thought that Wright might be queer, a thought that had crossed his mind when he'd met him at Irene's birthday party. He certainly didn't look at Hope in the way Hope imagined he did. Innocent little Hope, she made him smile sometimes, she was so sheltered, and then she would shock him – even him – with the things she did. He hardly knew what to make of her, had to concede that he didn't know that much about girls, given his upbringing. He did believe he loved her though. He believed it more each time he saw her, as she became more familiar to him.

The lightning flashed again, making the prince's face look suddenly animated, as though his horse had startled. Guy turned away, remembering that Hope really believed Wright wanted her – and it puzzled him that she could misread the signs so badly. It was obvious to him that Wright loved her as a father would. Guy frowned, thinking of the likeness between Hope and Peter Wright. Then: 'Christ,' he said aloud. Then, more softly, '*Christ*.' Of course – Wright was Hope's father! Their alikeness spoke for itself. No wonder this house had felt so haunted to him; it was stuffed full of this great enormous secret.

Guy opened the wardrobe, the drawers in the chest, searching for clues, wanting to find evidence to back up his new theory, realising that he wanted Wright to be Hope's father rather than that idiot Jackson. He went downstairs, began on the desk in the sitting room, working his way steadily through the house. It seemed as though someone else had done this before him: most of the drawers and cupboards were empty. Finally, the rest of the house searched, he stood in the scullery at the top of the cellar steps, breathing in the smell of damp walls and coal dust.

He felt along the wall, hoping to find a light switch just as there was on the cellar steps of the derelict house that had been his retreat from the world before he met Hope. Thinking of that house now and the hours he'd spent alone there, he began to feel the pressure of his own strangeness, a feeling he'd had less often since Hope but one that still had the power to unnerve him. Perhaps he would never be in step with the world, would always be an outsider looking in on other people's lives, wondering at the insignificant things that seemed to matter so much to them. He made himself think about Hope, the kindred spirit he had found; they were outsiders together, especially if his hunch about her was true. His fingers found the switch and the steps were bathed in a dim yellow light.

The cellar contained only gardening tools, neat and tidy where he had expected to find the usual accumulation of rubbish and spiders' webs. Guy walked along the corridor that led from the main cellar to the outside steps. There were doors along its length. The third door hung open and Guy could see that in the space behind it, a paving-slab had been lifted and someone had been digging into the exposed dirt floor. Two small metal spades – the kind children used to dig sandcastles – lay beside the hole, and beside the spades was a pile of small bones.

Guy squatted down to look more closely. He thought at first that they were animal bones – those of a rat, perhaps, or a small dog. He picked one up and examined it. After a moment he went to fetch the spade he'd seen hanging on the cellar wall.

Harry lay beside Ava; she was sleeping, the doll Danny in her arms. Guy had given her the doll the first time he had visited her in hospital. His arm had still been in plaster, his face so pale still that Harry had believed he would never truly recover but would remain forever this wan, frightened little boy. He was eleven years old and had lost his odd, cocky confidence that had always made him seem so much older and so independent that Harry would feel totally superfluous to his son's needs. This feeling had helped ease the guilt Harry had carried around with him since he left Guy at his first boarding school – even before that, if he was being honest with himself. He realised he couldn't remember a time when he hadn't felt guilty over his son.

Harry had never asked how Guy had come by the dolls. He had had an idea – one that he was ashamed of – that his son had stolen them from the children's ward where he'd stayed for a week after the accident. It was only recently that he had overheard Guy telling Esther that he had bought the dolls from the hospital's little shop. Guy had laughed that easy, careless laugh of his. 'They cost me all my pocket money – even then I didn't have enough. The woman in the shop let me off. I think she felt sorry for me.'

Harry had gone into the kitchen then, wanting to embrace his son, to beg his forgiveness for doubting him. Guy had glanced at him, smiled in that knowing, supercilious way he had that was such a barrier between them; it was as if Guy had known all about his suspicions – even as if he had made up the story about spending every penny he had on the dolls because he knew that his father was eavesdropping. Harry experienced the same irrational anger he often felt around his son; he returned to his belief that the dolls had been stolen. This belief fitted with everything he knew about Guy, all his bad behaviour that had Harry travelling up and down the country looking for schools that would take him on.

Ava stirred in her sleep and Harry stroked her hair, murmuring to her that he was there, that everything was all right. Danny stared up at him with his big, smiley blue eyes – amazing how much expression could be stitched into cloth. He remembered how Guy had placed Danny and the other doll at the foot of Ava's hospital bed and had stood silently beside him as Harry tried to explain that Ava might not recognise him any more. Guy had nodded. 'That doesn't matter. When she gets better we can explain who we are.'

'We think this is the very best we can hope for, Mr Dunn,' the consultant neurologist had said. The man had glanced at him, returned to the pages and pages of Ava's medical notes. Harry waited, although he knew the consultant didn't have anything else to say – really couldn't be bothered any more now that there were no more operations to carry out, no more experiments he could try to shock his wife's brain into behaving. At last the man looked up at him. 'I'm sorry. Take your wife home, take care of her – there's nothing more to be done.'

And he had taken care of her – he had – to the very best of his ability, the very best way he knew how: he threw money at the problem. He had paid for the finest nursing home he could find. But Ava had deteriorated in the Home, despite its gardens and lawns and views of open countryside, despite its lovely public rooms that were full of the demented old. Whenever Guy was home he would insist on accompanying him on his weekly visits to the place, and on the way back his silence bore down on Harry like a Panzer division. He had wanted to ask Guy what he thought he should do, because didn't he have to work every day to pay his school fees? He had to work, resolving other people's problems with each other – how was he supposed to look after Ava? But Harry never said any of this, never tried to make excuses, only bore the terrible silence.

Then one day the nursing home wrote to advise him that it was about to close; apparently there were more profitable uses for such a large amount of real estate. The closure had set him on the path that eventually led to Esther.

Harry sighed. As he'd put Ava to bed he'd entertained the idea that he could possibly change Esther's mind. But then he'd thought about how she'd told him she was too young for this job of caring so much and so relentlessly. The young needed to see progress and rewards; they needed something to aim for. And Harry had seen the way Esther looked at Guy, and soon Guy would be leaving and his unpredictable, rare visits home wouldn't be enough to sustain the girl's hopes.

How easy it was to blame everything on Guy, Harry thought, and how perverse, when the boy was innocent of everything Harry wanted to find a scapegoat for.

Getting up as quietly as he could, he laid the female rag doll down in his place and stood over Ava, ensuring that she slept on. He was tired; he thought that in the morning he would be able to think more clearly. For tonight he had no idea of what he would do or even how he would live, now that his life had hit the buffers with such dull predictability. Not that he had predicted any of it; he'd believed Esther would stay for ever, that Val would go on loving him so selflessly. Laughable, really, if he felt like laughing at all. He hadn't realised he was capable of such self-deception. He had always thought rather better of himself.

Leaning over his wife's bed, he kissed her, catching the scent of the soap with which he'd washed her face. 'I love you,' he whispered, and it wasn't a lie, not a true lie. He loved her in ways he couldn't even explain to himself, ways that he was sure he could trace back to that rat-infested room in Berlin, when the memory of a beautiful, blond boy swinging on the end of the hangman's rope was all too fresh in his mind.

Chapter 27

I shouldn't have spoken to Val the way I did. Now she believes that I must hate Jack, for why else would I say the things I said? I have made a fool of myself; I suppose I feel the sting of this more than anything else.

I couldn't sleep and so went downstairs to work, although the same thoughts that kept me awake now kept me from concentrating on the job in hand. I thought of Val, of course, the look on her face after my outburst; I could see that she pitied me. And why shouldn't she? After all, I seem to have so little; even my family must seem second-hand to her. And now she even knows how I spent my war. God alone knows what possessed me to tell her, except that sometimes I crave sympathy. Pathetic. In fact, I feel I am becoming more pathetic, the more time passes.

Ironically, in the camps I was known as the one who always looked on the bright side; I geed everyone along. There I was with beriberi or dysentery or with ulcers on my legs the size of saucers, weak with exhaustion and hunger, encouraging the others! I suppose I felt I had so much to live for. Perhaps if I'd known about Carol and Jack, about Hope, things might have been different.

Carol and Jack. I think their marriage was a happy one, as far as any outsider can tell. She bore her secret stoically until I came home and her desperation for another baby became too much. I remember they would touch a lot – yes, even in front of me – and they had pet names for each other. He called her Pudding because she became quite plump in the years before the twins were born.

I remember how self-conscious she was about her body because it had changed so much from that of the young, virginal girl I'd known. She would undress in the dark, the not-quite dark because it was always afternoon and so a little sunlight sneaked through the gap in my bedroom curtains. I would still be able to see how pale her skin was, the blue-blood veins showing on her belly and thighs, see where her skin had stretched tight during her pregnancy only to shrink back, a little of its elasticity gone for ever, pock-marked as an orange. Her breasts were heavier and less dense, there was a softness to her so that when her body was released from the reinforced moulding and flattening of her matronly underwear, marks were left on her skin, red welts and indentations as though she had mortified her flesh. I think that, had I allowed it, she wouldn't have undressed at all, only taken off her knickers and laid down, flat on her back, eyes closed tight as against some unpleasant gynaecological procedure.

She guessed at the days when she would be most fertile and would tell me a few days in advance that I should expect her on that Tuesday or Friday or Wednesday afternoon; there was no way I could flatter myself that she desired me. She believed that I desired her though, that I was quite mad for that body that Jack had pounded and pummelled night after night after night. She was right, but it wasn't passion that fuelled my madness, only rage over what she had done to me – was doing to me. I fucked her and pretended I was making love because I could kiss her and suck at her and work my fingers and lips and tongue to make her come despite herself; I could feel her holding back, her dismayed shuddering before I tipped her over the edge moaning and yelping, a real adulteress at last. I would slip inside her so easily then; there was nothing to push against as there had been that first time. She was so slack, so wet; she would always have to wait far longer than she would have wished for my climax. Sometimes I just couldn't reach those heights at all; my desire – my rage – would simply die, shrivelling me. I'm sure she thought I did this deliberately.

When I was successful though, when my seed was safe inside her, she would lie on her back for a while, managing to imbue her stillness with such portentousness that once I asked her if she would like to raise her legs and hips, give the sperm a fighting chance against gravity. She made a face as though I had said something filthy, shifting even further away from me in case I should compound my vulgarity by brushing against her. She would lie still on her back and so would I, our nakedness exposed to the ceiling, my badly used cock flaccid and sticky against my thigh. I could smell the talcum powder she used to sanitise her genitals before she visited me, a sharp, flowery scent of Lily of the Valley mixed with my musky cum, so that the first thing I would do after she'd gone was open my bedroom window. I couldn't wait for her to leave so that I might open my window and then go straight to the bathroom to bathe. But I would stay lying on my back on the bed until she got up because it seemed to me the most gentlemanly thing to do.

I was as much of a stud as she'd hoped; it took only a few tries of this carefully timed fucking before she stood me down. When Jack discovered she was carrying twins he became cock-of-the-walk, forgetting for a little while that he hadn't wanted one other child, let alone two. Hope had been enough for him.

Hope. I would have called her Grace, and my sons would be John and David if I'd had any say. But I was just one among many at the christening, not a godparent because she believed, with a perceptiveness that was rare in her, that I would be insulted by such a title. I watched strangers hold my boys, passing them around so carelessly, used to small babies as I was not. I was shy of them. They were the most beautiful, perfect little creatures I had ever

256

seen and I wanted to run away from them before my heart became too badly damaged and fell apart. But I've written before of how strong my heart is, how much it can withstand. I stayed: where else was there for me to go?

Nowadays, I sometimes say that I am their godfather because people are suspicious of me, a bachelor who loves children with whom he has no blood tie; but people also think artists are eccentric and can be excused certain behaviours. Also, I am Jack's poor friend who has been made harmless by a lifetime of bullying – in the eyes of some I am little more than a child myself. So, I have my camouflages. And Jack has never suspected. Even when I stand beside Hope and her eyes and mouth and nose are mine, and the way she carries herself and the way she smiles and laughs . . . He doesn't see her except as his; it's perfectly understandable, he's human after all. The boys are less like me; they are more like my father, and I see him in them sometimes. I believe he loved Martin and Stephen more than he loved anyone on earth.

There has been a storm tonight, a quite spectacular thunder and lightning show. On nights like this I'm afraid the boys may be frightened, because I was at their age. 'The angels are moving their furniture about' – isn't that what fathers are supposed to say to reassure their little children? Most likely they're sound asleep and not disturbed at all; they are such confident creatures, so certain that they are loved and protected. This is how it should be, of course.

I slept eventually and the noise of the rain invaded my dreams because I dreamed of the rain in Burma, its relentlessness. I imagined that if I died beside the railway track, my body would be pounded into the ground by the rain, returned to the earth before they had a chance to dig even a shallow grave. In reality we were allowed to bury our dead with a little dignity. I believed I remembered much of the funeral prayer, although I let most of it go and asked

God only to welcome the deceased into heaven. I believed in God at those gravesides, although most of the time He had slipped away from me; I thought that if only I could concentrate hard enough, I would win Him back, having finally grasped the concept that everything was in His plan. Perhaps if I hadn't been so hungry. Perhaps if that first Japanese officer I met had slit my throat I would have been accepted into heaven with my faith intact.

I made breakfast – porridge, tea and toast and marmalade. I thought about going next door to Val and asking her to forgive my outburst, only to wonder at the explanation I might give – that I was hurt and angry because my daughter believes I am nothing more than a filthy pervert – a good enough excuse after all for allowing my emotions to run away with my mouth.

Or I could tell Val that whenever I'm close to her I imagine how beautiful she would look naked, and how much I want to make love to her, and these thoughts interfere with my sense of propriety. I'm not myself around Val. I imagine few men are because, even clothed, Val's body is perfection, breasts and waist and hips in classical proportion. It's a body for bearing babies and a part of me wants to warn her about Jack, the truest reason for my outburst last night. But it's not my place; besides, I need to protect my children. All the same, I think of her despair in the future as the babies fail to come along, despair that no doubt will be as raw and ugly as Carol's was, just as clamorous and demanding, consuming her love for Jack until there's nothing left.

There was a knock on my door and I left my second cup of tea to answer it. Guy stood on the street, hunched and furtive as a runaway, his head turned as though he was afraid he'd been followed. His clothes were filthy and there was a smear of dirt on his face. I stood back, opening the door wider. What else could I do, after all? Brave boy – he only hung back a moment before he followed me inside.

Chapter 28

Guy sat at Wright's kitchen table watching as Peter made him tea and toast. He asked, 'Do you like jam or marmalade, Guy?' as he placed the tea pot, toast-rack and butter on the table.

'Neither.' Guy cleared his throat. 'Thanks.'

Wright sat down. The table was placed beside the window and he glanced out at the small back-yard where puddles of last night's rain had collected. 'Quite a downpour we had, but at least you weren't caught in it. You found somewhere to shelter.' Turning to Guy he said, 'It's obvious you stayed out all night. Won't your parents be worried?'

Guy avoided his gaze. He felt about five years old, shaky and fearful; he also thought that he stank of sweat and dirt and worse. He closed his eyes, sickened all over again by what he had found beneath the cellar's earth floor. His fingers went to the metal box in his pocket only to draw away, repelled. He said, 'May I wash my hands?'

Wright kept a bar of carbolic soap by the sink and Guy worked it into a lather, welcoming the soap's harsh scent.

Taking a clean towel from a drawer, Wright handed it to him. 'Sit down,' he said. 'Drink your tea. Perhaps you should have some sugar in it. Isn't sweetness meant to be good for shock?'

Guy did as he was told, his newly clean hands shaking a little as he picked up his tea cup. For all the soap he had used, he could still smell the cellar's terrible stink. He knew that Wright was watching him, that he must be curious at least, but the man remained calm, that gentle air of his unruffled. After a while Wright said, 'Why don't you tell me why you're here?'

Guy laughed brokenly and thought how appalling it would be if he burst into tears. He couldn't remember ever crying and perhaps he was in shock as Wright had said, not just appalled and disgusted, but in shock as though it was an actual place you went to get away from yourself and your horrible imaginings. Because he had been imagining quite a lot: the terror and the panic and the sheer bloody horror of what must have gone on in that house. He looked at Wright, making himself meet his gaze for the first time. He thought of the picture of the beautiful knight and the goblin grimacing from its lair. The man who drew such a picture must know about wickedness; he must have known everything about it just from living above that cellar.

Looking down at his tea cup, Guy said, 'I'm sorry.'

'About?'

'I broke into your house.' He managed to look at him again. 'Last night, when the storm started . . . I knew it was empty.'

'Because you'd been there with Hope.'

Guy nodded miserably. 'Yes. I'm sorry.'

He expected a lecture but Wright kept silent; he had never known a grown man to say so little, who allowed so much silence.

Falteringly, Guy said, 'I found this.'

He placed the metal box on the table. It was silver, a little longer and wider than a man's hand, its lid intricately engraved with flowers. Soil had collected in the grooves of the pattern and the metal was tarnished; there had once been a lock, but this had been broken, its catch hanging by a single tiny screw. Inside there was a lining of blue velvet, the deep colour preserved from the light so that it had kept its richness. Guy glanced at Wright, wanting to see if he displayed any sign of recognising the box. But he only looked puzzled.

Catching his eye, Wright said, 'Where did you find it?'

'In the cellar.'

Wright raised his eyebrows so that he looked more puzzled still. 'Really? Then it was well hidden – I've never come across it before. You must have been searching pretty hard. What were you searching for?'

Guy gazed down at the box. 'You need to look inside. There's a photograph.' He gulped. 'Your mother – I think it must be your mother – and you – when you were a baby. I'm sorry.'

Wright picked up the box, hesitating for a moment before opening it. Guy imagined he smelled the grave again and held his breath as Wright took out the photograph and absently placed the box back on the table, his eyes fixed on the picture of a young woman posed in front of a studio backdrop, a baby on her knee. He turned the picture over and read what was written on its reverse: *Emily and Peter, July 1922. My darling girl and boy.*

Wright placed the picture down gently beside the silver box. After a moment he picked it up again, turned it over again to read the inscription. The handwriting was an old-fashioned copperplate, neat and controlled. The name of the photographer was printed in the bottom left corner, alongside the studio's address on Thorp High Street. Putting the picture down, Wright turned to him, his face pale and troubled.

'Where in the cellar did you find this?'

'In one of the storerooms along the passage. A paving slab had been lifted – I think the twins had been digging. There were some bones, so I started to dig . . . ' Shaking his head he said again, 'I'm sorry . . . I'm so sorry.'

'There were bones?' Peter stared at him. Then sharply, he said, 'Tell me! Tell me what you found!'

'A grave – it was quite shallow. There's a body, a skeleton – I think she must have been pregnant.' He looked away, remembering the tiny bones of the unborn child within its mother's pelvis, and heard Wright gasp in shock.

Guy suddenly thought how stupid he was to have come here. For all he knew, Wright had buried the body himself; maybe it wasn't his mother and the photo meant nothing. But Wright was staring at the picture. He seemed hardly aware that Guy was there at all; his expression showed only a deep, despairing grief.

'Have you told Hope about this?' he managed.

Guy shook his head.

'There was nothing else? Only . . . ' Wright closed his eyes. Painfully he said, 'Only the box and . . . '

'Nothing else.'

Wright seemed not to hear him at first, his face expressionless as he gazed down at the photograph. At last he looked at him. 'I'll go now, see for myself.'

'Would you like me to come with you?'

'No.'

'I will – I don't mind.' Guy stood up. As calmly as he could so that he might seem older and sensible and not the child he suddenly felt himself to be, he said, 'I don't think you should go alone.'

Guy could hardly bring himself to go down the cellar steps again. He remembered how he had dug into the square of earth exposed by the lifted paving slab, and found more of the hand and finger bones that the boys had already uncovered. He lifted out the next slab and the next until the whole floor of the coal store was exposed; sweating with the effort, his muscles aching with the strain, he felt compelled to go on, possessed by a terrible fascination. As he began to dig, the spade hit against the box; he crouched down and his hand brushed bone as he lifted the box out. On his knees, he put aside the spade and began to uncover a skull with his hands, gentle as an archaeologist excavating ancient treasure. He saw how shallowly the body had been

262

buried and fetched a garden trowel, carefully digging away the two or three feet of soil until the whole skeleton was exposed. It seemed that only then he realised the horror of it. He staggered to his feet, his legs stiff with kneeling for so long. Snatching up the silver box, he ran from the house.

He went home. In his father's study he poured himself a Scotch from the decanter Harry kept topped up and thought that perhaps he had imagined the skeleton, that his mind had played some trick, a kind of waking dream. Then he looked at the box that had just fitted into his jacket pocket, remembered how it had bounced against his hip as he'd run home. He took it out and opened it and looked and looked at the photograph of the shy-looking, beautiful young woman and her baby. She looked like Hope, just like Hope, and it occurred to him that this was the evidence he'd originally been searching for.

He read the photograph's inscription over and over as though it might be a code, as if it held back some vital information he could decipher if only he wasn't so befuddled. His fingers scrambled around the box, feeling through its lining in case something was hidden behind it. There was nothing, only that stink of earth and what he imagined was decaying bone.

He went on sitting in an armchair as the dawn broke and the garden became alive with birdsong. He must have slept, fitfully, afraid each time he jerked awake. He heard his father get up, and knew he had to leave the house, unable to face him. Remembering Hope had told him that Wright had moved to Inkerman Terrace, he went there, knocking on doors until he found one of Wright's neighbours who knew who he was and the number of his house.

Now he stood at the top of the cellar steps, and Wright said, 'You can stay here, if you can't face it.'

'No.' Guy thought that he should face what was down there, knowing that he had made it even more terrible in his

263

imagination and that he needed to see it again, to tell himself that it was only the sad remains of a human being, if he wasn't to be haunted by the horror of it for the rest of his life. Close to tears, he looked at Wright, who smiled at him painfully.

'Shall we do this together, Guy?'

Wright had brought a torch. In the cellar's passageway he shone the light onto the exposed skeleton, and then crouched down just as Guy had done. Guy stood a few feet away and it was as he had hoped: a little of the horror was dispelled, only to be replaced by an overwhelming sense of pity as he watched Wright touch the skull with such tenderness. Feeling that such private pain shouldn't be witnessed, Guy turned away and went to wait on the cellar steps. After a moment, Wright came to stand in front of him, placing a hand on his shoulder.

'Let's go upstairs,' Wright said hoarsely. 'Into the fresh air.'

Guy cried; he couldn't help it, the tears just came and Wright put his arm around his shoulders and led him to a bench in the garden, not saying anything but only keeping his arm loose around him as he wept. At last, wiping his nose on his sleeve, pushing the heels of his hands hard into his eyes, Guy said, 'I'm sorry. It must be the shock or something.' He thought of the photograph, the woman who was so like Hope, and drew a shuddering breath, holding back a fresh wave of tears. Wright held him closer, but Guy edged away from him, ashamed of himself.

At last Guy said, 'Is it your mother?'

'Yes, I think so.' Wright had been staring out across the garden and now he turned to look at him. 'My father told me that she ran away with another man. I was a year old when she left – when he killed her.'

'Maybe he didn't. Maybe it was an accident or something.' This suddenly seemed absurd to him. 'I'm

264

sorry,' he said, and because sorry seemed such an inadequate thing to say, he shifted uncomfortably, aware that Wright was gazing at him.

'Guy, tell me what you were looking for in the house.'

'Nothing.'

'Something valuable to steal?'

'No! I'm not a thief!'

'Then tell me why you were searching my house.' He shook his head. 'It doesn't matter. Nothing much matters any more. That poor girl, my mother . . . I can't think of her as my mother – that girl in the photo looks nothing like I imagined her to be.'

'But she looks like you.' Forcing himself to meet his eye, Guy said, 'She looks like Hope. You're Hope's father, aren't you?'

Searching his face as though trying to decide if he could trust him, Peter said, 'Promise me that you won't tell her.'

'What if she guesses?'

'She won't.'

Wright stared out over the garden again, such pain in his eyes that Guy had to look away; witnessing such grief made him feel like a voyeur. Eventually, awkwardly, he said, 'I won't tell her. I promise.'

Looking towards the cellar's outside steps, Wright said, 'I should go to the police.'

'What good would that do?'

'I can't ask you to keep this to yourself.'

'But I will.'

'Why?'

'For Hope's sake – and for yours, because of what you mean to her.'

Wright turned to him. At last he said, 'I think you should go home now.'

'What will you do?'

'I'll bury her properly, decently. Out here in the garden

265

– beneath the lilacs, I think.' He closed his eyes, bowing his head. 'Oh Christ,' he murmured. 'Sweet Christ . . . '

Guy stood up. He blew his nose, finished with tears now; he felt as though he had cried all the tears he should have cried for the whole of his childhood, and that the tears had made him stronger. For the first time in his life he didn't question what he was about to do, knowing only that it was right, without any of the shades of grey that had always clouded his decisions.

He walked towards the house, taking his time, wanting to give the older man a little time alone. There were sheets in one of the bedrooms; he would take one, using it as a shroud before carrying the remains to the grave he would dig beneath the trees.

Chapter 29

That lunch-time, Jack was waiting outside the typing-pool door for her. As soon as he saw her he grinned. 'Come on, be quick. I'm taking you somewhere special for lunch.'

'Oh?' Val smiled at him, even as she was reminded of the guilt she felt over Peter. Last night, the guilt had her tossing and turning, although she told herself that of course she would never have actually allowed herself to be seduced by him. When Peter wasn't with her she found it impossible to imagine what she saw in him that made her behave so shockingly. Desperate for sleep, becoming more and more irrational, she could almost believe that he was some kind of sorcerer, bewitching her with just a look. Now, after a morning of the down-to-earth bustle of the typing-pool, she only felt this twinge of guilt. After all, they had only shared a look; he had only held her hand for a moment. And the look and the hand-holding were nothing, not enough to hurt her relationship with Jack.

She linked her arm through his and he patted her hand as he led her along the corridor crowded with their fellow workers heading for the canteen. All at once she realised he wasn't wearing his suit and tie, but his weekend clothes. 'Haven't you been working today?' she asked.

'Day off.' He smiled at her. 'And I've arranged with Davies for you to have the rest of the day off, too. There – am I a wonderful husband-to-be or not?'

A sudden sense of freedom made feel exhilarated. 'Very wonderful. So – where are we going?'

They'd reached the front offices where Stanley Davies

himself leaned against the receptionist's desk, watching Jack's sons run around. Davies called out when he saw Jack, 'Two fine boys you've got there, Jackson.' Then he leered at Val, looking her up and down in that lecherous way he had. 'Are we going to see a couple more like them in nine months or so, Miss Campbell?'

Jack squeezed her hand. To the boys he said, 'You two, didn't I tell you to sit quietly and wait for me?' Glancing at Davies he said, 'Good afternoon, Mr Davies.'

'Good afternoon!' He clapped Jack on the back. 'And I hope it's a *productive* one with your lovely lady.'

Outside, the boys running ahead of them, Jack stopped to light a cigarette. Looking back at the sprawling building that was Stanley Davies & Sons, he said, 'Old bastard. I'm going to leave.' He grinned at her. 'I'm going to tell him to stick his job and his dirty-minded bloody comments where the sun doesn't shine.'

Returning his grin she said, 'And then what will you do?'

'Oh, I don't know.' He drew her into his arms, kissing her mouth lightly. 'I think I'll find enough to occupy me in the short term.'

'And in the long term?'

He stepped back from her, his voice more serious as he said, 'Maybe I'm wealthy enough now not to have to work for a while. Maybe I can have a think about what I really want to do with my life – *our* lives, seeing as we're in it together.' He laughed self-consciously. 'Come on. Before the boys get too far ahead of us.'

Jack thought that what he most wanted to do with his life was take Val and his children and move far away. He'd thought about Australia, and then about Canada, a place that seemed somehow less foreign to him. And he had flown with Canadians; he remembered how they talked about the huge open spaces, the glorious summers at the lakes. He thought that Canada was a country where the boys would seem less contained than they were in England. He thought too about all the sadness he would leave behind, and how he could begin again where no one knew him and no one would look at him as if they were so sorry for him and his poor, motherless children. In Canada, Val would be their mother, no questions asked.

Only he wasn't sure if Val would want to leave England; in truth he wasn't sure if she loved him enough to give up everything familiar. He knew she half-loved someone else still, that fat, hail-fellow-well-met friend of Davies, Harry Dunn. He remembered the night of the Christmas party two years ago now, how Val and Dunn had danced and laughed together, how they had left together, provoking so much gossip that she just didn't seem to care about. Whenever he thought about Dunn and what he had put Val through with such lack of regard for her reputation, he wanted to go round to the man's office and smash his teeth down his throat. And now he knew exactly where his office was: the address was printed in fancy, self-important print on the letter he'd received from him, advising him just how much his inheritance from Peter's father was worth. Ironic, really, that it should be Dunn who was the bearer of such news – news that had once and for all made up his mind about accepting his inheritance.

Her arm linked reassuringly through his, Val turned to him as they walked towards Peter's house. 'Where are we going?'

The boys ran towards a junction and he called to them to wait, the note of panic in his voice making him sound too harsh. They ignored him, as usual, and ran into the road so that his heart almost stopped. When they were safely on the other side, he gave a sigh of relief before turning to her.

'Peter's house,' he answered Val. 'I've decided that if he really doesn't want it, well . . . the old man left it to me. He wanted me to have it.' He glanced at the boys; they'd

269

reached the house and had run into the garden. Seeing that they were safe, he stopped and turned to face her. 'If you like it, we'll live there. If not . . . '

'If not?'

He smiled, hooking a strand of her hair back from her face. She was so lovely, and so straight with him. He thought of Carol, a woman he had come to believe lately he'd barely understood; Carol had kept too much back from him, he'd been sure of that since he'd known Val, since he'd started to compare the two of them.

Unable to resist her, he kissed her mouth. 'I love you.' He felt himself grinning, and wondered if he had ever been this happy in his life. Taking her arm he said, 'All right – let us go and inspect our estate!'

Jack felt his grin slipping when he saw Peter in the garden, and he had to force himself to be civil to this man he had known for almost as long as he could remember. He wished only that Wright would clear off, leaving him to show Val the house in peace.

Already the boys were throwing themselves on Peter. Jack called to them but Peter was scooping them into his arms, kissing first Martin and then Stephen as he carried them towards the side gate where he stood with Val. Jack was reminded how strong Peter was – he doubted if he could lift the boys up like that and walk with them without an embarrassing show of breathlessness. Peter had always been stronger than him. When he came home from the POW camps and everyone else wondered how he'd survived, Jack knew that he was tenacious and strong enough to live through almost anything.

As Peter set the boys down, Jack said, 'Is it all right if I show Val around?'

'It's yours, Jack. You don't need to ask my permission.'

Jack laughed, knowing how forced it sounded. 'Is the

key still under that plant pot outside the back door?'

'The door's open,' Peter said. He glanced at Val, his voice brisk as he said, 'I'm afraid I had to break in this morning – I must have mislaid that spare key. I was just about to repair the damage.'

'There's no need.' Jack took Val's hand, wanting only to get away, but also wanting to show Peter that Val was his; he had noticed how the two of them looked at each other. He couldn't blame Val, most women looked at Peter like she did, their eyes big with surprise that someone like him even existed, their mouths smiling independently of their brains. He blamed Peter. Even though he knew he would never take Val from him, he believed he should keep his bloody eyes off.

Jack led Val towards the house. He called to the boys but as usual they preferred to stay with Peter. But it seemed that for once Peter didn't have time for them.

'Go on, boys,' Jack heard him say. 'Go inside with Daddy. Show Val your new house.'

Jack watched Val's expressions as he showed her around. She didn't give very much away. For his own part, he had forgotten how gloomy the house was, how much in need of modernisation. It seemed the place hadn't changed since his childhood, when he had first visited Peter here. He remembered how frightened he had been of Peter's father in those days. The old man had such a nasty tongue and seemed to know exactly what to say to cause the most hurt. He wondered how Peter had stood the old bastard for so long.

He led Val upstairs, the boys racing ahead. In the largest bedroom at the front of the house he turned to her, suddenly exasperated by the house, realising he would never want to live in it, that it tied him too much to a past he wanted to escape. Quickly, afraid she might disagree, he said, 'It's horrible, isn't it?'

To his relief, Val laughed as though she had been thinking the same thing. 'Maybe if we redecorate . . . '

'Maybe if we knock it down and start again . . . '

The boys ran in and began bouncing on the bed, the metal frame creaking and rattling beneath their combined weight. Val smiled at them, and he tried to read what her smile might mean – if she loved his sons or only found them amusing for the short time she was with them. He knew they were a handful and he would never have dared – never have dreamed – of behaving as naughtily when he was their age. His father would have thrashed him. He had spoiled the boys since Carol's death, everyone had. Watching Val watch the twins, he had to suppress the urge to ask her what she thought of them, just as he had asked her about this house. But some questions couldn't be asked, their answers only to be found in looks and gestures and the tone of her voice; he would have to go on studying her, looking for clues.

Stepping towards the bed, Val held out her hands to the boys. 'Hop down now, come and show me your favourite room.'

'Oh, that's easy, isn't it, boys?' Jack smiled at her. 'The toy room.'

They followed the twins into the room Peter had set aside for the children. Val looked around. 'It's as if this room belongs to another house. Like stepping into sunshine from the gloom.'

Going to the picture of the prince on the wall above the fireplace, she took her time studying it. At last she said, 'He's very good, isn't he?'

'You think so?' Jack went to stand beside her. 'I suppose he is. Never really thought about it.'

'Uncle Peter's father said that his drawings were silly.' Martin frowned up at him. '*Are* they silly, Daddy?'

'No.' He glanced at Val. Quietly he said, 'You might have gathered that Uncle Peter's father was an SOB.'

She nodded thoughtfully. 'Sounds like it.'

From the rocking horse Steven said, 'Uncle Peter's father said that we were very clever boys, too, so there.'

'Did he? Now I know you're telling fibs.'

'I am not! He said we were very clever and he knew we could find buried treasure if he gave us a clue about where to look.'

Martin glared at his brother. 'We said we wouldn't tell.'

'So – it doesn't matter if you break a promise to a dead person. Besides, it's only an old box with a letter in it.' Stephen got down from the horse, pushing it hard so that it knocked a dent in the wall, only to meekly slip his hand into Jack's. 'I think the letter's for you, Daddy. You're Mr John Jackson, aren't you? That's what proper people call you, isn't it?'

'Yes, it is. So, you found a letter addressed to me. Where?'

'In the cellar.' Stephen looked guilty. 'We didn't read it or anything. The writing was too hard.'

'In the cellar? This isn't one of your stories, is it?'

He looked affronted. 'No.'

Val said lightly, 'Where's the letter now, Stephen?'

Martin said, 'If we tell you, can we have some proper treasure?'

'No! Really, you two – you're the limit.'

But Val only laughed. 'Oh, Jack. They were *promised* treasure. Here,' she went into her purse and held up two shillings. 'One each, once you've given Daddy his letter.'

'No, Val, that's too much. They don't deserve it.'

She smiled at him with such warmth and tenderness that all his irritation with the boys was forgotten. He shook his head, pretending despair. 'All right. But the money will exchange hands only when the letter is delivered to me. Now, off you go and fetch it.'

When they'd run off downstairs, Jack pulled her into

273

his arms. After he'd kissed her he said, 'You know this letter doesn't actually exist, don't you?'

She gazed at him. Softly she said, 'This is a lovely room for children, isn't it?'

'Yes, although the boys have almost grown out of wanting to play in here.'

'But for younger children, babies . . .'

'Oh.' He laughed a little at his own slow-wittedness. 'Yes, I see, for babies.' Kissing her again he said, 'Of course.'

Hesitantly she said, 'Of course?'

He stepped back from her. 'Of course. Unless you think I'm too old to be a father again?'

She laughed. 'No!'

He reached out, pressing his hand against her cheek because she had blushed suddenly. 'Come on,' he said. 'Let's go and see where those little monkeys have got to.'

The boys were up in the tree-house, a complicated construction that was just one more example of why they thought Uncle Peter was the most wonderful person alive. Jack couldn't compete with Peter's ingenuity and patience when it came to toys and stories and games. Jack thought that he was too much like his own father, a man who worked his forty-hour week and was too knackered each evening to do anything but grumble and grunt from behind a newspaper. Except his father had a wife – his mother – to cook supper and supervise homework and bedtime; he never had to worry about taking time off work to look after a sick little boy, or comfort a bereaved child when she woke up crying in the middle of the night.

On nights like that, when he'd returned to his own bed at last and found he couldn't sleep for the empty space beside him, he would take himself back to the skies over Berlin and by reliving a certain mission moment by moment, make himself concentrate only on getting his crew

274

home safely. He never believed he would return there. Before Carol's death he tried to forget that he had ever flown, afraid that he'd find he missed it too much. He found he missed the adrenalin; that tremendous, fearful rush was far preferable to the constant ache of loss. And then he would feel ashamed, because his children needed him to be steady and not to go chasing after the excitement of being twenty-one and in charge of a huge, exploding sky.

Standing on the ground beneath the tree-house, Jack called up and saw the short-trousered, no-longer-chubby legs of one of his sons begin the descent of the rope ladder. 'So,' he said. 'Where's this mystery letter?'

Both boys dropped at his feet. 'Where's Val with our money?'

'Why are you such demons? Val's inside, powdering her nose. If you have a letter – which I doubt – you'll have your money when you hand it over.'

'Here.' Martin thrust an envelope at him.

Jack frowned. Just as Stephen had said, the letter was addressed to him in an old-fashioned, copperplate hand. The envelope had been torn open across its seal and he took out the single sheet of heavy velum. It felt gritty and smelled as if it had lain buried under earth. The boys were watching him, mildly curious.

'Go and play,' he said.

For once they didn't argue, but went off to find Val and her shillings.

There was a garden bench and Jack sat down. He took his reading glasses from his pocket and put them on, his movements slow and deliberate as an old man's. Like an old man's his hands were shaking a little, his guts churning in the kind of state they'd get into just before a take-off. Since the moment he'd seen his name on the envelope he'd had a creeping sense of what it contained; after all, he had always known how vile and malicious Peter's father was and how he would revel in the chance to rub his nose in all

275

that had gone on in the past. Jack scowled. Softly he said, 'Even from the grave, you old sod.'

He didn't have to read the letter, of course. He could rip it to shreds and toss it over this bloody garden, a place he was certain he would never come back to. But of course he couldn't help himself, like doing any other disgusting, sickening thing you knew was bad for you but was nevertheless compelling. Unfolding the letter, he pushed his glasses further up the bridge of his nose and began to read.

Chapter 30

I despaired when Jack arrived. All at once the garden was full of the boys, their noise and energy, full of Jack and Val, too, holding hands and smiling like adolescent sweethearts, greedy for each other. I wanted to ask them to leave. I wanted to cut some of the roses from the garden and lay them on the grave. I wanted to kneel there and try to piece together a prayer for my mother. Most of all, I wanted to be alone. I had sent Guy away and before he left, he embraced me. I was afraid he would cry again and couldn't bear it so I stepped back from him too quickly and perhaps I appeared cold, but I only wanted him gone. I smiled and told him he should go home to bed and try to forget. I thanked him. Perhaps I should have kept silent, but it seems I know only one stiff and narrow way to behave.

My father used to say I was like her. Just like her: wicked and immoral.

He killed her.

He killed her and buried her body in that terrible place and for years and years he had coal stacked over her and had me go down there time and time again, knowing I would stand on her grave. He made me believe she had left me willingly, thoughtlessly; that she had never loved me: how could she, to leave me like that? He put her photograph in a box and buried it beside her, and he buried me there, too, along with everything I might have meant to him.

I stayed by her new grave, guarding it, I suppose, waiting until Jack saw fit to leave. I had made the earth quite flat again, so that no one would suspect she was there.

I have seen so many graves without markers, or marked with only the most flimsy crosses I knew would quickly succumb to the rain. The flimsiness of those crosses only mattered to me at first, when dying seemed the worst that could happen to us.

The boys came out, running towards the tree-house. Then Jack, not noticing me, calling to the children, his voice full of his new happiness. I watched him because I have always watched him, looking for the differences between us.

He took something from the boys and they ran into the house, leaving him alone with me. He sat on the bench; after a little while he put on his spectacles so that all at once he looked young, like the shy little boy who was once my ally. He read what the boys had given him, and then laid it beside him. After a little while he stood up and walked across the lawn towards me.

Jack cleared his throat, afraid that his voice would break, that he would let himself down. He felt a kind of numbness, the same disbelief he'd felt when he was told that Carol was dead. He realised he couldn't think of a single thing to say. What he had just read had knocked all the sense out of him.

Val came out of the house, holding the boys' hands. He turned to them, surprising himself with the steadiness of his voice. 'Darling, would you take the boys inside for a while? I won't be long. I just need a private word with Peter.'

She led the children away, laughing at something Martin had said. He watched them and told himself that nothing had changed, that his sons were the same as they were a few minutes ago. Nothing had changed, nothing of any substance or worth. He realised he would have to tell himself this for the rest of his life, and all at once he felt weak with the thought of such endless effort; he doubted he had the strength left. Then he thought of Hope. She had always been his; from the moment he had held her in his arms he was her father. He wouldn't listen to the whispering voice in his head that told him that this was unimaginably different.

He made himself stand up straighter. Turning to Peter he said, 'I've decided to sell this house. I've been wondering what would be best for the children once Val and I are married, and I've decided we should all make a new start. We're emigrating. Canada. We're going to Canada.'

Peter looked dumbstruck, as though he couldn't believe what he'd just heard. 'Canada? No . . . You don't mean it.'

'Yes, I do. It's best.'

'Best? No, you can't –'

'Why? Come on, Peter, you tell me. Why can't I take my children away?'

Peter glanced towards the letter he'd left on the bench and Jack followed his gaze.

Turning back to face him, Jack said, 'Your father left it for the boys to find. It's addressed to me but it's all about nothing, really. Read it, if you like.'

He had to go. If he didn't get away from Peter at once he would say all the things he'd always believed must be kept to himself. And then he'd have no pride left, only the hollow satisfaction of having finally given voice to his hatred. He turned away but Peter caught his arm, his grip strong.

'Jack.' He let go, leaving a filthy mark on his sleeve. Painfully he said, 'You wouldn't take them. You wouldn't.'

'Why wouldn't I?' He couldn't help himself. Intensely he said, '*I'm* their father. It's *my* name on their birth certificates. You're nothing to them. You were always nothing!'

'Please don't take them away.'

Jack gazed at him. He thought how pitiable he was; there was a part of him that had always thought this, despite Peter's physical strength. Despite the way women looked at him. He thought of Carol, who had never lost her obsession with this man, the unsettling, agitating effect he had on her. And yet he seemed not to understand the power he had, like some beast that had been kept in chains and beaten every day of its life. Unable to look at him he turned away, but once again Peter caught his arm.

'You're their father, Jack. And you're right – I'm nothing to them and every day they grow older I become even less. They're slipping away from me, every day a little further. Hope has already gone – you've seen the way she looks at me. Please, Jack, please don't take the boys away, too – not yet . . . '

Jack shook him off, his skin crawling. 'I have to.' He thought of saying that putting an ocean between them was the only way he could stand it, but the words seemed too pompous, too measured and controlled when really all he wanted to do was lay into him with his fists. Instead, he met Peter's gaze, seeing Hope in him just as he always had. But now he saw the boys too, and he thought that he would kill him if he ever had to look at him again.

This time, Peter let him go. Jack began to walk towards the house, only to find himself running as he saw the twins come out into the garden. He swept them into his arms.

Val smiled at him. 'So, what was in the mystery letter that cost me so much?'

'Nothing,' he said. 'Stuff about the past, that's all.' The boys were squirming, wanting to be put down, too big to be held like babies. He kissed them, holding on to them still. 'Come on. Let's go home.'

I read the letter, of course I did – who would not? Who, if they found that their life had suddenly collapsed, would not want to try to make sense of it? The letter was quite short and to the point.

Dear Jack,

If you are reading this, then the boys are as clever and curious as I expect them to be – or rather, as I know them to be, given that they are my own flesh and blood.

I'm certain that Hope is my son's child: it's so obvious, isn't it? Hope takes after him and his mother. The twins' likeness to him is less obvious – one would have to know my family to see it. I recognised them at once, the first time your wife showed them off to me. Perhaps she thought that because they don't look so much like him, their secret would be kept safe. But Martin and Stephen so resemble my twin brothers, both killed in France in 1916. Seeing my grandsons was like having my brothers back – I can't tell you how much that has meant to me.

Until I saw them I thought my son wasn't mine, that I had been cuckolded as you have. But Martin and Stephen are undeniable proof that Peter is my son, for all that he has shamed me, for all that often I wish he'd never been born.

Perhaps you know already that these boys are not your blood. Perhaps your wife was as honest with you as my own wife was dishonest with me. But if you didn't know, if you doubt the truth of this letter, all you need do is ask my son. He longs to tell you they are his. Remember though, that they are yours. He is no more than their fool, their entertainment. You have shown yourself to be a good father; a far better father than my son would ever make.

Through you, I've left everything to my grandchildren, and I know that you will make the most of the opportunities money allows for; this was the reason why I have not left it in trust for the children as at first I thought I might. I want you to know that I have always admired you for your steadfastness and loyalty to Hope, for taking her on as your own, just as I know you will continue to accept the boys as your own.

Forgive me for the curious way you came across this

letter. All I can say is that courage has often failed me and part of me still wants secrets to be kept, even after I am dead. One never quite believes in death anyway; even as I write this, I can't bring myself to question my own immortality.

I am ten years old and it is Christmas and we are alone, my father and I, because there has only ever been the two of us; all we have is each other. I love him and want him to be happy and I've drawn him a picture – the first that I believe is even half-decent. I know that he is drunk – not too drunk, I tell myself, no worse than usual. But, as usual, I underestimate him. He must have been drinking all day. He takes my drawing and stares and stares at it, and all at once tears are falling onto it. He lifts his head and looks at me and says, 'I should have killed you, too. And Christ only knows why I did not.'

I could tell myself that I knew then that she was dead, but I didn't. I was too afraid for myself. Fear has stalked me all my life. I think I'm tired of it now. I think I should put a stop to it.

Chapter 31

Harry had dressed Ava, keeping up a stream of words, trying to get over the self-conscious feeling that he was talking to himself. When the words had dried up, he sang, nonsense songs from his childhood that his father had sung to him. Harry stopped mid verse of 'Lily of Laguna' to laugh bleakly. 'You know, Ava, he was such a kind man. I've never really thought about that before – how kind he was. Even when he'd had a drink or four, people loved him. Life and soul. They loved him, but they thought he was a buffoon – a silly old bugger.' He'd snorted. 'Am I like him? Oh yes. I am under no illusions.'

After a morning spent reading to her and working on a jigsaw she seemed to have no interest in, he imagined that if he spent another hour like this he would go mad with boredom and frustration. He thought about the Home he had found, run by the nuns whose existence Val had not believed in. But they did exist, and Sister Agnes had been thoughtful and sympathetic as she'd shown him round her quiet, cloistered asylum. In her office with the statue of the Virgin holding out Her arms to him, she told him that she understood how difficult it was for families to leave their loved ones, even there, where they would find peace and safety. He had felt ashamed of himself, could never admit to this woman, a woman he was beginning to think of as a saint, that he would only feel relieved. All the same, he said that he was merely considering his options.

Val had believed he wouldn't shut his wife away again and he was afraid to insist that he would, because how would such insistence appear? In his heart he believed Val only loved the man who wouldn't give up on his wife, a man he'd created only with Esther's help.

He led Ava out into the garden because after the night's storm the sun was shining in an innocently clear blue sky. They would eat lunch outside where she liked to listen to the birds. Because he had forgotten Danny and Martha, he went back inside to fetch them.

Guy was in the hall, quietly closing the front door as if afraid to be heard. It was obvious he had been out all night. Dishevelled, his son looked at him, only to look away, making to side-step him. But Harry had seen his expression and was shocked. Wanting to sound concerned, instead alarm caused his voice to rise as he said, 'Guy? What's happened?'

Guy tried to slip past him to the stairs but Harry stepped in his way, his bulk of occasional use, at least. More gently he said, 'Guy, I can see you're distressed . . . ' He noticed how dirty his son's clothes were. His anxiety increasing, he repeated, 'What's happened? Tell me – you look like you've been pulled through a muddy field.'

Guy kept his face resolutely turned away. 'Nothing's happened.'

'You were out all night, weren't you?'

'Most of the night. And so?' He seemed to force himself to look at him. 'What the hell do you care? Don't start pretending you care now! Just don't – it's too bloody late! You should have cared years ago, but you were too busy befriending fucking Nazis!'

'Keep your foul language to yourself!'

'Should I say it in German? No, that would make it sound even more *foul*, wouldn't it? Funny, isn't it, that all you care about are the words I used and not what I actually said.'

Harry sighed. 'Guy, Ava wasn't a Nazi.'

'No? Well, you keep telling yourself that.'

'Why are you saying these things now? Something's happened. Tell me what's happened.'

Guy shook his head, smiling as if he'd been told a bad joke. 'Oh, what's happened, Dad? Where should I start? When I was four and you left me in the care of total strangers? You don't want to hear about them, believe me.'

Harry felt his guts contract, a combination of guilt and regret and a shameful unwillingness to know more than he had to about those years when he had lost touch with his infant son. His excuse was the war, of course, and as excuses went it was certainly adequate. But he could not excuse his own heart, his own lack of connection with that little boy he'd left with the matron of that first prep school.

Dully he said, 'I'm sorry.'

'Sorry? Yeah, I bet. You always looked sorry when you were walking away. Christ, sometimes you actually ran, you were so *sorry* to leave me!'

'That's not true, Guy.'

'No, you're right – it wasn't quite running. You were always too fat to run.' He bit his lip and Harry could see that he felt he'd gone too far. Besides, Guy would normally think such childish insults beneath him and it worried Harry that he was upset enough to stoop so low.

He became aware that he was holding Danny and Martha in his arms as if they were real children. He laughed bleakly, shifting the dolls so that he held them less carefully. 'I wasn't so fat in those days, was I? If I was and I embarrassed you, then I'm sorry.'

Still seemingly unable to look at him, Guy mumbled, 'Don't say sorry again.'

'No, all right. But can I say that you were always so brave, and you never cried when I said goodbye?' When Guy didn't respond he said more softly, 'I was grateful that you didn't cry – you made me feel that you were all right. I was grateful when I should have realised you were unhappy. There,' he ducked his head to smile into his son's

285

downcast face. 'Now I want to say that word you don't want me to say.'

Guy made to brush past him only to turn to him abruptly, his face pale, his eyes full of tears that fell down his face unchecked. 'Dad . . . ' Guy crumpled and became a little boy again, rocking himself backwards and forwards as he wept.

It took a little while for Harry to coax the story from Guy. Halfway through, with many apologies, he had to leave him to check on Ava, only to find her dozing in a deckchair. Sitting the dolls at her feet, he returned to his son, feeling as sick as if he had uncovered the bones himself. And he was afraid for Guy; the walls his son had built to keep the world from touching him had collapsed, breached by this one, traumatic event. But those failed defences had kept other traumas at bay and now Guy was as overwhelmed as any of the shell-shocked soldiers Harry had seen, those men who had witnessed one horror too many. Some of Guy's horrors he knew about; it was those he was ignorant of that scared him.

They sat side by side on the stairs. Harry had given Guy a small measure of brandy and he seemed calmer. Wiping his nose on the handkerchief Harry had pressed into his hand, he looked down at his drink. 'I shouldn't have told you.'

'Yes, you should have.'

'It was against the law, wasn't it, what we did?'

'No one's going to go to the police.'

'I shouldn't have told you, shouldn't have got you involved.' He began to cry again and Harry put his arm around him, holding him so that his head rested against his chest. Stroking his hair, he said, 'It's all right, Guy. Everything's going to be all right. You don't have to worry about anything – I'm here now.'

Suddenly Guy said, 'I can't stop thinking about how

frightened she must have been.'

Harry held him still closer. 'Have you thought that it might have been very quick? She may have felt nothing, known nothing.'

'She was pregnant.' Guy struggled from Harry's embrace to look at his father. 'How could he have done that?'

'I don't know.'

After a while Guy said quietly, 'Hans would have known; *he* would have understood how someone could murder a pregnant woman.'

Harry kept silent; he felt as though he was holding his breath. Guy had never mentioned Hans before, and he wondered how much Ava had told him – whether he really did know more than he knew himself. Often he wished he had forbidden Ava to talk about her brother to Guy, but he had never been able to bring himself to be so heavy-handed; could never, in truth, bring himself to speak his name. He regretted such weakness now. Guy should have been kept innocent of a man he seemed to understand so well.

Guy said, 'Esther found out about Hans. It's why she left.'

Harry sighed. He had found Ava's diary and the photograph of Hans on Esther's stripped bed, the two speaking to him far more eloquently than her stilted resignation letter. He had read the diary, of course, years ago, looking for clues as to what had gone on in that spring of 1946. He had found none, only a reaffirmation of what he already knew: that Ava had loved her brother more than she loved anyone, with the possible exception of Guy.

Guy swallowed the mouthful of brandy he'd given him. 'I should go to bed, although I don't think I'll be able to sleep.'

Harry got to his feet. 'Then would you sit with Ava? I need to go out. For an hour or so, that's all.'

Guy looked up at him. 'You're going to see him, aren't

you?'

Harry hesitated. Eventually he said, 'Yes. I think he may need someone to talk to.'

After all, hadn't he always been the one to talk to? Hans had always insisted on talking to him and only him. Many men would have called their exchanges confessions but Hans would never allow himself to be so craven. Hans was only telling a story, nothing more.

'You've been a good listener, Harry,' Hans had told him at the end. 'Rapt. But then you'll leave this place and the spell will be broken. You'll wonder how you could have believed a single word.'

'No. I'll go on believing you.'

Hans studied his face. 'Do you think others will believe as you do?'

'You've left enough evidence.'

He sighed. 'You're always so blunt, Harry. It's good that you don't let me get away with my whimsies. Keep pointing to the evidence – you're right to do so. Truly, I'd despise anyone who denied what we did.'

Harry stopped outside Wright's house – not the house on Inkerman Terrace, for he guessed that Wright wouldn't return there just yet. At least, he hoped he wouldn't. He didn't want to be so close to where Val lived. He had been trying valiantly not to think about Val, but he knew how far he had to go before the pain of being reminded didn't feel like it would kill him. Even now, looking at a house that might only be part of her future was difficult. But at least he hadn't made love to her in its rooms; there would be no scent of her, no sense of her presence to distract him from his brave efforts at forgetting. He would concentrate on Wright; he would offer him his services as a listener, although he guessed at how condescending he would sound and wondered if Wright wouldn't see right through him, to his insatiable curiosity, that same curiosity that Hans had recognised with such glee.

He walked up the path, following it along the side of the house to the garden, half-expecting and dreading the sight of the newly dug earth. But the garden seemed undisturbed and rather beautiful for the way it had been left to the wild. He allowed himself to stand at the garden's edge, catching his breath, composing himself. A robin flew down at his feet; he watched it for a moment before letting himself into the house through the open back door.

He called out, once again self-conscious at the sound of his own voice seeming to go unheard. Going from room to room he became aware of the terrible stillness, the deep, oppressive silence. He called out again, more urgently, his heart quickening as he climbed the stairs. He had experienced such a silence before, when he had found Guy asleep beside his mother's body. It was as though the dead left behind an aura that only the frantic blundering of the living could disperse, because when he burst into Wright's bedroom, the silence became ordinary, was suddenly broken by birdsong. The window was open, the breeze from the garden scenting the air.

For a moment Harry imagined dropping to his knees, tearing at his hair in a fit of histrionic grief and rage, and it crossed his mind that it would be a relief to finally let go like that. Instead, he began to talk softly, not caring now that there was no one to hear him, but keeping up a soft stream of reassuring words as he righted the toppled chair. Climbing up, he lifted Peter's body into his arms.

Chapter 32

One month later

Hope waited until after her father's wedding to tell him that she wouldn't go with him to Canada. He was alone in their garden when she went out to speak to him. Val had taken the boys out to buy ice creams from the van. The van's chimes had reminded Hope of the last time she'd seen Peter that Sunday, a lifetime ago, and she'd had to be stern with herself to stop from crying. Even so, when her father saw her, he glanced away as if he couldn't bear to look at her.

'Now what? Can't I have a moment to myself?'

Jack had aged suddenly; he smoked more and said less, although he and Val talked and talked until late into the night, and one evening they went out into the garden for ages. It was obvious when they came back inside that they'd both been crying. Since then Val seemed to be forcing herself to be happy and only the boys didn't notice her sadness. Martin and Stephen loved their new stepmother. To Hope's relief she seemed to love them in return. It made what she was about to say easier, knowing the boys didn't need her any more.

Her father lit another cigarette. She stepped closer to him, inhaling the smoke greedily. He frowned at her. 'Do you want one?'

'Could I?'

He held out his silver cigarette case. 'Help yourself.'

She took one shyly and he lit it for her, tossing the spent match down as though he could hardly contain his contempt for it and everything else in the world. Already nervous, Hope drew on her cigarette heavily, feeling her father's eyes on her. She managed to smile at him.

'They're a bit nicer than the ones I usually smoke.'

'They're expensive. Don't smoke cheap cigarettes. In fact, don't smoke at all.'

After a moment she said, 'I need to speak to you.'

'I'd gathered.'

He had stopped loving her over the last few weeks and this was so strange and horrible that she kept telling herself she had to be wrong. Now he looked at her and there was something in his eyes that made her believe she could be mistaken, a struggle against that part of him that had been keeping such a distance from her. More gently he said, 'What is it, Hope?'

She drew on the cigarette again. Afraid to try his patience for long, she said quietly, 'I can't go to Canada.'

He was silent for such a long time that she said timidly, 'Dad?'

'Yes, Hope. I heard you.'

'And?'

He laughed emptily. 'And I know you don't want to go. Why would you? But *can't?* Do you think I need you to give me some big excuse?' He turned to face her, tossing his half-finished cigarette down. 'You can stay here, if you like. I can't make you come with us.'

'I don't know what to say.'

'How about goodbye and good luck?' He turned away, fumbling in his pocket for his cigarettes. As he took them out she saw that his hands were shaking so badly he couldn't open the case.

'Dad . . . ?' Fearfully, she said, 'Please don't be like this.'

He spun round to face her. 'Like what? Haven't you got what you wanted? Haven't you *always* got what you wanted? Between us, we spoiled you half to death! Well,

291

now you're seventeen you can have this last big *want* and I'll leave you to get on with it!'

'Jack!' Val had come outside without either of them noticing. Looking at Hope, she said, 'I'm sorry, love. Perhaps it's best if you go and see what your brothers are doing, and later we can discuss this calmly.'

'No.' Her husband sighed. 'No, Val. I've had enough. She can stay here if she wants to.' To Hope he said, 'And you do want to, don't you? You want to stay with this boy – Guy. Isn't that right?'

She nodded, unable to speak because she knew she would give her tears away.

'Will you marry him?'

'For goodness sake, Jack, she's too young to be married.' Val shook her head. 'Hope, your father's upset. As I said, we can discuss this later –'

'There's nothing to discuss,' Jack said.

'So you're just going to leave your seventeen-year-old daughter here alone?'

Her father gazed at Val. At last he said, 'Maybe I should tell her the truth.' Turning to her he said softly, 'Let's go inside, Hope. Upstairs in your room so the boys won't disturb us.'

'I loved you,' he said, 'since the moment you were born, and before that, because you were part of your mother and I loved her with all my heart. You were the only two people in the world that mattered to me. And we were so happy together, I didn't want anything else. When the war was over I thought only of us, the best life I could make for my wife and baby.

'The war was over, my war, at least, and I didn't want to think about what was happening in Asia – too afraid that they might send me there. I tried to forget about Peter. I believed that he was dead.'

They were sitting side by side on her bed and all the

time he'd been speaking he had held her hand, his gaze fixed on their entwined fingers. Her room smelled of her, of her perfume and cosmetics, and of something else, more fecund and even more telling of the young woman she had grown into. Hers was such a small room, the rosebud-patterned wallpaper making it seem smaller still; her clothes spilled out of the childish wardrobe he had built for her, nylon stockings and garter belts trailing from its drawers to the floor.

He closed his eyes, afraid of the way his emotions had overrun him lately. He was afraid that Val would leave him, despite her reassurances, and this fear made him feel as helpless as a baby; and then, only a few minutes ago in the garden, he had felt hard and bitter and angry enough to hurt Hope, to make her hate him, and that had felt like punching a fist into an open wound. In all his life he had never felt so adrift, so in thrall to unruly feelings. He dreamed of taking the boys away, flying them away in a machine he had control over. He thought of Peter often, trying to convince himself that his death really wasn't his fault.

Looking down at Hope's fingers clasped in his, he said, 'Do you remember when Peter came home? You would have been about five. I remember the first time he saw you, how my heart stood still when he lifted you into his arms. I thought he couldn't fail to notice . . . I wanted to hide you from him, take you far away. Your mother wouldn't hear of it.' He looked up at Hope. 'She loved him.'

Hope drew her hand away from his, wiping her eyes quickly. 'She loved *you*.'

'Yes. But Peter . . . Peter was from her childhood, from all the stories she invented for herself when she was a little girl, all alone in your grandparents' big old house. She told me that when she first saw him . . . ' He hesitated; even now the memory was painful. After a moment he said, 'When she first saw Peter, it was as if the prince had stepped out of her storybooks. You know how handsome he was. And she had this romantic idea of him. But she knew that's all it was, a romance, a fantasy. What she and I had together . . . Well, there are stories and then there's real life.'

'She didn't love him! She couldn't have!' Hope turned to him, her eyes fierce. 'Why did you allow it?'

He stared at the wall, the repeat pattern of flowers beginning to blur. He had no answer for her that didn't make him seem weak. He thought of his father who had always impressed on him the importance of honesty, whose life had been uncomplicated enough for him to keep to his rigid standards. His own life had been based on a lie, a lie that at times seemed too insignificant to even count as white, and at other times too huge to bear. Aware of Hope's angry gaze on him, he said, 'Peter was a good man, Hope. He loved you so much –'

'No! I didn't want him to love me!'

He turned to face her, taking both her hands in his. 'You're my daughter, Hope. But you were his, too. You knew that, didn't you? You knew in your heart . . . '

'No.' She shook her head in disbelief. Pulling her hands from his she cried, 'You're lying. You're lying because you don't want me any more.'

'No, Hope.' He held her face between his hands, gently sweeping her tears away with his thumbs. 'I love you more than ever, but I think you should know the truth.' He dropped his hands, unable to face her any more, afraid that his voice would let him down. At last he said, 'Hope, I need to leave – I have to. I have to start again with Val, with the boys. And you, if you want to come with us, my home will always, always be yours. But I think that perhaps you're old enough now to make your own decision.'

'You don't want me!'

He shook his head. 'Oh, you're wrong! So wrong. I want us to be together and happy as larks.' He smiled at her sadly. 'I want to say *come with us*, because I'll miss you so badly.'

She stood up. 'Did he know? Did he know I was his?'

'You're mine, Hope. But if you mean did he know he fathered you, yes. He did.'

She nodded; she seemed calm, the kind of tightly reined-in calmness that takes such concentration, such effort. Wiping her eyes impatiently, she said, 'I can't go with you. Guy's asked me to marry him and I've said yes.'

He thought how he might have reacted a month ago, how he would have raged. She was so young, after all, still his child, too young to be married. But now he didn't have the energy for outrage or bombast. He only searched her face, looking for proof that this was what she really wanted.

Hope spoke in a low voice. 'I thought you'd be angry. You should be angry.'

'Why?'

Meeting his gaze, she said, 'I'm pregnant.' She began to cry.

Jack stood up to take her in his arms, only for Hope to throw herself against him, the sudden force of her embrace making him stagger. 'Please don't leave me, Daddy. Please don't go.'

He held her as she cried. He saw his plans fall around him, all his big ideas for a new life far away from the small sameness of England. Perhaps he'd always known he wouldn't go; perhaps all he'd needed was something big to think about, to take his mind off the hurt.

Kissing the top of her head he whispered, 'I won't leave you. Of course I won't.'

Chapter 33

Hope wore a plain white dress and Jack thought how young she looked, and slight; no one would guess at the life curled safe inside her. In the car on the way to the church they had kept silent, the day's importance making them shy of one another. He found himself staring out of the car's window at the passing streets, the familiar places of his life. From time to time he had glanced at Hope and saw that her face was serious and composed; he imagined that she was rehearsing her lines, determined not to let Guy down. He thought of the boy who was to be her husband. At first he had thought that Guy was too plain, too ordinary for Hope; lately though, he had come to see what she saw – his brightness. Hope changed when she was around him, reflecting back the light that animated his eyes whenever he looked at her. Jack wondered if he had ever been so much in love. He pictured Guy, standing waiting for them now at the front of the church, his uniform so new, so pristine. If there was a war, he would hide him away.

Now though, they stood outside another church, the driver in his peaked cap waiting, the engine idling because Jack had told him that they wouldn't be long. At the lych-gate that led into the churchyard, he stopped and took Hope's hand.

'Would you like me to wait here?'

She shook her head. 'Could we go together?'

He smiled, squeezing her fingers. A breeze caught her short veil and he put his hand to it, smoothing it down. He wanted to say how beautiful she looked but there was that shyness still. Instead, he turned and led her along the gravel path, the swaying shadows of the trees changing the pattern of light at their feet.

Harry Dunn had seen to it that Peter's grave was far away from his father's. Dunn had come to him, had said, 'I need your help. You knew him; I know that he cared for you. At least tell me the hymns that he liked.'

'"The Lord's My Shepherd",' Jack had told him, and Dunn had looked at him as though this was the first hymn that had come into his head, making no effort to hide his contempt. But Jack knew that this was what Peter would have wanted; they had sung it at Carol's funeral. He remembered how Peter had held him upright when he thought that he would collapse with the weight of grief. He remembered all his careful words and silences. He remembered Peter's strength, how he had imagined that he could go on and on leaning so heavily against him and that Peter would never tire, never allow him to fall into that pit he knew he would never crawl free from.

Forcing himself to meet Dunn's gaze, he'd said, 'You don't have to do this. I will.'

Guy's father had sighed. 'We'll do it together.' Then, more gently, he added, 'There are only the words left. I didn't know him well enough to put him into words.'

To the tiny gathering at his funeral, Jack had said that Peter Wright had been the truest friend. He felt like a hypocrite, a liar, because his pain was still so raw; at least his children weren't there to hear him.

Hope walked ahead of him, her pace quickening as she approached the as yet unmarked grave. She stood, and Jack watched as she took a rose from her bouquet and crouched to place it on the earth. Her dress billowed around her, she bowed her head and her veil hid her face from him. And he thought how beautiful she was, and so like her father, who had loved her so truly.

About the author...

Winner of the first Andrea Badenoch Prize for Fiction in 2005 for *Paper Moon,* Marion graduated with distinction and won the Blackwell Prize for Best Performance for the MA in Creative Writing at Northumbria University in 2003. She currently teaches creative writing through the Open College of the Arts and has had poems and short stories published, most recently a pamphlet of poetry about her father and childhood entitled *Service.* Her first novel, *The Boy I Love*, was published in July 2005 to much critical acclaim. *Paper Moon* was followed in January 2007 by *Say You Love Me.*

Marion is married with two children and lives in the Tees Valley.

www.marionhusband.com

The Boy I Love

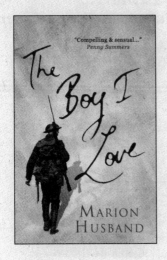

ISBN 1905170009 £6.99

Superbly written with engaging characters that are simultaneously strong and weak, compassionate and flawed. The book is a controversial but compulsive read and readers will find their sympathies tugged in unusual directions as they engage with the lives of the characters.

The Boy I Love is the first of a two book series – the second book, Paper Moon is set in World War 2 and follows the life of Mick, now a war poet, his son and Robbie, son of Paul and Margot.

Paper Moon

Winner of the Andrea Badenoch Fiction Award

ISBN 1905170149 £6.99

Following on from *The Boy I Love*, Marion Husband's highly acclaimed debut novel, *Paper Moon* explores the complexities of love and loyalty against a backdrop of a world transformed by war.

The passionate love affair between Spitfire pilot Bobby Harris and photographer's model Nina Tate lasts through the turmoil of World War Two, but is tested when his plane is shot down. Disfigured and wanting to hide from the world, Bobby retreats from Bohemian Soho to the empty house his grandfather has left him, a house haunted by the secrets of Bobby's childhood, where the mysteries of his past are gradually unravelled and he discovers that love is more than skin deep.